From the author of *Comes the Rain* . . .

TOUCH THE SUN

The life of a warrior's woman was a harsh one. From the moment the young, innocent Eagle Voice was given to Walks Far as a wife, her duty was to the tribe . . .

But when her heart is captured by Fire Wolf—a proud, rugged fighter bound to the land of his people—Eagle Voice must measure her fierce desire against the demands of the tribe. For Fire Wolf had awakened a passion more powerful than any warrior—and sweeter than anything she had known before . . .

In a novel of passion and survival, Beverly Bird presents an unforgettable story of one proud woman and the destiny of her people . . .

TOUCH THE SUN

BEVERLY BIRD

BERKLEY BOOKS, NEW YORK

TOUCH THE SUN

A Berkley Book / published by arrangement with
the author

PRINTING HISTORY
Berkley edition / April 1994

ISBN 0-425-14156-X

BERKLEY®
Berkley Books are published by
The Berkley Publishing Group, 200 Madison Avenue,
New York, New York 10016.
BERKLEY and the "B" design are trademarks of
Berkley Publishing Corporation.

PRINTED IN THE UNITED STATES OF AMERICA

10 9 8 7 6 5 4 3 2 1

1

Moon When The Horses Get Fat, 1863
Red Shield River

I

The excitement in the camp felt alive; Eagle Voice fancied it like a crouched and hungry prairie fox ready to hurl itself into motion. Though the air was warm with springtime, her skin prickled up in a shiver.

The people! she thought. Never in all her thirteen winters had she known so many to gather for a hunt. Cheyenne lodges, and even some of Little Raven's Arapaho, hugged both sides of the river, stretching too far for her to see them all. They crept over the low, rolling hills like ants.

The lodges closest to the water were the most important ones. They sheltered the *Vehoo'o*, the People's council of civil chiefs, and the four revered men who governed them. Surrounding these were the hundred or so tepees of the *Hotame-taneo'o*, the Dog Soldiers warrior society. Their black, fringed smoke-flap ornaments whipped in the wind like a bunch of frenzied crows.

This hunt was indeed important, Eagle thought, if the *Vehoo'o* had chosen the Dogs to police it. There were other societies, but the *Hotame-taneo'o* were the best of the fighting men. As though reading her mind, her mother, Small Blanket, paused as she and her sister worked to raise her lodge.

"My husband says there are more buffalo gathered here than he has ever seen before. We will all eat well and have new lodges and robes when Cold Maker comes again."

Little Moon frowned. "The *ve'ho'e*, the white spider trickster men, have left them little land to roam," she muttered. "That is why there are so many of them together, and why they are farther north this season than they have ever been before."

1

Eagle had heard some of the other adults worrying about the same thing. "What does it matter?" she asked. "They are here and we have found them."

"It matters because the buffalo fear white men just as they fear white horses, silly girl. They will not go where the *ve'ho'e* put their trails and their shelters. Next season we will have to travel all the way into Sioux country to find them," she warned darkly. "I have spoken. You heard me first."

Eagle bit her lip. Her mothers were very different. Little Moon was as fat and grumpy as Small Blanket was pretty and placid. She decided to change the subject.

"I would like to go to the Dog camp to visit my brother," she ventured.

To her surprise, Small Blanket nodded.

"Take my daughter and my littlest one," Little Moon put in. "Keep your eyes down. Do not shame our *Wu'tapiu* band by flirting with any boys."

Eagle nodded obediently and hurried to Little Moon's tepee, already up and sitting close beside the site Small Blanket had chosen. The door flap was pegged aside, inviting guests, so she ducked in without calling out first. Sun Roads lay on her belly, tickling a squealing toddler.

"We can go to the Dog camp to see if we can find Bear!" Eagle said. "Hurry!"

Sun Roads was on her feet in an instant, balancing little Pot Belly on one broad hip. The trio wound their way through the *Wu'tapiu* lodges, past women hoisting poles to dry all the meat that would soon be theirs, and clusters of old men gambling and muttering over their buffalo bone chips. The sweet smell of prairie grass mingled with the richness of tamped earth and ponies and sun-warmed humanity. Soon there would be the tang of blood as well, Eagle thought, and the heavy, pervasive odor of raw meat.

They came upon the Dog Soldier camp, and a thrill of excitement scooted through her. It did not matter that her own brother was *Hotame-taneo'o* or that he visited the *Wu'tapiu* with some of these warriors every summer. She never got used to them or their air of fierce superiority. Their wives inspired her awe as well. Most women remained with their bands after marrying; their new husbands came to live among mothers and grandmothers and sisters. But the *Hotame-taneo'o* were a band unto themselves. They were the only warrior society who left their wives' people to live together. Their women sacrificed everything familiar in their own worlds to follow them. To Eagle, it seemed both brave and terrible.

As she looked for one she recognized that she might ask for Bear That Goes Alone, there came the tattoo of hooves approaching behind her. She whirled to find a Dog coming off patrol.

"Walks Far!" She grinned. She had never been afraid of this *Hotame-taneo'o*. He was a close friend of her brother's. But to her consternation, he frowned down at her as he reined his pony to a stop. Then she thought she understood his dull mood.

"Someone has scared off the herd!" she breathed.

Walks Far looked startled, then he shook his head and dismounted. "No," he said, "it is still there, a short, hard ride just beyond those hills." Finally he grinned.

"You have grown, little sister, since I saw you a summer ago."

Eagle looked down at herself. Her doeskin fell loosely to her calves with a pretty row of fringe there. She was proud of that fringe. It matched the trim little lines that ran down each side of her leggings.

"Yes, my mother had to make this new for me this season," she answered, "and—"

She broke off with a grunt as Sun Roads elbowed her in the ribs. She rubbed the sore spot and frowned at her cousin. Sun Roads was looking determinedly at the ground.

Do not flirt with any boys.

Walks Far? Eagle's eyes widened and swept back to him. Walks Far wasn't a boy. He was . . . he was . . .

Suddenly her chest grew hot and strangely tight. The warmth seemed to creep up her neck until even her ears burned with it, and she looked quickly away from the warrior. It came to her then that maybe he hadn't been talking of how tall she had grown, because that wasn't really the reason Small Blanket had had to cut her a new doeskin this season. Maybe he was talking about how the old one had finally become tight across her hips and her breasts.

Was he trying to flirt with her?

"We look for Bear That Goes Alone," she heard Sun Roads say, but she didn't want to see Bear now. She moved away, dazed, her legs feeling clumsy and wooden.

When the crier's voice rang out to signal the start of the hunt, she became aware of her surroundings again in a disorienting rush. Sun Roads and Pot Belly had vanished. Men were spilling from the lodges now, and boys shouted to each other as they ran to bring in the best hunting ponies. When they were driven back into the camp for the hunters to choose their swiftest mounts, there would be chaos.

Eagle changed direction quickly, heading out from the camp. When she reached the low hills that rolled up from the river valley, she dropped down on her haunches to look back.

Oh, the Dogs looked mighty! Straight-backed, strong, and solemn, they rode among the bands, their favored raven feathers decorating their ponies and guns and lances. She finally caught a glimpse of Bear. Her brother was taller and broader than anyone Eagle knew, with a big hook of a nose and brawny muscle moving under his skin.

He would not be happy if he found her alone. He, too, would notice that she had needed a new doeskin, and he would be even less tolerant than usual of her wandering about unchaperoned. She pushed quickly to her feet again, keeping her eyes on him as she began backing away.

He paused in a clearing in front of the *Vehoo'o* lodges, and another Dog joined him there. Eagle squinted, recognizing Bear's funny friend, Night Fighter. Then Bear pointed in her direction.

She dropped quickly, falling into the tall grass with a thud that jarred her teeth.

They rode on. She glanced over her shoulder, wondering what they had been discussing. No one was there; the grass twitched and danced in the wind, undisturbed by human trespass except for the flattened places where men had crawled up on their bellies to peer over.

Bear must have been gesturing toward the herd, she realized. These were the hills Walks Far had said they were grazing beyond. That was why there were no lodges here.

Her pulse gave a funny little hitch. Her mother had said there were more buffalo this season than even Caught the Enemy, her father, had seen before.

Suddenly she was moving, pulling herself up and backward with her hands. Then she flipped over onto her knees, crawling fast through the grass, nervous sweat beginning to trickle down her ribs. She would be exposed at the top of the hill, she knew that, but how long could it take her to peek just once?

She reached the top of the hill and dropped flat on her belly. The wind here was ripe and gamy with animal scent. A brown blanket spread across the far horizon, but occasionally the near outline would change shape, and she knew that she was watching something very much alive. She could not see the end of them. Eagle gasped, a rush of breath that came all the way up from her toes. Then the sound of movement came from behind her, the irregular rhythm of a pony fighting its way up the slope.

She twisted around. The horse was reined in at her feet, black as night and dripping sweat from its belly. She scrambled backward, appalled at being caught.

"Not that way! Are you stupid as well as reckless?"

Eagle froze. Her gaze skittered up the pony's short, sinewy limbs until she came to its rider, and then she moaned. She could expect no clemency here. She did not know this Dog. If he was one of Bear's friends, he had never come to *Wu'tapiu* country with him. She would have remembered him.

His eyes were strange, a rich brown instead of the familiar black of the People. His onyx hair was unkempt and spilled down over his chest, as though he had no wife to brush and braid it, and he did not care to do it himself. He wore no shirt, either, only a breechclout and leggings, their fringes and rattles and enemy scalps stirring in the wind. His smooth chest tapered down to a lean waist, making her think of one of the scrappy camp dogs that could move like lightning when provoked.

"I was—"

"If you had run that way and scared the herd," he snapped angrily, "you would be dead. You are too puny to survive a beating!"

Her skin flamed with embarrassment, and hot tears began to burn at her eyes. There were many ways of chastising someone who disturbed the buffalo before every man had a fair chance at the game. She had known men to be beaten, whole pony herds to be slaughtered, and lodges to be slashed. But she was just a girl!

"No!" she cried suddenly. "You leave my brother's horses alone! And if you touch my mother's lodge, I will—"

The *Hotame-taneo'o* warrior leapt off his horse. She gulped back the rest of her words and began scrambling away from him again. This time he grabbed her ankle to stop her.

"You will do what, little girl?"

She jerked her foot away from his grasp, pushed to her feet, and ran.

She was nearly to the bottom of the hill before he caught up with her, his hands closing around her waist with impossible quickness. He lifted her off the ground and pinned her against his chest. She squealed, kicking and writhing, until he clapped one hand over her mouth and caught her flailing arms behind her back, against his hip. She slid down until her feet touched the earth again.

"I could tie your legs, too, or would you be quiet now?" When she didn't answer, he took his hand away. She sucked in breath.

"Who is this brother you speak of?"

She would not tell him. She would not.

"I will carry you to every camp until someone recognizes you," he went on grimly. "I will find out."

Of course he would. She was Black Kettle's niece, and Black Kettle was one of the four most important *Vehoo'o*, the ones who governed the Council. There were many who would know her. Hot, shameful tears began to burn at her eyes again.

"Bear," she whispered wretchedly. "Bear That Goes Alone."

"A brother of my society?" The Dog's voice hitched upward in surprise.

"Yes."

He let her go.

For a single, befuddling moment she missed the heat of his chest against her back. She had felt some odd measure of security that way, perhaps because he could do her little harm while holding her so. But the warmth of him was gone now, and Eagle turned cautiously to face him again.

His features were so hard and chiseled and dominant he should have been ugly, she thought, but he was not. He had a strong nose, but it wasn't hooked like Bear's, or sharp and aristocratic like Walks Far's.

"You are Eagle Voice?" the Dog asked.

He did know Bear, then. Eagle managed to nod.

He turned away to get his pony. "Stay here," he ordered. "Wait for me."

She stared after him. Then, for the first time, she noticed the *ho tam'tsit*, the dog rope, he carried on the waist string of the breechclout that hung over his leggings. The length of it was neatly coiled, its eagle feathers and porcupine quills dancing and shining in the bright sun. Its little red picket pin hung down to bounce against his thigh as he walked. Eagle's eyes widened.

Only one Dog could carry the *ho tam'tsit*. In a losing battle he drove the pin into the ground, tying himself to Grandmother Earth, pledging not to retreat. The action rallied his brothers to greater effort, and they came back to fight fiercely at his side. But sometimes even that desperate measure failed, and then the dog rope warrior would be obligated to remain tied there, fighting on to his death alone as the others fell or fled.

The carrier of the *ho tam'tsit* was the most fearsome of them all. He who carried it must use it, and to use it was to face the death road coldly and without regret.

The warrior vaulted onto his pony and whipped it around toward her. Eagle turned and ran back toward the *Wu'tapiu* camp as fast as her legs would move.

II

Fire Wolf was still scowling when Bear That Goes Alone rode up and joined him.

"That is everyone, I think."

Bear frowned sharply. He thought his friend's voice sounded strangely absent, and it was his opinion that a man's thoughts should be on this hunt.

"If anyone is so lazy that he still dallies," he answered, "then he deserves to be left out."

Fire Wolf shrugged, and they rode onto the nearest hill to

join the *Hotame-taneo'o* waiting at the top. As they approached, a woman broke away to meet them.

Several of the men glanced enviously at Bear. He didn't notice. His gaze was on his wife's appealing smile, and his big face softened for an unguarded moment.

"I wish you would put a babe in me so I would not feel obligated to join these hunts," Walking Spirit teased. She spoke quietly so that none of the others might hear her, but Fire Wolf was close. He turned away abruptly as sharp memory of another woman speaking those words clawed at his gut.

Then, almost immediately, the familiar pang splintered into confusion. It was not just the old and painful picture of Sweet Grass Woman that leapt in his mind this time. She faded in and out with another image, that of a frightened child with the same fleeting blaze of defiance in wide, ebony eyes.

Bear's Eagle reminded him of his wife, Fire Wolf realized. That was why he had been so lenient with her, why he had allowed her to run away. Sweet Grass Woman had possessed a heart of willful determination that had led her to be with him, the spawn of an unknown father, despite her family's objections. It would take the same sort of pluck for a child to risk the censure of the Dog Soldiers to glimpse a magnificent herd, Fire Wolf thought.

Now, as then, he felt a disturbing rush of amusement and approval that the little Eagle had dared it. Then the Dogs began moving again, and he nudged his pony to follow them.

Below them, on the plain, three thousand men and a smaller group of women were strung out in an uneven line. The *Hotame-taneo'o* warriors moved down to position themselves among them. After a long, breathless moment their hunting chief, Tall Bull, warbled out an imitation of a kestrel.

At once the Dogs' mounts flowed into easy, simultaneous motion. The others followed.

A heartbeat before they got close enough for the bulls to catch their *muh'ko ta'mins*, their man-smell, Tall Bull gave another cry. This one was a sharp, shrill order to charge. The buffalo reacted in the same instant. A close bull lifted his massive head from the grass and snorted. His mate gave a rumbling query in response, then heaved her big body around. The entire herd erupted into motion.

They were fast despite their dangerous size and strength. But the hunting ponies were faster.

Fire Wolf hung back a moment, as he always did. He watched and prayed to *Ma'heo'o*, the Wise One Above, that he might recall the sweet, heart-thumping urgency that carried the other men into the herd. Perhaps this time it would return to him. But as he swung his pony aside to allow Night Fighter to sweep past him, he felt only a familiar, cold weight pressing against his chest.

Flecks of foam were spattering from Night Fighter's pony. The crazy warrior rode up hard on a cow, hooting to gain the others' attention. Suddenly he sprang from his horse onto the back of the beast.

She leapt and spun, and her bull charged to her rescue. Night Fighter dug his fist into the remnants of shaggy, winter pelt that still covered her hump. He clung with long, strong legs, bare of the leggings that would have hindered such a ride. So he had planned this antic, Fire Wolf thought, and managed to smile as the other man pulled his knife from the sheath on his breechclout and reached down to slash the cow's throat.

His pony had remained close, running against her side. When the beast stumbled, the horse slowed, and Night Fighter vaulted onto its back again. He used his lance to strike the raging bull that had finally reached them.

"*Ah haih'!*" he gave the coup cry. "I am the first!" Then he drove his lance deep into that beast's heart, killing him, also.

There were crows of approval from the men close enough to witness the feat, but even as it was accomplished, the storm of dust and rumbling chaos grew farther and farther away. Fire Wolf touched his heels to his pony and galloped after them. He chose a bull; they were much fatter than the lactating and pregnant cows in this spring season. Riding close, he angled his lance across his body, allowing the buffalo to move slightly ahead. Using both hands, he thrust his weapon down, through fur and flesh. He put all his weight behind the lance, his muscles straining until they quivered and put up a sweet ache of pain. Finally the animal began to stagger. Fire Wolf yanked the weapon back as it dropped.

Sweat trickled down his forehead, burning his eyes. He

blinked and looked for another bull without glancing at his first kill.

Beneath his pony, Grandmother Earth continued to moan and tremble with the buffalos' flight. Walking Spirit and Night Fighter's woman came along behind him, stripping off the pelts so that other Dog squaws could take the meat and the offal. Fire Wolf finally reined in as they worked, his breath short and steady.

He watched a boy of about fourteen winters beat his pony to catch up with a runaway calf. The youngster struck once, then twice without hitting a kill zone before the animal dropped. Fire Wolf trotted over to him.

The boy was winded, but he beamed with satisfaction. Fire Wolf recognized him; he was another of Bear's *Wu'tapiu* family. That made him think of the little Eagle again, and he dismounted abruptly.

"Who are you?" His tone was shorter than he had intended it to be. The boy opened his mouth to retort, then he saw the *ho tam'tsit* on the warrior's breechclout.

"Blind Fox," he answered. "I am son to Little Moon and Gray Thunder of the *Wu'tapiu*, and nephew to Black Kettle."

"This is your first kill ever?"

"Yes."

Fire Wolf pulled his knife out. He stooped and sliced the calf's neck. When the blood spurted, he caught a handful of it, then he straightened to smear it over the boy's face.

"I honor you, brother."

Blind Fox's jaw dropped. Fire Wolf watched him and searched his heart for the memory of his own first kill, for the time when, as a boy, he had been congratulated so. Although it had happened only six or seven summers ago, he could not get that feeling back, either, could not share it with this child.

He turned away.

"Wait!" The boy worked furiously to strip some of the hide away and cut a sizable portion of the meat. It was always a good thing to give some to a powerful man to secure his friendship and the benefit of his prayers. Blind Fox could think of no one more appropriate than this elite soldier who had taken the time to honor him.

But Fire Wolf shook his head. "Find a man with many children, with many relations. Give it to him."

Blind Fox stared, hurt and confused. "You have no family?"

The sharp, hard pain came to Fire Wolf's gut again, and this time there was no one but Sweet Grass Woman in his heart. He had failed her and their babe. Now his meat went to the Dog woman, who shared their cooking paunches with him and tanned his hides. Now he was alone.

"A man with many children," he repeated, mounting again, rubbing his bloody hand along his pony's shoulder to clean it. This time when the boy called after him, he did not stop. He rode hard toward the camp on the Red Shield River, his past chasing him cruelly as it always did.

III

"I am hungry," complained old Medicine Wolf. He looked toward the *Wu'tapiu* lodges where Walks At Night, his wife, was working to butcher and roast the family's kills. None of the men at the *Vehoo'o* lodges commiserated with him, however. This council was far more important than food.

"Tell again exactly what this paper talk said," someone demanded.

"The white man called Bent read it to me," answered White Antelope. Like Black Kettle, he was one of the four principal chiefs. "He said that it came from the place they called Wash-ing-tone where their biggest chiefs live. It tells of an invitation to go visit and eat with the white chiefs in their city."

"Why?" Stone Forehead asked suspiciously. He was the most respected of the four principal chiefs; he was Keeper of the Sacred Medicine Arrows and a shaman of much renown. "We have already given them the mountains," he mused. "They put their Den-ver village there, and they seem quite happy with it. Why do they want to visit with us again, and why do they ask us to travel so far?"

The fourth principal *Vehoo'o* spoke up. "The paper talk said it is because we are friends now," explained War Bonnet. "Even among these white men, friends share their feasts. We travel to share with the Sioux and the Arapaho when they invite us," he pointed out.

Suddenly a man standing outside the circle gave a growl of dissension. He was Bull Bear, the first *Hotame-taneo'o* chief, the counterpart to Stone Forehead in matters of fighting and war. "If you believe that is all the spider tricksters want, then you are fools!" he spat.

The Council erupted into a cacophony of indignation and protest. Black Kettle raised his hand, palm out, to quiet them. "We will let every man speak his opinion."

Bull Bear left his gathering of Dog brothers and stepped forward. He was a relatively young man, arrogantly handsome, and he made an impressive figure as he paused to gather his words.

"You all remember the stories of when our grandfathers were boys," he began. "They did not even live here on the prairie then. The *Tse-Tsehesestahase*, the Cheyenne people, dwelled in the place of the big lakes, the land where Sun comes from at dawn. The *ve'ho'e*, the white spider trickster men, arrived there first. They filled up that land and drove our grandfathers here to this place. They made us leave our corn and our fields behind.

"But the *Tse-Tsehesestahase* are strong! We adapted! The spider tricksters took our corn, so we learned to hunt buffalo. Our warriors are the fiercest, the most cunning! We fought the Comanche and the Crow and claimed hunting grounds for our own! And then," he added more softly, "after we did all this, the spider tricksters began to appear even here.

"When first they came, they said they wanted only to cross these hunting grounds we fought so hard for. For a few circles of seasons, they kept their word. They passed through like a howling wind, going to the land where Sun sleeps to dig up their yellow metal. But like the wind leaves behind flattened grasses, so did these *ve'ho'e* leave behind signs of their trespass. They left all their dirty sicknesses in their wake.

"You remember this!" he charged. "What man among us did not lose a loved one to the *ve'ho'e* cho-ler-a?"

There were more mutters, and even Black Kettle nodded.

"I ask you to think," the war chief went on. "I ask you to remember what happened next, when our warriors were sick and our numbers were decimated. That was when some of the spider tricksters decided they did not want to go after their yellow metal after all, that they wanted to stay right here in our country! And you, our *Vehoo'o*, thought that that would be okay if they stayed up in the mountains. You said that buffalo do not go high into the mountains, so our hunters did not need that land.

"Now," he finished bitterly, "there are even more of them. They have stayed and spread and spawned like mongrels. If they were to stay in the mountains, they said, then they must have roads leading to those mountains. And if there were roads, then they should have forts and blue-coats to protect them from our younger, hotheaded men. When they wanted each of these things, they invited us to feast with them. They gave us useless presents, then they asked us for everything they wanted. Now they want to feast with us again, and I say it is because they want something more.

"I ask you to think of this before you act. What else do the *Tse-Tsehesestahase* have to give them? We have given our corn, our mountains. Should we hand over our buffalo? Our women? Our ponies? We have nothing left that it would not break our spirits to lose! We must stay away from these white men, or soon they will take everything from us that makes us proud to call ourselves Cheyenne!"

He turned haughtily away from the Council. His men broke to follow him, but Bear That Goes Alone stayed behind. Night Fighter, Walks Far, and Fire Wolf remained with him.

When the vote was in, Black Kettle announced it. "Our brother Bull Bear is right about all the things that have happened in the past. These *ve'ho'e* can be as greedy as spoiled children. But it is the opinion of this Council that we must placate, not antagonize them. We will go to their Wash-ing-tone and eat with them. It is a small thing, really. War Bonnet has agreed to represent the four principal *Vehoo'o*. Lean Bear and Stands In The Water will represent the rest of the Council."

Bear swore under his breath and strode angrily toward the *Hotame-taneo'o* lodges. He was halfway there when his gaze angled sharply toward the river and those of his own family's camp. Suddenly he knew it was time.

He went to Bull Bear's lodge. Falling Bird, the chief's wife, stepped back to let him enter, and Night Fighter, Fire Wolf, and Walks Far followed him inside. Bull Bear was seated by the fire trench, ripping into a hunk of meat with his teeth. When he saw them, he put the food aside.

"Get the others," Bear said shortly. Falling Bird looked at her husband. Bull Bear nodded.

Within moments the two other *Hotame-taneo'o* chiefs arrived. Tangle Hair appeared deceptively old, his face thin and haggard, his body scrawny. It was an image he cultivated, for it led unsuspecting adversaries to their deaths. In truth, he had only just passed his thirtieth winter, and he was faster and more deadly in a fight than any man.

The other chief was Tall Bull, the established leader of the band's hunts. His angular face was shiny with grease, and it was clear that he would rather be celebrating his success this day.

"So," he said. "The *Vehoo'o* will go east to twitter with the white men as though they were all women. Who among us doubted it? But there is nothing to be done about it now."

"I thought Stone Forehead would vote against it," Tangle Hair mused, settling in for a long discussion. "He does not usually endorse any action that involves the spider tricksters."

"Perhaps he learned of this invitation at the last moment, just as we did," Bear snapped. "Perhaps he did not have time to get his thoughts straight."

"That is probably true." Bull Bear nodded thoughtfully. "I myself did not learn of it until just after we came in from the hunt."

"We must put an end to these surprise councils," Bear declared, then he hesitated. He was not an eloquent man, and this was important. "Here," he said, thumping a fist against his broad chest. "In here, I feel . . . a darkness about this trip. It is worse than we think. It will start something terrible, if giving those mountains hasn't done so already. Think of this! Each time the *ve'ho'e* come with their hands outstretched, our *Vehoo'o* fill them. If we could simply go out onto the prairie and ask a buffalo to fall dead, soon they would all be rotting on the earth and we would starve. Do you see?"

Tall Bull straightened. Such a scenario unnerved him badly.

"I think . . . we must learn of the *Vehoo'o*'s plans sooner," Bear went on. "We must have time, and a means to sway the

Council once that time is ours. I think we need a spy among them."

Stunned silence fell in the lodge. There had always been subtle friction between the *Hotame-taneo'o* and the *Vehoo'o*. One comprised hot-blooded fighting men; the other consisted of elders who rarely picked up their bows. But each faction knew that the People could not survive without the other, and they had always trusted each other to act in the bands' best interest. To violate that trust was, at first, unthinkable.

Then Night Fighter recovered to poke gingerly at the idea. "The *Vehoo'o* are chosen from among their own numbers, and they all know well where our sentiments lie. They would never elect one of us to join them."

"No," Bear argued. "They would not. But they listen to their women."

He watched their faces carefully in the dim, smoky lodge. He knew the precise moment when each man understood. There was a sense of fraternity among these seven *Hotame-taneo'o* that was fierce and inviolate. Now he would trust one of them with a most precious responsibility. He would give him his sister.

"She is Black Kettle's beloved niece," he pointed out. "She could easily act as a liaison between him and us. She could be sent into the *Wu'tapiu* camp to visit her mothers, and while there she could learn all of what is currently weighing on Black Kettle's mind. Then she could work to bring the *Wu'tapiu* women around to the *Hotame-taneo'o* point of view. When they start yammering at him like magpies, Black Kettle almost always bows to their wishes."

"I like it," said Bull Bear thoughtfully.

"But will *she* like it?" muttered Night Fighter.

Bear shrugged. "She is an obedient and malleable girl."

He broke off at the strange sound that came from beside him. It was not one he had ever heard before, though he had been a Dog for many circles of seasons. At first he thought Fire Wolf was choking. But there was no meat in his hand, nothing to cause such a problem. And then he understood.

The dog rope warrior was laughing.

The other men exchanged glances. None of them could

recollect ever witnessing this, either. One by one they joined him until eyes were streaming and bellies hurt.

Only Bear remained silent. He was confused, and that made him irritable.

Finally Fire Wolf shrugged to indicate that his surprising reaction was unimportant. If the girl possessed more spirit than her brother was aware of, then it was too late to tell him so.

"You will take her?" Bear demanded.

For a moment Fire Wolf entertained himself by thinking about it. He saw her again, those strong, slender limbs pumping as she fled from him, her black eyes flashing at the thought of him doing any damage to her mother's lodge. He remembered high cheekbones in a delicate face and thick black braids. How would that hair look unfettered, spilling free over his buffalo robes? How hot could that secret, inner fire burn?

Something faint and whispery moved in his gut at the promise of it. The conversation began to eddy around him, distant and unheard.

"You should have the first opportunity to claim her," Bear decided. "You carry the *ho tam'tsit*. And you"—he glanced at Tall Bull—"you hold a position of some honor. I would defer to whatever you two decide."

"And what of the rest of us?" asked Tangle Hair. "I agree that she would make a pleasant addition to any lodge."

"I am asking much of her," Bear answered carefully. "I must give her something in return."

Tangle Hair was startled, then he understood. He had a wife, Cherries In The Snow. He knew little enough of this Eagle, but she was from a good family and deserved more than to be relegated to the position of second wife, a rarity among the Dogs in any event.

"So be it," he murmured.

Tall Bull thought a moment, then he grunted and nodded at Fire Wolf. "I give you first choice, friend. I do not want her. No disrespect intended, but I think I would rather be hunting than initiating a child. I think I will stick with those squaws whose husbands have divorced them, thrown them away. They are randy and well learned."

Silence fell, expectant and poised. Fire Wolf became aware of it suddenly, and memory returned to him to tear away at the softness that had pooled in his gut for an unguarded moment. Damn the contrary part of him that would always remember black hair spilling over night robes.

"No," he said and shook his head. Never again. He pushed rudely past Bear and ducked out the door.

They all glanced at Walks Far.

That warrior felt a strange sensation grab his gut. Tall Bull hadn't claimed her. Fire Wolf hadn't, either. Impossibly, the offer had reverted to him, the only other unwed warrior among them.

He wanted her; he could not deny that. He remembered the way she had looked just this sun, standing there in her new doeskin. When had she grown up? The summer before she had been flat-chested, with scabby knees and a fumbling lack of grace. He could almost remember her as a toddling babe. He had been born to the Ridge People, was White Antelope's grandson, and the Ridges and the *Wu'tapiu* had always been closely associated.

It was natural for him to ask for her. He gave a lopsided grin as he considered how poorly the hunt had gone for him; he had spent much of it considering when and how he would approach Bear with the matter. He had finally decided to wait until the end of this gathering. Somehow, even with the strict chaperoning of such a girl, he would get time alone with her to ascertain her feelings on the matter.

Now she was being offered to him, regardless of her feelings.

"Our boy is romantic," Night Fighter teased, clutching his heart. "He wants a wife who loves him."

"She will learn to," Bear insisted.

"No, no, he has a point," Bull Bear cautioned. "What wife would embrace this *Hotame-taneo'o* life if not for the man she has chosen to follow?"

"I will tell her to follow, and she will follow," Bear said stubbornly, and suddenly Walks Far was angry.

He pushed away from the taut hide of the lodge wall. Bear was two winters older and outweighed him considerably, but he stood chest to chest with the other man, his jaw hard.

"I will think on this," he said tightly, "and give you my

answer when Sun comes again." He pushed past the hide that was still askew from Fire Wolf's abrupt exit.

Tall Bull shook his head worriedly. Nothing was right. First there was the dog rope man's laughter, and now this, a pup of a warrior, swelled up to face down one of his own.

"I am beginning to fear that nothing good will come of this night," he said glumly. "Oh, I fear it greatly."

IV

"Wed Walks Far?" Eagle whispered. He must really have been flirting with her yesterday, she thought wildly. He must have gone to Bear and asked for her. Bear would not waste time trying to arrange a marriage for her otherwise, not when she had not even bled yet.

As the seasons had passed, she had fretted over whom her brother might give her to when the time came. At least she knew Walks Far, she thought. He was not a stranger, and she liked him. But she did not want to join with *anyone* yet, and, oh *Ma'heo'o*, she surely did not want to follow a Dog!

How could Bear ask that of her?

A sense of betrayal swept through her with such force it made her shake. She launched herself to her feet and fled from the lodge.

Walks Far felt a quick stab of hurt in his gut as he watched her run from the *Wu'tapiu* camp. He grunted softly, and Walking Spirit looked over at him from where she was stringing up strips of meat to dry.

"Do you want her, truly?" she asked.

Walks Far nodded without hesitation. In the night that had just passed, he had indeed thought about it long and hard. Without Bear's plan complicating the issue, he could have waited, could have taken the time to coax and woo Eagle through her reservations. But Walks Far knew that Bear would not wait. He would find one of the other Dogs to take her, and eventually, Eagle would bow to his wishes. If he stood on principle now, he would lose her.

Walks Far did not want that to happen. Somehow, she felt like his. She had from the moment she had smiled up at him, her breasts straining against even that new doeskin.

"Well, then," said Walking Spirit. "I will see what I can do." She started off toward the river, where Eagle had gone.

She found her far down the bank, where the spare trees gave way to tangled, wet grasses. "It is not terrible being a Dog wife," she said softly. "It is only different."

Eagle started and twisted around, scrubbing her hands over her cheeks to erase the signs of her tears. Walking Spirit came down to squat beside her.

"I will tell you all of it, truthfully," she went on, "and then you can decide. If you still do not want Walks Far, I will try to make both him and Bear forget it. But I think Walks Far will be very disappointed."

"He would?" Eagle squirmed as a strange onslaught of butterflies came to her belly. She was not sure she liked them at all.

"Yes. Even *Hotame-taneo'o* fall in love, more fiercely, I think, than other men." But that, she thought privately, was something Eagle would have to learn for herself.

"It is lonely at first," she admitted, "leaving your family and going to live among strangers. But you are not alone, because everyone else has done this, also, and we all know how it feels.

"Some seasons we have to move more than other bands, if the Dogs are needed to fight or guard many hunts. And the women all pitch in to take care of the men who are not wed. But that is just a little extra work.

"There are not many babes. Perhaps *Ma'heo'o* does not bless us as often as other women because he gives only the strong children to us. They must be sturdy and healthy to survive the war camps when they come, and all the demands that are made upon their mothers.

"But think of the freedom! Think of it! There are no mothers or grandmothers to fuss over how you fill your parfleches or clean your skins. There is only you, and your man, and your friends, following the wind."

Eagle looked at her brother's wife. She always seemed so quiet and well-mannered, but high color had come to her cheeks as she spoke.

"You . . . you love it," Eagle breathed.

Walking Spirit grinned. "Yes, I suppose I do."

It did not truly sound that bad, Eagle thought. And really, truly, what choice did she have? She knew that some girls managed to resist their brothers' choices, but Eagle trembled at the thought of screaming and holding a knife to her breast in protest. She did not think she could do such a thing.

"I will be there for you," said Walking Spirit. Though she barely knew her, somehow Eagle was sure that Walking Spirit spoke true.

"I . . ." she began, but she could not actually say the words.

Walking Spirit nodded understandingly. "It is okay," she said. "I will tell them for you."

2

Moon When The Cherries Are Ripe, 1863
Flint Arrowpoint River

I

The night was too hot for this, Eagle thought miserably. Her hair, unbraided, clung to her neck. She was naked, but the buffalo rope draped over her shoulders was suffocating. The endless prairie wind blew its torrid breath against the walls of her grandmother's lodge, and the fire threw off its own heat inside. Sweat began to bead on her upper lip and trickle down her ribs, smearing the red paint on her skin.

She watched as Walks At Night removed a coal from the flames and carefully sprinkled sweet grass, sage, and juniper needles upon it. The lodge filled with cloying incense. Then the old woman placed the ember on the ground in front of her, and suddenly Eagle felt her throat squeeze tight.

The moon had waned three times since the *Wu'tapiu* had returned home from the great spring hunt, and she could no longer remember why she had given Walking Spirit her promise to wed. Her brother's wife's face was distant and murky in her memory now, no matter how hard she tried to recall it. *How could she trust someone whose face she could not even remember?*

But she had to trust, because she had finally bled this sun. While her grandmother performed this ceremony, Blind Fox was riding for the Dog camp on the Smoky Hill River to tell Bear and Walks Far that it was time. She and Walks at Night would go to the women's moon lodge for four sleeps, and when they came out, Walks Far would be waiting for her.

"I cannot . . . do . . . this thing!" she bleated suddenly.

"Bah!" Walks at Night snapped. "What is this foolishness? Do you want the birds in the trees to sing songs of your love?

21

A child can know nothing of love. That does not come until you are old, until your knees hurt and your teeth ache. Then you know love, when your man has been beside you through everything, when you have patched his wounds and bled for him. And then the birds are only silent in awe of it.

"You cry because you think you will lose your family. That is silly, also. You have kin with those people, and they visit us at every spring hunt and every summer.

"You are a woman of the People, and I pray to *Ma'heo'o* that this is the hardest thing you will ever have to do, but it will not be. So now you must tell me. Will you whimper through these sleeps we spend in the moon lodge, or will you learn all those things it is necessary for a woman to know?"

Eagle colored, shamed at her behavior. "I will learn," she whispered. Of course she would. It was what Bear intended for her to do.

II

Eagle stood stiffly in the moon lodge as Walks At Night wrapped the chastity rope around her waist. It was passed down and backward between her thighs, then each branch was wound around her legs. The rope was worn by all women when they reached puberty, as long as they were unwed or whenever they were away from the protection of their husband. While it was in place, no man would violate it.

When it was secured, she tied on her leggings, then a lovely new doeskin was dropped over her shoulders. This one was fringed along the hem and across her breasts, and a row of elk's teeth ran down the outside of each sleeve. Her breath caught as she smoothed it over her hips. She had never owned anything so elaborate and beautiful. Her mothers and grandmothers must have been working on it ever since she agreed to be wed!

She flashed Walks At Night a grateful look even as she began to inch toward the door. "I can go now?"

Walks At Night nodded, and she hurried outside.

She shielded her eyes against the brilliant blue sky and began wandering through the crowd. As her eyes scanned the visitors, she felt another cold trickle of alarm at the sheer

number of them. Her marriage to a Dog was just unorthodox
enough that she had expected Bear and Walks Far to simply
come and whisk her away. Now it seemed that all of the People
had come to watch that happen.

Visitors' lodges stretched all along the river. There were the
mingled smells of too many cookfires, of buffalo and venison
and the pungent tang of berry cakes. Children squealed and
raced among it all, and dogs barked after them.

Finally Eagle's gaze fell upon the *Hotame-taneo'o* lodges.
Her brother was there, speaking with Night Fighter. There was
no sign of that dog rope warrior. As for Walks Far, he would be
off somewhere making his own preparations for this day.

Walking Spirit waved to her, and she went hesitantly toward
them, to the tepees with their black smoke-flap ornaments. The
women clasped her hands warmly, then she was turned toward
the men, the fearsome *Hotame-taneo'o* themselves.

For a moment her knees felt weak. They all seemed so
young and proud and arrogant. How, oh, how was she to
become one of them? She wasn't anything like them at all.

Bear placed a hand on each of her shoulders. She had not
spoken to him since fleeing from her mother's lodge at the
hunting camp. Though she had finally capitulated to his
wishes, she still expected a reprimand. Instead, his voice was
low, as though he searched for words.

"*Na'sima*, little sister . . . I wish to thank you. This is a
very good thing you are doing, for our family and our people."

Her eyes widened. Thank her? Then she heard her mother
calling to them.

It would begin now.

Her heart hurtled upward, and she swallowed against it.
They went back to her mother's tepee, where her whole family
had gathered, even Black Kettle.

"Oh!" Sun Roads gasped, and Eagle whirled. A procession
approached them from the Ridge People lodges, and her own
eyes widened at the sight of it. She had not been expecting this,
had not dreamed of anything so grand. Walks Far would not be
coming to live with her people, so there was no call for his
family to gift hers so richly. But the ponies that trotted toward
them were laden with supple doeskins and trade blankets.

There were guns and bows and arrows. At the end of the line was the most beautiful mare Eagle had ever seen.

She guessed immediately that the pony must be from White Antelope's prized herd. She was a glorious copper brown, shining red in the sun. Her points were black, and her eyes were big and expressive and dark. But more than that, her legs were strong and her chest was deep.

A warrior she did not recognize handed the lead leather to her. "She is Wind Runner," he said. "She has seen several winters and she is trained, not a filly. Our uncle, White Antelope, hopes she will serve you well."

Eagle was speechless. This was a better animal than anyone in her family, except maybe Bear, had ever owned.

"*Ha ho'*," she finally whispered. "Thank you." Then Bear boosted her up onto the mare's back.

Wind Runner pranced at her sudden weight, making the hawk bells on her bridle jingle. Small Blanket took the leather to guide her on the traditional journey back to the Ridge People camp. Behind her, the other ponies were quickly stripped of their burdens, then repacked with gifts for Walks Far's people. Eagle tightened her legs delicately against the mare's ribs and grinned, delighted with her response. Then she looked up and saw Walks Far.

She had not seen him since that first day of the spring hunt. She had not known that he had earned a scalp shirt, that he had that many coups. The circles of hair laid in a V across his chest, and rich strips of quills glistened along the outside of each sleeve. His black hair was greased and his braids shone in the sun.

She managed to slide off Wind Runner's back, though her legs threatened not to hold her. But then Walks Far disappeared again, lost behind the crowd of his relatives who descended upon her. The women pulled her into a nearby lodge to finish dressing her while the Ridge men took the reciprocating gifts off the ponies.

Inside the tepee the air was close and warm. "Ow," Eagle complained. She tried to pull away, but hands continued to poke and prod at her. Strings of bright blue trade beads were wrapped through the slits that had been cut through her ears as a child. Copper bracelets were pushed onto her arms, and a belt of slick, shiny antelope hair appeared around her waist. Stripes of vermilion and yellow were painted across her cheekbones. Then the crowd began jostling her again, leading her outside.

Sun hid low behind the prairie now, throwing pink and purple shadows back across the buffalo grass. Eagle looked around desperately. Oh, how she needed someone familiar to hold on to! Where was Sun Roads? Then there was a touch at her elbow, and she whirled into Walks Far's arms.

Her heart began thudding.

"I have always wondered what goes on in those women's lodges when a girl is wed," he said. "Do you know what it sounds like from out here, with all that squealing and giggling and thumping going on? But whatever they did to you, I am glad. You are very beautiful."

Beautiful? Could he truly think so? Eagle's breath caught painfully in her throat, then he grinned, cocking his head to the side the way she had always remembered. Suddenly it didn't matter if he was fibbing just to make her feel better. This was Walks Far, happy, handsome Walks Far, and he was her friend.

She slipped her hand shyly into his and clung to it.

III

The moon was yellow and low when Bear cracked a delicate antelope bone in two and sucked out the marrow. He sat outside Walking Spirit's lodge, staring at the embers of the cookfire that smoldered there. It was far too hot to cook indoors, not to mention that the camaraderie of such an occasion would not allow it.

But Bear was not in the mood for camaraderie. Only Night Fighter sat beside him, gnawing the last of the meat from his own bone. He tossed it aside abruptly and stood. In a lightning reflex he flicked his knife from its sheath and hurled it into the earth close to Bear's knee.

Bear bellowed and leapt to his feet. "That was crazy!"

Night Fighter laughed. "Ah, but it got your mind off your troubles, did it not?"

Bear grunted and looked at the big, white *Vehoo'o* tepees pitched in the center of the camp. Outside them stood Black

Kettle and White Antelope. As he watched, the two chiefs shared a smoke.

"I am wondering," he mused, "if arranging this marriage was the wisest thing I could have done. This union of their kin melds those two together more than ever."

Night Fighter shrugged. "You worry too much. I think we should see to it that there *is* a union of their kin."

He started off toward the center of the camp. His wife, Wind Woman, jogged up beside him and held out a painted robe. Night Fighter gave a short laugh.

"It will do no good if we cannot find the bride."

"She and her mother are with Walks Far's people, on the other side of the water."

Night Fighter set off in that direction. Behind him, Bear lengthened his stride to catch up. They splashed into the river, leading a growing procession of Dogs and their women.

Eagle saw them bearing down on her and felt her tummy roll over.

"Daughter," said Small Blanket. "I would tell you this now, quickly, before they reach us. You have always been taught to be modest, and you have been a good daughter. Now you must forget all that and be a good wife. It will be scary and mysterious the first time, but you must be willing. Soon it will become a joy."

Soon? Eagle thought wildly. When her bones ached and her teeth hurt, as Walks At Night had said? She moaned and looked back at the *Hotame-taneo'o* coming cheerfully toward her.

The painted robe was whipped out to its full length, and Wind Woman, Cherries In The Snow, Falling Bird, and Walking Spirit laughed as they herded her toward it. Night Fighter lifted her in his strong arms, spinning her around foolishly as the others hooted their approval. All around them the steady, throbbing beat of drums began. Suddenly it seemed to Eagle that there were so many cookfires that the whole night glowed a frightful orange. Then Night Fighter deposited her upon the hide, and the Dog warriors gripped it to lift her and carry her off to the *Hotame-taneo'o* part of the camp.

They lowered her to the ground again in front of Walks Far's lodge. There was no hooting and laughter now. Wind Woman gave her shoulder a little push.

"It will be fine," Walking Spirit whispered. "You have known him forever."

Eagle managed to nod. She wanted to ask her about what Walks At Night and Small Blanket had said, but there was no time. Night Fighter pulled back the hide door flap, and the opening beyond it yawned at her like a black hole.

Eagle pushed to her feet and stepped clumsily inside. For a moment she simply stood, her fists clenched at her sides. There was a fire in this tepee, low and banked into embers, laid deep in a trench in the ground to confine some of its heat. Still, it threw off meager light, enough that she could see.

She had never been in a lodge so . . . so manly and stark. The tepee lining that was gaily decorated in her mother's lodge was bare of design here. Along its upper edge hung a bow, a shield, a quiver full of arrows, and a medicine bag. There were no well-worn, comfortable backrests of hide strips laced over cottonwood branches. There were no parfleches, no altar for burning sweet grass, just some clothing and a lone pile of buffalo-skin bedding against one wall.

Walks Far sat upon it. He had taken off his scalp shirt, and his naked chest was smooth and broad in the red light from the fire. His unbraided hair streamed down his back now, still slick and shiny from the fat he had rubbed into it.

He pushed to his feet, and Eagle jumped.

"I could . . . I could maybe not take my rope off." Oh, *Ma'heo'o*, had she said that aloud? Her mother's advice came back to her, and she felt her skin flame. She would never bear the gossip and shame if Walks Far was instantly dissatisfied with her and threw her away.

Instead, he came to her and tucked her hand into his own, much as she had placed it there earlier. She shivered at his touch, wondering how it could feel so different now. When she had clung to him before, it had been strong and protective. Now it seemed hot, and his hand was as sweaty as hers.

Her tentative grip made something tight and panicked clamp itself around his own belly as well.

Walks Far had had women, enough romping, fun-filled encounters with Sioux and Arapaho girls to know exactly what to do now, how to do it. He knew that he should bring his mouth down on hers, fast and fevered, in that exotic, strangely gratifying gesture his people had learned from those spider women. But this was Eagle, lanky, sloe-eyed Eagle Voice, who had always giggled at his teasing.

He wanted her with an aching, pulsing need that sluiced through his blood and settled in his groin, but he could not think what to do about it. Her eyes stayed on his, waiting, needing him to guide her.

Impulsively he moved her hand to his hardness.

"Oh!" She jerked away. For a horrified moment he thought she would run straight out of the lodge. But then her gaze dropped and her eyes grew huge.

She had not asked for this, had never wanted it, but he had asked for her. He had chosen to hunt and fight for her, and she wanted desperately to please him. She put her hand out again and touched him gingerly.

A low, moaning sound came from his throat. He reached out and pulled her against him.

When his mouth first tried to cover hers, she threw her head to the side, not understanding. His hand cupped her jaw and brought it back. His tongue dived past her teeth, tasting, seeking. She opened to him and cautiously met it with her own.

His hands moved down her hips and caught the hem of her doeskin. Slowly he began drawing it upward. "All right?" His voice was raspy, strange.

"Yes," she managed. "Yes, all right."

She felt dizzy as the warm air began to lick at her skin. Then the doeskin was gone and her leggings slid down her thighs. He tugged at the rope underneath and it began unraveling.

"My . . . my feet."

He felt stupid. *Ma'heo'o*, he thought, despite the scalp shirt, despite the coups, was he that much of a boy? He knelt hurriedly and tried to unlace her moccasins, but the leggings were in the way now, pooled around her ankles, and the rope was becoming tangled through it all. He swore.

A whimper escaped her, pained and mortified.

"No! It is not your fault!" He lunged to his feet again, his arms strong around her. "Here, sit." When she didn't move, he put pressure on her shoulders. "Sit."

She dropped quickly to the buffalo robes. Somehow, he managed to free her feet of all their confines.

Rising up, he covered her body with his own, lowering himself upon her carefully. He was warm, she thought. Slowly, in spite of herself, she relaxed. When he reached down to push her legs apart, she did not stop him. Her limbs felt heavy, liquid, more inclined to respond to his will than her own.

She felt his fingers probing, and suddenly the heaviness swam upward, filling her belly. She whimpered again, but this time it was a plea for something she did not understand, a need so demanding and mysterious she could do nothing but beg for it. It swelled even more when she felt his hardness pressing and questing against her most secret flesh.

That, she thought, yes, that was it, knowing with the age-old wisdom of woman. Instinctively, she arched up against him, only to have him pull back.

"Once," he managed. "This once I will hurt you. Then I promise, my woman, I will never do it again."

Her eyes flew open wide. How could that be? Where had she gotten the notion that this was always and forever, every sleep in their robes? But before she could reason it out, the pain came.

It was sudden and jolting. She gasped and recoiled, then there was a flood of warmth, easing the hurt. He moved within her, filling her to the point where wanting, reaching, was agony. But then he left again, pulling back so that she had to chase him, press up against him. Could she ask for more? Could she ask him to stay inside her?

She wrapped her arms around his neck to hold him close, and then, as suddenly as it all began, he moaned and thrust into her hard. There was a ripe moment of inconceivable pleasure, and then he fell heavy atop her.

Finally the last of the light from the fire died, and Eagle felt the delicious new tension slide reluctantly out of her body as well.

3

Moon When The Water Begins to Freeze, 1863 Smoky Hill Country

I

Eagle's yawn broke off into a shiver as she paused in the chill dawn. The steep hillocks of the Dogs' lush Smoky Hill camp were cloaked in mist, thick with cottonwoods and grasses and the last of the season's berries. A pheasant darted out from under cover, startled by her presence.

She missed the unbroken prairie of the *Wu'tapiu*'s southern lands so much she ached with it.

She went to the river and hunkered down to plunge a buffalo heart sac into the frigid water. Gathering the top closed, she lugged it back up the slope. Walks Far popped out of their lodge just as she reached it, heading down for his morning bath with the other men.

"The river is as icy as a *mis'tai*, a ghost," she warned. "Cold Maker moved closer while we slept."

Walks Far's heart jumped in his chest. Her eyes were as dark and bright as obsidian stones, he thought, and her hair was wild and free from sleep. He knew that she truly did not appreciate how beautiful she was. He knew, too, that she was not happy here, but he had seen her narrow chin jut out determinedly time and again, and she had never murmured a word of complaint.

"Then I hope you have a warm fire going when I get back," he answered, touching a wisp of her hair.

Her eyes widened. "You will eat with me?" Since she had come to live with the Dogs, Walks Far usually left her in the mornings to go council. But this time he nodded.

"Then we are riding up to the Red Shield," he added.

"To hunt? Will everyone go?" Her heart yearned at the thought of a familiar place with familiar faces, but she knew as soon as she asked that it was doubtful. The huge buffalo herd that had gathered there in the spring would have broken up into smaller foraging groups by now. Autumn grasses were too thin to sustain such numbers.

Indeed, Walks Far shook his head. "No. Skinny Toes said he saw some white spiders up there. He is going out to find Fire Wolf's party. We will meet them, and together we will track the tricksters to find out where they are headed."

The dog rope man was counciling somewhere in the Sioux country. Eagle had heard that he had been there since before her wedding.

She nodded and turned away. If Walks Far was eating with her, then she had more important things to worry about than the dog rope warrior and spider tricksters.

Inside, she pulled her cooking paunch off its tripod branches and hauled it to the door to spill out the dead water that had sat in it overnight. She filled it again with the living water in the heart sac and built up the fire, pushing a few round, heavy stones into the flames. Then she dug through a pile of vegetables she had gathered just before the last of yesterday's sun. She tossed a handful of wild peas and tuber roots into the water, then added the last of some elk meat as well.

The stones were red-hot. She tried to balance one atop two sticks to drop it into the paunch to set the stew to boiling, and seared her finger so badly she yelped.

The icy river water would help. She went outside again. The camp was awake now; the warriors were coming up from the river, hooting, shaking water from their hair. Fragrant ribbons of smoke eddied up from every lodge. Two Feathers, the *Hotame-taneo'o* crier, strode along the pathways, chanting the news of the ride to the Red Shield. Beloved war ponies snorted as sleepy squaws led them out to graze. But there were no elders, and the only child in sight was Skinny Toes, the aloof orphan who had attached himself to the Dogs.

Eagle sighed and headed down the bank again.

As she came around a patch of trees, she found Walking Spirit, Wind Woman, and Falling Bird squatting near the water's edge. Walking Spirit was straining to fill her sac while the others hooted with laughter.

"Here," Wind Woman said, "let me do that for you. I had the

good sense to accept a small husband with sensible appetites."

"I do not see what one has to do with the other," Eagle ventured, plunging her sore hand into the water.

The others snickered again. "Bear is trying to put a babe in me," Walking Spirit explained kindly.

"And I think his cock is probably as big as everything else about him." Falling Bird laughed. "Look at this one! She can hardly move for the hurt it brings."

Eagle's eyes widened. The closest she had ever come to hearing women talk of such things were those cryptic exchanges just before her wedding.

"You say he hurts you?" she asked Walking Spirit, shocked and fascinated.

"Oh, no. There is just so much of him, and sometimes he forgets his own strength, but I never realize it until later."

"And what of you, Eagle?" Falling Bird winked at the others. "I would guess that Walks Far is very small or very weak, because you have seemed agile every sun you have been with us."

"Walks Far!" Eagle gasped and pushed to her feet again. "He said he would eat with me this morning!"

She hurried back to their lodge. He was there, peering down into her cooking paunch. *Very small or very weak.* She did not think he was either of those things. His young body was lean and hard. His shoulders were broad beneath his straight, black hair, wet now and clinging to his back.

But he had never caused her to be stiff and sore. He *had* continued to come to her sleeping robes after the night they were wed, but only sporadically.

Something unsettled sank in her belly. She must be doing something wrong.

She gathered up two horn bowls that Medicine Woman Later had gifted her with and filled them. They sat near the fire. Her gaze angled toward Walks Far, watching him as he ate.

Suddenly she put her bowl aside. "Would you . . ." She licked her lips, then rushed on. "We could be together before you left," she blurted, waving a hand at their robes.

To her horror, he laughed. "Is that what is making you so fidgety this morning?" He put a hand on each of her shoulders, pulling her closer.

"Oh," she breathed.

She wanted to try this again, to make it be the way the other women had described. She reached for him, and he tumbled her beneath him. His breath was hot on her neck, then his hands were beneath her doeskin, sliding sweetly over her skin.

He had learned her body so well, better even than she knew it herself. He slid down and touched his tongue to the hollow just inside her hipbone, and she heard herself whimper, though she had never consciously thought that she liked him to kiss her just there. She arched to his touch, but then he moved on, up her ribs, to her breasts.

Quickly there, because the sensation of his mouth on her nipple made her writhe. She wanted to tell him not to stop, but the words clogged in her throat because he was up near her collarbone now, behind her ear, and yes, that was good, so good she forgot what she wanted to say.

He nudged her legs apart with his knee, and she opened to him willingly. There was no pain this time when he entered her, because he did it slowly, with maddening care. Suddenly desperate, she pushed up against him, capturing all of him.

"Ah, yes, wife, that is good." He groaned, as he always seemed to, and then he stopped.

Eagle bit down hard on her lip. When he touched his mouth again to that spot behind her ear, she sighed. Slowly, tremulously, she let out all the breath that she had been holding.

II

"There," Night Fighter said. He laid on his belly atop one of the rugged ravines that slashed through this country northwest of the Red Shield. Below him, three coyotes trotted his way, tongues lolling. Then they paused, looking back the way they had come.

"White spiders," Walks Far agreed. "Still west of us."

Night Fighter nodded. They had picked up the *ve'ho'e* tracks near the site of the old hunting camp and had followed them for four suns. The *ve'ho'e* were moving toward no fort he knew of, and their tracks told him that they were an odd mixture of blue-coats and little-buffalo-men, the ones who raised the strange, squat animals they called cat-tul.

He pushed to his feet after Walks Far, and they returned to their ponies. Throwing their heads back, Night Fighter and Walks Far howled like wolves, grabbing the attention of the rest of the *Hotame-taneo'o* scouting party.

They rode in circles, communicating what they had learned. Further sign of the enemy had been discovered, and the enemy appeared to be moving, for there were no smokes on the horizon to indicate that they had camped.

Strangely, the other Dogs did not turn in their direction. One warrior laid his quirt into his pony's hide instead, his horse plunging into a sudden gallop. The others followed. Night Fighter and Walks Far exchanged glances.

"They have found them," Night Fighter muttered.

They kicked their ponies into a run as well. When they finally caught up with the others, they saw that Skinny Toes had rejoined them. It was the first they had seen of the orphan since leaving the Smoky Hill camp. The boy's ugly little paint strained beneath him.

"The spiders are stopped at a south branch of the Moon Shell River," he gasped as he rode. "Fire Wolf is nearby, waiting for you. There are fifteen white men."

The dog rope man had only four warriors. "We must hurry," Bear snapped.

The Dogs began yipping their approach. They found Fire Wolf's party a hard ride later. Twenty head of horses milled white-eyed in the shallow river behind them.

"Where did they come from?" Bear demanded.

Fire Wolf rode up to meet him. "I stumbled upon them on my way here. They were roaming free. Who am I to refuse such a gift from *Ma'heo'o*?"

Night Fighter grinned. "The Wise One is feeling generous this sun. He has even given us white mongrels to kill."

Fire Wolf did not smile. He whipped his black pony around and positioned the butt of his Remington .44 saddle carbine against his hip. "I think I would like to start with that fire-haired one."

Bear, Night Fighter, and Walks Far looked at the *ve'ho'e* who were gathered downriver. One of them, a little-buffalo-man, had dismounted. He had a face full of orange hair, and he strode excitedly back and forth in front of the blue-coats. Then, unaccountably, he pointed straight at the ponies Fire Wolf had captured. The wind snatched his voice and hurled it back toward the *Hotame-taneo'o*, but they could not understand his *ve'ho'e* words.

"They've got my goddamned horses!" he bleated. "Bunch of them bastard savages run right through my corral last week and stole 'em all."

He made a move toward the Indians. An officer dismounted to stop him.

"Easy now. There's no reason for you to be running over there and giving them your hair." Dunn's eyes stayed on the Cheyenne, but now he spoke to his men. "I don't want to engage them unless I have to. All I've been instructed to do is recover this civilian's stock and disarm the thieves. With any amount of luck, they'll oblige. We've got them red-handed. Even Indians know when it's best to shrug and tell the story." He began to move off on foot up the river.

"Jesus Christ on a mule!" shouted a soldier. "What's he doing?"

"What is this?" Walks Far echoed the white man's question as Dunn approached them.

Bear looked at Fire Wolf. "It is your call, my friend." None of the *Hotame-taneo'o* chiefs had accompanied them. Leadership of this mission fell to the dog rope man.

Fire Wolf's eyes narrowed as Dunn stopped thirty feet away and waved at him, sensing his authority. He lifted a leg over his black's head and sprang to the ground.

Dunn motioned to the ponies as Fire Wolf approached him. "Where'd you get them?" he asked. "One of my men here says they're stolen from his property."

He took a step toward the horses. Fire Wolf laid his carbine in front of him, blocking his way.

"Now, look here," Dunn said, forcing a smile. "I'm authorized by the United States Government to retrieve this stock. Give it over, boys, and we can all be on our way."

Fire Wolf did not move. "Every animal here was taken from my land," he said, his Cheyenne tongue rolling gutturally into the tense silence. "If ever they were yours, they became so no longer when they trespassed."

He moved away, then turned to stone as the *ve'ho'e* grabbed his gun, tugging on it.

"Your weapons, please, and the ponies," Dunn demanded.

"You are a fool."

Fire Wolf wrenched his rifle free. Hot fury built in his head, but before he could act on it, the report of a *ve'ho'e* gun cracked out into the quiet.

A curdling war cry rent the air in the next moment. Fire Wolf brought up his carbine. Dunn dived safely down the bank.

It did not matter. The fire-haired one was bellowing and running toward him, and Fire Wolf had sensed from the first that this man was the force behind this particular invasion of his land. He squeezed off a shot, and the civilian dropped. Then he gave a shrill cry, and his black stallion broke from the confusion and surged to a stop beside him.

Fire Wolf vaulted onto him, straddling backward, bringing his rifle up again. Dunn was a useless target, still crawling through the grass. Fire Wolf aimed for the soldiers pressing on and fired again.

Behind him, the Dogs spread across the prairie, galloping north, east, and south. Raven-feathered arrows hissed through the air, finding flesh. But gradually the remaining blue-coats fell out of range as they charged haphazardly, trying to pursue an enemy who would not stop and fight according to any West Point strategy.

Only then did Fire Wolf reach behind him for the black's mane. Gripping it, he hurtled around again to face forward. He threw his head back, his unbraided hair tangled and whipping in the wind, and screamed once in unquenched fury for an enemy who had taken everything from him and would not even give him the peace of a warrior's death. Then, his heart cold again, he motioned to his men and turned for home.

III

Eagle squatted outside her lodge, crushing bull berries for cakes and sausages. The muscles along her shoulders put up a steady ache of complaint. She paused, rubbing her neck, just as a piercing scream vibrated through the crisp autumn air.

Gasping, she pushed half to her feet and looked around. The

other women hurled their fleshers and tools aside as the warriors in camp began hooting in response. On a nearby rise, black now against the fading light of the sky, the returning warriors appeared silhouetted with their lances held high.

They came down to gallop in a victory circle around the camp. Screaming again, they stood on the backs of their ponies; others hung low below their bellies. Their faces were symbolically blackened with charcoal.

Enemies killed. They had fought. Oh, sweet *Ma'heo'o*, they had fought someone!

The shock of it made Eagle's head swim. She followed the others to the camp center, slowly at first, then faster and faster. She raced to Bull Bear's lodge and stopped, searching for Bear and Walks Far, then her breath froze in mid-burst.

The dog rope man came in first. He discharged one precious round from his rifle and reined in where Bull Bear stood. He was close enough that she could smell the acrid odor of the charcoal he wore, even the pungent tang of his sweat.

He had not changed in the two seasons that had passed since the spring hunt. Though the air nipped with cold now, his chest was bare as it had been that day, and his long hair spilled wildly over it. His eyes were as strangely colored as ever, and his disparate features still came together with hard, forbidding symmetry.

No, he had not changed, but something pounded suddenly at her temples, because she had. Now she was wed; now she knew what a man and woman did in their robes at night.

And she remembered.

Her palms started to sweat. She thought of the sure strength of his hands when he caught her from behind that sun, and the heat of him as he had held her against him. His hands had been hard and uncompromising, gripping her waist. Had she felt *comfort* at that? It seemed crazy now, because this was not a safe man. Suddenly she knew that he would not love a woman as Walks Far loved her. He would not be gentle; he would not ease into her with care. With this warrior, loving would be more furious and shattering than anything the other squaws had ever known or talked about.

She took an unsteady step backward. *Why was she thinking this? She had to find Walks Far.*

As though reading her mind, the dog rope man's odd brown eyes swiveled around to find her. Recognition flared there and a corner of his mouth quirked. Then he looked away again, dismissing her, but he did not do it quickly enough. For one unguarded moment, she saw something else in his eyes, something that made her gasp and reach out instinctively to touch his thigh.

Appalled at herself, she snatched her hand away. She turned and ran, but she could not block it out, that unbearable emotion she had seen so briefly in his gaze. Somehow, she knew it as impossibly and intimately as she knew what loving him would be like.

It was torment. His soul was aching.

4

Big Freezing Moon, 1863
Smoky Hill Country

I

Bear's lodge was stuffy with the damp fur of robes and the musky scent of too many bodies. Except for the chiefs and their women, all his closest confidants had gathered. Outside, a storm was building. To sit alone without shared body heat on a night such as this was unthinkable.

Even the dog rope man had joined them, and Eagle stole a peek at him. His eyes were hard with angry thoughts now, but she still scowled in memory of the pain she had glimpsed in them back in the Freezing Water Moon.

"The spiders shot first, and many of them died for it," he said as the conversation turned again to the skirmish of that sun. "What troubles me more is that they were in our country in the first place." He glowered at Bear. "I found those stray horses, but how did they get here for me to find? I will tell you. Pawnee Killer says that his Sioux lost them when Orange-Hair chased them. They raided his corral, and that corral was right on the western end of the Red Shield! The spiders are beginning to crawl down from the mountains our *Vehoo'o* gave them. Not just to pass by on roads, and not just to camp in forts beside those roads. Little-buffalo-men are coming down to live and feed their cat-tul on our grasses!"

"Our Dog warriors will not be restrained when the thaw comes," Walks Far answered thoughtfully. "They will sniff out those little-buffalo-men and try to kill them, and that is not the answer."

"Any dead *ve'ho'e* is an answer," snapped Bear.

"No. It is not enough. I will tell you why. It seems to me that the little-buffalo-men, if you count the ones in their Den-ver village, must have more than our hundred lodges. If they join forces with the blue-coats, the *Hotame-taneo'o* could lose to them, no matter how superior we are. Each one of us would have to kill five, maybe ten, for us to stay even."

Bear scowled at him. "So if we are to restrict these *ve'ho'e* to their Den-ver mountain place, we must have more men."

"Yes. We must urge all our warrior societies to fight behind us if we are to work to push these mongrels back."

Fire Wolf nodded, his eyes narrowing. "Pawnee Killer would help," he added. "His hunting grounds are just north of our western ones. That is why he raided Orange-Hair. He knows that once the spiders invade those western lands of ours, they will keep spreading, right into his country." He stood up. "I will ride tomorrow," he decided, "and tell our other societies to be ready."

Eagle gaped up at him as he began to step past her. Was he crazy to go now? The thaw was at least three moons away. Then his foot came down squarely on her toes, peeking out from under her thigh where she had curled her legs beneath her. She yelped, scrambling to move. Startled, he jumped away, and his gaze fell to her.

"I apologize."

She nodded quickly and gathered up the moccasin leathers she had been working on, her hands trembling.

He scowled, puzzled by her reaction. Surely she could not still be distressed over the secret of their first meeting. How many moons had passed? Was she that silly? Feeling strangely disappointed in her, he stooped and pushed his shoulder through the door flap.

II

In Denver that evening the snows were building to a blizzard. Piles of white clung to the waxy window paper of the cabin among the soldier tents at Camp Weld. Inside, a fire threw warm shadows over the rough wooden furniture, but the air ached with cold.

Governor John Evans lowered himself into a chair, tightening his coat against the wind that eddied through the cracks in the walls. His voluminous gray beard lay atop his lapels like a ratty animal.

"A territory on the verge of statehood should certainly boast better accommodations than this," he complained.

Across the desk Colonel John Chivington shook his head. He appeared to be a friendly bear of a man until one met his eyes.

"We are not on the verge of statehood," he snapped, "nor will we ever be, until this damnable Indian situation is dealt with."

"If you'll pardon me, Colonel, we've had only one significant 'situation' with the rascals since the Treaty of Fort Wise was signed two years ago. I think the plains have been admirably quiet of late," said Edward Wynkoop. Chivington scowled at him impatiently. Chivington was commander of the United States Army in Colorado Territory, while Wynkoop merely controlled nearby Fort Lyon.

"I am not referring to actual altercations, Major," he said. "Our campaign to win recognition as a state will never be won while the Indians are *here*."

"It is difficult enough to be heard by Mr. Lincoln with the war back East demanding his attention," Evans mused. "But to compound that dilemma, even were we to gain an audience with him, we have nothing with which to plead our case. Such a large portion of this territory—the entire *eastern* portion— belongs to the Cheyenne."

"Precisely!" Wynkoop declared. "It was awarded them in the treaty. They retained it because they hunt there."

"*They hunt there*," Chivington repeated. "That is precisely my point. There is no one actually living there."

"Well, they move through when they're following the buffalo," Wynkoop explained. "To my knowledge, there are several herds, lately coalescing into one large one that's been feeding along the Republican River—they call it the Red Shield. It probably numbers over a million, and it is, I believe, the major source of Cheyenne interest in that country."

Chivington's eyes narrowed to pinpoints. "I am not interested in geography lessons, Major. The fact is, that land is presently vacant of *human* inhabitants."

"Presently, yes. But it's winter," Wynkoop persisted. "The

Cheyenne generally move their hunting camps through there in the spring and early summer, when the herd gathers together."

"It is my contention that the plains east of us are being wasted," Chivington grated. "For statehood, we need population. And for population, we need land! I've been thinking lately about that altercation Lieutenant Dunn engaged in last fall. It can be used to our advantage. I agree with Major Wynkoop that the Cheyenne won't let go of their so-called hunting grounds easily. Even those chiefs we sent to Washington last summer mentioned how much they coveted them. Therefore, we need ammunition to convince both the chiefs and Washington that the tribe must relinquish the territory. Dunn's skirmish proves that such things will happen as long as white citizens and Indians are living in close proximity to each other. We need barrier lands between us. The Cheyenne *must* move farther away from Denver if there is to be peace between us."

Evans smoothed his beard. "Then further altercations would not be . . . unwelcome."

"No, sir. In fact, I intend to have my troops step up surveillance in that area as soon as the weather allows." He glanced at Wynkoop. "Were you ever able to have those arrows examined?" he asked. "The ones that killed the unfortunate members of Dunn's party? They *were* Cheyenne, were they not?"

"They were, Colonel," Wynkoop reported. "My Arapaho at the fort tell me they bear the markings of the Dog Soldiers."

Chivington shook his head. "My Lord, they even name their killers after the animals that spawned them."

The Fort Lyon commandant moved toward the door, but in good conscience he had to turn back.

"Colonel, I understand your need for new lands, but I might recommend that you look to the north for them, or the south. Engage the Sioux or Comanche."

"More geography, Major?"

"I simply suspect that the Dog Soldiers are considering Dunn's debacle as well as we are."

Evans chewed the silver hairs tickling his lower lip. "You're saying these, uh . . . Dog people are more bloodthirsty than the Sioux or Comanche? Are they plotting and planning now, do you think?"

"Most definitely. These Dogs aren't mongrels, gentlemen. They are the Cheyenne elite. Provoke them further, and you may end up with a full-fledged war on your hands."

Evans shifted his weight uncomfortably when the other man had gone. "He could be troublesome."

"Then I shall remove him. I want that land."

III

Eagle squatted beside the fire trench in her shelter. She cracked a branch in two and fed each piece into the fire, then she shivered. It was the last one of her supply. She would have to go out and get more wood. She pushed to her feet and took her heaviest robe, thick with a winter pelt. She was so tired from these endless chores that its weight nearly folded her legs again.

Outside, the snow had picked up. She tucked her chin close to her chest and hurried down the bank. Kneeling in the growing drifts, she gathered some fallen branches, then hurried back to the camp.

She stopped in front of Walking Spirit's lodge and called out, thinking to share her fresh supply. The other squaw pulled her quickly inside. Walks Far was there; he gave her a quick grin that seeped warmth through her again.

"Do you have enough for Fire Wolf?" Walking Spirit asked. "It is my turn to take some to him."

Fire Wolf. He had not gone with the dawn after all, then, Eagle thought. She began to hand over some of the wood, then she went still. She was already cold and wet. It made no sense for Walking Spirit to go to the dog rope man.

Her belly rolled nervously at the prospect of encountering him again, but she ducked outside. The bitter, wet wind hit her hard. She pushed her way into it, angling toward the dog rope man's lodge. At the door flap she opened her mouth to announce herself, and something strange, something not at all like her own voice, came out.

The flap was whipped aside, and suddenly he was there, scowling.

She pushed past him to the fire and dropped her burden. "I . . . this is from Walking Spirit."

"It was not necessary. I did not expect anyone to go out in this weather for me."

Indignation grabbed her without warning. She had not wanted to come here, either. "Then you should choose a wife," she snapped, "and the rest of us would not have to worry about your chores as well as our own."

His expression darkened dangerously. She stood and took a step back, frightened, then her chin came up. If he had not punished her at the spring hunt, then he would not do so now. Somehow, she was sure of it.

"Well," she muttered, "you should."

He laughed.

Eagle gaped at him. He looked younger this way; suddenly the pain and anger were gone from his strange brown eyes. He scrubbed a hand across his jaw and looked at her.

"So we meet again, little Eagle," he said finally. "I was wondering if that spring hunt-girl was a mirage."

She did not understand. She shrugged and made a quick move toward the door flap.

The wind caught it just as she reached it, billowing it inward with a great gust. Snow spilled inside. She grabbed the hide and looked out. Clouds of white moved along on Cold Maker's frozen breath. She could not even see the lodge she knew was directly across from them.

"The worst of this should pass before long," he said quietly. "Warm yourself while you wait."

She shook her head, but she knew he was right. If she went out there now, she would not find her way. She pulled the flap back into place, but she kept her nose at the crack so she would know the moment the weather eased.

Fire Wolf went to the fire, feeding some of the new wood into it. *So long. How long had it been since he had laughed?* He thought it had been the night in the Fat Horse Moon when Bear had offered her to the Dogs. She did not appear to have changed much since then, he thought, looking up to study her idly. She was still lean and long, her ankles tiny even encased in her sturdy winter moccasins. High cheekbones, a sharp chin. Her eyes . . .

Her eyes had changed, he realized.

He could not see them fully now, but memory, from the moment she had faced him, served him well. They were quieter than he remembered, with the mark of a woman who had been given to a man she had not necessarily chosen. That did not puzzle him, but there was something else there as well, something that he could not quite put a finger on.

As though he had somehow willed it, she peeked over her shoulder at him.

Recognition hit him suddenly, like a fist in the gut. Now he understood. Walks Far was not satisfying her, and there was enough woman within her to ache over it.

She did not, after all, remind him so much of his wife. Sweet Grass Woman had always been sure of what she wanted. This one was innocent, her eyes guileless. He guessed that she did not know exactly what she was lacking. It would be a shadowy and obscure thing just out of her reach, he thought, but her body told her she might find it with a man who challenged her and made her pulse quicken.

When he spoke again, he did not recognize the hoarse sound of his own voice. "The storm is coming from the north," he said.

Eagle glanced back at him and nodded again. "Yes. I see that."

"Keep leaning to your right," he went on. "You will come upon another lodge before you know it, but I cannot guarantee which one."

Still, she did not move.

"Go!" he snapped.

Startled, Eagle fled. Fire Wolf shook his head.

He was not the man for the chore, but there was just enough kindness left within him that he knew he would protect her from herself.

5

Light Snow Moon, 1864
Northern Dog Country

I

It was the richest river valley Eagle had ever seen. Angular cliffs guarded it on both sides. To the north, Turkey Creek was so close she thought she could hear it chuckling along. The Cedar River tumbled by at her feet, narrow but icy and full. Grandmother Earth pulled a great deal of moisture from the two waterways; in return, she gave forth red cedars and cottonwoods, soapweed and rich blue gramma on the plains that stretched between them.

Walks Far came up behind her as she took it all in. "Now do you think there are some good things about being wed to a Dog?"

Eagle smiled and leaned back into his comfortable warmth. "It is all right here, I suppose."

"All right? It is a choice camp. It thaws here early, and the buffalo and elk and deer all come with the first green. Soon we will have fresh meat again."

Her belly rumbled in anticipation. Perhaps it was the extra work of being a Dog wife, but she was always hungry. And she was so tired of the leathery, dried meat that sustained the People through Cold Maker's moons.

Walks Far moved away with the other warriors, and she joined Walking Spirit where the squaw crouched on a knoll, tugging up the tough, frozen gramma by its roots. When they had cleared two large circles, they walked over them, stamping their feet, compacting the soil. When their lodges were raised, there would be less loose dirt to find its way into their bedding and cooking paunches.

Despite the chill, Eagle was sweating and breathing hard

46

when she looked up and saw Tall Bull approaching. Tall Bull still declined to take a wife, and it was her turn to see to his needs.

She started toward him wearily when a hard, inflectionless voice stopped her.

"I need her. I have brought meat, and I owe her some."

Eagle whirled, her heart giving an odd little jump. The dog rope man had come back.

He had finally begun his travels after the blizzard, and he had been gone, off and on, for the better part of three moons now. He was like a man with a *mis'tai* at his heels, restless, always moving. But the Dogs had thought he would come back soon, and they had left sign to tell him that they had gone to their spring-thaw camp.

Now he sat astride his sinewy black pony, an antelope slung over its rump, his strange eyes level and steady on Tall Bull's. Eagle rubbed her forehead where a dull ache was building. She did not remember him owing her any meat, but she went to his pony anyway and used her teeth to gnaw open the thongs that held the carcass in place.

Fire Wolf watched Tall Bull turn away, then he swung to the ground, his eyes moving to Eagle. This sun, at least, she would not turn that sloe-eyed, questing gaze upon a man who might greet her invitation.

Or had she already, while he was gone?

She felt him staring at her and looked up, her eyes troubled and curious. "You wish something else?"

His tension disintegrated like a prairie puffball in the wind. Nothing had changed. She was still hungry. He did not question how he knew that; he merely did.

"I will sleep near the water. The meat is yours if you will put up my lodge. Just leave a steak and something good over the fire. The tongue or liver, maybe."

Eagle's tummy rolled again hungrily. He would give her the whole carcass! She nodded quickly and lugged it to her clearing before he could change his mind.

Its gamy, ripe promise goaded her with new energy. She heaved her lodge covering into place, then she carried her parfleches and their bedding and backrests inside. When her horses were unloaded and Walks Far's war pony was scrubbed down with grass, she set to butchering the kill.

When she was finished at her own lodge, the twilight was deep blue and purple, the sky littered with big, strong stars. The hum of conversation in the camp had turned sleepy and intimate. She went to find out who had transported the dog rope man's lodge and worked to raise that as well.

Finally she ducked inside to dig a trench and start a fire. She was squeezing the delicious green ooze of the gall over the liver when he touched her shoulder, startling her.

She leapt to her feet, an odd, prickly sensation running along her skin where he had touched her.

"The moon is up. You should have been finished long ago."

She turned her back on him and hunkered down again to finish. "Who are you to judge how long a woman's work should take her?" she muttered. "Contrary, crazy jackrabbit . . . it is no wonder you are unwed. Who would have you?"

"What?" But he had heard her.

"Nothing. I speak to the flames."

Then, incredibly, laughter hit her. She dropped down onto her bottom and threw him a quick glance; he was looking at her as though she was crazy.

Fire Wolf scowled at her. He knew that she laughed because for one precious moment she had lashed out in temper against this arduous life her brother had chosen for her, and it felt good. *Make her go. Do not encourage her.* Instead, he watched her hiccup while the flames threw shiny, orange light over her greased braids. The other wives always moved through his lodge quickly and distractedly, their thoughts turned ahead to their own man, their own chores. How very long it had been, he thought, since one had stayed a moment, losing herself to her own uniquely feminine emotions.

Yes, it felt good. He took up the liver, chewing it without tasting.

"I did have one . . . once." A hard rhythm of surprise came to his heart as he heard his own voice, but the need to tell it was suddenly strong.

"What?" She looked up at him.

"A wife."

"What happened to her?"

"I killed her."

Shock flew through her, then fell like a dead bird from the

sky. "No." Instinctively, though it suited every harsh, wretched edge she had seen in him, she did not believe it.

His voice grew hard. "She was *So'taa'e*," he said, "the last to come here from the land of the lakes. I was not a Dog then."

"You lived with her people."

"Yes, at the time the *ve'ho'e* gold-seekers attacked them."

He ripped the meat apart and handed her some, and Eagle gnawed at it hungrily. She vaguely remembered this story. The blood-hungry Pawnee had led the spider tricksters to an unsuspecting *So'taa'e* camp and had massacred many.

"She was full with a babe then, close to pushing it out," Fire Wolf went on. "She could not run with the other women when the attack came. She was too slow. I chose not to cover her retreat myself when she fell behind. I sent her to a hollow under the banks of the river instead, to hide there so I could go back to the fight and kill their maggot hides.

"I returned with Pawnee scalps and spider ones. My blood was going strong and fast. I would show her the coups, the triumphs. But she was dead."

Eagle flinched, her meat suddenly tasting rancid in her mouth.

"Her own hair was gone. So was the unborn one. They had cut her babe out and taken it." He focused on her again. His eyes were icy now, as dull as the frosted water at the edge of the streams. "You say no other woman would have me. I know only that I would have none of them. I failed the one who deserved the most from me, and I will not risk such responsibility again. Do your work here, little Eagle, and return safe and sanely to a man who makes wise choices. Sweet Grass Woman was a fool. She stood by me when her people scorned me for a father I do not know. She loved me when I was young and my head was hot, and I did not give her the kindness or care she deserved. You are not that unlucky or stupid."

Eagle scrambled to her feet, nearly choking on her meat. "*Stupid?*" she echoed incredulously. "She gave you all that and you malign her, when you are the fool? What warrior would not have gone with his brothers to fight that sun? It is for the old men and the boys to lead the women away, to cover the slow and the sick. If you had done that rather than fight, you would have been shamed, and justly so!"

Surprise skipped through him at her vehemence, then his face hardened. He had not sought understanding. He could not bear it.

"You are a child," he snapped. "You know nothing."

She recoiled. "Perhaps," she said tightly. "But I am learning much, and I know you are right. I am glad for the one who chose me, and that he is far wiser than you."

She left in a blur of motion. The heat of her, of her indignation, seemed to linger. He felt it curl around him, touching the cold that had filled him and protected him for so long.

Angrily he hurled the neatly cut hide she had brought into the fire. As the moist skin curled and smoked in the flames, he laid back on his bedding and stared up at the smoke hole, damning her and her innocence.

II

Before the moon waned, the snow melted in the Cedar River valley just as Walks Far had promised. Game began to appear at the water. At first the elk and mule deer stopped right on the far bank, poised and curious, their nostrils sniffing the air for scent of these human intruders. But soon they learned that to drink there meant death as the *Hotame-taneo'o* warriors made competitions of launching their raven-tipped spears and arrows across the water.

Raucous laughter and good-natured ribbing always accompanied the sport. After one particularly loud burst, Eagle looked up from the hump bone she was dressing, and a grin spread slowly across her lips.

She thought of Small Blanket and Sun Roads, poking at their memory gingerly as she would a sore tooth. She waited for the grief of their separation to swamp her again, but now there was only a soft ache of yearning. She knew she would be seeing them very soon, when the buffalo came together. And while she waited, life had begun to seem good.

The diverse personalities of the Dog people had become almost as predictable and precious to her as those of her own family, she realized. Walking Spirit was her closest comrade, but she had come to appreciate Falling Bird's bawdy humor as well. Wind Woman was practical and could always be counted on. Night Fighter was a glorious prankster, and she had learned that her own husband told the best stories.

Of them all, only the dog rope man continued to disturb her.

Her gaze sought him out now and found him alone at his lodge. His strong, dark shoulders were hunched over his carbine. She had heard him tell of a plan to saw down its barrel, making it more accurate when shot from a pony. His cold moon travels had convinced him that the other warriors were not very concerned by the prospect of trouble arriving with the thaw. Fire Wolf was determined that he himself would be prepared.

As though feeling her eyes on him, he looked up. Eagle felt heat creep up her neck, and she pushed to her feet.

She needed more of the soapweed that kept the bone from drying out after it had been heated and bent into a scraper. She hurried to the cliff wall, grateful for the excuse to leave camp. It had been many suns since she had visited the prairie. She was amazed at the wealth of vegetation that had burst forth since then. She collected the soapweed she needed, then took an extra few moments to explore. She found some wild licorice and hesitated, then she hunkered down and uprooted it, munching it slowly.

Her scraper could wait. There were no mothers around to chastise her for leaving it.

She laughed aloud—and nearly missed the low rumble of sound that came from behind her. She glanced over her shoulder, then froze beneath a cold wash of fear.

A boar glared back at her with red-rimmed eyes, its tusks cracked and yellowing with age. Such animals were not common in *Wu'tapiu* country. She did not know what it was, but instinct prickled the hairs at her nape, warning her that it was dangerous.

Her first instinct was to scream, and too late, she knew her mistake. The animal lowered his head and charged her. She lunged to her feet, but not fast enough; his tusk caught her leg, and pain seared down her calf.

She cried out again, then her fingers fumbled for the knife tucked into her belt. She hurled it without thinking, and to her astonishment, the weapon hit the boar in the throat. Enraged, he turned his attention to it, shaking his head in an effort to dislodge it.

In the next moment there was a popping sound and the

animal dropped. Dazedly Eagle looked up to see Fire Wolf lower his rifle.

He strode lazily toward her, his long hair catching and dancing in the wind. Her knees turned to water, and she dropped to them gracelessly. The dog rope man nudged the carcass with the toe of his moccasin, then squatted to pull her knife free. A gush of blood erupted after it, soaking the prairie grass. He tossed the weapon in her direction.

"He would have died anyway, as soon as he shook that out. Good kill."

"Good . . ." she began incredulously. "I did not . . . I never . . . killed anything . . . before."

His hard eyes studied her. "You acted on survival instinct, then. That is lucky, because he would have killed you. But it is far better to rely on skill." Suddenly he took up her knife again. "Show me how you held it."

She did, awkwardly, biting her lip and willing her hand not to tremble. He was the dog rope man. He should not be taking the time to teach a squaw how to hunt. Yet that was exactly what he was doing, and suddenly it seemed very important that she be worthy of the effort.

"No, like this," he said, snagging her wrist, bending it. Her eyes darted from him to the blade again.

"Flick your hand up and outward. At the last moment release the weapon. Do not look at your hand. Watch your target. Move with it. Face it always."

She did as he told her. The knife spun up in the air, then dropped at her feet. Her skin flamed.

"Practice every sun," he finished, turning away, "and you will learn to hit a squirrel scampering at forty paces."

The Dogs and their women began scrambling up the cliff, anxious to see what the commotion was about. When Walks Far helped her to her feet, Fire Wolf was gone from the crowd.

"You are bleeding." Walks Far could not take his eyes from the crimson-stained gash in her moccasin. He looked down into her face, then he gathered her up, holding her hard against his chest.

Oh, *Ma'heo'o*, how he had come to love her!

She began squirming, and he finally put her on her feet again. Eagle looked back at the carcass. No matter what Fire

Wolf had said about this monster-animal dying anyway, she owed him some piece of this kill for his help in saving her.

"It is edible, then?" she asked when Walking Spirit dropped to her knees to begin butchering it.

"They are very fatty animals, but some parts are all right, and the grease makes good seasoning."

"What is the best part?"

"Here." She sliced off a hefty portion of the loin.

Eagle took it from her. "If you finish for me, you can have half the meat."

"Go. You should have Four Ponies look at your leg."

Eagle nodded. It was beginning to throb steadily now.

Fire Wolf was not outside his shelter, so she stopped at the closed flap and called out to him. He came and motioned her inside, scowling at the meat.

"It is not necessary."

Eagle gave a little snort and hung it from his tripod. "You always say that. If we listened to you, you would live cold and hungry."

"Your time would be better spent putting something on that leg."

"I will see Four Ponies when I leave here."

"That healer will want to trade for your whole kill. All you need is a little *pat se'wots*, that salty onion that grows near the water. It will stop the bleeding and keep pus from coming to it."

Eagle felt her jaw drop. She turned back to him. "How do you know this?"

He pushed, not gently, against her shoulder, so that she dropped hard onto his pile of bedding. When he began pulling her moccasin off, pain shot through her ankle, and she gasped and tried to wrench away from him. He did not apologize, but his touch gentled.

Somehow, that was worse. Something trembled deep in the pit of her tummy.

"My mother was wed to a healer," he said finally.

"Your father?" she managed.

"No. I told you once. I have no father."

She considered that as he went for his warrior's medicine bag, thinking of his odd-colored eyes. Suddenly it did not seem at all preposterous to her that he had been spawned by some mysterious spirit-being. She shivered, then he put the *pat se'wots* against her open flesh, and the sting made her jerk away from him again.

"It will stop hurting in a little while and feel numb."

She nodded and tried to take her mind off it. "Where is your mother?"

"Above the Moon Shell River," he answered shortly. "I am *Ohmeseheso*, born of Dull Knife's Northern People band."

That did not surprise her, either. To the *Wu'tapiu*, who dwelled so far south, those of the *Ohmeseheso* were nebulous, unknown kin.

"Why did you not go back to *them* after the *So'taa'e* fight?" she blurted.

His deep brown eyes came up sharply, then he looked away, slipping his knife free from the sheath on his breechclout. He cut a strip of leather from her moccasin and tossed the rest into her lap.

She knew then that he was not going to answer her question. Perhaps he had spoken of his wife once, but it had been a rare and isolated moment. He would not do it again.

He wrapped the strip around her calf to hold the medicine in place, then he rocked back on his heels and stood. Eagle scrambled to her feet as well.

"*Ha ho'.* Thank you." She clutched the ruined moccasin to her chest and hurried for the door.

"For the same reason I did not stay with the *So'taa'e*," he said suddenly. He spoke to her back, his words low and quick. "Neither band tolerates failure well. The *So'taa'e* could not honorably cast me out as long as I continued to hunt for them. I had been wed to one of their own even though my error in judgment cost them a daughter. But their eyes were a constant reminder of my shame, as living with the *Ohmeseheso* would have been a constant reminder to my mother of hers. She was unwed when she birthed me, and she has never told who her lover was."

She turned back to face him. "So you came to the Dogs?"

"The *Hotame-taneo'o* do not care about a man's lineage and past. They judge only his coups, his courage. They gave me sanctuary. In return, I carry their rope. I give them a man who no longer cares if he dies."

But he did care, he did.

She knew it with sudden emotion. She even knew now why he had not punished her on that hunt so many seasons ago. His warrior's rage was for himself, not for others. He carried the rope not because he wanted to die, but because he needed to suffer its deadly responsibility.

She very nearly reached out to him, as she had on that sun when she had first seen the cruel truth in his eyes. Instead, she dug her fingers deeper into her tattered moccasin and shook her head.

"No," she whispered.

His smile was abrupt and hard. "You think you know my heart better than I know it myself?"

"You are my friend," she blurted. "I do not think your heart is that cold."

She was embarrassed as soon as the words were out. She jerked around toward the door again.

Silence followed her as she pushed past the flap. It was not until she was outside that she heard him speak again, and then she was not at all sure she had heard him correctly.

"So goodbye, friend," she thought he said.

III

The suns became gently warm before the buffalo finally appeared in their annual migration to find the rest of their herd. They were neither as dim-witted nor as curious as the elk and deer. They did not come close to the *Hotame-taneo'o* camp to drink. Instead, Eagle was awakened one morning by the rumbling of Grandmother Earth as she whispered to her children that the beasts were passing nearby.

"*Eeeeiaaa!*" came a shout from outside the lodge. Before she could blink the sleep from her eyes, Eagle found herself buried beneath Walks Far's bedding as he hurled it aside.

She fought her way free and stood, wrestling into her doeskin. Grabbing Walks Far's lance, she dashed outside. He had his pony's bridle in place and was astride. He grabbed his weapon and galloped off.

Finally Eagle looked about the camp through the murky dawn. In contrast to the other men Fire Wolf was only now vaulting onto his black. That stony look had returned to his face.

She called out to him without truly considering her instinct to do so. "I need horns for bowls and spoons," she said. "Please, will you bring me some? I will cook for you tonight."

His hard eyes swiveled to her. "I think your husband will manage a couple of horns."

"I need many. For gifts. For his family when I see them again." Fire Wolf measured her, but he finally nodded and rode off.

Eagle turned away and found herself confronted by Wind Woman's thoughtful gaze.

"You should stay here," the other squaw decided.

"I—"

"No." Wind Woman cut her off. She pulled herself up onto her mare and nodded toward the squaws' moon lodge. "Walking Spirit bled last night. Someone must take food to her. You can do that. Falling Bird, Cherries, and I will see to the kills of our men."

Eagle watched her go, feeling strangely chastised. She had only wanted to take the pain out of Fire Wolf's eyes, to distract him from whatever memory had been haunting him this time. What did Wind Woman think?

In spite of the warmth of the dawn, something cold rushed her and she shivered.

She hurried to get some live water and make a stew, then she filled a bowl and carried it to the moon lodge. Outside the door another thought struck her, and she stared at the rudimentary tepee as though seeing it for the first time.

She had not been to this place since well before the camp change.

Her heart skipped suddenly, and she dropped the bowl. Dazedly, she wandered back in the direction of her own lodge. She tried to count, to consider the moons that had passed, but her head swam. It did not matter. It was true.

She had Walks Far's babe inside her.

"Thank you," she murmured. "Ah, Wise One, *ha ho'*."

She grabbed another bowl and filled it, hurrying back out of the camp. She stomped her feet, doing an impulsive little dance, and laughed aloud. Then, abruptly, she sat down hard beneath another cold sweep of fear.

What had Walking Spirit told her about *Hotame-taneo'o* babes? "*Ma'heo'o does not bless us often. He sends us only the strong ones.*" But that was crazy! Life had been simple and unthreatening since she had joined the Dogs.

She gave another prayer anyway, this one swelling up from her very soul. "Please," she whispered. "Please grant me a son, a healthy one. Oh, *Ma'heo'o*, let him live that I might give Walks Far this blessing."

She did not consider why it seemed so very, very important that she do this thing for the one she had wed. But it soothed something inside her, something dangerous that filled her whenever she thought of a troubled warrior with hot, brown eyes.

IV

The hunt was a propitious one for an early spring trailing herd. Not a man was lost to the pummeling hooves of the beasts, despite the disorganized rush, and there was enough meat that some could be spared for a modest feast. While the men savored the rich tallow of the bulls' loins, the women worked outside in the last of the sun. Falling Bird and Wind Woman roasted slabs of hump meat, while Cherries and Eagle quickly fleshed the hides to prevent them from becoming stiff and useless overnight.

All around the Dog camp, knots of people formed at one lodge or another to share and celebrate. Two Feathers roved about, chanting of how many animals had fallen, and who had had the most kills. The pervasive aroma of the meat made Eagle salivate. She paused in her work to put a hand to the babe in her belly, then she glanced up at Walks Far.

He paced back and forth in front of the other men, reenacting his problems with the hunt. His hair streamed freely; his stride was long and sure. He glanced her way, and his lopsided grin made her heart roll over.

She would tell him of the babe later, in their bedding, she decided.

Then pale leggings trimmed with enemy scalps broke her

line of vision, and two bloody horns were dropped beside her. Her heart knocked up into her throat.

She looked up at Fire Wolf.

"You have enough to do with Walking Spirit indisposed. I will not hold you to our bargain. Wind Woman has enough meat cooking for all of us."

Eagle nodded and pushed abruptly to her feet. With an urgency she did not understand and did not want to examine, she left the dog rope man and hurried to the circle of the other warriors. They quieted as she approached and stood at Walks Far's side.

"There is something I would say," she announced.

Walks Far looked startled, then he laughed. "Do not chastise me, wife. It is bad enough that I was bested by a cow, not a bull."

The others hooted, then quieted as the other women joined them as well. They already knew, Eagle realized. But of course they would have guessed; they had not had to pitch in to do her work during her moon time for quite a while now.

A cold shiver tickled her spine. That they had not mentioned it indicated that they did not take for granted that this wee one would survive.

But it would. *He* would. She gave the squaws a strong smile and turned back to her husband, whispering in his ear.

For the space of a heartbeat, Walks Far looked stunned, then his triumphant shout filled the air. A clamor erupted and the women pressed close to pat and hug her.

"So much for love, my friend." Night Fighter laughed. "You made up for things quickly."

Bear stood, looking more dazed than she had ever known him to be. Then he shouted from the bottom of his deep chest, announcing the gift of a pony to honor the occasion. Other *Hotame-taneo'o* arrived to jostle each other over the unexpected present.

Tangle Hair pressed a pipe into Walks Far's hands. "Good," he said. "We will let this young buck supply the smoke tonight."

Walks Far looked at her, his black eyes so full of emotion that Eagle felt her own heart thump hard. "When?"

She had figured it out. "I think you put it in me around the time of the blizzard."

He touched her cheek so gently it felt like his breath when he laid on top of her. "I . . . I have to get smoke," he managed.

"I will do it."

He made a vague gesture as though to stop her. Wind Woman nudged him hard in the ribs.

"Do not start that," she scolded. "She must do everything as she has always done it, since you first put it in her. Do we stop riding mares when they carry?" She gave Eagle a little push. "Go."

Eagle hurried back to their lodge and took Walks Far's medicine bag from its rawhide thong on the tepee lining. When she brought it back, the crowd had quieted a bit. Walks Far filled Tangle Hair's pipe with sage first; such smoke carried the People's prayers to *Ma'heo'o*. He raised it and offered it to the Wise One's servants who dwelled in each of the four directions, then he tamped in a more tasty weed and took the next smoke himself, handing it finally to Bear.

"*Ha ho'*," Tangle Hair said to *Ma'heo'o*.

"*Ha ho'*," echoed Bear, passing the pipe to Fire Wolf. Eagle followed it with her eyes, then found herself trapped in his.

The naked pain that flared there made her cry out. *What had she done?* Even as she had given joy to her husband, she had driven a knife into the soul of this man who was her friend.

"No," she whispered, but Fire Wolf only smoked and passed the pipe to Night Fighter.

"Enjoy, friends," Fire Wolf said. "I travel tonight."

There was a murmur of confusion. "Now?" Bear demanded. "Why?"

"Do you see snow on this prairie?" the dog rope man demanded, his voice suddenly harsh. "It is good that you celebrate, but you do not need me for it. I can be of more use elsewhere right now, seeing what the spider tricksters are up to with this thaw. Besides, I want to know where that herd goes." He turned away before anyone could stop him.

He did not turn around again, and she could not take back her announcement, could not do it over again, less rashly, so that the reminder of his own unborn one was not as abrupt. She let him go as hot tears burned at her eyes, blurring his image.

Walks Far touched her arm, and she blinked carefully.

"You are okay?" he asked.

She managed to smile for him. But before she could answer, Wind Woman interjected smartly.

"Women get this way when they are full," she said. "There is not much to be done about it."

V

Night fell and made the black's hide glisten in the moonlight. Fire Wolf drove the animal hard, moving faster, faster. Still the image lingered in his mind, sharp and taunting.

Long, strong limbs. Not sprawled in death, but bent at the knees, entwined over Walks Far's hips. He thought not of his wife's womb ripped asunder, but of his brother burying himself deep in the sweetness of Eagle's innocent flesh . . . her hair spilled back and loose . . . her head thrown back . . . her narrow chin lifted as she cried out her release . . . the release, the yielding, the giving that had allowed room for a babe to grow.

Whatever had been lacking in Walks Far's loving, the little Eagle had finally found it. She was not his any longer; she would not need him again.

Jealousy hit him in a stunning ambush. He pulled his pony in suddenly so that the animal reared and plunged, then he dropped his head and let guilt swim over him. It was nearly as mocking, as strong, as the other he had lived with for so long.

She was his brother's woman. Even were Walks Far to drop in the next fight, Fire Wolf knew he would not claim her. She had put a treacherous warmth in his belly with her staunch outbursts, her blushing grins, her sloe eyes. But she was not his, would never be his, because not even she could melt the cold in his soul.

6

Moon When The Horses Get Fat, 1864
Northern Dog Country

I

Eagle licked the sweat off her upper lip and levered her dibble stick under a ripe prairie turnip. Behind her, warriors' voices drifted up from the camp below the cliff. One voice hinted of the rough, hard timbre of the dog rope man's tone, and she straightened and looked back, knowing it was not him, looking anyway.

Where had he gone?

More than two moons had passed since he had galloped away from them. An ache swelled up in her, and she went back to her work. She had moved on to the next promising clump of weed before the steady tattoo of galloping hoofbeats finally reached her.

She looked up again distractedly and saw him coming out of the west. *Fire Wolf.* Her heart gave a kick, and she hurried to meet him, leaping over prickly pears and nettle weeds, running, running, even when her breath grew short.

"Where did you go?" she demanded when she reached him.

There was a pure, uncomplicated happiness in her voice that clawed at his gut. She fell behind him a bit, struggling under the ungainly weight of her babe. A grunt of frustration escaped him, and he finally reined his pony in.

"The herd has gathered near the Red Shield again," he answered tightly. "Some of our people are there already. It is a big herd, bigger than last spring season. Even the *Ohmeseheso* will join in the hunt this time. They are among those who are there now."

Eagle gave a joyous little squeal. They would go now, finally. She would see her people again. Unconsciously she put a hand to her belly, bulging more than gently against her doeskin in this sixth moon of the child's growth. His eyes veered to her sharply.

"Your *Wu'tapiu* will know soon. They will come north, and your mothers will learn of your babe."

Something in her warmed and yearned toward him. "I did not know how hard it would be carrying someone," she blurted. "He moves now sometimes, and he gets in the way, making even simple chores difficult."

"And so you no longer practice with your knife."

She looked at him blankly for a moment, then her skin colored. It was true. She had been so flattered by the attention he had shown her that sun, but honing the skill had not seemed so very important anymore once she had learned she was full with someone.

His voice turned sharp at her expression. "There may not always be someone to look out for you and your babe," he snapped. "You should be able to defend yourself if need be. You have it within yourself to learn. You would be a fool not to do so."

She gaped at him, stung by his censure, and suddenly Fire Wolf felt his own thoughts grow thick and confused.

He had watched out for her until she had no longer needed him, until not being needed had been like a knife in his gut. She was sweet with her husband now, and it was good and right for him to turn away from her. *Let her go.*

But he could not. It was both too much and not enough that she should huddle happily beneath another man's protection. He needed to know that she could survive on her own as well, if Walks Far and the Dogs were suddenly gone from her.

"We will speak of it more with the next sun," he said shortly. "And I will show you how to follow trail as well. Then you can find what you need to kill."

He touched his heels to his black. The pony surged ahead again, and the others pressed in on him, calling out greetings and mild rebukes for his long absence.

"He found somewhere warm to put that worm of his," Falling Bird whispered conspiratorially. The other squaws snorted and laughed.

"You did not bring her back with you, Dog Rope Man?" she asked more loudly. "Are we to care for you forever?"

Eagle understood suddenly, and a pain came to her chest. Is that why he had been gone so long? Had it had nothing to do with her after all?

Wind Woman caught her elbow, scattering her thoughts. "Where are your turnips? Where is your dung?"

Eagle opened her mouth to answer, then closed it again helplessly. *The game.* Even with their imminent journey to the hunt, it would not be forgotten.

The men came over the ridge, alerted by the commotion. She hurried to gather her turnips and form piles of them, then she grabbed up some dried pony manure and squatted down behind her cache to defend it. The warriors ran laughing into the pony herd, catching up the slowest ones.

She saw Walks Far in the throng, and suddenly a laugh gurgled free of her. She forgot all else as she watched him try to throw his leg over the back of her oldest pony. The mare struggled with him until he finally landed on his belly and managed to trot toward her piles that way. She had not braided his hair for him that morning, and it streamed down, obscuring his vision, so that when he made a grab for her prizes, he missed. She pelted him with her dung, hooting.

There was a shriek from behind her. She whipped around to see Night Fighter galloping toward them, standing astride one of Wind Woman's young fillies. When he reached the turnips, he dropped low, slinging one arm around the animal's neck. He swept the earth with his free hand, and the squaws descended upon him, pulling him to the ground in a skidding thump. They pummeled him with manure, laughing.

"*Ah haih!*" Wind Woman shouted the coup cry. "I am the first!"

"But we have the victory!" crowed Night Fighter.

Eagle whirled again to find that Walks Far had managed to claim all her piles while she was distracted. He alerted his friends, released her pony, and scrambled back down the slope. He could eat and share all her turnips if he chose to, but she knew he would not. They made her stews thick the way he liked them.

Breathless, she followed after him. True to her expectations, most of the roots were dumped in front of their lodge. He sat outside Walking Spirit's shelter with Bear, happily chewing the remainder.

Eagle dropped down beside him. "That was sneaky."

He wiggled his brows at her. "It is hard to best the *Hotame-taneo'o*—"

He broke off suddenly. Bear lowered his own turnip and scowled. At the river, where Night Fighter had been washing the dung from his skin, that warrior straightened, also.

"What is this?" he wondered aloud.

The orphan Skinny Toes appeared at the top of the crest, his pony foaming from a hard ride. As though *Ma'heo'o* had thrown a blanket over the camp, smothering their ebullience like flames, the people quieted. Eagle watched the boy-warrior ride to them and drop to the ground.

"What has happened?" Fire Wolf demanded.

Eagle pivoted to find him in the crowd. Her heart began moving hard with premonition. She dug her fingers into Walks Far's arm; he stood like stone, not seeming to feel her grip.

"It was the man Dunn again," Skinny Toes blurted. "On the Red Shield. The hunting camp—those already gathered—he attacked them this dawn."

The *Ohmeseheso* were already there. Eagle's head began to swim.

"How many dead?" Fire Wolf asked roughly.

The orphan showed all ten fingers of both hands three times. "And twice more than that wounded."

"Kin?" Bull Bear asked. Every man and woman present had family scattered over the plains.

Skinny Toes looked reluctantly at Fire Wolf. "Your mother."

The dog rope man did not move.

Night Fighter recovered first. "*Pack up!*" he roared. "We ride." But Bull Bear grabbed him to stop him.

"First let us hear everything."

Skinny Toes nodded. "The people slept, mostly women and small ones. The men were down the river, keeping the buffalo in sight. Two women were killed, two babes as they were running. Fourteen old men, covering their retreat. The rest were their warriors of other societies, returning at the sound of the fight to defend. All their lodges were burned as well, and a hundred ponies taken."

The women reacted in a surge of motion, heading for their lodges to begin tearing them down. Bear's voice bellowed out, stalling them again.

"No! The mongrel tricksters will be back in their Den-ver by the time we get there."

Some of the men shifted their weight impatiently, but Bear went on, looking to Bull Bear for support.

"We should council," he urged. "Walks Far was right. We are going to need the help of the other societies now."

Bull Bear nodded curtly. With quick stabs of his finger, he selected those men closest to his hearth. Only Fire Wolf remained where he stood after the first chief signaled to him.

Pain and primitive rage struggled in his deep brown eyes. Eagle whispered his name helplessly, but he only whipped around, finally, and disappeared into the tepee after the others.

II

At Camp Weld, Colonel John Chivington grinned as he dipped his pen into the inkwell on his desk.

President Lincoln, sir. You will find enclosed further proof of the terrible dilemma in which the brave citizens of this Territory find themselves. On this inst. Lieutenant Dunn once again engaged the Cheyenne Dog Soldiers not one hundred miles from this settlement. The Lieutenant feels that these marauders were intent upon committing depredations against Denver, and I must say my suspicions are compatible with his. Only one of our own lost, I am happy to report, and one wounded. Thirty Indians killed, young men of prime fighting age. I would say the Cheyenne were severely punished in this affair.

He scowled a bit, then shrugged. The children killed would have grown into warriors, and as far as he knew, the savages called all their fighting men Dogs. He enclosed a brief clipping from the evening's newspaper, waxed the seal, and handed it to his messenger.

"Send word to those friendly chiefs as well, Lieutenant, the ones who went to Washington. Get their names and whereabouts from Major Wynkoop. I do believe they'll feel differently about giving up their Red Shield River now."

III

In the suns that followed, Bull Bear's door flap remained closed. The warriors remained inside, counciling. Eagle did not see Fire Wolf to talk more about her knife, nor did she expect to. There was a sharp feeling of waiting in the camp, like smoldering coals ready to burst into flame, and no one had any patience for trivialities.

The squaws worked outside in little fits and starts, pausing frequently to look toward the chief's shelter. Eagle kept her eyes down, because to watch and wait for news was almost unbearable.

She would not be seeing her Wu'tapiu *now, nor Walks Far's Ridge kin, either.* She picked up one of the new horn bowls she had made for them, feeling dazed.

"None of the bands will venture near the Red Shield with the spiders in the area."

Her head snapped up at the dark voice speaking her own thoughts. *Fire Wolf.*

Her pulse stirred in surprise, and she looked quickly to Bull Bear's lodge again. The flap was still down. The dog rope man must have left just long enough to relieve himself, yet he had paused to talk to her.

A shiver went through her, but then all the despair and confusion of the last several suns erupted inside her, and she forgot everything but the treacherous spiders again.

"I cannot remember a time when there was not a spring hunt!" she exclaimed. "What will we eat? We can subsist on elk and deer and small game until the buffalo herd scatters again. But that will only pull us through the summer and autumn. Without a big hunt, there will not be enough meat to dry and store. How will we brace ourselves for Cold Maker's moons? We cannot make lodge covers out of elk skins!"

He lifted one shoulder in a shrug. "So we will sleep beneath our old ones, and patch them with elk skins. It is as I told you.

You must learn to survive, because maybe you will not always be well provided for."

In her belly her babe seemed to roll over. She put a hand to him. "It will be his first, most vulnerable winter." Suddenly a wealth of hatred rose up in her throat, strangling her. "How do they dare this? I hate them! Why will they not go away and leave us our food?"

"Because they want what we have," he said flatly.

Suddenly there was a flutter of movement on the prairie bluff. Fire Wolf turned sharply, and her eyes followed his. Yet another rider had appeared there. She scowled until he drew closer.

Blind Fox!

A glad cry escaped her, and Eagle ran for him. He stopped near her, eyeing her swollen belly and grinning.

"They are fine, everyone is fine," he said before she could ask. "It was a good winter. We lost no one, not even the oldest grandfathers."

At his words they both sobered. It would be different this season.

"I have news," he went on as the dog rope man came up behind her.

"We have already heard of the fight on the Red Shield," she told him, but he shook his head.

"It is more than that. That white man Bent has been to see Black Kettle again. My mother is angry and has sent me to make sure the Dogs know of this latest audacity."

Little Moon has not changed, Eagle thought narrowly, but the realization was fleeting, washed away under another cold sweep of fear. *This latest audacity.* Something else had happened. *What?*

"Come," Fire Wolf ordered, leading the way to Bull Bear's lodge. Eagle hesitated a moment, then followed. Falling Bird and Walking Spirit fell in behind her, and they squatted outside, listening where the lodge cover was rolled up to allow the warm spring air to circulate inside.

They heard Blind Fox's rushed explanation first. "This message comes from the Den-ver men, not those in Wash-ing-tone. They want another treaty."

Bull Bear reacted furiously. "They are fools, those *Vehoo'o*!

I told them this at last spring's hunt! I said that if they complied with that Wash-ing-tone visit, the tricksters would demand more!"

"Yes," Blind Fox agreed. "Now they say they want us to stay away from the land near the mountains as well. Black Kettle thinks it would be a good thing to do. He says that if we stay away from Den-ver and the *ve'ho'e*'s country, there will be no more fights. Our women, children, and old ones will not be killed as on the Red Shield several suns ago."

"And does he think, too, that we can tap the buffalo on their shoulders and tell them to follow us to a more convenient place?" Night Fighter snapped.

Eagle leaned low and saw her cousin shrug. "I know only that he will first move our *Wu'tapiu* to Smoky Hill country. He is calling upon the other principal *Vehoo'o* to bring their bands there and join him. He wants to council with them about this, and he feels that Dog country will be a safe place for such a gathering."

There was a roar of disbelief from the *Hotame-taneo'o*. "He wants our protection, but he will not take our advice!"

"Another treaty cannot be allowed," Bear spat.

"But if the *Vehoo'o* vote to do this thing—" ventured Blind Fox.

"They will not. Not this time."

There was rock in his voice. The others seemed to understand, even if Blind Fox did not. Eagle scowled. She could not fathom such conviction, either.

"Eagle Voice and I will depart for the Smoky Hill with the next sun," decided Walks Far.

"I think we should all go," added Night Fighter. "We can work to influence the other societies."

Bear grunted. "So be it. You and I will take our wives and go, also."

"I will lead a small party back to the Red Shield," Fire Wolf decided. "That is where the *ve'ho'e* are currently moving. I will show them that this will not be tolerated."

Eagle stood, her head hurting. She would be seeing her family after all, but that leap of excitement was fleeting. Beneath it, something else nagged her. She looked at the other squaws.

"This does not make sense. Why would Fire Wolf want to fight if Bear, Walks Far, and Night Fighter are going to the *Wu'tapiu* camp to make strategy? I thought those four men always acted together."

The others looked startled. "The dog rope man always travels," Walking Spirit answered finally, faintly.

But this was different, and they all knew it. Fire Wolf rode alone when the others remained in their home camp, not when the Dogs were acting in defense of their people.

IV

The warriors left Bull Bear's lodge when Sun went down. Blind Fox and Fire Wolf returned with Walks Far for their evening meal. Blind Fox could not be sent back to Little Moon without food and rest, and it was Eagle's turn to share with the dog rope man.

She shredded some of her turnips and added them to her cooking paunch, listening as the men hunkered down on the far side of the fire trench she had dug outside her shelter. She picked up just enough of their conversation to become more confused.

"It is good that Little Moon sent you," Walks Far mused. "Who knows when we would have been alerted otherwise?"

"She will expect a prime pony for this, in-law."

Walks Far laughed and stood up. "Come to the herd with me. You can tell me what will best suit her needs."

They wandered off, Walks Far moving jauntily despite the trouble. Eagle watched him go, then she looked back at Fire Wolf.

"What is happening?" she demanded. "Why do you go to fight when your brothers go to my people?"

He was rubbing grease into his bowstring, his strong fingers working the sinew. His gaze came up slowly.

"How brave are you, Little Eagle?"

Eagle felt her tummy roll over at his odd expression. "I . . . I do not understand."

But she thought she might.

"I have said that I will teach you things, and I will do that. How much more time would you have us spend together? Do you not feel the danger? I, for one, think it is best if I often stay out of camp."

His hard smile mocked her. This could not be, she thought, shaking her head. He could not be speaking of what she thought he was. Like Wind Woman, he seemed to think that she . . . that she . . . wanted to know what loving him would be like, because she knew that he would not touch her with exquisite care that left her aching and wanting more. She wanted to know if even then the shadows would stay in his eyes.

Oh, *Ma'heo'o*, she wanted that! She dropped her knife and rocked to her feet. Her skin flamed, and her eyes went to the pony herd, where Walks Far and Blind Fox bent over a colt's leg.

Fire Wolf followed her gaze and his voice became harsh. "You are happy with him now, and that makes it better, but I am still only a man. You haunt me, little Eagle. You taunt me with what I do not, should not want."

Her eyes flew back to him. Treacherous excitement rushed through her, curling hot in her belly. Was he saying that he wanted to touch her, too?

"Your marriage may have been arranged," he went on, "but you have found peace in it nonetheless. You no longer need what little I could have given you. You do not need Tall Bull, or any of the others."

"Tall Bull?" she repeated faintly. She shook her head, then felt a jolt of shame. What did he think? "No!" she cried. "It was only you!"

He came to his feet so suddenly she staggered backward, frightened of him as she had not been for a long time.

"Do not say that to me."

"But I speak true!"

"Speak it to a man who believes it!"

An ache filled her, hurting her throat.

He saw the tears threaten, then her chin came up. He swore violently and turned away. But he could not escape the sure, sudden knowledge that he was doing her a terrible wrong. Guilt, that vicious beast so old and familiar to him, clawed at his gut anew. He needed desperately to believe that she would have gone to any man when Walks Far was failing her, and he knew he would never be able to believe that again.

He heard her move behind him. He glanced back to see her dodge toward her tepee, then veer and head the other way, like an animal running from some terrible pain within. Then she went still and turned back to him.

Her eyes were suddenly wide. "My marriage was *arranged*?" she repeated. "Why do you say such a thing?"

He knew then, too late, that while she might have settled in with Walks Far, no one had ever explained to her why that marriage was fixed.

He was torn between frustration with his brothers and the flashing fire that was in her eyes now. *Ma'heo'o*, they were stupid to think that this girl would accept their arrangement with docile indifference. He had always known she would follow her own heart. How could they not?

She would learn the truth soon enough, he thought. Someone would have to tell her why she was being taken back to her people. She would hear of it elsewhere . . . and their odd, growing friendship would never again be the same. He would be alone again.

And that was best.

He turned away only to look back. He could not do it to her. He could not do it to himself.

"We need someone to learn what Black Kettle and the *Vehoo'o* are planning," he said carefully. He would not spare his own part in this arrangement. "You are a Dog wife. You must go to your people and learn from your grandmothers and your kin what that chief is thinking. Then you will report back to us and try to bring the *Wu'tapiu* women to support our plan of action."

Eagle felt a terrible stillness. Suddenly it all made sense. What had Bear said when she was wed? *"It is a good thing you are doing for our people."* She had not pressed him to explain, because she could not ever imagine pressing Bear. But perhaps she had known, somewhere deep inside, because she still remembered his words now after all these seasons.

She stuck her hands under her armpits to still their trembling. "I need to know," she said carefully. "Did Walks Far volunteer to . . . to . . . bring me into this band?"

The silence was long. "Your brother would not relegate you to second wife," Fire Wolf finally muttered.

"There are several other unwed men among us."

"Not so many in our circle."

"So my husband took me when no one else would."

"It was not like that."

"Ah. You and Tall Bull fought him for me?"

Curse her, he thought, even as he knew fresh respect for her as she angled the truth from him. "Tall Bull feels he is too busy hunting to take a young wife," he snapped, "and I will never wed again. You know why."

She gave a barely perceptible flinch, so vague that he was not sure he had seen it at all. Then there was movement on the bluff, Walks Far and Blind Fox returning. This time she jerked back noticeably.

She ran from the camp, her belly sick. She did not see Walks Far pause as he returned to their lodge. His eyes narrowed as he watched her, then moved suddenly between her and the dog rope man who was his friend.

7

Moon When The Buffalo Bulls Rut, 1864
Smoky Hill Country

I

Eagle woke stiff and sore, her body carefully angled away from Walks Far. For one moment she reached out to him, but her fingers stopped a breath away from his skin. Shame overwhelmed her again.

He had not asked for her. It had only been a plot that the Dogs might best the *Vehoo'o*.

She snatched her hand back again and pushed her robe away. Outside, the People were waking. She brushed her hair from her eyes and hugged herself, looking around. The Smoky Hill was Dog country, but for a while the *Wu'tapiu* would claim it, and she let the familiar scene soothe her heart.

"It is always the same, just a different river."

Startled at the echo of her thoughts, she spun to find Sun Roads. "Yes," she breathed. But already she heard voices raised in dissension near Black Kettle's lodge. There had never been councils like that before, she thought, not on empty bellies, before the first smoke of the new sun.

Sun Roads called to Pot Belly, toddling now on strong, sturdy legs, and they went downstream to relieve themselves. Eagle put the Dogs' manipulations from her mind. It was good to be back among her kin. She would let no one take that from her, she thought grimly. But as they returned to the camp, she saw Bear moving down to the water for his bath. She froze, staring at him, her throat growing tight with anger again.

Oh, brother, what have you done? She was trapped by his arrogant whim, like a hare in the claws of a hawk. It was done.

It was done.

She could not throw Walks Far away. Oh, *Ma'heo'o,* she had

73

thought of that, in the dark of some nights! She had thought of defying, of fighting back, of showing them all. It had been a wild, dangerous idea, making her pulse scramble hard. Had she dreamed that the dog rope man might claim her then? She gave a short, high-pitched laugh and pressed her hands to her cheeks. That would not happen. Perhaps he wanted to touch her, too, but he would never wed anyone. She would only hurt most the one who had hunted for her, who had warmed her, all through Cold Maker's last moons.

She swallowed, her throat aching. Walks Far cared for her; she knew it in a place deep in her gut where no lies could live. No matter how or why it had started, he provided well for her. In the end, she could ask no more than that.

She closed her eyes briefly and let embarrassment and regret ache in her for the last time. Then she straightened her spine and went to find him.

He was still sprawled upon his bedding, sleeping restlessly. She dropped to her knees and let herself touch him this time, laying her palm flat against the smooth planes of his chest. He came fully awake with a start, then a wariness came to his eyes that pierced her heart.

He knew; of course he would know that Fire Wolf had told her of the *Hotame-taneo'o* plan.

"It is all right," she blurted. "I see now. I see."

It was not all she wanted to say, but he understood. He came up on his elbows and caught her hand, gripping it so tightly that she thought her bones might crack.

"You are mine? Still mine? I have to know."

Her heart moved hard and jerkily. She must not, could not, think of haunted brown eyes that spoke of hurtful truths. There were only these black ones, sharp and searching and bright.

"Yes," she whispered.

He pulled her toward him, finding her mouth. She opened to him quickly.

"The babe," he managed after a moment.

"Perhaps we will scare him into coming out sooner. I would not mind that."

"You are sure? That would not hurt him?"

She wasn't sure at all. But the babe was strong and moving inside her, and she did not want to rush outside their lodge to find a more experienced woman to ask. Walks Far had not come to her at all since the wee one had begun swelling, but she knew it was important that he do so now.

She shook her head. "No . . . no, he will be fine."

"Roll over," Walks Far urged, and she did until he was behind her.

He slid her doeskin up her hips and over the mound of their child. The warm summer air moved over her skin. She shivered, tilting her head back into him, holding her breath, waiting, waiting . . .

His mouth, warm and wet, touched her neck the way she liked best, the way only he had learned to do. The hardness of him pressed against her bottom. She wriggled closer to him, and his hand closed over her breast, so sensitive now that she cried out. He jerked away again.

"I hurt you."

This time she did not try to deny it. She took his hand and put it back. He did not protest. It had been so long, too long, since he had loved her, and somehow, in that separate time, she had almost slipped away from him, like mist being burned off by the dawn.

Eagle felt it, too, a need that was different and deeper. She reached behind her and found him, guiding him inside her. He entered her in a new way, fuller and somehow stronger. He thrust in deep again, and she squealed, but this time he did not stop or ease back. His hand found the damp warmth of her, teasing and urging her, jolting something inside her.

Finally, finally, she knew the peak. It ripped through her, tense and hot, and she dug her fingers into the strong arms that had been chosen for her, knowing she would never, could never, push them away.

II

Later, as Sun climbed, she went to work with Small Blanket and Little Moon. The Smoky Hill camp was swelling now as Black Kettle's runners brought in the other bands. The Ridge People, the Scabby Village People, and the Flexed Knees Band arrived, led by the *Vehoo'o* White Antelope, War Bonnet and Stone Forehead. Lean Bear, a lesser *Vehoo'o* of the Ridge

People, was there too, showing off a shiny medal that had been given him on his visit to Wash-ing-tone.

Eagle listened to her mothers' gossip as they watched the new arrivals, thinking it was far more banal than the Dog wives' provocative conversations. For the first time in suns, she felt herself grinning. Then she looked up to see Walking Spirit approaching them, and the good feeling inside her shattered.

"Bear would see you," Walking Spirit said, shrugging to indicate that she did not know what was going on.

Eagle pushed to her feet with meticulous care. Bear was not alone in his lodge. Night Fighter stood behind him, and Walks Far sat cross-legged at his side. Her husband would not look at her.

"I wonder," Bear began, "what our mothers and grandmothers think of this treaty idea. You have heard them talk?"

Her heart moved with a quick, hard flutter. "What would you have them think?" she countered. "Is that not what I must know if I am to do your bidding?"

His face went slack with surprise. Suddenly temper was big and alive inside her. Oh, it was so good to finally say it!

"You betray me, brother!" she cried. "You go beyond your rights! You can say the one I should wed, but you cannot tell me what to feel, what to think! If you had been true with me all those seasons ago, I could have told you then that I would not promise to help you if I did not agree with your Dogs' schemes."

Bear shook his head vaguely as though *Ma i yun a huh'ta*, the dream maker, was whispering impossible visions into his head. As quickly as Eagle's anger gripped her, it whispered away again.

"I can tell you what our kin want," she went on more quietly. "Except for Little Moon, they desire peace at any cost, that is what I hear. They do not want to be caught as the *Ohmeseheso* were on the Red Shield. But I cannot say that I disagree with them, and I will do nothing to sway them until I understand, until I am sure. Tell me why you do not want this treaty signed."

Bear scowled, but he answered. "If Black Kettle can be delayed long enough by the disapproval of his women, I do not think the other *Vehoo'o* will sign without him. The *Hotame-*

taneo'o will have time to incite the warriors of the other bands. We would urge them to join us in this fight. We need to form a larger, stronger coalition of our societies."

She had heard them talk of this before, but now Eagle felt something quake in her belly. For the first time she truly considered the magnitude of such a fight.

Walks Far finally spoke. Her eyes darted to him.

"I think the spiders could be like the leaves on the trees, wife," he said quietly. "If they crawl down from their mountain, they will be all over. We will need many men to meet them. If our *Vehoo'o* do not sign this new paper talk and give them the land they want, they will be angry. A war will almost certainly come then."

"No! They will have to go back to that Den-ver place if they do not get the Councils' marks on their paper!"

"I do not think so. Their last paper talk promised they would not come down from their mountains, and they are trying to do that now."

Her gaze flew back to Bear. "Our mothers will not listen to me."

"They will. You are one of us now. They respect that."

The truth of that suddenly made her feel strange, as though she wore someone else's skin on her body. "I . . . I will think on this," she managed.

"Think?" Bear growled angrily. "What is there to think of now that you know what we would achieve?"

A pulse throbbed hard at her temple. "You," she said, then she looked to her husband. "And you."

And, *Ma'heo'o* help her, the dog rope man. *Do not think of him. Do not.* But she could not help it, and her breath felt short as she considered that a fight such as the one they spoke of would certainly force him to use the *ho tam'tsit* he wore in arrogant defense of his memories.

She could not allow that to happen.

Then her babe moved, kicking hard against her belly. She could not allow the spider tricksters to take his homeland, either, to steal away even more of his food.

As though reading her mind, Night Fighter finally spoke. "If your uncle attempts to put more land between the People and the *ve'ho'e*, that peace will last only as long as it takes the *ve'ho'e* to fill up the land they have taken. Then the tricksters will start more visiting and fighting so that they can ask for still more. It will go on and on until our people have nothing. These *ve'ho'e* must be stopped. They can never be permitted to leave their Den-ver. If they come down from there, we will never be able to push them back."

She nodded politely to let him know that she understood, then she pushed past the door flap. Behind her the lodge rang with a silence as profound as Night Fighter's prophecy.

"Will she help?" Bear asked finally. He felt foolish. He had arranged this, and at the crunching moment, he did not know after all what his sister might do.

But Walks Far only shook his head, bewildered. For the first time he realized that he truly did not know his wife at all.

III

Eagle hurried for the pony herd. The boys there stepped back, startled, as she hauled her cumbersome weight onto Wind Runner's back. She put her heels to the mare's flanks and galloped away from the camp.

She did not know what to do, did not know what was right, and she hated them, hated them all, for making her think about it.

Finally she slowed to a trot, circling back toward the camp. She rode through the golden-green grass that swayed lazily, toward a low hillock where four spindly trees twined their branches together. Ours, she thought, this is all *ours*. The *ve'ho'e* could not just ask for it and take it away. What did they think?

She reined in on the hillock, then heard hoofbeats behind her, frantic and fast. Wind Runner pranced nervously beneath her, and she pulled her around.

The riders did not notice her as they galloped past. *Wu'tapiu* men, she thought, returning from an effort to flush out some game. But their haste bothered her. Something was wrong.

She looked back the way they had come, and her heart staggered. *Ve'ho'e.* She had never seen them before, but she knew them now. For once the wind was still, and the relentless sun made the prairie shimmer beneath them, throwing up a reflection of blue from their clothing. They were mounted, but they were moving slowly. They were dragging two big guns along behind them, like big, hulking black metal beasts on wheels.

"No," she breathed. "*No!*"

She whipped Wind Runner around and smacked her rump hard, racing back down to the camp. Panic swelled there at the hunters' news. The Dog men were painting themselves, harassing the other warriors into doing the same. There was a sour smell of fear in the air as Black Kettle, White Antelope, and Stone Forehead gathered at the central *Vehoo'o* lodges. Black Kettle stood with his hands raised.

"All is well, all is well," the chief called, and, sweet *Ma'heo'o*, the people believed him. Eagle looked around disbelievingly as they quieted and the men began to drop their weapons again.

"These *ve'ho'e* only come to see what we have decided," Black Kettle reassured them.

"No," she burst out. "No! That is not the way it is!"

The crowd stared at her, stunned by her rudeness, but Black Kettle took the assault with calm dignity, as was expected from a man of his station.

"If we meet them with our weapons, we will make them angry and our women will die," he said quietly.

"If you meet them with nothing but your crazy medals, we will *all* die!" Night Fighter suddenly challenged.

"They have guns, big guns," Eagle whispered helplessly. "I saw them."

No one listened to her. Already Lean Bear was fumbling with his present, the shiny coin with the picture of Linc-on given him by the men in Wash-ing-tone all those seasons ago.

"We will show them who we are," that old man insisted. "We are good friends of the United States. This white medal says so."

"Arm yourselves," Walks Far said quietly to his brothers. "I believe my wife. These old men are wrong."

Lean Bear and Black Kettle hoisted themselves astride, Black Kettle clutching a tattered American flag. It had been given him at the Wise Treaty, with the instruction that if his people were ever set upon by white men, he need only show it to them to divert trouble. Proudly he draped it over his shoulders, positioning his loose braids neatly atop it, and then he rode out.

"Get the women out! *Get them out!*" Bear roared.

The Dogs tore the tethers from their war ponies. A handful of other warriors defied the *Vehoo'o* to go after them. Walks Far reached the hillock first and stared. The forms of the blue-coats were clearer now. Black Kettle's startling red, white, and blue shoulders bobbed with his pony's trot.

Lean Bear was faster, eager. Oh, how he loved that stupid medal, Walks Far thought bitterly. He held it high, waving it at the white men.

A shout punched into the tense quiet, *ve'ho'e* words that Walks Far could not understand. What sort of people came to this country without even learning the signs that could let all tongues speak together? He pressed his heels to his pony's flanks and moved down the slope, wanting to keep close to the two chiefs who were his grandfather's comrades.

Ahead of him, the *ve'ho'e* formed a line. That was not good, he thought. They fought that way. Then, impossibly, the harsh spit of bullets rent the air.

Lean Bear fell, first across his pony's neck, then sliding slowly to the ground, his old body tumbling, making the grass splay. Walks Far's muscles were knotted in readiness, but he could not move. Not this way, he thought, stunned. He had not thought even they would cut down the emissary who would have taken their hand in friendship.

For the lethal space of a breath, he stared as the *ve'ho'e* came on. They paused to riddle Lean Bear with more bullets. His old body twitched and jumped in the grass.

"*Noooo!*" Walks Far roared.

He rode hard for the fallen chief. There was a wet-sounding thud, and a boy beside him fell backward off his pony. The Dogs' moment of shock had given the spider tricksters an advantage.

Bear and Night Fighter fanned north; Walks Far screamed a war cry and drove his pony south. And now others were coming, Hair Rope and Flexed Knee warriors streaming over the hill at the sounds of the fight. The *ve'ho'e* cannons boomed thunderously, with huge belches of smoke, then fell silent and abandoned as the blue-coat cowards began to flee.

There are many of them, Walks Far thought. They could best us, but now they run. Why?

He coiled his strength beneath him and eased down to cling against his pony's side. He swept among their lines and fired from beneath its neck. Then, as he circled for another drive, his pony veered. His fingers lost their grip in its long mane, and he fell hard, his breath punching out of him, his carbine jolting free of his hand.

He rolled back to his feet, looking about sharply, ready to fight with his knife if he had to. His medicine was strong and hot inside him; he knew he would not die this sun. But it was not a *ve'ho'e* who had brought him down. Black Kettle stood in his pony's path, his own mount lost in the melee, his flag sadly askew now.

"Go, Grandfather! Go back! The *Hotame-taneo'o* and the warriors will deal with this!"

But the old chief did not acknowledge him. "No more! No more!" he screamed to his *Wu'tapiu*. "Let the white men go! Peace! We must not give them cause for war!"

But Walks Far knew that war was already upon them. There would be no time for calculation and an organized coalition now. In their strange, deadly hunger for more land, the stupid *ve'ho'e* had murdered a friend, one of the few men who might have given it to them.

Walks Far caught his pony, screaming, and went after this incomprehensible enemy again.

IV

Eagle sat astride Wind Runner amid the confusion in the camp, scowling at the hollow pop-pop-pop of bullets. She did not want to know what that sound was, could not bear to know . . . but she did, she did.

The spiders had come to kill them. They had come right into Dog country—*Dog country*—and they were firing their guns at the warriors who had gone out there to stop them.

Then a boom came that seemed to make Grandmother Earth tremble in horror. Eagle knew it was the big guns on wheels, and she screamed and clapped her hands to her ears. A grandfather slapped her mare's rump, sending her trotting toward the knot of women and children gathering at the center of the camp.

Where was everyone? *Where were her kin?*

She saw Blind Fox first, a bow clamped in his fist, hollering a war cry, tears streaming as he raced from the camp. Her grandfather, Medicine Wolf, moved bent and stooped among the women, urging them into a safe retreat. Then Black Kettle came back, staggering under the weight of a body. The eerie, shocked wails of mourning began to rise. Another body was brought in, then another. The grandfathers began herding the women east, prodding and pushing them. They moved, howling.

The bodies lay at the edge of camp, too cumbersome to be carried any farther in this time of terrified flight. Eagle could not pull her eyes from then.

Walks Far? Bear? *Who were they?*

She dropped heavily to the ground. Clutching the ungainly weight of her babe, she ran. She stumbled to her knees beside them, pulling one head up, then another, letting them drop. They were both *Wu'tapius* she knew only barely, young men who had recently married into the band.

Her breath came out short and ragged as she pushed at the third body, rolling it so that it flopped onto its back. A keen started deep in her chest, swelling there.

Lean Bear.

She had not loved him, had barely known him. But she knew the way he had ridden out, so proud and sure, and her head swam. The wretched *ve'ho'e* medal was still clutched in his spidery fingers.

There was something wrong about that, so very, very wrong.

She lurched to her feet. The gunfire was soft now, sporadic, fading. *"You cannot do this to us!"* she sobbed. *"You cannot!"*

And she knew then that she would not let them.

8

Moon When The Cherries Get Ripe, 1864
Smoky Hill Country

I

The wind moaned like a man dying. Hot and restless, it tussled with the fire in front of Little Moon's lodge until the flames popped and the wood settled with a shower of sparks. The women gathered there jumped and flinched.

"There, you see!" Little Moon snapped. "This is how it will always be if those spiders come down from their mountain. We will never know when they will come again and kill us all! We will be like rabbits, noses twitching, waiting for the hawk. I have spoken. You heard me first."

Old Walks At Night looked up from her sewing. "If they want to come down and we resist, there will be fear anyway, daughter. The *vehoo'o* say it is best to give them what they want. Then they will leave us alone again."

"No!" Eagle cried. "This way, at least, they fear us as well."

Their eyes came around to her disbelievingly.

"That is what the Dogs say," she insisted. "When our warriors went out to fight that sun, the spiders ran. Walks Far has thought about this, and he thinks it is because they did not truly intend to do war, but only scare us into signing their papers. Now they have sent another message, and the *Hotametaneo'o* think it is because they do not want to fight us at full force unless they have to." The word had come suns ago, an invitation for the friendly chiefs to bring their people into the forts where they would be protected from the blue-coats' attacks. So far, Black Kettle remained undecided.

"Bah," Medicine Woman Later said mildly. "They want us to come to their fires because they fear us? Even *ve'ho'e* are not that contrary."

Eagle scowled. How could she make them see? "If they lure us to their fires, they will break our numbers," she tried. "They will weaken us so they will not have to fight us when we are strongest. If some of us go to their forts, and others stay to fight, then we will be divided. There will not be so many warriors on the plains for the *ve'ho'e* to conquer."

Little Moon put down her quill work to cross her arms militantly across her breasts. "If our *Vehoo'o* say we should go, I say we should refuse."

Small Blanket murmured a thoughtful agreement, but several other squaws shook their heads worriedly. Eagle closed her eyes. Some of them were changing their minds about this treaty, but would it be enough? She did not see how she could sway enough of them to have any effect on her uncle.

Suddenly, despite the parching wind and the fire, she felt cold to her bones. She stood again, gathering her sewing to move off to another fire and keep trying.

II

Eagle and Sun Roads squatted close to the river, digging up wild onions. Eagle thought grimly that their bellies were already twisting with hunger. Some straggling buffalo had finally roamed south, and there was other game, but it was not enough. She closed her eyes and fought the urge to pop one of the onions into her mouth. They would make the meat last longer if they were put into stews and sausages. Deliberately she dropped a handful into her gut bag just as a squaw screamed from somewhere in the camp.

In the same moment they heard the rolling tempo of galloping hoofbeats. Sun Roads moaned in fear.

"It is only one pony. Listen." Still, Eagle sank her fingers into Sun Roads' arm. She did not think any of them could stand another attack so soon.

"Wait here," she said. "I will go see what this is about."

She shrugged her bag off her shoulder and pulled her doeskin over her knees to scramble up the bank. The camp was quiet now; the scream had been reactionary. A lone rider came across the prairie, just as she had guessed. His wild black hair whipped in the wind, and his chest was bare.

Fire Wolf was back.

An invisible fist slammed into her chest. She had not seen him since he had told her the truth of her marriage. She had tried hard, so very hard, not to think of him. But now he was close again, and relief moved in her so intimately she swayed with it. He looked strong and unhurt.

He slowed to a trot, and she moved impulsively, letting emotion carry her. Oh, yes, she knew it was dangerous, every bit as dangerous as he had hinted for them to be together, to share time. Yet she slid her knife free in one quick motion and hurled it as he had taught her.

Her eyes narrowed on it, as though she could somehow will it to do as she intended. She had practiced, and more often than not now her aim was true. Still, she could not bear to err this time.

She did not. With a little, punching *chh* sound the blade drove into the ground at his pony's feet. She gave a whoop of satisfaction.

He reined in and stared at it, his jaw stony. Then his eyes came up to hers, and a slow grin spread over his face.

"Too bad that blade of grass cannot feed you."

"Ah, but I was aiming for that precise blade of grass."

His grin cracked wider, and he laughed. She shivered at the rare sound; she could not help it.

"You are well?" he asked finally. "It has been good for you here?"

She looked up and met his eyes, opening her mouth to answer. Then there was a shout from the lodges, followed by more raucous greetings that seemed very distant to her. Someone bumped into her as they came to greet their dog rope man, and she stumbled backward a few steps.

Walks Far caught her arm to steady her. His grip seemed too hard, too tight.

She looked up at him, feeling herself flush guiltily. *I have not done anything wrong.*

But it felt like it. Oh, *Ma'heo'o*, it did.

"I . . . came to hear, to tell the others . . ." she managed.

He nodded and led her back to Bull Bear's lodge. But his hand stayed possessively on her wrist even after they were inside, so that she finally had to pull away from him.

Everyone's attention was riveted on the dog rope man. There
was a sense of triumph and tension about him as he crouched
on his haunches. For the first time her thoughts turned honestly
to the news he would bring, and her blood seemed to pump
harder.

"I need you to come back north with me," he said without
preamble. "We have devised a way to drive the *ve'ho'e* out of
even their Den-ver place, but we need more warriors."

There was a cacophony of voices and questions. Fire Wolf
shouted to be heard above it.

"We have been fighting far north in *Ohmeseheso* country, at
the place the spiders call their Platte River Road. The *Ohmeseheso* societies have joined with the Dogs who are with me,
and Pawnee Killer is helping with his Oglala Sioux. There are
Lakota there and some *So'taa'e* warriors. We have taken
control of that trail. No *ve'ho'e* wagons have gotten through for
six suns now, except those we have emptied and sent on as a
message to the mongrels."

Bear leaned forward, his eyes avid. "I have heard of that
road. It is how they get their paper words and their food into
Den-ver."

"They have no other way in?" demanded Night Fighter.

Fire Wolf shrugged. "If they did, they would not be fighting
so hard to regain this trail. The last wagon to attempt to pass
before I left was protected by blue-coats. It took half a sun's
fighting to kill them all and strip the load this time. That is why
I have come to you. We need all the Dogs, all the societies now,
and we will triumph."

He was sure and arrogant, and his promise of victory incited
the others. A fury for vengeance, an edge of hungry hope,
began to shine in Walks Far's eyes.

Eagle saw it.

"No," she whispered, but it was too late to stop it, and no one
paid her any attention in any event. She had done her part.
Black Kettle had not signed the treaty, and his *Wu'tapiu* would
not go to live at the forts. Now the Dogs would band the others
together to tear the hearts from these *ve'ho'e* who thought to
rob them.

An angry hunger moved in her heart. *Yes, kill them,* she
thought. *Make them pay for all they have done.* But as her eyes

moved from one face to the other, to all these men who dwelled in different corners of her soul, fear filled her.

The *Tse-Tsehesestahase* were at war, and somehow, impossibly, she had helped put them to it. She had offered up the lives of her brother, her husband, her friend.

And her babe? Walking Spirit's words came back to her yet again. *"They must be strong to survive the war camps when they come."*

Nausea pushed up in her throat, and she pushed her knuckles against her teeth and fled the lodge.

III

Walks Far slept.

Eagle lay on her side, watching him. He is *Hatame-taneo'o*, she thought. Of course he sleeps. His path is clear, chosen long ago. He would defend the People, and I must follow him.

A shudder went through her, and she put a hand to the swell of her child. As though sensing her touch, the babe kicked back heartily.

He will survive this, she thought. Surely he will. And if he does not? Then I have killed him. *Oh,* Ma'heo'o, *what have I done?*

He was almost ready to be pushed out; despite her inexperience, she knew that. He felt lower, harder against her private parts. He would come out long before the Dogs drove the *ve'ho'e* from Den-ver, no matter how many allies they had. If she went with them, her babe would be birthed just as Lean Bear had died, amid bullets and screams, with the Grandmother trembling.

If she went with them.

She sat up and grabbed her doeskin. Struggling into it, she went outside. She went to the river, where she cupped her hands and brought up a bowl of water to splash against her feverish face. A rustling sound came to her beneath the wet noise of her splashing. She stiffened, wanting to be alone.

It came again, a sibilant echo in the night as feet moved through the grass. She stood and turned about, and then she saw him.

Fire Wolf.

He wore only his breechclout now, and the moonlight bathed his burnished skin. As she watched, he drove his fingers through his hair and looked up at the sky, his eyes restless. He was so very different from Walks Far, she thought, and oh, *Ma'heo'o*, she loved them both!

The thought wrenched a groan from her. She clapped a hand over her mouth with a sound that snicked out clearly into the night. He whipped around, his eyes narrowing on her.

"Thank *Ma'heo'o* you were born a squaw and we do not need your stealth in a fight," he muttered.

She almost giggled at that, but her emotions were too raw. She made a quick move back toward the camp instead.

"No," he said quietly. "Do not go. Not yet."

He wondered if it was there in his tone, a distant uneasiness that perhaps this time it would happen, this time *Ma'heo'o* would grant him peace and he would go up the death road. *What had this little one done to him?* Before she had scoffed at his guilt, his will to die had been his most intimate friend. Now something very tiny and very weak kicked inside him in protest when he thought of falling.

She hesitated, but she came on, closing the distance between them. He looked down into her face, and what he saw there was the worst thing of all.

She still needed him. There was a storm in her eyes, and Walks Far could not ease it. That warrior had perhaps put this babe in her, had maybe met her ache to love fully and well, but there was still a place within her that needed him, a rogue warrior who could, in the end, give her nothing.

"Is there food there?" she asked. "I must know."

At first he did not understand, then it came to him. She was worried about the war camp.

There was, after all, one thing he could give her, and it was why she had come back to him now. As always, he would grant her the truth.

"When Cold Maker comes, it will be better than anywhere else," he answered. "We take much off the *ve'ho'e* wagons we stop. They have some little cakes that are thin and dry and salty, but they fill holes in your belly. There is the fatty meat they eat and some of their sweet powder and that cof-fee."

Eagle nodded and shivered. "Do you have time to hunt?" she persisted. "Is there game?"

He shrugged. "Sometimes yes, sometimes no."

"You are hungry."

"We all are."

He was right. She was beginning to crave meat so much that her mouth sometimes salivated with it. The Dogs would fare best with that strange *ve'ho'e* food. It was, she thought, one reason to go with them.

The moment she thought it, she realized that she had already decided to stay.

Fire Wolf saw the panic flare in her eyes. "What?"

"I cannot do it. Oh, sweet *Ma'heo'o*, I cannot birth this child there! But staying behind would be like throwing Walks Far away!" She grabbed Fire Wolf's arm. "I . . . I have come to love him," she blurted.

He nodded, and if there was pain in his eyes, it was hidden by the darkness. But she felt the muscles beneath his skin harden, and a pang went through a different part of her heart, the part that was his. She felt so shredded, so torn.

And then she felt angry.

"I am only a woman! There is so little I can do about any of this trouble! You have all asked me to work against this treaty, and I have done that. But now there is something more important. I will not give my babe's life to Bear, to the *Hotame-taneo'o*, to *any* of you!"

"Then stay. Follow your heart. You will survive, little Eagle. You always do, because you are strong."

She shook her head, hurt. Could it be that even he did not understand? Then the moon moved out from behind a cloud again, and she saw the truth in his face.

She laughed aloud, a thin, cracking sound. If she stayed behind, Fire Wolf could play no part in that decision. He would not wed her if she was free. She saw it now as she always had, in that set to his jaw and the *mis'tai* ghosts in his eyes.

She thumped him hard on the chest with the heel of her hand, then she moaned, because the choice was for her babe, it had always been for her babe, and it was not his fault at all. She spread her fingers across his warm skin, because he would go and she would stay, and perhaps she would never see him again. Her eyes were drawn to the dog rope he wore even now, and suddenly the wanting inside her was a physical ache.

"I am so tired of thinking what everyone else wants of me!" she cried. "Just once I would like something for myself before it is too late!" She wanted to know what love was like with this strong and broken man who knew that the world was not gentle. Then she would release him back to his demons and the death he seemed to crave, if only she could taste him just once.

Beneath her palm, she felt him stiffen. Carefully he took her hand from his skin.

"No," she whispered. "You said you wanted me, too."

He cursed darkly, struggling with himself a last time. Then he raised her hand to his face, and she yearned toward him. His grip was hard, painful. He took her fingers into his mouth, first one, then another, nipping and laving the sting with his tongue.

The wet warmth of him burned through her, curling about her belly, making her shake. But she knew it would end here. They would not, after all, betray the man who slept.

He dropped her hand and gathered her to him. And for a moment, she had that, too, the precious, hard solidity of him, his arms finally warm and strong about her. "Yes," she whispered. Then quietly, quickly, he stepped away from her, putting her arms back to her sides.

It was almost, almost enough.

IV

So many of them would go.

The clatter of lodge poles rang everywhere, and the air was full with shouts and whinnies and dust as the People broke camp. Eagle felt her gut tremble. Had she made the wrong choice? Nearly all of the warriors would go north to increase the Dogs' stranglehold on the spiders' road. She knew there would not be enough fighters left among the *Vehoo'o* bands to protect the women and the babes if the tricksters came back.

But the *Vehoo'o* were planning to migrate south now, away from the strife. Stone Forehead had invited Black Kettle and White Antelope to join his Flexed Knees People at their Medicine Lodge Creek. Stone Forehead always kept his people far away from the white men. He had their Sacred Medicine Arrows to protect.

That would have to be enough.

Her gaze moved to Walks Far as he bridled his pony. He did not understand this decision she had made, and she ached for him. She went to him, touching his arm, trying to reach him one last time.

"I speak true," she managed. "Hear me. I do not throw you away. I will be here, waiting, if you will return for me."

Walks Far felt his gut twist. He knew in that moment that if she waited for him it would be because she chose to, not because she was vulnerable and lost without him. For a wild, fleeting moment he regretted taking her. She was not anything like he thought she was when he had wed her. She was not like any wife he had ever heard of! And yet he wondered if he might love her more for it.

He hugged her to him suddenly and hard, and she grabbed on to him.

"I will return," he vowed. "Keep that wee one safe."

She managed to nod against his shoulder. Then he pulled away, shouting something hoarse and harsh to the others.

Eagle's eyes followed all of them as they mounted and rode out. Deep within herself, she thought she felt something fracture, but she turned away and went back to the place where her *Wu'tapiu* waited for her.

9

Cool Moon, 1864
Medicine Lodge Creek

I

A single golden leaf clung to the aspen despite the moaning autumn wind. Governor Evans watched it, his stomach feeling sour. It occurred to him that soon the snow would come to blanket it, and still that damnable leaf would hang on, surviving long after it should have laid down and died.

It reminded him of the Indians.

"I never anticipated that this would be so difficult."

Chivington worked at his desk and answered without looking up. "The end is in sight, sir."

"In sight? Not a single teamster has made it along the Platte Road in nine weeks! My word, how intelligent they must be to figure out that we need that trail!"

Chivington stood calmly and pushed a piece of paper across his desk. "I've needed soldiers to push the Indians off the Platte. Now I shall have them, and I can meet the heathens even at their full strength. This arrived just today. Washington cannot grant me cavalry with that blasted war going on back there, but I've been authorized to mount and arm as many hundred-day men as I can enlist."

Evans felt a strange foreboding. "Hundred-day men? Nothing less than trained militia will dislodge those bucks from the Platte. You'll have discipline problems, zealots, if you enlist irregulars!"

"Farmers will suffice if guided by the proper military strategies," Chivington argued. "In the meantime, I'm sending Major Anthony to relieve Wynkoop at Fort Lyon. The time has come to put someone in there who will cooperate with our efforts. Then you must appeal to the citizens. Urge the men to enlist as my hundred-dayers, but short of that, you must impress upon them the necessity of defending their homes and towns against these merciless savages. Authorize them to kill and destroy as enemies of the country all Indians remaining outside the forts. The Cheyenne failed to respond to my peaceful overtures, Governor. Now I believe that we must make a commitment to war with them, which must result in exterminating them."

The commander's eyes were sure and hot. Evans looked into them and found himself nodding in agreement.

It would work. He refused to consider the consequences to his political career if it did not.

II

The wind had a hollow taste to it, Eagle thought. It was not so much cold as it was empty of warmth . . . and any trace of animal smell. A pain gripped her belly, and she turned away from the creek, toward the People's lodges again.

Oh, she was hungry. *What had she done?* Suddenly the pain inside her moved to her heart. She had thought of everything, of Fire Wolf dying by the rope while she was gone, of the best place for birthing her babe. But she had not known that she would long for Walks Far's chuckle, a sound that soothed even her worst fears. She had never been truly hungry before, and she had not known it could hurt so.

She hugged herself as she stepped carefully over the dried moss of the creek bed, then she stopped, staring at riders who had appeared on the plain.

It was silly, just her hunger and despair tinging everything, but she felt a terrible foreboding. She hurried toward them, five men with shirts mangled and torn. Another pain stabbed into her, stronger than the first. It made her stumble. It was not hunger, not this time, she thought. Her babe was finally coming . . . but what were these men doing back here? *If these warriors were here, then who was fighting for the* Hotame-taneo'o *coalition?*

She clenched her jaw against the low, growing urgency in her body, reaching the warriors as they dismounted at Black Kettle's lodge. Their women jostled her, crying out in their gladness, then keening when their fingers touched the crusted blood.

"What is happening?" she demanded. "Tell me!"

Something in her voice made one man pause and address her. "The Dogs are holding the road," he explained. "They do not need us so much now, so we have returned to try to bring in some food."

Eagle shook her head. That lost spring hunt would be the wretched *ve'ho'e*'s biggest coup. The surety of it made her head swim, and she could not tell herself that it was the appeal of her babe trying to escape her belly. Hunger would be the thing to release the Dog's hold on the Platte Road.

"The blood," she managed. "Tell me about this blood."

The warrior flinched, then his features settled into rocky impassivity. "We lost a man on the way here. It is strange. There are bands of cat-tul men, not blue-coats, roaming our land, looking to fight. But they are inept in spite of their hunger for our scalps. We kill them for trespassing." He stabbed his lance into the earth. Pale hair flowed from its tip and down its shaft.

Eagle spared it a glance, then pushed on. "And the Dogs themselves? They fare well?"

"Who do you ask for?"

Oh, so many. "Walks Far of the Ridge People?"

Recognition lit on the man's face. "That one is well."

"And Bear That Goes Alone, one of ours?"

"Him, too."

Suddenly her body gathered itself again, demanding that she pay attention to it. But there was another name, another man. She should not ask, but she had to, had to know.

"The dog rope man?" she gasped.

The warrior nodded. "He is well, too."

He lived.

"Ah," she whispered as she felt everything within her gathering, getting ready, tightening again. She put a hand to her child.

Now she knew. Now she could push him out.

III

The pain savaged her until her thighs screamed and trembled with it. Eagle could not stand it and she could not make it go away, no matter what she did. She shoved weakly at the woman who gathered around her and crawled back to her bedding.

"What is wrong?" she heard Sun Roads ask. "Why is it staying in there?"

Little Moon's face swam into her line of vision, big and red and shiny with sweat. "It was like this with her mother when she pushed Bear out," she answered grimly. "This girl is too skinny, like Small Blanket. They should not be making babes."

Eagle scowled at her, and then she understood. Her aunt was saying that this babe couldn't get out.

"No," she protested. "No!"

But, oh, *Ma'heo'o*, he felt so big! He filled all of her, and she knew he could never pass through that small place between her legs. She would go up the death road because Walks Far had put him in her, and she did not want to go.

Terror and denial rushed up in her, and she screamed, though she had not thought she had the strength for it. Then she grew angry. Always Little Moon thought she was right, always she thought she knew everything.

But this time she was wrong.

Eagle struggled to her knees again on the thick grass and the buffalo robe that had been laid down for her. "I will show you that I do not have to be a cow to do this."

Little Moon nodded smugly.

Eagle stared at her, agape. Had she made her angry because there was no other hope, challenged her because all that was left was her courage? It robbed her of her pique, but not her terror. She grunted and let the woman brace her with her bulky body, pushing desperately as the pain came on her yet again.

It rode her in wave after wave of excruciating demand. She moved her hands to the birthing posts they had driven into the ground, gripping them with all her strength. There was a snapping, splintering sound and then a different pain, wood slashing into her palm. She cried out and jerked away, falling to her hands and knees.

"Here! He comes!"

But she knew that, because it felt as though her very body was rending, fracturing with the huge force of him. She screamed again, with the last of herself, and felt a warm, wet rush, the beginning of a slow emptying. Sure hands caught him from beneath her, and Little Moon gathered her up.

She let the darkness rush in on her and felt another trembling contraction so distantly that it was not like it was happening to her at all. Then she heard him, a tiny voice pinched with anger, growing stronger. She fought back, out of the darkness, and twisted around to look at him.

Small Blanket wrapped the cord once around a shaking finger, slicing him free of her. Eagle stared at him, elation rocking through her.

She had known him forever as he hid within her. She had sacrificed and defied for him. But now . . . now he was here. And he was real.

His little face was mottled and red, and for the first time she loved him with overwhelming force, *him*, not just the mound of her belly that demanded responsibility and agonizing decisions. She reached out for him, gathering him gently to her, trembling as the blackness finally swam over her.

IV

Eagle pulled sinew thread carefully through the buckskin bag she was making. Shaped into a lizard, it would hold the dried stump of the babe's birth cord. It would dangle from his cradleboard, and then, when he walked, it would be worn about his neck. The cord contained the essence of him, and she knew it was strong and robust. Already, after only seven suns, it had dropped off him and the spot on his tummy was healing well.

She put her sewing aside and gathered him up. "Ah, little one, what did you do to me?" she whispered. "You could have survived that war camp, but I am not sure I could have. I am lucky you did not split me in two!"

She shrugged out of one shoulder of her doeskin to feed him, and he nuzzled even as her gut twisted hollowly. She rubbed her forehead against an ache there. In one more moon the streams would begin to freeze. There would be even less food than ever.

"Hurry, husband," she murmured. Surely he would come back for them by then.

She pulled the babe away from her nipple, afraid that he would deplete what milk she did have. Then a voice beckoned to her from outside.

The warrior who came in was one she did not know. He held his arms out for her child, and emotion swept her. This would be done according to *Ma'heo'o*'s wishes despite the war.

"*Ha ho'*," she managed. "Who has sent for him?"

"White Antelope."

"Ah." Walks Far's kin. That was good.

As they moved through the *Wu'tapiu* lodges, people broke away from their chores to follow them. There would be no feasting, but at least there would be talk and smoking. In the Ridge People camp, White Antelope sat outside his lodge, wrapped in his best painted buffalo robe. Black Kettle was present as well. He took her babe from the messenger.

Together the chiefs unwrapped the soft doeskin swaddled about him. There were grunts of approval from those gathered. The babe's swarthy little body had already been greased and dusted with finely ground manure and the sweet-smelling powder of the prairie puffball. But now sage was sprinkled over him as well, to inspire a long and productive life.

Finally White Antelope bundled him up again. "I will give him this name. I have thought about it long, and it is not for one of our kin. It is for this." From the folds of his robe, he withdrew a splintered stick.

Eagle scowled, not understanding. A boy-child was almost always named for an older, honored man in the band. That one would change his own name and give the wee one his old one. Then she remembered distantly, as though the birthing had happened to someone else. She had strained against that post when she had pushed him out, and she had broken it.

There were murmurs and nods as the story was passed around. Then White Antelope spoke again.

"There will be power in this name, just as though it were passed on from a man of courage and wisdom. I call this child for his mother's strength and his own. I call him Broken Stick."

It pleased everyone. They began talking louder, and Eagle could feel them darting appraising looks at her. She felt her skin heat. She was not strong. She had just not been willing to die.

Her babe was given back to her, and her own kin pressed in, Small Blanket and Little Moon, Walks At Night and Medicine Woman Later. Eagle looked down at her little one.

"If only my husband would come back and feed us," she murmured, "all would be well indeed."

Medicine Woman Later's gnarled fingers touched Broken Stick's brow. "There will be food enough when we get to the fort," she soothed absently. "They have promised."

"The fort?"

An awkward quiet fell. Eagle felt her heart kick.

"What is this?" she demanded. But she knew. Seven suns! she thought wildly. She had been confined to her mother's lodge for only seven suns, but somehow she had lost all of them! They had turned back from the *Hotame-taneo'o* to the *Vehoo'o*.

"No!" she protested. "You must think of all we talked about, of what will happen—"

Walks At Night interrupted. "I know your heart is with the *Hotame-taneo'o*, Granddaughter, and that is as it should be. But this is best for everyone. Black Kettle does not think it is wise to defy the *ve'ho'e* any longer now that even their cat-tul men are trying to attack our camps."

"Yes, yes, I have heard that. But they are fools, not good fighters—"

"They are dangerous enough," Medicine Woman Later said with some authority. "We will go where we will be safe, where their chiefs will protect and feed us."

Eagle whirled to Little Moon. "*You* do not want this! I know you do not!"

"No one else will stay," the woman answered tightly. "I must go."

She turned away. Eagle chased after her.

"You are not so stupid as to believe what they are saying!" she burst out.

Her aunt turned on her, angry red color staining her face.

"What would you have me do? I cannot squat here on the prairie all alone! They will go. I must follow."

"No! You can send Blind Fox to the Dogs! Tell them what is happening. You did it before. They will help! They will stop this!"

Something flared in the woman's eyes, a brief hope, and then it was gone. "That was before these bands of cat-tul warriors." Then she looked down at Broken Stick with a sly, calculating look. "Would you send *him* out there alone to face them?"

Eagle felt her throat close, and her arm instinctively tightened around her babe.

She had left her husband so as not to birth him in a war camp. But he was a wee one, vulnerable and defenseless. If he were nearly a man, if, like Blind Fox, he had seen sixteen winters, would she send him?

"If I did not have him, I would go myself!" she gasped, her chin coming up. "If we go to those forts, we will lose everything."

"She is right," said Blind Fox belligerently.

They turned to find him behind them.

"I wanted to go to fight on the Platte Road," he went on. "You would not let me. Now, this is something I can do. I want to go. I am too old for you to stop me."

Little Moon let her air out with a *woofing* sound, as though someone had punched her. But Blind Fox only flinched and hardened his jaw. Eagle sank to the ground where she stood, overcome with a need to sit, to rest, to weep at the insidious way the *ve'ho'e* were tearing them all asunder.

The worst part was that she had done all she could. She did not think there was anything left she could do to stop them.

10

Moon When The Water Begins To Freeze, 1864
Medicine Lodge Creek

I

Stone Forehead's cottonwoods raised naked limbs to the gray sky. Eagle paused beneath them to shift Broken Stick's cradleboard off her back. He bawled relentlessly, a harsh wail stitched now and again with wet little gasps.

It had been four suns since she had put anything but bark in her tummy, and she did not dare feed him until she managed to eat something herself. She was afraid if he suckled one more time, he would drink her dry. Without food, her body could not seem to supply milk.

Grimly she hung his cradleboard on a tree limb the way her mothers and grandmothers had told her to do. She pushed her fingers against her temples and stepped back.

"You must learn not to complain so," she murmured. "You must stay here until you learn to be quiet. When you are good, you will have my attention again, and perhaps, if we are lucky, I will even bring something to eat."

She left him and went down to the creek, pulling a long, sharpened stick from her belt. At first she did not see any of the fat fish she had noticed during her earlier treks here, then she found one hovering languidly against the bank. Her pulse picked up. It was just as she had noted before—with the water growing cold, they seemed more lethargic now than they had back in the Cool Moon.

She had never heard of eating fish, but she could think of no taboo against it, and it was food . . . food.

She raised her stick, her hand trembling with weakness and desperation, and brought the pointed end down hard. Almost immediately she knew she had misjudged. The water distorted things. With a surge of his tail, the fish sped away.

100

"Noooooo!" she wailed. She hurled the stick aside and splashed in after him.

He veered into a little cove formed by a bend in the bank. Instinctively she dropped flat on her belly, splashing to block his way. With a slippery hand, she worked her knife from her belt. This time she pinned him to the bottom with it.

"Eiiaaa!" she squealed in triumph. She scrambled to her knees, instinctively working her fingers into his gills. She pulled the knife free, and in the same quick movement flipped him up onto the ground.

She would eat. She would eat!

She splashed out after him, the cold biting into her sodden doeskin, and gathered him up again. Then she half ran, half stumbled, back to the tree where Stick waited.

"I did not know," came a voice from the swell of ground above her. *"Ma'heo'o,* had I known, I would have dragged you with me by the hair to make you leave this south!"

She screamed in shock and lost her legs beneath her. Scrambling, she twisted around to look into the trees.

Walks Far . . . Walks Far had finally come back for her.

She gasped with emotion she had not known she could feel for him. Then he was upon her, and she touched him frantically, her mouth on his face, her hands in his hair.

"Blind Fox found you—"

"We found him—"

"The road—"

"We are losing it—"

"No! No!"

"There are other ways." He paused, standing again to take the babe from the tree. "He is mine! You pushed him out."

He stared at the round, red face of the wee one. He did not know if he was more moved by this life he had known only as a lump in her belly, or by the fact that she had indeed done it, that she had birthed him alone.

Eagle would not let him think about it. She pushed to her feet after him and touched her fingers to the crinkled skin around his eyes, shocked by the gauntness about him. His smooth, *Vehoo'o*-bred looks had roughened, hardened.

"What has happened to you?" she breathed.

"Do I look so bad?" He laughed, a short sound, then he caught her hand. "It is hard fighting, wife."

"Tell me."

But he shook his head. "Later. You can listen when we talk to the *Vehoo'o*. Now we must take this wee one to the others. They will want to see."

But she hung back against his strength when he would have tugged her toward the camp. "The others . . ."

"They are mostly well."

Mostly. Her heart plunged hard. "Who . . . who is lost?"

"Four Ponies, our healer, but Fire Wolf knows some about wounds and broken bones."

She closed her eyes. So the dog rope man lived . . . still, this time, one more time. She looked at her husband again.

"Who else?"

He hesitated. "Cherries."

"Aiy-ee." The sound slid from her, and she thought her legs might melt. Walks Far caught her.

"How?" she breathed.

"On the way here. We fought on our journey."

So they had met the little-buffalo-men warriors. She looked up at Walks Far and saw his jaw go hard.

"They are nothing to fear if we are careful. They can only kill women and weak ones, when they stray too far from our warriors. But Cherries did that. She saw a hare one dawn when she was the first to rise. She chased after it and ran into the False Soldiers." His fingers dug deep into her arms. "We killed them all and put their faces down against the earth so that their souls will be forever trapped inside them."

There was that. She clung to it, knowing that Cherries had been avenged, and followed him back to the camp.

The knot of *Hotame-taneo'o* was at Black Kettle's lodge. Many, many of them had come to ward off this weak choice of the *Vehoo'o*. Blind Fox stood at their fringes, his chest puffed and proud. And the others! Walking Spirit cried out and rushed to greet her. The other squaws came on as well . . . everyone but Cherries. Her absence was a sharp, empty place among them, and Eagle's heart went to Tangle Hair.

Bear took the cradleboard from her, grunting as he pulled the laces apart and looked down at the babe. Then a broad grin took his face.

Walking Spirit hooted. "He will dote on this one. I have spoken. You heard me first. Look, he is in his image."

Falling Bird chuckled and elbowed her in the ribs. "He is big. The grandmothers say that babes grow best when their mothers walk before dawn. You must have walked a lot in the darkness, little Eagle."

Eagle's feeling of gladness vanished abruptly into something shaky. As though *Mai i yun a huh'ta,* the Dream Maker, had blown in her ear, she remembered the single night when she *had* walked, remembered the moonlight as though she were back in it now, and the wet warmth of Fire Wolf's mouth at her fingertips. She looked up at the crowd again. Walks Far had said he lived. So where was he? *Where?*

She found him standing back from the others, as he always did. His brown eyes were steady upon hers. He lifted one brow, but she knew he could not have heard Falling Bird's words, and his arrogant face was unreadable. Then he finally came in among them and took the cradleboard from Bear.

He touched the babe's round cheek, and something almost soft came to his tortured eyes. "A son as strong as you are," he murmured. "Yes, you survived your choice."

A little shiver went down her spine, then he handed the babe back to her.

"Now, where are these *Vehoo'o*?" he asked.

II

"So, you have come to stop a dull old man from behaving foolishly. There was a time when you honored my choices, but now it seems you do not trust me. Who sent the boy to you?"

Black Kettle's hooded gaze moved around his lodge. It was crowded with *Vehoo'o* and *Hotame-taneo'o*, the elders huddled close to the fire trench, the warriors standing stiffly against the taut lining. Eagle was pressed in between the two factions.

"You speak of trust!" Bull Bear charged angrily, and Eagle jerked around to see him. "What of honor? Would you have told us yourself that you planned to crawl into those forts on your bellies?"

"It is not your concern," White Antelope said mildly. "This is not a decision for the Council. We are not saying that all of the People should go in. I am planning only to take my Ridges. My friend would take only his *Wu'tapiu*. These choices are our right, as leaders of our bands."

"No," Bear growled. "If any of our people go there, it will destroy us all."

Black Kettle drew himself up. "I have had words from Little Raven, of the Arapaho. He has been living at one of those forts, and he is doing well. His people eat. They receive food in exchange for staying out of the fighting."

"Tell me of this fighting," prompted White Antelope. "I have heard that it is no longer going well."

There was a sudden tension among the warriors, and Fire Wolf stepped forward. Watching him, Eagle shivered. He was the dog rope man again, deadly and cold.

"It is true that the spiders loosen our grip on that road," he answered. "The warriors of the southern bands have left us to feed their people, because it is mostly their people who are hungry. The *ve'ho'e* have mounted more fighters at the same time. These new soldiers are crazy and stupid, but they know enough to join hands while we muddle about, bumping into each other.

"The buffalo are north of the Red Shield this season. Elk and antelope are there, also. I have seen them. But none of them will move south of that river because of the spiders that you, our *Vehoo'o*, have allowed in our midst. If your bellies groan here, it is because you invited it upon yourselves by taking the hands of those mongrels! Now you speak of giving them even more, and I say that if you do, we will lose not only the road, but the buffalo will never come back while the spider tricksters swarm here."

"We are giving the *ve'ho'e* nothing more," White Antelope answered wearily. "No one is speaking of putting our marks on their paper talk. We will only take our women and children away from the fighting until all this is finished."

There was a long, impossible silence.

"You must vow not to put your marks on anything," Bull Bear finally challenged.

Eagle's eyes flew from Fire Wolf to the first Dog chief.

Surely he was not conceding this fight! Then she glanced back at Black Kettle, and she understood.

The *Vehoo'o* would not be moved. His proud face was stony but calm. For a wild moment she thought she could feel the ripping, the rending, as these two strong factions of the People finally pulled apart. Bull Bear would negotiate for all he could against these grandfathers who had become his enemies.

Black Kettle nodded. "We will agree to no treaty without a full council first."

"Stay there only until the thaw," Bull Bear countered. "Then there will be game again, even if you have to travel north to find it."

Black Kettle hesitated. "We can agree to reevaluate the situation come the thaw."

"So be it," growled Bull Bear. "There is nothing else I can say. But know I will continue to fight those men until they are gone!"

He left the lodge abruptly, his Dogs following. Eagle squeezed through the throng after them. She caught up with them just in time to see her brother's jaw harden stubbornly.

"I would see this place. I would see them safely there. They are my kin," Bear said. "Do what you like. I will travel with them to this fort and meet with you later."

Eagle stared at him, thinking her brother was being uncharacteristically sentimental. She did not know that the very thing he had feared at her wedding had come to pass. Black Kettle and White Antelope had indeed drawn closer since the union of their kin. Would one of them have gone in without the other? Bear did not think so, and he felt responsible that such a large portion of their people would be at the mercy of the spiders.

Eagle looked to Walks Far, begging him silently that they should go with him, whatever his reasons.

Walks Far nodded. "I will join you."

Fire Wolf felt his blood pump hard and impatiently with a sensation close to pain. He wanted to get back to the fighting. But there was something to be said for knowing more about this enemy, for seeing how they lived. "So be it," he said. "I will travel with you, also."

Night Fighter shrugged. "You think I would go fight without all of you? Who would drag my body out onto the prairie for Coyote to scatter my bones if I should fall?"

"Your bones would make Coyote gag," muttered Bear, and there was tense laughter. Then Bull Bear nodded as well.

"They are fools, these *Vehoo'o*, but someone must protect them from themselves and the False Soldiers. That is what *Ma'heo'o* has appointed me to do."

Tangle Hair was ambivalent and hollow-eyed, but he joined them. In the end only Tall Bull declined, anxious to return to the war camp and hunt so that the Dogs might eat when they finally returned there.

As they began to move away to their own lodges, the sky above them rumbled eerily with winter thunder. Rain broke in a downpour. Eagle felt her heart shudder. It was almost as though *Ma'heo'o* were moaning and crying for them.

III

Major Wynkoop stared slack-jawed at the two young bucks who stood just inside the gates of Fort Lyon. Beside him, John Smith scratched his beard thoughtfully. He was a crusty, grizzled old trader who had lived out the best of his life on the prairie, and he knew just enough of the native Cheyenne tongue to translate.

"Black Kettle's gone and changed his mind, wants to come in," he reported. "White Antelope, too."

"They want to come in? Here? Now?"

Smith mumbled in Cheyenne again, and the bucks nodded. "They say the bands are on their way."

Wynkoop's stomach dropped fast and nauseatingly. "Oh, Lord," he murmured. It was far too late.

"Remind them that that offer of sanctuary was made in June. My word, this is autumn. Chivington has his hundred-day men. He'll never go for this now."

"It's what he says he wants," Smith muttered, "to get 'em off the Territory."

Wynkoop shook his head reflexively. He did not think Chivington had given his offer of sanctuary because he wanted to clear the land in a humane manner. More likely it had been done because he had not had sufficient soldiers at hand to ensure a victory over a consolidated Cheyenne tribe.

That had changed now.

"He'll kill them," Wynkoop mused aloud. He looked miserably at the bucks. At the moment they were sullen, but there was an arrogant, admirable pride in their faces as well. "I am not God," he muttered to himself. "I cannot sentence them, no matter what they may have done, not if they seek peace now."

He looked for his captain. "Mount me a hundred men as quickly as possible. We'll warn these damn fool chiefs before they get here. Intercept them. Tell them they're not going to find the sanctuary they expect."

IV

Wynkoop's horse danced nervously beneath him as he held back and watched the procession cross the scrubby prairie. Two howitzers and one hundred twenty-seven men. I will either be a hero when this is over, or a dead man, he thought. A cold runnel of rain worked its way beneath his collar, and he shuddered.

John Smith came up to park his mount beside him. "I don't reckon these Indians is going to like all this military-type stuff," he warned.

Wynkoop scowled. "This is a military expedition, mister."

"Not according to my calendar, it ain't. Wasn't you relieved and sent to Fort Larned?"

"Until Major Anthony arrives to take over at Lyon, I can hardly abandon my post. Besides which, I don't see what concern it is of yours."

Smith shrugged. "Just can't see you givin' up your hair for something that ain't your responsibility, is all."

"That's why I've surrounded myself with all this military-type stuff," the major responded dryly.

Smith gave a coarse, cackling laugh. "Well, I reckon we'll find out how they're gonna take it soon enough. Lookee-there. Guess we found 'em."

The trader took off his battered hat and waved it at the horizon. Wynkoop immediately felt his stomach turn sour.

He rode up onto the nearest rise and put his spyglass to his eyes. Sweet Jesus, he thought, so many of them. The Cheyenne came on, easily six hundred of them in a series of endless lines that wavered out onto the prairie. Dogs ran around them, snarling and nipping at each other. Short, wiry ponies dragged cross-beds impossibly laden with bulging hides.

Wynkoop moved the glass over them, bringing it back to the front of the caravan, and then his mouth went dry. The men had stopped there, and many of them had dismounted. God help him, but Wynkoop saw black raven feathers dangling from some of their lances.

Dog Soldiers.

"Smith!" he roared.

"Beside you here, Major."

"Send one of those messenger bucks over there to tell their people we mean peace. Tell them that we're here to help them. Now, damn it! *Now!*"

V

Blind Fox spotted the soldiers first. He had been riding wolf, going ahead to make sure the trail was safe and clear. When he saw the blotch of dark movement on the horizon, his bowels went soft.

Blue movement. Blue-coats.

He tried to howl, but his throat was closed and tight. When finally his voice erupted, he rode frantically around in circles. *Enemy. Enemy.*

Behind him, a squaw saw the sign and keened in fear. The others took up the howl, a ululating sound.

Bull Bear stopped his pony in front of Black Kettle's.

"Send the women back," he hissed. "Would you have their blood on your hands? Do not lead them into slaughter!"

The old chief paled visibly, but his narrow chin came up. "Promise me you will harm no one, and I will do as you suggest, at least until we see what this is about."

"It is about death! It is always about death! But you are wise enough, old Grandfather. You give the choice of the blood back to me. Then so be it." Bull Bear whipped his pony around. "For now."

He galloped back to his Dogs, the Ridge and *Wu'tapiu* warriors seething around them now.

"Let the white maggots shoot first," he snapped. There were roars of disbelief. Bull Bear sneered. "You think one bullet will win this battle? Are we that weak? I gave my word for the lives of your children." He galloped off, leading the way. Ahead of them, on the plain, a single rider approached.

"It is Coyote Singing!" one of the *Wu'tapiu* men called.

The young warrior came on, riding hard. "They are here to take us back!" he gasped when he reached them.

"With guns-on-wheels?" Bear asked incredulously.

"Fan out," Bull Bear agreed.

The warriors spread over the prairie. Behind them, the *Vehoo'o* came on stolidly with a small retinue of their own. The blue-coats formed their long line of battle formation.

Eagle watched from atop Wind Runner, fear churning in her gut. *It would happen again. They would come on and kill them all this time.*

Something rose up in fury inside her. They had no right here, no right to come killing! She galloped to catch up with the *Vehoo'o*. The Dogs and the warriors surrounded the soldiers, but their guns remained poised, their arrows notched. No one fired.

The blue-coats came on, and she watched them with sick amazement.

They moved confidently, trapped within their deadly escort. Her eyes darted to the soldier at the head of them. He had dismounted to walk beside his pony. His eyes moved like fear was inside him, she thought, but when he held his hands up to tell his men to stop, they did not tremble.

A little-buffalo *ve'ho'e* came up to stand beside him. To Eagle's shock, he spoke a rough, garbled version of the People's talk.

"The Major wants to talk to Black Kettle," he said in Cheyenne.

"If you draw him into this circle to kill him, you will die after the first shot," Bull Bear challenged.

"You gave your word, young brother," Black Kettle said, reaching them. "There will be no dying this sun."

He raised his hands in quiet dignity. Eagle felt her throat squeeze tight. He moved among his enemies—both those of his own people and the *ve'ho'e*—as though he were stepping into a council where everyone would honor him.

"Tell me why you come here," he said quietly to the spider leader. "You scare my women, irritate my men. They do not trust you. You should not be here. This is our country, even if we choose to winter near you."

For the first time the Tall White Chief looked uncomfortable. Eagle saw the lump on his throat go up and down, up and down.

"I . . . do not have the power to offer you peace terms or sanctuary. I came to tell you that I cannot take you at my fort. You must go back."

Smith translated, and there was a murmur of angry confusion among the People. Desperate, Wynkoop tried again.

"I will do everything in my power to get you that peace! But there are other men, more important than me. They told you to come to me, to my fort, a long time . . . many moons ago. That time has past now. You must understand that they have waged war against you! That complicates things."

White Antelope rode up, conferring briefly with Black Kettle.

"My friend thinks you do not understand," the *Wu'tapiu* chief explained patiently. "We do not choose to fight. We would like peace, food."

"For Christ's sake!" Wynkoop cried, exasperated. "Of course *I* understand. But I'm trying to tell you that those other soldiers want to fight you!"

"Chiefs of honor do not change their minds," Bull Bear growled into the stunned silence.

No, Wynkoop thought as his words were translated. No, they don't. "Nonetheless, that is what mine have done." He scrubbed a hand over his face, then lowered it again thoughtfully. "Maybe I have an alternative."

He conferred briefly with his blue-coats.

"These men can escort your women to Fort Lyon," he said impulsively. He looked around and found most of the squaws distant, hovering a mile away on a low hill. "They'll be safe enough there for the time being. And you, those of you with authority, should come with me. I can take you to Denver. You can talk to my chiefs yourselves. Further discussion regarding sanctuary should take place with them."

"Den-ver?"

The word murmured through the warrior ranks, humming and deadly. No one had mistaken that single white word as soon as it was spoken. Eagle felt her heart go cold.

"Bah!" roared Bull Bear suddenly, stabbing his lance in the direction of the Tall Chief. "You think I am a fool? I tried to live, long ago, in good faith with you *ve'ho'e*. My council gave you the mountains, and I bowed to that. Then you took them to your Wash-ing-tone and put crazy medals in their hands and stupid thoughts in their heads! You accosted my Dog brother and tried to take away his coup of ponies! You attacked a sleeping hunting camp on the Red Shield, and came into Dog country and *killed a Vehoo'o* when he went out to council with you! Now you tell me you will take my chiefs to your Den-ver, and you think I will trust you? I do not trust you! I spit in your faces!"

Someone howled in agreement, but Black Kettle's voice rose above it. "No! No! We should go there, talk. If this is the way they make peace, we must do it."

Bear stared at his uncle, his big face ruddy with rare emotion. "If you believe that, Grandfather, then your thoughts have gone crazy," he said roughly. "But once again I will go with you, see you safely to this place, and protect you when they try to put their bullets in your heart."

Fire Wolf and Night Fighter and Walks Far gathered behind him. Eagle felt a thin scream of horror rip from her throat.

They would go, too? They would *all* go?

She trotted to them and slid weak-kneed to the ground. She clutched Walks Far's leg. "No!" she cried. "They will be all around you there! You said there would be many of them, and they will all be in this Den-ver place!"

A flash of pain crossed his eyes, then his expression settled. "This is your grandfather, and mine. Fools though they are, I cannot let them go alone."

She stepped back numbly. Overhead, thunderheads gathered, hiding Sun and all his life-giving rays. Bull Bear screamed a war cry and careened off across the plains, the others following. Only Fire Wolf held back for a moment, his eyes seeking her out. His gaze was steady and hard.

"You will survive this, also, little Eagle. Go to the fort, and keep the truth of that in your heart."

Then he, too, galloped off. Eagle sank to her knees, a helpless scream trapped in her throat. She did not believe him this time.

11

Freezing Moon, 1864
Colorado Territory

I

Fire Wolf watched Black Kettle as he took his morning meal with the spiders. Old man, you are a fool, he thought. You think they can be friends. Friends are men who have killed beside you, for all the same things you believe in.

Then he thought of a woman who had killed nothing more than a cantankerous boar, one who trusted in the heart he did not have. She will live to tell about that fort, he thought. He had told her so, but he did not wholly believe it himself.

He whistled for his pony, and the black broke from the warrior herd. Fire Wolf vaulted onto his back, galloping around the blankets of the blue-coats who were still sleeping. He tore close enough to a soldier tent to clip it and bring it down. An astonished Wynkoop struggled out from beneath its cavernous folds, and Fire Wolf reined the black in at his feet.

"Den-ver," he pronounced. Before Sun truly arrived, they were moving again.

The mountains were blue-black against the sky, but as they drew closer to them, they became laced with white and thick with trees. It was a magnificent but crowded land, and Fire Wolf felt a painful, ready tension settle into his muscles as he rode among it. With the coming of the next sun, they went into a valley embraced by the verdant peaks. At the sun's zenith they arrived at the Den-ver home of the spider tricksters.

Fire Wolf had seen the *ve'ho'e* forts, had expected nothing less from the mongrels than this. Yet anger began to throb at his temples as he looked about their seething village.

Ahead of him the spiders' wagons and the parade of war ponies moved down a wide, rutted strip of dirt. On either side stood big dwellings, more ornate than those at the forts and some as tall as ten men. Between them, Grandmother Earth struggled valiantly to thrive again.

Fire Wolf drew close to one of the vacant lots, and a ripe smell assaulted him, dragging his belly up into his throat. The winter-parched grass was splayed in places. He frowned at that, squinting, but his nose told him what his heart did not want to know.

Easily ten hands of skinned carcasses were discarded there, rotting and putrid.

Hatred and fear filled his throat. Suddenly he understood a new truth, why there were so few buffalo south of the Red Shield this season, why so many of his people were starving.

The white men were killing the beasts, too.

But the *ve'ho'e* were wasting them.

II

Walks Far's eyes were on the spider people as they reached the council place. News of Win-koop's astounding arrival had spread through the town, and white men on ponies and women in wagons had come to the fledgling talk-fort they called Camp Weld, gawking and staring at them.

So many of them, he thought. Walks Far felt sick with the truth of it. There were more, so many more, than even he had feared.

Their chiefs came out from a squat, logged dwelling, and the *Vehoo'o* and the Dogs were herded beneath a flapping piece of canvas to wait for them. The wind howled wildly through the open sides.

Walks Far felt the chiefs' anger first, so strong it came off them in waves. The big, balding man had spots of hectic red on his face, and his eyes burned with it. The other man, one with a tangled, white mess of face hair, had tiny eyes so caught in folds of wrinkled skin that Walks Far could not truly see them.

The big man with the bad eyes spurred the talk. "What is it you wish to say to us?" he demanded, and the little trader translated.

Black Kettle was startled. "There are no smokes?"

"This is not a party, mister."

For a brief moment a thump of hope knocked up against Walks Far's ribs. Black Kettle seemed to turn away in irritation, but the old *Vehoo'o* sighed.

"It is an important council, and there should be smokes. But I will talk, if that is what you want."

He drew himself up. "We have come to you with our eyes shut, following your man here like coming through the fire. All we ask is that we have peace with the whites. The sky has been dark ever since this war began. I want to take good news back with me to my people. You must make the chiefs of the soldiers here to understand that we are for peace so that we may not be mistaken by them for your enemies.

"My people must live near the buffalo or starve. We cannot stay near your soldier forts all the time, but we are here now, freely and without fear, to stay by you until you settle this war."

Walks Far watched the eyes of the gray spider chief move to those of the other one. He felt something cold worm its way down his spine. They were the eyes of men with secrets.

"I am sorry you did not respond to our appeal at once," White-Hair-Face muttered. "However much you few individuals may want peace, as a nation you have gone to war."

Black Kettle shrugged. "I cannot speak for all my people without a council, but my *Wu'tapiu* will not fight you, and the Ridge band will not, either. We will stay with you until the thaw."

"The thaw!" erupted the big bald man. "The time when you can make war best is summertime. The time we can make war best is the winter. You have so far had the advantage, but our time is fast coming."

John Smith recited carefully, repeating. White Antelope once again trusted in misunderstanding.

"You need no good time to fight," he said patiently. "We will not fight you."

"If you continue to try, you will be destroyed. You think because we are at war among ourselves, you can run us from this country. You are wrong. The Great Father in Washington has enough men to drive all the Indians off the plains and whip the rebels at the same time. And the war with the rebels is ending. Now the Great Father won't know what to do with all his soldiers except send them after the Indians."

A confused murmur went through the warriors. Fire Wolf went rigid in his disbelief.

"He would trick us with words. I have seen these soldiers of his. They do not fight each other. They fight together."

White-Hair-Face waved his hand to quiet them, and the ice-wet wind howled through the shelter.

"Our offer to the friendly Indians has already gone out. We should be glad to have them all come in under it, but I have no new proposition to make. My advice to you is to turn on the side of the government. It is utterly out of the question for you to be at peace with us while living with our enemies and being on friendly terms with them."

A strangled sound came from Bull Bear. "Say what you mean, *ve'ho'e*. These words you speak now are like snakes, wriggling about everywhere, going nowhere."

"My rule of fighting white men or Indians is to fight them until they lay down their arms and submit to military authority!" the big bald man shouted. "You are nearer to Major Wynkoop than anyone else. Go to him whenever you're ready to do that."

He moved out of the tent abruptly. After a moment White-Hair-Face followed him.

Black Kettle turned to the man Win-koop. "We should go with you," he said, nodding and motioning to make himself understood.

The Tall Chief's eyes slid away. "No . . . no. I must go to another fort now. You should go back to Lyon and collect your women."

"Listen! Still they say nothing!" Bull Bear snapped.

White Antelope's chin came up. "That old white man said we should not live with his enemies. I heard that. I will go to that fort where my women are waiting and stay there."

He moved back to his pony. First Black Kettle, then the Dogs, broke to follow him.

Only Walks Far remained behind, staring thoughtfully at the place where the spider chiefs had stopped to confer with each other. Win-koop hovered tensely just outside their parley.

"If they come in, what are we going to do with the

hundred-day men you told Washington we needed?" Evans fretted. "We've declared a state of emergency. My word, we'll look like fools to the entire country!"

Chivington's nostrils flared. "My plans are fixed. I am ready to kill Indians, and I believe it is right and honorable to use any means under God's heaven to kill Indians." He turned on Wynkoop. "As for you, Major, I can scarcely believe you orchestrated this debacle. I intend to see to it that you never again command a post in this West!"

Walks Far melted silently away after the others. He did not know what those men had said, but he knew the sound of frustration and anger. Suddenly the need to get back to the women was a violent urge within him.

III

Eagle stood on a high bluff, the cold wind buffeting her as it wailed over the basin below her. The north side of the Sand Creek bed was flat, unbroken prairie, with nothing to obstruct the gusts. They hit the steep, eroded banks on the south side and tunneled upward to where she stood, tugging and pulling on her robe.

She moved Stick around to her back, blocking him from the weather.

"This is where the *ve'ho'e* at the fort say we should stay?" Sun Roads asked doubtfully. "This is not a good place."

"That old chief from the Cloud People, the Arapaho, says it is right. Look, they are putting up their lodges." Eagle pointed across the rugged table of high ground to where those other women worked, but she could not convince herself. *Why? Why had Little Raven been asked to move his people out here?* Black Kettle had said that at the fort the Cloud People were getting food, but there would be none here.

Below her the creek bed was tangled with cottonwoods and grass, some of it still showing green. But here, on the south cliffs, Grandmother Earth was barren. Her dirt was crumbly and rocky, with spare shoots of tough rabbitbrush thrusting up. Nothing could live up here, and the flare of vegetation below her was too isolated to sustain life.

Eagle shuddered and looked around for the Dog wives. She

found them frowning out at the landscape just as she was, and she went to them hurriedly.

"I think we should put our lodges here, close to the bluff," she urged. She did not know why it suddenly seemed so important, but she knew in her gut that they had to remain close to the thick trees down in the bed. They seemed to groan in the stiff wind, calling to her.

There was safety there. She stared at them, her heart moving, then she brought her babe around again to hug him tight.

IV

The soldier fort sat hunched beneath an eerie quiet. There were no squeals of children, no murmur of hundreds of conversations going at once. There were no camp smells of smoke and ponies, tallow and grease and hides. There were not even any lodges, just lines of the squat, flat *ve'ho'e* buildings. They were defiantly spread out, as though to blemish as much of the stripped land as possible.

Bear turned in fury to the man he had once respected as a grandfather. "What is this? *Where are our women and the babes?*"

Bull Bear was already in Black Kettle's face. Spittle sprayed from his contorted lips. "You said the Cloud People were here, doing well. There is no one. What trick is it that your friend spiders have led our families into?"

Nearby there was a scrambling in the tall grass. The warriors surged that way, weapons drawn, lips drawn back in feral snarls. But it was an Indian youth who stood.

"I can tell you that. My grandfather, Little Raven, has sent me to meet you." He paused to lick his lips. "The blue-coats have a new chief here. My grandfather wanted you to know so you would be careful. Win-koop gave us food, but they say he will not be permitted to come back here, and this new one has strange eyes that speak of lies.

"He sent us away from the fort, to camp half a sun's ride from here. He said there was hunting there, but there is not. Your women are with us. My grandfather waits for you to come and get them, but then he is leaving to go back to our own country. His spirit-talker says it is no longer safe here. Hurry! I will take you to them."

He began running back the way he had come. Fire Wolf felt his blood run to ice.

"Yes, it is a trick," he spat. "And she waits there alone for it to unfold."

He drove his heels hard into his black's sides, taking off in pursuit of the Arapaho buck. Behind him, Walks Far sat very still.

She waits alone.

His heart thrummed with the sudden pain of it, but he knew; it seemed he had always known. He had seen it when he had watched them together. A rogue warrior could only laugh with a woman who was as strong and independent as the wind he chased. He could only love a woman who would never truly need him.

A woman like his Eagle.

Walks Far beat his pony into a gallop as well. He slowed only long enough to wrench up the Arapaho boy as he passed him, dropping him hard behind him on his pony. At that moment it did not matter who reached her first. He had come to love her so deeply, so wholly, he only cared that one of them did, before the evil perfidy he felt in this white man's air finally festered and burst open.

V

The moon was yellow and high when Tangle Hair finally rode into the Sand Creek camp. Eagle spotted him as she came from her lodge, and her heart stuttered. She knew he had remained with the *Vehoo'o* at the fort to talk to that new white man. She snapped into movement again, following him to Bull Bear's lodge. She ducked into the tepee just as he lowered himself to sit beside the fire. He tossed a brace of rabbits behind him. Falling Bird grabbed them and began skinning them, but for once, Eagle's mouth did not water in anticipation.

"I think there is going to be blood and death," Tangle Hair began.

There was a rumble from the men. Eagle sat clumsily, her legs going lifeless beneath her.

"When?" Bull Bear demanded.

"That I cannot tell you. How long will it take those blue-coats to pull their guns-on-wheels out here? It took me half the darkness to get here, but I stopped to bring food. I think we have several suns before they reach us."

He shifted his weight to make room for Falling Bird to spit the rabbit carcasses over the fire. Then he rubbed his wrinkled face and told them.

"The new chief at the fort is called An-to-nee. He has red eyes like I have never seen. They are far apart"—he motioned to either side of his head—"and small. They do not stay in one place very long.

"He says that he is here to take the place of Tall Chief Win-koop. He says that his white chiefs tell him not to have anything to do with us. He will give Black Kettle and White Antelope no food. He says he cannot have any of us at the fort because we have been raiding again in this area."

Bear staggered to his feet in fury. "That is a lie! There has been no raiding here! We only just arrived from Den-ver, and our brothers are still harassing the road!" He turned on Fire Wolf. "What of Pawnee Killer? What are those Lakota and the Brule and the Oglala doing now?"

The dog rope man shook his head. "Cold Maker is breathing ice down our smoke holes. The Sioux have no war now. They would be home and warm in their lodges."

"Yes, the red-eyed one lies," confirmed Tangle Hair. "That is what I am telling you, why I know something is very, very wrong."

He waved a hand in the air. "Our *Vehoo'o* told him that it was not our people who were fighting here, that it was no people we know of. An-to-nee said he will tell his big chiefs this, that we should stay here and wait for word from him. But Black Kettle and White Antelope said they could not remain, waiting for food. Our people are too hungry. The red-eyed one got very upset and angry about that. He said we could hunt right here if the *Vehoo'o* were sincere in their wish for peace. He said he has heard of buffalo nearby, and if the People will stay just a little while longer, he will straighten out this trouble and give us more food."

"He does not want our people to leave this place because they make very convenient targets here," said Walks Far.

Night Fighter gave a chilling grin. "Especially when our men are out hunting invisible buffalo."

"What do the *Hotame-taneo'o* do about this?" Bull Bear looked to the women, who had been out and about this whole sun. "Who is here now?" he demanded. Many had come in here when word reached them that Black Kettle and White Antelope sought sanctuary.

"War Bonnet has come in with his Scabby Village People," Falling Bird answered, "and Sand Hill is here with his Closed Gullets. Yellow Wolf came with his Hair Ropes. But I saw some Ridges and some Closed Gullet People leaving again for the Smoky Hill. They say they believe Little Raven's medicine and do not want to stay here."

Bull Bear scowled, the weight of responsibility sitting on him as heavily as a rain-sodden robe. "We will divide our strength," he finally decided. "We must stay to feed these people here and protect them, but one of us should go to the Smoky Hill to bring back those other men. We should get the other Dogs, too. We will need them here. I am tired of trying to talk sense into those *Vehoo'o*, and I do not think we can get them to leave. This time we will do things the *Hotame-taneo'o* way. We will meet the spider blue-coats when they come, and rid ourselves of them once and for all."

There was a sudden moment of tension when he finished; it made the air feel hard to breathe. Eagle looked up from Stick, expecting to find the fire of battle in their eyes. Instead, she saw a look pass between Walks Far and Fire Wolf, and her heart staggered.

The heat there had nothing to do with the trouble. They were like two bulls pawing the ground, facing each other over a female that breathed sweet scent between them. It was there in their faces, a stunning knowledge between them of her heart . . . the heart that loved and needed both of them.

She choked, but the sound went unheeded. Fire Wolf stared into the eyes of the warrior across from him.

So you know, old friend, so you saw inside me. Distantly he remembered uttering those naked words at the fort. He felt the power of the dog rope against his thigh, hot and heavy, seeming to burn with the force of his obligation to it. He saw the challenge in Walks Far's eyes.

Fear was so sudden and emasculating it made his belly feel rotten. Suddenly he understood what this brother, this friend, would have him do. He would ask him to choose again, between a woman and the fighting he had vowed to lead.

He could not do it.

Then the old, hard weight came to his chest again, nearly suffocating this time. He had no choice to make, not any longer. He had already chose, long ago at a spring hunt in a Fat Horse Moon. He had done it when he had turned the offer of Eagle away, passing her on to this warrior.

He shot to his feet, nodding curtly to Walks Far. "I will go to the Smoky Hill."

She is yours, friend. Protect her.

He did not look at her when he left the lodge. If ever his heart had writhed, he was the dog rope man again now. The tension went out of Walks Far like a wind dying, but as Eagle clutched Broken Stick, her heart bled for all of them.

VI

It was nearly dawn when Sun Roads made her way back from the creek. Grandmother Earth was pitched in a still, icy blackness, and she wished more than anything that she had been able to hold her water until sun came. She moved forward again, more quickly. Finally the trees broke, and the craggy slopes of the south bed loomed before her.

Her teeth chattering in the cold, she tucked her hair behind her ears and clawed her way up. Then she paused, crouched on the high ground, scowling.

The People's lodges spread out on either side of her, running the length of the bluff, segregated into bands. In front of her the arid grasslands rolled out in a swath left between the Ridge tepees and those of the *Wu'tapiu*. There, far away, a single light bobbed, up and down, up and down.

It was like nothing she had ever seen before.

Suddenly, on the prairie below her, there sounded a wild rumble of hoofbeats. It has scared the ponies, she thought, but the light was to the south, and most of the herds were north of the camp.

Then one of the boys who had been with the horses hauled himself up the slope behind her. She heard him grunt, and she twisted around to face him. Blood ran down his forehead.

"What?" she breathed. "Oh, *Ma'heo'o,* what is this?"

He gave a long, curdling howl of distress.

The camp began to stir into fumbling, sleepy activity. Squaws pushed their way past their door flaps to stare, clutching their bedding robes about their shoulders and their wee ones against their legs.

"Run to the trees!" Someone screeched from behind her. Sun Roads whirled again to find Eagle working frantically to fix her babe's cradleboard against her back.

"Is it *ve'ho'e*?" She moaned. "But they told us to come to this place. *They told us to!*"

And they had told the men to hunt.

She looked around wildly, but even now, with everyone bursting from the lodges, there were so very few warriors. All the *Wu'tapiu*, and even Bear and Walks Far, had been forced to go out on a quick search for game, and that dog rope man had slipped away earlier in the darkness.

Her old uncle's voice boomed out over the commotion, and she spun toward him.

"It is good, this is good!" he promised. "Do not be alarmed. The white chief has learned that we speak true, and he comes to make peace. Probably he even brings food."

Yes, that was it. Of course that was it, Sun Roads thought. She began to hurry toward him.

He was outside his lodge, and Medicine Woman Later was dragging a lodge pole toward him. She lashed it busily to his tattered striped flag. The pole was braced in the dirt, and the banner went up to hang limply in the still dawn.

Sun Roads stared at it, her mouth dry.

Suddenly she saw it again as it laid over her uncle's shoulders on the sun that Lean Bear had been killed. She remembered how it had hung askew when Black Kettle had carried back his old friend's body. Black Kettle had spoken words like this then, too, but they had not been true.

She changed direction suddenly, veering for the bluff. Then she came up hard against her grandmother.

"Where do you go, child? It is best to stay with our *Vehoo'o*. We have enough confusion just now without our young people running wildly about."

"No," she moaned, struggling against her.

"Come, we must go help them carry this food in," her grandmother muttered. "We must show our gratitude and offer them hospitality."

She moved off toward the long line of soldiers. They were close now, so close, in the streaked gray light.

The first blue-coat Walks At Night met brought his rifle up. There was a knife on the end of it, and it struck into her hard, her old body jerking. The *ve'ho'e* pulled up on his weapon, and Walks At Night hung there on it, her gray head falling back, her limbs twitching grotesquely.

Sun Roads screamed.

Their raucous laughter, belching into the dawn, drowned out her voice as a False Soldier came on and slashed his knife down the back of Walks At Night's doeskin. He ripped it off her shoulders and dug his fingers into her fleshy buttocks, hooting. Blessed blackness pressed in on Sun Roads' mind, and she fell into the darkness.

Another soldier leapt from his pony. He wrestled the hundred-dayer to the ground, and the body of the old woman came with them, wrenching free of the bayonet with a sucking sound.

"Jesus, oh, sweet Jesus," he moaned, pushing it away. "Stop this! *This is an army!*"

Chivington trotted up, his mount's breath coming in hard plumes of white. "Enough!" he ordered.

The soldier staggered to his feet again. "Thank God," he muttered. "You've got to stop this, Colonel . . ."

He turned toward the Indian camp, where Black Kettle stood beneath his American flag, his people pressing in on him, seeking the banner's protection. "That's no enemy tribe there," he managed finally. "He's that friendly chief Major Wynkoop had to turn away from the fort. I know him. I was there on that mission. I brought their women back to Lyon myself before

Anthony sent them away—" Then he broke off as stunned realization came to him.

"You know that," he said softly. "You met their men in Denver. You . . . you set these people up for a slaughter."

"I cannot be responsible for their actions after they departed Camp Weld!" Chivington snapped. "They are not at the fort! This is a mission searching for recalcitrant savages, and we have found them, so step aside. Damn any man who has sympathy for the Indians! You and Wynkoop have no place in the United States service!"

He turned back to his troops, to the spattering of Fort Lyon soldiers he had commandeered to join his five hundred irregulars.

"Charge them!" he bellowed.

VII

Eagle reached the edge of the bluff and hunkered down to drop over it. Then a roar sounded behind her, a thunderous ovation of men's voices swelling out over a rumble of hooves. It was like nothing she had ever heard before, and she whipped around again, her heart slamming.

They came on, hundreds of *ve'ho'e*. They swarmed over the *Wu'tapiu* camp until the little knot of her kin, hovering around Black Kettle's lodge, was lost in the melee.

Eagle screamed helplessly. She had begged them to leave, to follow her to the creek bed. Why had they not listened?

She lunged to her feet again and angled toward the wretched, striped flag that hung high over her uncle's lodge. Something slammed into her with impossible force, pitching her forward, and she went down, her breath pounding out of her. She hugged the ground as the air above her began to crack and explode with bullets.

The People passed her, screaming, stumbling, dragging their young ones. Beneath her the ground trembled as the soldiers rode hard among them. Their bullets spattered the taut hides of the lodge walls. From inside a few thin wails of women and babes fell starkly silent.

Eagle lurched to her feet again and ran.

She saw her kin finally, blessedly, leaving. Black Kettle had deserted his precious flag. He rode with Medicine Woman Later, trotting clumsily away from the fray. Small Blanket and Little Moon ran beside the pony, and her grandfather, Medicine Wolf, shuffled along dazedly behind them. Blind Fox, Gray Thunder, and Caught The Enemy tried to cover their retreat.

It would not be enough, she knew it would not be enough. They were fleeing across the open, high plain.

"Not that way!" she screamed. She ran for them, her breath thick and burning in her throat. Then a herd of blue-coats intercepted them.

Behind Black Kettle, Medicine Woman Later began jumping on the pony as though she danced. Her big old body jerked crazily as red spread over her doeskin. She fell, hard and gracelessly, and then Gray Thunder went down, his chest ripping violently apart.

Little Moon fell to her knees beside her husband, slashing at her braids and her arms, the wailing sounds of her grief carrying impossibly over the gunfire.

"No," Eagle moaned. "You must go on."

Small Blanket pulled at her sister helplessly, then a bullet came to her, too, mangling her soft, black eyes.

"Aiy-ee!"

Her mother. They had shot her mother.

Eagle staggered away and moved blindly into the Ridge camp. The acrid stench of burning hides seared her eyes and her throat. The *ve'ho'e* were setting the lodges to flame, and the last screams from inside were inhuman. She moved past them, keening wordlessly.

Then she found White Antelope.

"Please, the others . . . my mother . . . You must do something."

He began to sing his death song.

Rage exploded in her, and she lunged at him, clawing her fingers into his robe. *"Nooooo!"* she screamed. "You cannot go! You did this! You did this to us!"

He focused on her slowly. "There is nothing I can do now. There is no hope for our people against these men, no chance for the *Tse-Tsehesestahase* by their side. It is over."

He turned toward the *ve'ho'e* march, waiting for them, chanting his way to his death road.

"Nothing lives long,
Only the earth and the mountains . . ."

Gunfire sounded close again. The old *Vehoo'o* collapsed at
her feet without singing anything more. The soldiers raced by,
some on foot, some on ponies.

"He did not hurt you!" she screamed at them.

One of the blue-coats heard her, veered for her. She dragged
herself back to her feet and ran for the bluff.

Her feet hit another body, and she tumbled. Gasping, she
crawled to her knees again and looked over at the crumpled
form of Sun Roads. Her, too. Oh, sweet *Ma'heo'o*, they had
gotten her, too. Then her sister stirred, sitting up to look about
vacantly.

"Where is Pot Belly?" she mused. "Have you seen Pot
Belly?"

She had only fainted. Eagle groaned and started to crawl to
her, then she shrieked and crabbed her way backward on her
bottom again. A *ve'ho'e* ran up to them, yanking his strange
blue leggings down as he moved.

Eagle understood what he would do, and she howled and
threw herself at him. She hit him with her full weight as he
buried his hand deep in Sun Road's sleep-tangled hair, and he
lashed out at her with the repeater in his other. The gun cracked
solidly into her head. The pain exploded, shimmering. She
sprawled in the spare, dry grass, but she came up again,
staggering, groping for her knife.

She caught a glimpse of Night Fighter. "Help me," she
moaned, knowing he could not hear her.

But as he came around the side of the lodge in front of her,
he saw. He came upon them with a bellow of fury. There was
a clicking sound, deadly and sure, and he shot his carbine so
that the spider fell obscenely across Sun Roads.

The girl screamed and clawed her way free, and Night
Fighter went on. Gagging, Eagle pried the dead *ve'ho'e's*
fingers from his gun, then she ran again for the bluff.

Grief filled her, so raw and primitive it swelled over
everything else. Somewhere, Walks Far and Bear and Fire Wolf
lived, safely away from this carnage. She held to that, ignoring

the stench of gunpowder that burned her nostrils and the stinging-sweet smell of blood freezing on the icy air.

Her hand shook so badly she could not get it around the little hook on the gun. But she had to, because she knew the warriors squeezed that spot to make it spit death. She stopped, fumbling until her finger curled there. Clutching the weapon, she slid down the bank.

Still, the blue-coats came on.

They stood on the high ground, riddling the slopes with their weapons. Squaws hid beneath them, screaming and cowering, and blood flew as the bullets found them. Eagle wiped it from herself frantically as it sprayed on her. Then the soldiers came down, dragging the survivors from the caves they had dug in the sand for protection.

She twisted around again and pulled the trigger. The gun bucked crazily in her hands, flying free, sending her tumbling into the sand. But when she looked up again, a blue-coat had dropped.

"Yes," she sobbed, "die, yes, die."

She found her legs and began staggering across the bed toward the copse.

She passed an infant babe, his head pulpy and crushed. Retching, she moved around him, and then she passed some squaws, their limbs tangled together in a last embrace of kin. Something cold and hard and numb began to fill her head. She did not acknowledge that their breasts had been slashed from their bodies; she did not see their bloody, mutilated privates. She went on, past the *Vehoo'o* War Bonnet, his ears and genitals gouged away.

Finally she reached the secretive branches, stumbling deeper and deeper into their cover. She fell, pulled herself up, then fell again. At last she came up painfully against a gnarled old trunk. She wrapped her arms about it, sagging.

Over now, it was over. The gunfire popped distantly. The screams shrilled into whispers.

But the silence around her was too deep, too full, and her mother's heart staggered.

She moaned, wrenching Stick's cradleboard from her back to rip the laces apart. His face was pale, his left leg shattered and bloody, and then she remembered. Sometime, a nightmare ago, something had hit her hard, and she had fallen. A *ve'ho'e* bullet had come for her, but it had not found her. It had splintered the frame of the cradleboard instead, and the tender flesh wrapped within it.

"*Nooooo!*" Her terror echoed among the trees, but when she put her hand to his chest, she felt his heartbeat. It was tiny, erratic, like that of a baby bird, but it was there. They would not have her child.

She found her knife, slashing off the bottom of her doeskin. She bound the strip tightly to his leg, then she lurched to her feet one last time. This time she would not fall. This time she must keep going.

She had to get to the Smoky Hill, where the other, wiser people had gone.

12

Freezing Moon, 1864
Smoky Hill Country

I

The moon came again, white and cold and distant. As Eagle looked up at it, helpless tears of exhaustion burned her eyes. She had traveled in the creek bed all sun, leaving the copse at twilight when the trees had become so thin and scattered she knew they could no longer shield her. Then she had dropped to her belly, moving across the open prairie at a crawl.

Only now, in full darkness, did she stumble warily to her feet again. The night would shelter her as the trees had done. She turned herself to face the north and the east, then she struggled on as the cold came.

Once she heard Fire Wolf's voice, so clear and rough she staggered around to find him. *"This, too, you will live through . . . you will survive, you will survive, you will survive . . . ."* But he wasn't here, and she finally dropped hard and gracelessly to her knees, fighting the urge to give up.

She was alone, and Cold Maker would not let her go on. Fire Wolf was wrong. She would not survive. She would die, and Stick would die, unless they got warm.

She laid him on the frozen grass beside her. His blood had seeped through the soft wraps of his cradleboard. The doeskin was stiff and crunchy now as it turned to ice.

"I will make us warm, babe," she murmured hoarsely. "I promise."

She dug at the frozen ground with her hands until her nails bled. Finally she made a spot deep enough that she could crawl into it, tucking him close to her side. She pressed her warmth against him and pulled the earth and the grass back in on them.

Near dawn she watched unblinkingly as the sky began to

pale. She pushed the mounds of dirt off again and looked around. The plain was unbroken and open before her. She thought she had come far enough that she would not encounter any more spiders. It did not matter in any event. She had no choice now but to walk upright. Crawling was taking too long, and she had to get her babe to a place where there would be healers and warm fires.

She pressed her lips to his forehead, then she keened a thin, high sound. Cold, oh, *Ma'heo'o*, he was so cold, and suddenly she knew she had lost him. They could not win, not the *Vehoo'o* or the *ve'ho'e,* and take her precious child! She would not let them!

She moved instinctively, covering his mouth with her own. She could not think what else to do but push her warm life into him. Crazed, she breathed into him again and again, and when still he was silent, she brought her fist down hard on his chest, wailing.

She felt his tiny ribs crack, and she recoiled, sobbing. She had broken him, she had broken her babe, but it did not matter, nothing would matter *if he did not breathe.*

His air came to him again with a mewling sound of agony.

She collapsed beside him, shuddering. Then she gathered him up again, ever so gently, and got to her feet.

Dusk was gathering again, turning the sky to purple, when she thought she smelled meat. Saliva collected in her mouth, and trickled out one corner of her lips. Somehow, she managed to move faster. As the pitch of darkness closed in on her again, she saw the orange light of fires on the horizon. The naked, gnarled limbs of creek bed cottonwoods were etched eerily against the glow.

A camp. *Ma'heo'o,* it was a camp.

It did not matter if it was her own people, or if it was spiders. She could go no farther. She would go to them because if they were spiders, she would die anyway, trying to avoid them on this ice-crusted prairie.

She staggered toward the place of light.

As she drew closer, she saw the lodges. There were only a handful of them, but it was the Smoky Hill, a far western branch of it, the place the Ridges and Closed Gullets had come when they had defied their chiefs and left Sand Creek.

She waited for a feeling of relief, but there was only a cold, terrible exhaustion inside her. No one noticed her as she moved among them. She was just one more stunned and bloodied survivor who had made it back to Dog country.

The wails of the bereaved filled the night, grief undulating, peaking, fading only to start again. Eagle limped past one fire, then another, past scrawny rabbits spitted and roasting. The living pushed shreds of meat into the mouths of the near-dead.

Slowly, disbelievingly, she realized how many were missing.

She found the *Wu'tapiu* and the Dogs who had stayed with them, and then she swayed on her feet, staring. Little Moon sat by the fire, the dark crust of Gray Thunder's blood still staining her face and her doeskin. There was Sun Roads, keening loudly in anguished horror, and Wind Woman, rocking, holding her belly in grief. Falling Bird wandered, touching bent heads fretfully.

She saw her father. Caught The Enemy's eyes touched hers with silent pain that made her want to scream. She thought of her mother, but she could not go to him yet, could not grieve with him. First she needed to see it all, she needed to know.

She swiveled slowly, looking. Medicine Wolf shuffled about, tending the wounded with his healing skills. Black Kettle was there, crouched on a log. Eagle gaped at him, then at the body at his feet. Medicine Woman Later? She went to them, stunned.

Black Kettle looked up at her. He spoke slowly and carefully, as though he had told this tale many times.

"They shot her, but I went back for her. When the darkness does not claim her, she speaks. She told me the *ve'ho'e* shot her from my pony. Then they came back and shot her again to make sure she was dead. Nine. Nine bullets is what they put in her. Why? Why would they do that?"

Eagle shook her head. Medicine Woman Later lived, but Blind Fox and Pot Belly and Walking Spirit were still unaccounted for, and the others, so many others were dead.

Her throat closed. Only a few suns ago, there had been hundreds of lodges of *Wu'tapiu*. They had been one of the strongest bands.

Now she could count only two or three hands of survivors.

II

A feeling of doom came upon Fire Wolf as dawn spread. He should have ridden harder, faster, he thought. He should have sent someone else to the Smoky Hill and to the war camp. He should have come to the fort himself and watched the treacherous spiders so closely they could not have belched without him knowing.

He had let them find her. He had failed, had made the wrong choice *again . . . again . . . again . . .*

Finally, in its dip on the horizon, he came upon the fort. It was deserted as it had been the first time he had seen it. He pulled up hard, his pony heaving in exhaustion.

The Dogs he brought back with him surged up behind him. "What is this?" Tall Bull snarled, staring.

And Fire Wolf spoke the words aloud, though they strangled him. "The blue-coats have already gone to attack the Sand Creek camp."

"Track them!" someone shouted. "We sit here like old women when they could be killing our people even now!"

"No. It is done."

Fire Wolf had found the tracks, and his knuckles went white where his hand gripped his carbine. They were two suns old. Grandmother Earth was pummeled with the marks. There had been hundreds upon hundreds of ponies, of soldiers.

A bellow ripped from his throat as he finally gave himself to the rage inside him. The thought of losing Eagle was terrible, but the truth in his heart, the truth that even Walks Far had known, was somehow worse. She was not just his friend, a woman of spirited loyalty who believed in him. In his own scarred way, he loved her. She needed him now, and he would find her, no matter whose woman she was to protect.

III

The screams started again in the refugee camp as soon as the distant sound of hoofbeats grew clear and certain. The squaws reacted in terror, grabbing up their babes, dragging their howling children across the prairie. The men could not subdue them this time and no *Vehoo'o* tried. Black Kettle only stood, staring dully to the north where the sounds came from.

Eagle lurched to her feet at the *Wu'tapiu* fire, where she and Little Moon had been trickling a thin broth of fortifying medicine into Stick's mouth. She would lose him forever if another *ve'ho'e* attack came now.

"Do something!" she spat at her old uncle.

Black Kettle did not move.

She thrust her babe into Little Moon's arms. "Take him away. Take him and hide."

"Where do you go?" A faint glimmer of life returned to the woman's eyes.

"To kill them," she said flatly. "To kill every one of their maggot hides before they get the last of us."

She went to the log where her *Vehoo'o* uncle had dropped the belongings he had saved from the massacre. She pawed through them until she found his ancient carbine, ripping the feathers and the seasoned leather from its grip so she could find the trigger. Then she ran out onto the plain, a dull hatred moving at her temples.

But it was not spiders who approached.

Her fingers went suddenly lifeless, and she dropped the gun. She stared, unwilling to believe, but the sight remained the same. Blind Fox rode in, driving some salvaged ponies ahead of him. She saw Wind Runner and choked with emotion. Somehow, impossibly, the boy had escaped the slaughter to recapture some of the herds. And he had found the missing hunters. With him came other men, *Wu'tapiu* warriors, and Bear . . . and Walks Far.

Eagle felt her legs go out beneath her.

Thoughts of Fire Wolf had brought her to this place. Memories of his knife-sharp, passionate strength and his belief in her had driven her on. But she had no more to give. Now she needed the easy, sure steadiness of this warrior she had wed, needed it so much she ached with it.

Walks Far's black eyes searched the grasses until he saw her. He gave a crazed sound and leapt from his pony, then his hard arms were around her.

She was safe now.

Behind them, shouts erupted from the camp again as Fire

Wolf and his *Hotame-taneo'o* warriors approached from the other direction. Fire Wolf stopped dead as he saw them, his pony staggering with the sudden command.

Emotion surged up in him again, intense, sweet, so long forgotten. She was alive. His heart hurt with fierce, exultant pride that she had escaped. He knew she would have fought, snarling and killing her way to safety.

Then he understood what he was seeing, and reality crushed him like a bullet shattering his flesh.

She possessed her own strength now, and Walks Far still possessed her. Only one thing had changed.

He could no longer bear the mistake he had made in giving her to the other warrior.

IV

When Sun crept below the horizon again, the last of the Dogs finally arrived from the Platte River Road fighting camp. Their squaws moved among the other women as they huddled miserably in the cold darkness. They pressed upon them everything they could spare—an aged pony to carry a grandmother, a skin to warm a child who had lost his shirt, a handful of small, necessary tools. Then their black-fringed lodges went up, and their fires shone like beacons in the night. The People needed guidance, protection, someone to save them, and they flocked to the *Hotame-taneo'o*.

As they came, one by one, squeezing into vacant spots around the Dogs' big central fire, Eagle huddled close to Walks Far. She cradled Stick in her lap as she listened to the talk.

The war chiefs did most of it. Bear and Night Fighter had gone back to Sand Creek to search for anyone who might have survived, and Fire Wolf was off doing what he could to help the wounded.

She looked around to find him bent over a squaw, and an ache swelled up in her, almost distinguishable amid the despair that already filled her. Since he had come back, he did not even seem to care that she lived. He did not look at her nor speak to her, and it was as though she had only dreamed his rare, short bursts of laughter.

"We must elect new *Vehoo'o* to replace the ones who have

died," Bull Bear asserted, and she twitched and looked back to him. "You must tell your leaders that we want men of strength, or they will fill that council with more cowards who go to the spiders and beg them to kill us! I say we should put Dull Knife of the *Ohmeseheso* in as a principal. He has fought well with Red Cloud and Pawnee Killer of the Sioux."

There was a vague murmur of agreement from those gathered.

"A messenger has gone to Stone Forehead, and he approves of this choice."

"Sand Hill, too, would be good," said Tangle Hair. "I am born to his Closed Gullets, and I followed him when I was a young man. He will not take the hands of those spiders."

The old chief bent his head in modest recognition of the praise, and the hum of voices grew louder, stronger.

It died coldly and abruptly when Black Kettle moved into the circle. He bore the brunt of the warriors' guilt and scorn, that they had trusted his foolish faith. They avoided him, as though to look upon him was to remember their own wretched shame and stupidity.

"I will throw away my vote," he said quietly. "I have lost two dear friends. Fill their places as you see fit. But I caution you, please, to remember this is a civil council. Think with your heads, not with the fire and grief in your hearts.

"This is a tragedy, but it has proved something. We cannot fight this enemy. They are stronger than we are. They are crazy, and they do not speak true.

"With the new sun, I will go back to the *Wu'tapiu*'s Flint Arrowpoint River. I will stay away from these white men now, as Stone Forehead does.

"My camp is open to all those who would come with me. I beg you to follow me, to see the sense in peace now."

He began to turn away, then a bellow rent the night, terrible with rage and pain.

"Stay away from them, Grandfather?" Bear choked, appearing out of the darkness. He dropped a lifeless bundle beside the fire.

It was Walking Spirit, barely recognizable. Her scalp and nose and fingers were gone, and her belly was slashed, so that her dark, tangled innards spilled out.

"Aiy-ee!" Eagle howled, and her heart finally and fully shattered, leaving a cold, empty ache in its place. Walks Far touched her in comfort, but she did not feel him.

"Hide from this?" Bear raved on. "They have taken our women, those who give the People life! No, *Vehoo'o*, I will not turn away from that. I will hunt them down! For every butchered body I saw at that place, I will take ten! I will make them pay with their own women's blood!"

Then his body seemed to fold in upon itself, and the big *Hotame-taneo'o* warrior wept.

After a long moment, Bull Bear spoke again, his voice tight. "Let this *Wu'tapiu Vehoo'o* go south. We will carry the pipe to Dull Knife, that a man of strength and courage might smoke and agree to lead our council."

Fire Wolf joined the circle. "We must move quickly. We must scatter our women and children away from this place. I was at the fort before I came here. It was empty."

This time the heat of response was feverish. The white men who had murdered their wives, their children, their parents, still roamed the prairie.

A pipe was passed hurriedly among them. Sand Hill took it. There was a pregnant moment of silence, then the lesser *Vehoo'o* gathered among them began to nod their votes.

Sand Hill smoked deeply.

Bear and Night Fighter, Fire Wolf and Bull Bear, Tall Bull and Tangle Hair and Walks Far all jostled angrily around him. They inhaled the smoke and sent it back to *Ma'heo'o* as the others came on, men of all the societies. One by one they handed the pipe on.

The night huddled in endless cold, and the *Hotame-taneo'o* fire leapt and burned. But the single ember that was passed from hand to hand seemed the brightest. It glowed red in the night until Bull Bear knocked it gently from its bowl into the fire. The flames there flared and twisted as through feeding on its sacred power.

The *ve'ho'e* had found victory in a peace camp without warriors. Now they would meet the Dogs.

V

Eagle stood close to Wind Runner as the meager shelters of the Smoky Hill camp were torn down with the dawn. She began to pull herself up onto the pony, then her gaze fell on the tiny gathering around Black Kettle, those who would stupidly go south. Her family was among them.

Something very faint moved at the spot of her heart, a whisper of pain. She eased down from Wind Runner again, going to them, stopping in front of her father.

"You, who have lost so much, choose not to fight back, to hide instead?" she challenged.

Caught The Enemy's gaze moved to the others. Eagle looked as well, to Little Moon and Medicine Woman Later and to Sun Roads. They would go where they thought they would be safe, with the man who had always led them. In the People's tradition, it fell to Caught The Enemy to care for them, his dead wife's widowed sister and her kin.

Sun Road's eyes sought hers out. "I . . . I lost him, sister," she whispered. "He was with me, and then he was not."

Pot Belly. Little Moon's babe had not been found, either.

Eagle thought she would finally cry at that, but her eyes were dry and grainy. She went to her and pulled her head gently down to her shoulder instead, shuddering with her. But the others were leaving now, mostly on foot. Sun Roads pulled away to go with them.

Eagle looked back to the *Hotame-taneo'o*. An angry, vital crowd surrounded them, but as she watched, her grandfather stepped away, hobbling after the *Wu'tapiu*.

"No," she breathed.

She had been so sure he would stay with the Dogs. There would be war now, a terrible war, and he was one of the few men who truly knew how to heal. The warriors needed him. *She* needed him! Stick could not live without the medicine the old man held in his head!

The lethargy inside her crumbled under a hot stream of betrayal. She ran to him and clawed her fingers into his robe. "If you go, he will die!"

Medicine Wolf pried her hands away with surprising

strength. "Listen to me, Granddaughter! You must listen! I have seen more than sixty winters. There is no place for me in that war camp. Only the young ones can stand against the treachery of those *ve'ho'e* now. It is your fight."

Fury blazed through her. *Hers?* She was only a squaw, only a mother. What did he think?

But he kept talking, and his words gnawed a disbelieving hole in her heart.

"You think I betray your child, but you are wrong. You must let him go, Granddaughter. Let *Ma'heo'o* call him up the death road. He has lost far too much blood to ever be strong again. And he will never be a warrior. He will never have use of that torn leg.

"You know that; in your soul, you see. Do not waste your strength on him, not when so many others need you."

She screamed. "I . . . hate . . . you for failing him!"

And in that moment she did, oh, how she did! But she would not give up because *he* was a coward, because he chose to run and hide.

Fire Wolf said she was strong. She did not know why he, too, had turned away from her now, but it did not matter. He had shown her what was inside her, and she would use it.

"Those *ve'ho'e* should die, and I will help our men kill them. But know that I will keep my babe alive as well! Tell me how to keep the sores on his leg from going rotten. Tell me what you dribbled into his mouth to keep his skin from burning! *If you would go, then tell me!*"

He looked at her for a long time, then he untied his medicine bag from his breechclout. "It is all in there. It is the best I can give you."

Eagle snatched the leather sack from his hand.

"*Pat se'wots* makes the pus stay away," he said. "*To'wan i yuhk ts*, To-Make-Cold medicine, is for fever. And the *hoh'a-hea no is'tut* gives strength. Wrap the leaves in a small piece of skin, then chew them up good and rub them over his chest. But be careful with a wee one. It can make his heart pound so fast it could burst.

"I do not know if you can find these things where you are going. I have never been to visit the *Ohmeseheso*, and I do not know what grows in their land. But I will pray to *Ma'heo'o* with every sun that you succeed."

She licked her lips, wavering for the space of a heartbeat. He was her kin, and something inside her yearned to accept his powerful prayers. She made a little moaning sound, but the time for grief was over. Still her son lived, and still the Dogs could fight. Now she would have to fight as well, for both of them.

13

Big Hoop-and-Stick Game Moon, 1865
Ohmeseheso Country

I

The war drums were relentless in Dull Knife's camp, a steady *THUMP-thump-thump* that sounded in her sleep and when she woke. Eagle learned to shut them out, even when a raiding party came in and they became frenzied and faster.

They could not help her save Broken Stick.

She bent over him now in her lodge, a small hut very different from the one the blue-coats had burned at Sand Creek. It was Cold Maker's favorite moon, and there were not enough buffalo to create tepees for so many refugee families. She had improvised instead, fashioning rounded poles to accommodate the few precious hides Walks Far could bring her.

They were warm enough, but they were still so very hungry. Only the native *Ohmeseheso* and the Sioux ate well, because they supplemented their dried stores with bear meat. It was readily available now that the animals could be provoked from their hibernation places with a minimum of effort.

The *Ohmeseheso* squaws were eager to share their men's kills with their starving relations, but the southern bands could not accept. They still believed it was taboo to eat Grandfather Bear, and even the smell of his flesh roasting gagged most of them.

Suddenly Eagle went still, thinking on that. What would happen to Stick if she fed him bear meat? Her milk was so weak that fresh food could only help him grow stronger, but would *Ma'heo'o* strike him down?

The *Ohmeseheso* still lived, she thought. Fire Wolf still lived, and he had been birthed and raised here on such kills. She pushed hard to her feet, trembling with the possibility. She would ask him about it.

Then her hope splintered into painful confusion. Fire Wolf would not even look at her anymore.

She sat again, her legs folding clumsily beneath her, then her shoulders squared. She would just have to keep him alive with that heart medicine that her grandfather had told her to use.

She pulled the last of her supply from a parfleche, trickling it between her fingers. Medicine Wolf's pouch had run out long ago, but an *Ohmeseheso* healer had traded her for all the weed he had. Sleep after sleep, she quilled robes and sewed leggings for Blue Storm in exchange for his healing substances. The greedy man accepted all her work, although he told anyone who cared to listen that Broken Stick would not see the Spring Moon.

Eagle loathed the man.

She began chewing the bitter leaves, then she unlaced Stick's cradleboard and smeared the concoction gently over his chest. *Smile at me. Oh, little one, please open your eyes.* But he only blinked once, then slept again.

She dug for her robe, determined to go out and find more. Then she gasped, twisting around as the hide flap at her door snapped back rudely. Wind Woman entered without announcing herself.

"Our men have returned. They are all alive," she said flatly.

Eagle flinched. She had not noticed the drumbeats picking up their tempo. Guilt penetrated the dull focus of her mind on her child. Three moons had passed since they had come to this place, and she had always managed to meet the returning war parties, spurring them on for the next raid when they would kill even more *ve'ho'e*.

Wind Woman's face softened a bit at her distress. "Walks Far needs you as much as this babe does."

"*Needs* me?" Eagle blinked in vague confusion. "He is alive, walking, yet still I am always there for him. This babe cannot even crawl yet."

"He will never crawl."

For a moment she reeled at her friend's cruel words, then determination settled in her again. She gathered Stick up and made a move for the door flap. "I will join my husband as soon as I get the medicine I need for this one," she said tightly.

"You are killing yourself, driving yourself into the frozen

ground," Wind Woman snapped, angry again. "You push yourself, dark and sun, to keep the babe breathing and to do your other chores besides. Curse you for the friend you have become! I do not want you to die! I have lost too many others!"

Eagle hesitated. "Please," she begged. "It will thaw soon, and then there will be more food. Then I will be fine. Everything will be fine."

But she knew it would not be. When the thaw came, there would finally be precious hides to tan. There would be buffalo to dry. The raiding would pick up even more, and she knew, in a dark spot of her heart, that Stick would still need her just as desperately.

An overwhelming loneliness and exhaustion swept her, that no one understood, that she was only one woman alone to do it all. She swayed with it, but then she pushed past the flap, rallying herself another time.

The sky was deep and gray, hovering over the thousands of Sioux and Cheyenne lodges that filled the war camp. Eagle moved resolutely past them to the council fire. She would welcome Walks Far and love him. It would take only a moment, then she could go find that medicine.

Warriors hooted and leapt there, whirling and dancing in a frenzy of victory. It made her pulse pick up as they stomped their moccasins against the earth where the heat of the flames had thawed it to mud. The snows had been swept back from this spot, and they reenacted their raids there, sounding their war cries.

A ghost of a smile touched Eagle's lips. Many *ve'ho'e* had died.

Beside the place where she stood, there were heaps and piles of plunder. Blessedly, this time the raids had brought food. Bags bulged, spilling strange beans, and there were splintered wooden crates full of meat. This was covered with a crumbly white substance, and she touched her finger to it and tasted it curiously. It was salty, but not entirely repulsive.

There were long wooden poles, too, and she hunkered down to peer at them more closely. They had odd material wrapped around them. The stuff was like skins, but infinitely softer and more pliable. Had this come from an animal? Her mind reeled. She had seen other *ve'ho'e* clothing. She had even touched the scratchy blue wool of their soldier's coats when the warriors brought them back to camp. She had decided that they were made of the hairs of some animal woven tightly together. But this stuff was different, fine and seemingly nonporous.

Who were these white maggots that they could create such stuff?

"It puzzles me, too."

She leapt to her feet again to find Walks Far behind her. Then she stared and a laugh gurgled out of her. His aristocratic face was nearly hidden by the funniest headdress she had ever seen. She touched it gingerly. It was made of material like that on the pole, but a little bit stiffer. It had a wide, flapping brim and strings that hung down below his chin.

Walks Far grinned, a surge of good feeling rushing through him at her response. He took the bonnet off to work it between his fingers.

"I do not know how they do it, but their women take that material and they make these things for their heads. They are good trophies," he said, then he sobered. "For our women who died at the Creek, who will never own pretty things again." He put the hat back on.

"Yes," she whispered. For her mother and Walks At Night and Walking Spirit.

She shivered and looked around. Some of the warriors had taken bolts of the cloth and had draped them over their shirts and leggings. Their war ponies wore strips tied into their bridles and braided into their manes and tails.

She was able to fight off her exhaustion one more time. She slipped her hand into her husband's.

"Tell me about it. Tell me everything, and then I must go find more medicine."

A shadow crossed his eyes, but he raised their joined hands to motion toward a man standing in a place of honor near the fire.

"Do you see him? He is the mightiest warrior the People have ever known." If he begrudged the man that, it was not in his voice, in his face. She felt a rush of love for him, for his steady, unthreatened sense of himself.

"But he is not *Hotame-taneo'o*," she realized.

Walks Far shook his head. "He petitioned to the Elkhorn

Scrapers Society long before his power came to him. He is
loyal to those brothers and will not abandon them. His name is
Roman Nose."

A shiver took her as she watched the man's broad, sculptured
face. He was nearly as big as Bear, and very handsome. But it
was more than that. There was something vital about him,
something strong and unimpeachable.

"You see that war bonnet his wife holds," Walks Far went
on. "It is sacred. Once he did the Sun Dance, and he had a
vision. *Ma'heo'o* showed him that bonnet. Later he learned that
Stands On Clouds, the *So'taa'e* shaman, had a dream in which
that same bonnet appeared. He bargained with him, a vast
amount of ponies and hides, to get him to make this hat as they
had both envisioned it.

"Many taboos come with the possession of it. Roman Nose
can never eat any meat that has touched the white mongrel's
metal. He cannot dance when the moon is visible, or sleep with
his feet facing south. But in accepting all that, he has power
such as I have never seen before. That bonnet protects him
from *ve'ho'e* bullets. I saw it in this last fight when he rode
right through the white soldiers. They shot at him, but nothing
happened. He did not fall, and the *ve'ho'e* used up all their
ammunition firing at him. Then the rest of us could move in
and kill them."

A murmur of awe slipped from her. "Then we can destroy
them," she breathed. "With Roman Nose, we can drive them
out of Den-ver, make them go away."

Walks Far hesitated, but she did not notice. "Yes," he
answered. "Now that we are all together, now that we have the
help of Roman Nose and his society, we can kill every spider
we find."

If we can find them all.

But he did not say it aloud, because there was life in her eyes
again, and it had been so long since he had seen it. He pulled
her closer, savoring it.

She managed another smile, then her gaze slid away.

Walks Far followed it, and an invisible fist clenched abruptly
around his innards.

Fire Wolf was talking to Roman Nose, an old *So'taa'e*
comrade. As Walks Far watched, the dog rope man's gaze

moved to meet that of his wife. But his stony face did not change; if he saw her, if he acknowledged her in some part of his heart, it was not visible in his eyes.

Walks Far wanted to be glad for that, but he felt her stiffen in his arms.

Eagle pulled away from him as something hot and sharp pierced her in a place that could still bleed. *Why? Why has he betrayed me?* Suddenly she missed the warmth they once shared so much it was a physical pain.

"I . . . I need that *hoh'ahea no is'tut,*" she managed, then she ran from the hurt, doggedly setting out toward the frozen drifts and the trees beyond the tepees.

II

As the moon diminished, the aching cold of a northern winter came to crust the snowbanks with ice. Eagle pawed through them sun after sun, digging for clumps of the weed that Stick so desperately needed.

She found none.

On the night the moon finally waned, she dozed lightly, the babe at her breast. He slept sweetly in her arms, and it was his quiet that finally penetrated her shallow slumber.

She came out of it with a yowl that jarred Walks Far.

He came awake groping for his repeater, but there was no enemy in the lodge, only death. He thought he could smell it, a haunting sourness. Eagle bent over their babe, a crazed sound vibrating in her throat.

It chilled him more than Cold Maker's harshest winds. "Eagle," he said, then he called her name louder. "If he would go, let him leave!"

But she could not do it.

He tried to pull her away. She turned on him, clawing viciously, and he let her go, stunned that she had so little weight to her, appalled that she would turn on him so. She went back to their babe, putting her mouth over his.

Finally Stick's eyelids fluttered, and he mewled.

Eagle staggered to her feet, clutching him. "It . . . it only works if you do it right away," she explained. "You have to do it as soon as he stops breathing.

"The *hoh'ahea no is'tut*," she went on. "That is it. That is the difference, do you see? He has not done this since right after he was wounded, but I have been putting that heart weed on his chest every sun. I have to find more. It can wait no longer."

Her gaze sharpened. "You spoke of a *So'taa'e* shaman when you told me about Roman Nose."

"Stands On Clouds?" He felt dazed.

"Yes, that is the one."

She took the cradleboard and her robe, tucking the babe inside against her warmth, then she went outside. Walks Far watched her go, a heavy weight pressing against his chest.

This could go on no longer.

Oh, *Ma'heo'o*, he knew it, and he knew, too, that there was only one way to stop it. He held his head in his hands, grieving for the wee one, and for the first time he wished that the babe had died on that bloody sun, sparing them all these wretched half-hopes, this agonizing decision. Maybe, in the end, *Ma'heo'o* would spare him. But Walks Far knew that he would offer his son's life to the Wise One that He might spare his wife's.

He could not do it without the dog rope warrior.

He wanted to be vicious, to demand some great sacrifice of Eagle as well, but in the end he loved her too much to do it. His heart tried to writhe away from the truth, but he forced himself back to it again and again, until he could tolerate it. He grappled for the last time with the affection he had discovered between his wife and the warrior who was his brother, then he pushed to his feet again and went to find her before he could let himself cry like a boy.

III

Dawn was spreading a pearly pink color across the sky. Eagle looked up at it beyond the tree's highest branches, her breath puffing whitely in the air.

She had held Stick back from the death road again. *How much longer? How much longer could she do that?*

She steadied herself against a pine, then she straightened her shoulders and made off toward the *So'taa'e* part of the camp. The first squaw she met there was one she recognized, but she had to stop and scowl before she remembered why. Finally she recollected it; this was the woman who had held Roman Nose's bonnet the night of the last big Scalp Dance.

"Please, you would help me?" she managed.

Woman With White Child peered at the cradleboard clutched against her breast, then at her face. "You need our healer? He is five tepees down the line."

Eagle hurried on. Stick's little face was still faintly gray. Oh, *Ma'heo'o*, she could not be polite, could not wait, no matter what her mothers had taught her. She called the healer's name, slapping her hand against his door flap.

An old man came out. "A grandfather need his sleep," he muttered irritably.

Eagle swallowed. "Please. My son—"

"Have you no healer to help you? Who are you from?" he interrupted, scowling at her accent. The *So'taa'e* people spoke a slightly different dialect than the southern bands.

"I . . . no. I am *Hotame-taneo'o*."

He gave a sudden smile and waved her inside. "Sit then. Eat with us."

Eagle spared a fleeting glance for the squaw who was busy putting things into a cooking paunch. Her belly rumbled, but the medicine was more important.

"There is no time." She pushed her babe at him. He scowled down at him for a moment, then he gave him back at her.

"He is trying to get up the death road."

No more. She would not hear that anymore!

"I do not ask you to save him!" she cried. "I have kept him alive myself all this time. All I need is more *hoh'ahea no is'tut!*"

He watched her for a moment, then lowered himself to sit. "I cannot help you," he said finally. "I will not have more until the thaw. I sold all my heart weed to Blue Storm long ago. You should try that healer."

She gave a bitter laugh. Suddenly she knew that the greedy *Ohmeseheso* man had bought the weed from Stands On Clouds far cheaper than the price of all the beautiful quilling she had done for him. But it did not matter now, it could not matter, because Stick needed more.

"It cannot be found until the thaw?" she managed.

Stands On Clouds chewed his lip. "It will not be potent again
until the thaw. But I suppose you could try it as it is now. Just
use more of it, very carefully, to make up for its difference in
strength."

More. But she could not find any at all!

"I have looked and looked—"

He waved a hand in disgust. "You look for weeds. *Hoh'ahea
no is'tut* grows as a vine."

All those drifts she had dug through! She moved back for the
door, but his low murmur stopped her. *She had nothing for him.*
She had forgotten she would have to pay him.

"A hide," he said. "I could use a good, thin elk piece for
painting on. But do not worry about it now. I will take
recompense when the thaw comes."

The unexpected kindness, something she had met with so
rarely in this strange camp, nearly buckled her knees.

"Why?" she whispered.

He shrugged his bird-thin shoulders. "I admire the spirit of
someone who does not give up. This is a time when our people
have need of such a thing."

She could not find her voice to thank him, but her eyes were
full of gratitude. She pushed past the flap, into the cold again.

Thick trees buffered the camp rise here, shielding it from the
harsh prairie winds below. She moved into them, going from
trunk to trunk, running her free hand fretfully over the bark.
Her palm scraped and bled. Doggedly she pushed on as the
sounds from the lodges grew dim behind her.

She found no vines, and she pressed her hand to her mouth
to stop a sound of hysteria. Then another hand came down on
her shoulder.

She screamed, spinning about to face Fire Wolf.

"You?" she moaned vaguely. "Why?" He was not her friend
anymore. What was he doing here?

"Tell me what you need," he answered roughly. "I will find
it for you. Then go back to your lodge and send someone out
to find your husband. He is on the other side of the camp,
searching for you there."

Anger began to twitch inside her. It was the first grief-free
emotion she had felt in so long, and when it ignited, it rushed
through her, white and hot and clean. He had ignored her and

left her son to her own frantic care. Now he thought to tell her what to do, but she would not allow it.

"I . . . needed . . . you when he was dying!" she gasped. "I know how to fix him now. I do not want your help!"

She shoved past him. He caught her, his fingers closing easily around her bone-thin arm. Eagle howled in rage. She could not bear for him to touch her again. She could stand anything but that, anything but the sweet memories of an easier time when he had been her friend.

She wrenched violently against his strength, but she had none of her own. Finally she sank her teeth into the fleshy part of his hand where he gripped her.

He bellowed, shaking loose of her, and for a wild moment she thought he might strike her. But he was fierce and hard with others, never with her. When she could have run, she stood panting instead, and he crowded her hard against a tree to keep her still.

"Listen to me." He made a harsh, ugly sound deep in his throat. "I thought once the only thing I could not do for you was wed you. I was wrong. With or without those vows, I cannot turn away from you and let you kill yourself."

You have already turned away! She wanted to scream the truth at him, but suddenly she understood what his words had cost him. He did not want to care, but he did, he still did, and it was clawing at him inside.

Her anger left her. "I can do this," she assured him. "I am strong."

"No, little Eagle, you are not," he said wearily, "not enough to survive this road you travel."

She jerked as though he had struck her. His voice had carried her across the prairie. Even when he would not acknowledge her, the memory of what he had taught her about herself remained.

"That is what you gave me," she whispered. "You let me see my strength. Now you would take it back?"

Did she need his friendship so much? He could not allow her to ask it of him with those silent, aching eyes, because now she asked too much.

He turned away from her, then heard her give a little cry. She fell into the snow, drained to exhaustion.

For a long moment he only stared at her. Then he gathered her up carefully, almost unwillingly, fixing her babe on his shoulder.

She was so horribly light in his arms. Her cheekbones were gaunt, her elbows knobby. Her doeskin hung on her under the robe that had fallen askew.

He shifted her weight and moved out of the woods. The women were waiting at her lodge, Wind Woman and Falling Bird, and, inexplicably, Roman Nose's woman. As he approached, Walks Far jogged from an opposite copse, jolting to a stop when he reached him.

Falling Bird slid Stick's cradleboard from his shoulder. Woman With White Child and Wind Woman took Eagle from his arms, supporting her between them.

"Where did you find her?" Walks Far's voice was hoarse.

"Stands On Clouds told her where to find that weed. She was looking for it. I do not think she found it."

Falling Bird groaned. "Then she will go out looking again as soon as she wakes."

"No," Walks Far said hoarsely. "Not this time."

They all looked at him, expecting more. His tone was strange, thick with pain, with some kind of loss. They frowned at him, but he kept his eyes on the dog rope man.

"I would end this," he went on.

An instinctual urge to escape swelled in Fire Wolf. He wanted to shrill for his pony and run back to the rage that was bloodying the plains. That was where he belonged; it was the world he had chosen. He knew somehow that if he stood here a moment longer, all of that would change.

Walks Far's jaw hardened. "I have decided to pledge a Sun Dance. Smoke with me, brother."

The women gasped. A harsh sound came from Fire Wolf.

How many seasons had passed since he had first said no to the sweet, innocent lure of her? Now that he knew the bitter error he had made, it seemed that *Ma'heo'o* would put the offer back to him again and again, mocking him.

Take the promise of her now, or leave her forever this time.

He tried desperately to remember Sweet Grass Woman, but there was only a distant shimmy of pain this time, one so fragile and weak it shocked him. He clawed after her *mis'tai* ghost, wanting her back, needing the cold protection her death had always given to his heart. He wanted to once again be the warrior he was content to be before Eagle had defied the Dogs to sneak a peek at some buffalo. But Sweet Grass Woman had left him when he had begun to fear dying again.

"So be it," he said roughly. This time he would take her.

This time, he realized, he did not have a choice at all.

IV

The change was not subtle or stealthy. Eagle felt it as soon as the darkness around her began to ebb.

The voices in her lodge were quiet and conspiratorial. They were the first thing to reach her, and then memory came back to her. *Fire Wolf.* Hurt closed around her throat, and she yearned to slip back into the comforting blackness again where his betrayal could not touch her. But she thought of her child and opened her eyes to find Wind Woman pressing against her shoulders.

"Do not get up," she muttered. "Your babe is fine."

Angry, she craned her neck, looking. Wind Woman had no right to keep her from tending her son.

Then she saw her husband leaning against a backrest with Stick swaddled in his lap. He was dribbling medicine down his throat . . . he was helping her.

The door flap snapped back, and the dog rope man came in. Eagle started, feeling all the hurt and anger and disbelief again. He dropped some weeds at Walks Far's feet.

Her pulse began to move like the war drums outside. Fire Wolf spoke without looking at her, even as she began to fight against Wind Woman.

"Stop. There is truly nothing for you to do now."

But that was preposterous. There was always work; she had more than any other squaw. Then an intuitive feeling of dread began to move in her gut, and she looked around the lodge more closely.

Falling Bird was there, dropping hard grains into her cooking paunch, grains that could only have come from her own parfleches since Eagle had not had time to trade with the *Ohmeseheso* women for any of her own. There was a pile of wood near the door flap that had not been there earlier, and Walks Far was chewing the weed that Fire Wolf had brought.

Her heart staggered. It was *hoh'ahea no is'tut*. Fire Wolf had found some for her.

"What is happening here?" she demanded.

Their hands slowed, and then Fire Wolf stepped back for the door flap. Falling Bird pushed to her feet and brushed off her knees, and Wind Woman ducked outside.

When they left, there was silence between her and her husband, thick and uneasy.

"We will help you with your chores and keep this babe alive until the thawing moon," Walks Far said finally.

"Why?"

"Because then he will either live on his own, or he will travel up the road that calls him."

Fury slapped her with stunning force. It was a trick. All of it, this help she so desperately needed, the warmth of their friendship, it was all a trick! First her grandfather had urged her to let her child go, then even Fire Wolf had spoken of her failure to win this battle. Now her husband would side against her, trying to placate her into giving up.

She screamed and lunged at him, trying to wrest her babe from his grasp. The need to save Stick from their treachery rushed her until she sobbed with it. But Walks Far caught her, laying the babe aside to hold her still.

"Listen to me." His voice was hoarse and strange. "There is a way, only one way to help him now. We will do it, but then that will be the end of it. We will put it in *Ma'heo'o*'s hands then. You must promise."

Ma'heo'o's hands? Somehow, with those words, she knew. "You would ask Sun."

He pulled her into the steady warmth of his arms. She resisted, then she clung, tears coming to choke her. How could he do such a thing? How could he ask it of her? Then she felt a warm, wet slickness against her neck.

Her man, her dog warrior, wept with her. He would do this thing to save their child. He asked it of her, because he would do it himself.

She pulled away to touch his face. She loved him so much

more than she had ever credited, in a soft, profound spot at her very core. "It is not necessary," she tried. "I can—"

But Walks Far shook his head. "We must end this nightmare."

She knew in her gut that he was right, and that knowing terrified her. Sun was the most powerful, life-generating of *Ma'heo'o*'s forces. What it beamed down upon became strong and healthy. But the People did not seek its cure lightly. To receive Sun's benevolence, a man made the utmost of sacrifices.

Walks Far would lead the other men in the self-torture that would prove they were brave and worthy. And he would share her with another man. In the joining, outside beneath the sun, *Ma'heo'o* would give to her all the goodness and strength of Sun's power. Then she would in turn love her husband, and grant that power unto him, for the one in his prayers whom he would save.

If Sun and *Ma'heo'o* did not make Stick strong again, Eagle knew that Walks Far would not allow her to fight for him any longer.

"Ah, Eagle," he said, "I do not want him to die. But if *Ma'heo'o* deems through Sun that he should still travel up *Heammawihio*, then you must let him go and begin living again. You must stop these crazed efforts to heal him and let Sun decide."

He held her warm and close, but there was something hard in his voice she had never heard before. She pushed away to look up at him, and she knew that this time, this one time, he would give her no choice.

Stick cried feebly. She touched a hand to his chest, and a horrible weariness touched her deeper than her soul.

She brought the babe into her lap and felt the dull hurt the movement brought to her muscles. She had to believe that *Ma'heo'o* would save him, or dread would make her go mad.

"Who?" she managed. "What other man would you give me to? Who would take me?"

She thought of bandy-legged Tall Bull, or perhaps old, widowed Tangle Hair. *Not that.* But the others were all wed. Who else would be willing to take her and her child? To share her in this rite was so much more than to rut on the prairie. It was a vow. The warrior Walks Far chose would wait through all the seasons, bound to him closer than any blood kin. If Walks Far should fall, he would assume care for her in memory of the sacred moment they had all shared.

She could stand it, she vowed. Oh, *Ma'heo'o*, she could bear anything but losing her child.

Then Walks Far answered, and her skin blanched all over again.

"Fire Wolf," he said quietly.

14

Spring Moon, 1865
Ohmeseheso Country

I

Eagle paused as she worked over the elk hide she had
promised to Stands On Clouds. The moon had come for
thawing, but blessedly, winter hung on. The grandfathers said
the Sun Dance could not begin until the first squaw shrugged
off her robe because it was too warm to work beneath it. She
had time to pray that the rite would work, and to agonize over
what it would entail, time to fear that *Ma'heo'o* would destroy
her child rather than heal him when he saw the treachery she
hid in her heart.

She wanted this.

The thought had her fingers spasming around her flesher,
and she dug a gouge deep in the perfect hide. Groaning, she
hurled the tool aside, but she could not rid herself of her
despair. How could she touch Fire Wolf when she had loved
him so long?

The Dance was meant to be one of suffering and endurance,
but heat curled in her belly when she thought of the dog rope
man. She remembered the panic and the stunning awareness
she had felt in the beginning, and later, the rough-edged
comfort of being his friend. She remembered the times her
heart had hurt for his aloneness. Walks Far had felt the bond
between them; she knew that. Yet of all his *Hotame-taneo'o*
brothers, he had chosen Fire Wolf to smoke the Sun pipe with,
a man whose heart could not possibly survive what the vow
entailed.

At once she decided she could not allow either of them to do
it. Then Stick let out an odd, gurgling moan.

She had to do it, and she would live with her terror. She

would do it to save her child, but when it was all over, she did not think any of them would ever be the same again.

II

When spring finally came to the northern country, it was with a sudden eruption of life, as though the Wise One had only been waiting for the right time for the Dance. In the space of a few suns the lingering snows melted. Smoke-blue grasses appeared where the banks had been, and the agave on the plains opened their long, stalky arms to reveal flutterings of pink.

Eagle moved through the trees, her arms laden with the seasoned wood that had lain beneath the snows. Soon now, she thought, looking about. Soon it would all be over . . . the waiting and the dread, even her last precious breath of hope that the Dance would work.

An *Ohmeseheso* girl rushed past her, making her stumble and clutch the wood clumsily. Distractedly she looked the way the squaw had gone. The girl chased a toddling brother who trundled happily past the lodges. Suddenly hot envy twisted Eagle's belly. She wished fervently that for just one sun Stick could play like that while that other wee one lay bent and twisted in his place.

Just one sun.

Her skin flushed hot with shame as the squaw pushed her cumbersome robe off her shoulders to go after the child.

Eagle's heart staggered. *Stick, my babe, what have I done?*

The wood she held crashed and clattered to the ground. Terror swept her as silence fell over the camp. The people all thought that girl had started the Dance, but Eagle knew better. She had done it with her horrid, jealous thought. *Ma'heo'o* had heard her. It was a cruel omen.

She ran blindly for her lodge, shoving people aside. Behind her the word spread like a brush fire, treacherous and hungry. She dropped clumsily to her knees on the ground inside her tepee, her breath coming in harsh, gasping bursts.

"Eagle Voice."

Her flap rattled and she started. She squeaked a response, and Stands On Clouds moved stiffly into her lodge.

"I . . . it is not ready yet," she managed. In the end she had ruined the skin she had worked for him, like a girl tanning her first piece of hide.

But the old medicine man only shrugged. "I do not come to talk of what you owe me."

She began to feel dazed. "What, then?"

He sat as though she had invited him to. "I am a shaman as well as a healer. You husband has asked me to lead this Dance. It is time to discuss it now."

She shook her head helplessly. Walks Far had even found a priest she would feel comfortable with. It was not fair that he should suffer while she gloried in these rites.

"Bah!" the old man snapped, as though reading her mind. "You think you are the first woman who has done this with a secret in her heart? Do you think you are the first to cringe because her husband loves her and would ease her way?

"I counciled him in his choice," Stands On Clouds went on. "Walks Far gives you to the dog rope man because he knows of Fire Wolf's respect for you. Your brother gave you to your husband. Now your husband would know, if he falls, that such a thing will not happen to you again. Walks Far does not think Fire Wolf will force you to join with him, or anyone else, should *Ma'heo'o* deem that your husband die."

Old man, you do not know everything, she thought bitterly. Suddenly she understood. Fire Wolf trusted her *not* to wed him; that was why he had smoked. And it was like a knife in her breast to see that still, after all these seasons, her husband groped with the painful truth that she had not chosen him.

Then she looked into the healer's shrewd eyes, and she thought that maybe he did know, maybe he understood after all.

"I have seen more winters than anyone knows," he said, nodding. "I have Danced, and I have led others in the Dance, and I will tell you this. It will not be sweet for you, as you fear. You will suffer before this is over. You will do it not only for your babe, but for your people, because killing the spiders may bring vengeance, but only doing the Dance can renew life."

He thought a moment, and when he spoke again, his words

were eerie, the same ones her grandmother had said on that long ago sun when she had first been given to Walks Far.

"You are a woman of the People, and I pray that this is the hardest thing you will ever have to do, but it will not be. Now, will you let me teach you this Dance, or would you turn away from me like a child?"

Eagle heard her own voice repeat the words she had uttered on that sun.

"I will learn," she whispered, strangled.

III

She counciled with the old shaman for four suns while the *Hotame-taneo'o* stirred the camp to a feverish pitch outside. Eagle listened distantly to the disparate rhythms of many different Sun Dance songs being rehearsed. It occurred to her that for the first time since that bloody sun at Sand Creek, the People's voices hinted at hope.

Still, she shuddered when Stands On Clouds finally drew back her door flap and motioned her outside.

She stepped self-consciously into the sunlight, her hands fisted tight at her sides. Faces pooled together in her line of vision, and despite their fervent anticipation, they were all haggard and bereaved. Her heart stuttered as she picked out the people she loved best. She had been looking upon them since they had come here, but this time the haze of her own anguish lifted, and she saw their change. Bear's face was cruel and empty, and she understood with a pang that he had been that way since Walking Spirit had gone up the death road. Falling Bird's funny, bawdy tongue had finally gone silent.

Eagle knew then that Stands On Clouds was right. This Dance was for all the People dead and wounded and grieving. Something fierce flared inside her. She took a deep breath and moved after the shaman, into the crowd.

The lodges of the many band encampments had been spread widely over the bluff a few suns ago. Now they were squeezed close; everyone had moved in toward the central camp circle. As Eagle and Stands On Clouds reached that place, the last of the people came out of their tepees. The *Hotame-taneo'o* began opening their brother's Dance.

Singing deeply and strongly, Bull Bear planted several willow boughs at the center of the circle where the Renewal Lodge would be erected. Then the Dog chief danced around them, leaping and whirling so that his breechclout fanned out and the raven feathers on his headdress bobbed.

The Dog Soldiers came in on their ponies. Eagle felt her skin break out in gooseflesh. She had forgotten this. *How had she ever forgotten how fierce and haughty these men were?* The old awe came back to her, the kind she had known as a child before she had lived among them. The roar of their voices seemed to fill the earth, and the scalps on their shirts quivered with their owners' fluid, angry motion.

One by one the *Hotame-taneo'o* struck the boughs with their lances, counting coup on them. Their ponies reared and plunged beneath them as they held their weapons high and told of their most ferocious exploits. Quietly at first and then with more force, the People began yipping and cheering.

Next came the other military societies, all dressed in their own special shirts and bonnets and war paint. They galloped full tilt into the circle, whopping out their own coups. Roman Nose came last. He snapped an arrow out of his quiver and shot it into the boughs so that it lodged firmly in the earth between them. Then he charged at the spot to grab it back up again and wave it at the crowd.

"I am an Elkhorn Scraper! Twelve times I have ridden right through enemy bullets without being hit! I have touched the *ve'ho'e* while they lived, and then I have killed them. Now I will slay the rest so that they pay for what they have done and leave our land!"

The People howled jubilantly.

Finally the warriors retreated, and the women came on, a frenzied throng of them. The young ones danced and the grandmothers hobbled, but they all slapped the boughs, screaming as they counted their own imaginary coups on the white men. Like an abcess bursting and spewing forth poison, their hatred came out until one by one they stumbled away, clutching each other and weeping.

Eagle felt a hot, healthy wetness burn her own eyes.

From the corners of the clearing the leaders of various societies returned, bearing lodge poles painted to represent each of the four directions. They were erected and left to wait for the sacred hide cover of the Renewal Lodge. Then the most honored chiefs brought in the center pole.

There were Sand Hill and Dull Knife, the new *Vehoo'o*. Bull Bear came again to represent the Dogs, and Red Cloud of the Oglala carried in honor of the Sioux. The pole went up, and the People sighed.

Bundles of dogwood and cottonwood brush were carefully lashed to the fork at the top of the joined poles. Into the nest went the last symbolic items the chiefs carried. Bull Bear put in a broken arrow and a mangled shell casing for the enemy weapons which Sun would make useless. Dull Knife dropped a bit of buffalo meat inside for the food supply that kept the People strong. There was a clay, phallic image to represent the rebirth of their strength, and then finally the lodge cover was brought so that the tepee was whole.

It will be good now, Eagle thought fervently.

Stands On Clouds left her to move in front of the sacred lodge. He raised his hands for silence.

"I would remind you of *Tomsivsi*, Erect Horns, who brought this Sun Dance to our people. I would tell you this story so that the young ones might learn it, and our grandfathers might remember it all anew.

"It happened long ago, when the *Tse-Tsehesestahase* were first driven from their land of the corn by the white spider trickster men. There was terrible famine in this new place on the prairie when they got here. The grass was withered and the animals had starved. This land our grandfathers had fled to was barren and dry. They were forced to eat their dogs.

"*Tomsivsi* saw all this, and his heart cried.

"He was a good young man and a strong warrior, and he decided to fix this. He took the beautiful wife of one of his *Vehoo'o*, and together they slipped off secretly on a long journey to beg *Ma'heo'o* for help. They found a Sacred Mountain, and they went inside. It was there that *Ma'heo'o* taught them the Sun Dance, to be carried back to the *Tse-Tsehesestahase* for their salvation.

"*Ma'heo'o* told them this: Follow my instructions with care, and then, when you go forth from this mountain, all the heavenly bodies will move. The roaring thunder will awaken them, and the sun, the moon, the stars, and the rain will bring forth fruits of all kinds. All the animals will come forth behind you from this mountain, and they will follow you home. Take this sacred horned cap to wear when you perform this ceremony that I have given you, and you will control the buffalo and all the other animals. Put the cap on as you go from here, and Grandmother Earth will bless you.

"And it was just as *Ma'heo'o* had promised. When *Tomsivsi* and the wife of his chief emerged from the mountain, the entire earth had turned fresh and new. The buffalo came forth to follow them into their new homeland. There was an abundance of water, and good breath of the wind. *Tomsivsi* and the squaw laughed and danced. They loved each other, then they took this great rite back to her husband.

"That is how it was. That is how it shall be this sun."

Stands On Clouds turned into the sacred lodge. And then, from behind each side of it, Walks Far and Fire Wolf stepped out.

Eagle's pulse began to gallop again. For a moment she thought she might disgrace them all and faint. But Fire Wolf found her gaze, and what she saw there was not what Stands On Clouds had said at all.

In that moment she understood. Perhaps he trusted that she would never wed him; he knew his demons were safe with her. But he had also smoked the Sun pipe because, somewhere in his hard, wretched heart, he knew love for her. The health of her child was the most precious thing he would ever be able to give to her.

She looked to Walks Far and saw love there, too, in eyes black and bright. And there was no treachery among them then, no hidden, dark secrets after all. There was only the strength of the special bonds that had entangled her life with theirs.

She went to them and led the way into the Renewal Lodge.

Outside, all the warrior societies came to stand guard around the tepee. Walks Far went to the fire that Stands On Clouds had laid inside in the trench. He took a coal and brought it to her, and she sat behind it. He sprinkled sage upon it to carry their prayers to *Ma'heo'o*, then he lowered himself to sit on her left.

"For the child," Stands On Clouds murmured, and they all echoed him.

"For the People," intoned the shaman.

"For the People," they said.

"For those who follow us in pain, that we might be blessed and strong again."

Stands On Clouds moved to her. Eagle raised her arms as he had taught her, and he lifted her ratty dress from her skin.

"We give you Sacred Woman," he said and draped her head and body in a buffalo robe.

He moved to face Fire Wolf, and Eagle felt her heart jolt. She had not seen him carry the Sacred Horned Hat into the lodge after his story, and it had not been there before the lodge cover had been raised. She could not explain how it had gotten here, but Stands On Clouds held it now, the precious fetish of the *Tse-Tsehesestahase*, second only in sacrament to Stone Forehead's Medicine Arrows. It was the bonnet given to *Tomsivsi* long ago when he had visited *Ma'heo'o* in the sacred mountain.

Stands On Clouds placed it upon Fire Wolf's head. "We give you *Tomsivsi*, Erect Horns."

Eagle lifted herself up onto her haunches and bent over the coal. The sage incense wafted up beneath her robe, purifying her, and then she felt Fire Wolf move to a spot on her other side.

She turned her head and filled her eyes with him. Greedy, yes, she knew it was greedy and that it was wrong. But he wore only his breechclout now, and her throat ached.

His body was hard, like Walks Far's, but where her husband was all smooth planes, this man was chiseled. The ridges and valleys of his muscles played with the firelight and threw dark shadows back over his skin.

She had known that. She had always known, in her heart, that he would look just like this.

"We give you a man in your image," said Stands On Clouds, "that you might breathe Sun's power through him."

The shaman came to her with a horn full of blue paint. She shrugged her robe back so that it came across her arms and gathered above her waist, and he painted the sacred Sun emblem on her chest, an emblem of male, generative power.

"It is as You taught us," Stands On Clouds chanted.

"It is as You taught us," they echoed.

He drew the same design upon the faces of Fire Wolf and Walks Far.

Eagle rose to her feet. She took a deep breath and turned to go outside, then her gaze slid and met with Walks Far's.

Suddenly her heart writhed for him. The agony of sharing flared in his eyes, and she knew that she would ache with that look always.

She fled the lodge, Fire Wolf and Stands On Clouds following solemnly behind her. She knew where to walk, had been told time and time again over the last several suns. That was good, because now she followed the trail blindly. Fear clawed at her throat again, throwing back at her that last image of Walks Far's face. She stumbled, and Fire Wolf came up hard against her back.

As he always had, he spoke the truth that was in both of their hearts, though it was bald and harsh.

"It is for the babe, and for our people. But it is also the only way it can ever happen between us. Would you turn away from me now, little Eagle?"

She would not. She could not, and they both knew it.

They went on, moving behind the line of warrior societies who stood to block the sacred act from prying eyes. Out on the prairie, in the distance, there appeared a singular place where the grass had been stripped away. The Sun emblem was painted there as well, big and glorious as it caught the light of its father image.

Eagle stopped there, and Stands On Clouds moved around them to spread a buffalo robe upon the emblem. Then he seemed to vanish like smoke on a cruel wind.

She could not move.

Fire Wolf's hands came down on her shoulders. His fingers were hard and strong and callused from his bow. He touched her bare skin at the top of her robe, and something long denied, long dreaded, began to ache within her.

His voice sounded thick and raw. "Now, this one time, is ours, and then that is all there will be."

She turned on him fast. "I pray that! I pray you will never have to fulfill more than this moment!"

"But this moment is all I could ask."

His hand found hers. Because they had both wanted this

forever, because suddenly he feared it, too, it seemed easiest to do what he had done once before. He brought her fingers to his mouth, laving his tongue across her tense, white knuckles.

He did not do it gently. He touched, and then he closed his teeth around her bone.

Need screamed up in her, for him and for this moment she had always hungered after. She cried out and pulled her hand free to finally, finally, bury her fingers in his hair. And that, too, was as she had known it would be, thick and tangled, slick and soft.

She wanted to weep. He was her love . . . her fierce and strong friend, and, as always, he made her brave and strong.

She shrugged the robe off her shoulders and felt the heated kiss of Sun on her naked skin. He watched her face change. Her eyes were dark with turbulence, then brilliance caught them. She had made him feel when he would just as easily have died. And now, for this one time, she was his.

She hurled herself at him and closed her mouth over his.

He had wanted to love her with the care she deserved, with the reverence that *Ma'heo'o* demanded. But the heat of her punched into him, and he knew he could only be the man he was. He pulled off his breechclout and dragged her hard and suddenly against him. Eagle felt the smooth-hard texture of his body, then his tongue took from her the last of her air.

Rough, relentless, it sparred with hers and challenged her. She felt pain shimmy and fade as his lips crushed hers against her teeth. Then she dug her fingers into his shoulders and gave it all back.

Once, just once, she would know all of him, but he was all she had ever needed.

She felt him rise hard and rigid against her belly. Without moving her mouth from his, she sank to the robe, dragging him with her. They fell, limbs twined with limbs, and she writhed with the full, hot weight of him atop her.

He found the spot behind her ear, but he did not kiss it. He buried his face there as his hand closed over her breast. His breath, intimate and damp against her neck, made an agony of wanting settle into her womb.

She arched her back, pressing herself into his palm until his thumb found her nipple and stroked there. He did not ask her if he hurt her. He knew her cry for what it was. Her love, her wanting, rocked him. She would be his forever, even if all he ever had of her was the memory of this time.

He touched his mouth where his thumb had moved, drawing her in between his teeth, and she pressed his head there hungrily.

"Fill me," she moaned, "oh, please, please fill me."

It was something she needed more than she needed life. But even as the words broke from her, she knew he would not, not yet, not this man. He was her dog rope man, a scarred warrior who hurt and loved with ferocity.

His mouth moved, down the slope of her breast. His tongue touched that spot inside her hip, and she bucked. And then, impossibly, he slid lower.

She dug her fingers into his skin, above his hips, where the hard, perfect angles of his waist tapered down. And then her fingers were splayed over his chest, because he was easing away from her, moving until his tongue touched her wet, burning center.

Sensation shot through her, hot and shattering as a bullet.

She had not ever dreamed, had never guessed that it could be like this. He taunted and teased her until she sobbed out his name and her nails clawed frantic trails in his flesh. He rose above her, and his strong, hard face filled her vision. Now she knew. Now she saw. In the throes of this moment, his ghosts were gone.

He felt them go, the last of them. Even as his voice roared free of him at the loss that left him so naked and vulnerable, he plunged into her waiting flesh.

Sun burned. He filled her and she closed around him. He did not moan and move off her. Arms strong and straight, his back arched, he drove into her until there was nothing but the pounding crescendo of too many seasons of wanting.

Together, finally together, they fell into the sun.

IV

Back at the camp, the dying sun turned the horizon orange and red and purple. Eagle knew then that Stands On Clouds had been right.

He had tried to tell her, but her own sacrifice of this sun had caught her blind. She nearly cried out with sudden pain of it. Instead, she rolled hard and impulsively atop Fire Wolf again, skin to skin, heat to heat. But she felt the cooling of passion now as it faded into the old warm, ragged edge of their friendship.

"I would . . . remember you like this . . . always," she managed. "Whenever Sun goes down, I will remember."

She scrambled to her feet again and stood naked against the sunset, hugging herself. He knew he would never live a moment without aching to see her like this again.

Eagle bent to grab up her robe. She shrugged under it, and suddenly she was running away from him. She understood now. Knowing that she would never touch him or love him again was the cruelest sacrifice of all.

The crowd surged forward to meet her when she reached the camp, and Stands On Clouds caught her as she stumbled close to him. His grip was steadying on her arm, and she thought she saw pity in his old eyes.

She knew suddenly that she did not want it.

This hurt, this torment was hers. It was all she had to give to these rites, and it was both precious and monstrous. Her chin came up and her voice came out true when she turned to Walks Far. He waited for her, hovering like a *mis'tai* near the door to the Renewal Lodge.

"My husband, my prayers and wishes have been blessed by *Ma'heo'o*," she recited. "I have brought you back power."

Walks Far's eyes searched hers. *He could not see her pain, her loss.* If she could give him nothing else, she would give him that.

But he did; somehow she knew he saw it all.

"Now you shall have the power I have brought you," she managed, finishing.

He took her hand. His touch was slick and gripping as he led her into the Renewal Lodge once again, and if she moaned with something both more and less than desire when she went into his arms, he pretended not to hear it. He took her mouth hungrily and desperately, in a way he never had before.

V

Late into the darkness, after the moon came, the Renewal Lodge came down, so that only the sacred center pole remained. Long strips of leather were attached to it, and the *Hotame-taneo'o* began the last part of the Dance.

Eagle made herself watch. This, too, was part of the pain she owed.

Stands On Clouds took his knife to Walks Far's chest, gouging two holes just above his nipples. She moaned as skewers of bone were slid in beneath flesh and muscle, then tied to the leather thongs attached to the pole. The shaman did the same to Fire Wolf, and a howl built in her throat before she swallowed it. As the moon rose, other men joined them, chanting and dancing, pulling against their tethers.

Skin stretched and yielded, but it did not tear. The men would not allow it to happen this soon. Now there was only blood streaming and spraying, and their grunts of agony as the Dogs tortured their spirits into a world of hazy illusion where *Ma'heo'o* would talk to them.

She bled with them until Sun touched the sky again, until one by one they fell in exhaustion, ripping their flesh from the tethers. Then, finally, she screamed with horror, and with relief for the end of this nightmare. But most of all, the sound curdled with hatred for the white men who had brought them to this, forever altering her world.

15

Moon When The Horses Get Fat, 1865
Ohmeseheso Country

I

Though her head still felt fractured with worry, Eagle finally finished a hide for Stands On Clouds on her second attempt. But as she crouched in her lodge, smoothing it into neat folds to take to him, her hand faltered.

She studied Stick's small, round face where he sat propped against Walks Far's backrest. A whole moon had passed now, and still he lived. That was good, but her mother's heart needed so much more. She touched his cheek, aching to see his lips become pink like every other babe's she knew. It seemed to her that she had given everything to make it so, and suddenly frustration rose up in her for a Wise One who would not answer her pleas.

She made a sharp, angry sound in her throat, and Stick's black eyes shot open in surprise.

Her heart staggered with intuition. *Now, something will happen now, something will change.* But the babe only gave a stitching gasp that seemed to fall silent again without completion. Then his eyes closed, and he did not do it again.

She moaned, fisting her hands and relinquishing hope once again.

She forced herself back to her feet. She would put him in the sun, she decided. That would not be breaking her vow to treat him like a normal babe. All around the Sioux-Cheyenne-Arapaho encampment, wee ones played in the warm rays or hung from tree limbs to learn silence.

She gathered Stick up and took him outside to lean his cradleboard against the lodge. Sun's healing strength was nearly baking there; though she was not satisfied, it was enough. She made herself turn away, leaving him long enough to deliver the hide to the shaman.

She hurried through the *Ohmeseheso* and *So'taa'e* camps, her skin feeling itchy as hundreds of eyes watched her. She knew that squaws looked up from their work and grandfathers paused in their gaming to know that she was about, doing her chores. That meant that the babe who had brought about the Dance still lived, and that was a good omen for all of them.

She did not return anyone's gaze until Woman With White Child stopped her.

"Stands On Clouds is helping with a backwards birth. He is not at his lodge."

Eagle sighed. She would have to return later, then, leaving Stick one more time.

"I could give him that when he returns," Woman With White Child offered suddenly.

Eagle chewed her lip. There was no true reason why she had to deliver the hide herself, except perhaps that she wanted to. But she needed to be with her child more. She handed the piece over and began jogging back toward the *Hotame-taneo'o* camp. She dodged mongrels and children, but she still kept her eyes averted from the people she passed. She could not bear the squeals and cries of the healthy babes, and her heart lurched at the thought of any encounter with Fire Wolf.

She did not think she could bear falling into his eyes again. Not now, not when her heart and body knew what she would never possess again.

She did not look for the dog rope man, but she had no defense against the sudden, rare rumble of his laughter. As she came upon the *Hotame-taneo'o* camp, the sound carried across the warm spring air, turning her skin to gooseflesh.

He never laughed.

She stumbled, looking around in spite of herself. She found him outside his lodge, and his strong face was alive with a grin. Her heart leapt as she looked where he was pointing.

Stick?

Her babe's face was a swarthy red as he howled his displeasure at being left alone. A chugging sound tore at her own throat. Then her voice tangled with Fire Wolf's as tears began to burn down her face. *Stick was crying.*

The others poured out of their lodges, but the dog rope man caught her first, lifting her in his hard arms. And in that moment she could not think of the sweet danger of touching him again. She wrapped her arms around him and buried her face at his neck while the truth filled her heart.

Ma'heo'o had forgiven her the joy and passion she had known beneath Sun's rays. The powers had given her her son back.

It was the most blessed, sweet gift she had ever known, and she did not question it. She broke from Fire Wolf to race, laughing and weeping, to Stick's side.

II

Word passed from lodge to lodge, and the *Hotame-taneo'o* warriors began swarming out of the camp on impromptu hunts. Night Fighter and Tall Bull picked up the spoor of a trailing herd, and they brought down three fleeing cows. Night Fighter galloped back with the news, jubilant.

He said that the herd was big and healthy, and there were nods and murmurs of excitement. If anyone questioned why the animals were moving north again this season, they did not mention it.

Eagle watched it all as Sun gave the sky over to purple twilight. Suddenly her throat tightened until it ached. Oh, yes, Sun had blessed them in the Dance. They were healing; they were *all* healing.

Wind Woman collected her knives to go out and butcher the kills. Bear was out of camp on a vision quest, trying to understand a strange dream he had had in the Dance. But Walks Far was in camp, wrestling with the carcass of a pronghorn as he reenacted a tale about his own hunt. Warriors howled at his antics, and even Fire Wolf grinned.

Someone jostled her from behind, and Eagle turned to see Falling Bird.

"I think I will go out and help our sister with those kills. Maybe she will give me a piece."

Eagle was surprised. "What could you need?" This northern country had indeed been alive with game since the thaw. She had not thought any of them were bartering and exchanging meat any longer.

Then she recognized the squaw's forgotten, mischievous grin.

"The pizzle," Falling Bird answered. "Bull Bear raids so often now, I could use something to replace him."

Eagle stared at her, and then her laughter came rich and true. At her back Stick began a mewling sound that turned into a wail. She had to pull him off her shoulders and take him to a tree.

She did it with a grin that felt like it would split her face. And then Walks Far caught her up in his arms, twirling her back to face him. His long, muscled legs began to pump against the earth in a dance, and he urged her to join him.

Her heart exploded with gladness. She threw her head back, laughing, and moved into his embrace, so warm and steady. Together, they kept time with the powerful tempo of the drums beating at the camp center.

Word of Stick's recovery seemed to spread even further as the moon rose. *Ohmeseheso* and *So'taa'e* and Sioux came with pemmican and smokes, to dance and to eat on the kills. The old ones sat and murmured. Stick quieted and was brought back to be passed among gnarled old hands.

Then Eagle felt her good humor begin to splinter into anxiety as he was taken farther and farther from her reach.

She closed her eyes, willing herself to trust *Ma'heo'o*. Surely the Wise One would not give him back to her only to take him away. But what if the babe's breath spasmed again? Those grandmothers would not know what to do.

Finally, helpless to fight the protective urge any longer, she took a step after him. The rough, low timbre of the dog rope man's voice stopped her.

"He will be fine."

She spun to face him.

A half-smile lingered on his hard face. She knew he meant only to give her strength, to be the friend he had always been. Yet suddenly, in the moonlight, it seemed to her that he looked just as he had on that dusky twilight of the Dance. Her belly filled with soft yearning again. As the others swarmed about them, she felt the very center of her begin to tighten and ache with urgency.

She could not bear to remember, to want him again.

She took a clumsy step away from him, and his nostrils flared briefly in anger. Then he understood. She could feel his breath quicken as if it were her own.

"Go to your babe, then," he said tightly.

But before she could run for Stick, Bear rode in.

He stopped near the fire, and as the light of the flames caught his eyes, her blood went cold. For a heart-stopping moment, as she stared at him, she could not recognize him. His clothes were disheveled and torn, and his gaze looked as though it burned from a monster-soul.

Silence fell over the gathering, and his laugh rang out, crazed where once it had been rare and deep.

"I found it," he roared. "I found the answer to my dream, and to the death of those spiders."

Conversation erupted again in a curious buzz, but Eagle felt her throat go dry. *What has happened to him? Has some demon stolen his mind?*

A cold sense of premonition shot down her spine. She looked desperately to Fire Wolf for the reassurance he always gave, but he would not meet her gaze now.

Suddenly she knew she had been right all those moons ago when she had feared the Dance. So many of them had healed; many of them were whole again.

But some of them would never be the same.

III

As the moon rose high and swollen, Eagle felt the celebratory mood in the camp begin to flicker like flames dying out to embers. Inevitably tension came as warriors and squaws began darting surreptitious glances at Bear.

He sat alone beside the big fire, hunched and muttering to himself, stroking his carbine as though it were a woman. Pain twisted Eagle's heart. They murmured that he did not speak with full wisdom, but she knew that they would not risk the possibility that *Ma'heo'o* truly had talked to him out in the hills. As she watched, they began to gather around him cautiously, as they would a strange, three-legged beast.

Do not laugh at him. Whatever he says, do not laugh and poke and prod at him. She could not bear it.

Roughly she took Stick back from a grandmother, leaving the old woman grumbling. She shouldered her way into the crowd. He had manipulated her very life in seasons past, but Bear was her kin. She would not see him shamed.

But when he finally looked up to see those who watched him and waited, he spoke with surprising clarity.

"I followed my name-giver," he explained, looking about. "This bear led me east along the Moonshell River. He showed me a blue-coat place that was not there in the winter moons when this war started."

There was an uncomfortable shifting of weight among those gathered. The warriors had been raiding all along the Platte River Road. None of them had seen any such fort.

Then Walks Far rescued him smoothly and sensibly. "How far east did you go?" he asked.

Bear thought. "Five suns of riding."

"We do not often raid that far afield."

"No," Bear said complacently. "That is why we have not seen this place earlier."

The uncertain murmurs of the crowd turned to a drone of excitement.

"I dreamed of it, but it was not like any place we have ever seen, so I asked my name-giver to show it to me," Bear explained. "In my dream we destroyed all the blue-coats there and struck fear in the hearts of the spiders. They ran east again with their babes and their women. This fort is their strongest place, and we triumphed over them anyway. Killing the blue-coats there is better than taking every wagon that comes down that river road. They think they are safe from us in this fort. When we prove they are not, they will flee."

His voice grew stronger, with an echo of the conviction he had always been known for. "My dream of this place came in the Dance, so I know it is true. If we slaughter the *ve'ho'e* there, life will be good again."

It sounded so sure, so simple, yet a cold hand seemed to touch Eagle's spine. *My dream of this place came in the Dance.*

She heard herself cry out in denial. Walks Far caught her arm.

"What is it? Are you ill?"

His voice sounded so far away, although his face was close to hers. She tried to tell him, but her fear was so sudden, so great, there were no words for it.

It did not matter anyway. He would not believe her. No one would believe her if she told them that suddenly she knew the Dance was not yet over after all.

16

Moon When The Buffalo Bulls Rut, 1865
Ohmeseheso Country

I

The night was still and hot, and the war paint ran off the
warriors' skin in rivulets of red sweat that made it look as
though their blood was leaking from their bodies. It seemed to
Eagle to be another terrible omen as she watched the preparations for the raid on the fort in Bear's dream.

The mission would be a massive undertaking. Led by the
Dogs and the Crazy Dogs, their Northern counterparts, the men
of all three tribes had been making strategy for nearly a moon
now. With so much experience and cunning, nothing could go
wrong.

Sensibly, she knew that, yet she could not banish the strange
rolling feeling in her belly.

She watched as Bull Bear, Tangle Hair, and Fire Wolf carried
a *Hotame-taneo'o* flame into the camp circle. Wood for a
mighty bonfire had been laid there, and the most important
warriors from all the societies bore in embers from their
council fires to ignite it. As the wood caught, the flames threw
frantic light over their bodies. The heat became so great it beat
at Eagle's skin and made her eyes feel grainy and dry. She
retreated a few steps as more warriors came on in groups of
three and four, dancing around the fire.

They spun and stomped their feet, their sweat-slick bodies
shining in the feral light. Arrows were shot heavenward, and
precious ammunition was loosed from their guns. The night
reverberated with the weapons' fire.

When the moon set, the crowd began shifting. People drifted
back toward their own camps to watch their societies perform
their last, private rituals. She moved after the throng of *Hotame-*

taneo'o, glancing back once. The shamen among the *Vehoo'o* broke apart to follow, but the other council chiefs remained aloof. This night belonged to the warrior societies, to the men young enough to take vengeance.

She reached the Dogs' fire and hunkered down to see those rites which the women were permitted to witness. The men had begun tying fresh raven feathers into their bonnets and lances. The fur tails on their shields were shaken out and brushed meticulously smooth. With calm deliberation, Walks Far bound up his pony's tail, securing it with rawhide and tucking feathers into that as well.

If he felt fear, he did not show it. She could not remember a time when he ever had.

She squared her shoulders, determined to be as strong for him as he had always been for her. When he glanced her way, she forced a grin that he answered jauntily.

Then she looked beyond him and saw Stands On Clouds approaching.

She was not surprised that the *Hotame-taneo'o* had chosen him to bless their equipment and their mounts. He had worked for them before in the most sacred of times. *In the Dance.* Stands On Clouds looked her way and nodded solemnly.

He was not telling her that her fears were groundless. She knew, suddenly, that he felt it, too.

"No," she breathed, but it was too late. *Ma'heo'o* would, indeed, take something in exchange for the love she had gloried in on that glorious sun of the Dance. And now she thought she knew what that something might be. The shaman went to Fire Wolf, taking the *ho tam'tsit* from him. He moved around the flames with the dog rope, chanting over it, beseeching the powers to honor its carrier. Once she had been terrified of that rope, then she had forgotten it in her rush of feeling for the man who carried it. But always, always, Fire Wolf had meant to use it.

Eagle pushed suddenly to her feet, running from it now as she had when she had first seen it. But this time a wail of incomparable loss built in her throat, a cry filled with the fear she could no longer contain.

II

Fire Wolf stopped his black and frowned up at the sky. He did not like the clouds there, iron gray and bulging low as though to smother Grandmother Earth. If this was indeed a mission that Sun had endorsed, then it seemed to him that its strong, sure rays should accompany them.

He felt his belly twist, and put his hand to the *ho tam'tsit* at his hip.

In some part of his soul, he had expected it to vibrate with its life and its deadly message. It surprised him to find it cool and coiled under his palm.

He would not use it then, at least not on this sun.

Some of the tension in his body eased. He pushed his mount around with his heel to survey the scene before him. Bear had led the thousands of warriors to this culvert hidden among a swell of hills. To the south, where the mounds tapered down, he said the fort would be waiting for them.

The men were avid to descend upon it immediately, but that would not be the way of this raid. As Fire Wolf watched, Bull Bear and the other warrior chiefs began riding among the throng, hissing orders of furtive silence. They would camp here, then wait until dawn to attack with cunning and stealth. That had been agreed upon before the Shield Dance had even begun, but now, this close to their prey, the men were restless. Fire Wolf thought that they were like wolves who had not known they were hungry until their nostrils caught a blood-tainted wind.

"If he is wrong, they will kill him," Tangle Hair said, riding up beside him.

"No."

Fire Wolf did not dispute the men's mood, but he had been in that Dance, had been an integral part of it. He knew, somehow, that nothing that came of those rites would be a lie. Bear's vision would be accurate, and the mystery fort would be beyond the hills.

But Tangle Hair had not felt the sun in that Dance. "I would see for myself," he persisted, "before I am called upon to rescue his mangy hide."

He rode out again. Fire Wolf scowled. He trusted the dream, but it would not hurt to see this place, to know its every nook and cranny if *Ma'heo'o* would ultimately have him choose a spot at which to plant his deadly rope.

They trotted at a quiet, gentle pace, winding their way through the concealing swells of earth. Then Tangle Hair tilted his head back, tasting the wind. It was sour and heavy with the smell of excrement and old meat. In Tangle Hair's experience, nothing smelled quite like a white man.

Addled though he might seem, Bear had been right. There was some sort of spider camp just beyond this hill.

Beside him, Fire Wolf dropped lightly to the ground and began crawling up the next slope on his belly.

The Moonshell was a strong river, and it nourished a wide tangle of trees along its banks. But at one spot the earth had been denuded. The trees there had been destroyed until only their stumps remained. In their place was a rickety span of wood arcing over the water.

Bear had talked of that; he had said that the blue-coats used it to cross the river without fighting its currents.

Fire Wolf's gaze moved beyond the bridge to the encampment. More trees had been slain there to erect walls as high as three men. They hid the spiders' dwellings from his view, but there were telltale signs of their invasive life. Several thin rapiers of smoke rose above the fences. There was the sharp sound of metal ringing against metal, and the stink of the cat-tul that the spiders ate. Inside, Fire Wolf decided, it would look much like their Den-ver place.

He looked up at the sky again, and suddenly he understood the clouds. They had gone with the Dogs to Den-ver, too. They had begun this war, and they would end it. Soon, as it had started, it would all be over.

"I am ready now," he said quietly.

Beside him, Tangle Hair gave a breath of satisfaction. When a *ho tam'tsit* man said that, he was prepared to die that the battle be won.

III

The new dawn came heavy and damp with dew.

In the camp hidden by the hills, beads of moisture clung to

eyelashes and braids and the war ponies' coats. Only guns and
bows were warm and dry from the repeated stroking of ready
hands. The men began to stir among their mounts, rebraiding
feathers into manes, but the *Hotame-taneo'o* camp was still as
each Dog communed with his name-giver and spirit-protector
a final time.

Walks Far sat on his haunches, passing his fox-skinned
quiver from hand to hand as he considered his own. He had
been named for a warrior of his mother's people who had been
captured by the Ute. The man had survived starvation and
torture to escape home without even a pony to carry him. Like
that warrior, Walks Far knew that he could endure agony
without dying. It was his special medicine, that he would live
as long as he did not allow his heart to give up, and it had never
failed him.

But this battle, he knew, would be different from all the
others. This battle had been conceived in the Dance.

He pushed to his feet and went to join his brothers before the
thought could take hold of him. Fire Wolf and Bear and Night
Fighter waited nearby, neither speaking nor looking at one
another. Then a flurry of activity came at the edge of the camp,
and Blind Fox rode in, his grin slanty and cocky. He had been
appointed to watch over the fort, and after a season of
apprenticeship, it had been his first important duty as a young
Dog.

"They are moving now," he reported on a rush of excited
breath. "The blue-coats are awake."

Sun speared once through the clouds, then vanished again.
Bull Bear made a slashing motion with his hand, and his men
moved into position.

Now, finally, vengeance will be done, Walks Far thought. He
would make the white men suffer for all the lives and the
losses, for his crippled babe and the sunset when he had
watched his woman grieve for the loss of another man's
embrace.

Before any of the other warriors could react, he vaulted onto
his pony. As he rode for the south gap in the hills, the camp
behind him broke apart. The *Hotame-taneo'o* followed him to
lure the blue-coats from their fort. The Crazy Dogs split off to
the north, to a road Bear had warned of where the spiders

would surely try to flee. The Sioux and the Arapaho vanished with the other warrior societies, melting back into the concealing hills to wait for the ambush.

Only the Dogs made any noise, howling screams of taunting fury that bounced through the narrow valleys. They cleared the hills and rode hard down the last slope toward the river, releasing a flurry of worn and broken arrows. The sacrificial missiles rained down over the spider's plank walls, not expected to kill, but only to antagonize.

Walks Far gave a quick, hard grin at the chaos that erupted inside. The blue-coats' bellows rang with the unmistakable quiver of fear. Their big doors swung open.

Yes, come out. Come out here and die.

Beside him, Night Fighter laughed and leaned forward over his pony's neck until his legs were beneath him. Then he stood and rode straight for the open gate, hooting.

When he rushed past it, he leapt to face the other way, flashing his buttocks at the maddened blue-coats inside. Walks Far followed him, spitting his repeater-rifle through the doors.

They made another pass and another before they were rewarded with the appearance of a gun-on-wheels. Sweating spiders struggled to push it past the walls, their homespun underwear bagging and sagging, some with their suspenders tangled across their naked chests.

Night Fighter leapt around again to clutch his heart in mock terror, then they raced for the hills. Behind them, the tricksters hesitated, then began pulling the big gun-on-wheels backward until the wooden doors swung shut again.

Night Fighter reined in hard. "*Maivish,*" he spat. "Baby birds fluttering back to their nest."

Walks Far stopped as well and eyed the fort. It seemed impossible that they should fail to irritate the spiders into following their decoy, seething after them into the deadly hills.

"Again," he said quietly. "We will harass them again." He began to work at the small sack tied to his breechclout. He pulled out his fire stick and dropped to the ground. A moment later one of his arrows flared into flame.

Night Fighter bellowed to the others. One by one, they began igniting their own arrows.

When Night Fighter and Walks Far returned to the fort, a

hundred small fires already puffed black smoke into the air above the stockade. Walks Far shot toward the area where the animal smell was the strongest. Where there were horses and cat-tul, he knew the white men also kept their grasses, roped into neat bundles.

His arrow landed and there was more shouting. Walks Far saw orange flames lick up once, high enough to be seen over the fence. Then the gates swung open and the gun-on-wheels appeared again.

The warriors swung about, racing once more for the hills. Walks Far reached the first crest and stopped there, looking back. Then his jaw hung. The big fence closed again at their retreat. The fires that had burned so hotly now puffed innocuous white smoke as water doused their flames.

Frustration pounded at Walks Far's temples.

"They know it is their biggest strength," he bit out as Night Fighter and Bear and Fire Wolf skidded to a stop around him. "As long as they stay in there, they think they are safe from us."

Fire Wolf pulled out his fire stick again. "Then we will remove the wall," he said flatly. "We will burn it to ash until there is nothing left for them to hide behind."

He drove his heels hard into his black. Then Bear shouted, making him stop to look back at him narrowly.

"No! They will come to us of their own accord. That is the way I dreamed it."

The ponies began to mill restlessly, the other Dogs impatient and unsure. Too many believed now in the power of the Sun vision. Many others smelled blood on the wind and remembered the butchered wombs of their women.

Bull Bear's voice cracked out over their tense murmurs. "We will keep harassing them until this sun passes," he decided. "Then, if they do not come out, we will go in."

He raised his repeater, his finger at the trigger as though to warn off any man who would defy him. Then, impossibly, there was a roar of voices to the north of them, stitched with the sudden sound of gunfire.

The Crazy Dogs had found white men.

One Dog shouted, then another, though no one understood quite how it could be. The other warriors began to seethe up from their concealment in the hills, chasing after the commotion.

"No!" Walks Far bellowed as the Dogs moved to follow. *Ma'heo'o*, he knew it was wrong. It was some kind of a trick. "The blue-coats are still in their fort! We have watched them, and we know they have not left there!"

Suddenly Blind Fox's voice rang out, shrill in his excitement. "Look! Look! It is as Bear said. They are coming out on their own!"

Walks Far swung back to see the big gates open once again. But this time the spider soldiers came out on their horses, in the neat lines of one of their details. They dragged two guns-on-wheels behind them. But there were not enough of them, and they stopped inexplicably to fire one of the guns-on-wheels at the sky.

Beyond the hills, screams and gunfire and war cries still howled from the area of the road. Suddenly Walks Far understood.

"They are signaling something!" he shouted.

Beside him, Night Fighter's mouth thinned. "The blue-coats were not all in their fort to begin with," he realized.

"No. Many left before we arrived."

"And now they return."

"They have met the *Hotame-taneo'o*. The Crazy Dogs have found someone coming in, not trying to flee."

Below them, from the river, came a heavy, rattling sound as the spider soldiers began crossing their bridge, dragging their cumbersome weapons across its rickety spans. "Those other soldiers up on the road are coming back with food!" Bear shouted over the noise. "These men would warn them that we are waiting, blocking them from their fort. They do not think of their lives yet. They think only of their supplies."

"They will think of their lives soon enough."

Fire Wolf wrenched his pony around. The Dogs followed him as the spiders reached the earth on the other side of the bridge. The *Hotame-taneo'o* drove toward them in a fury, but the blue-coats did not swerve away. They met their enemy head on, occupying them long enough that their supply wagon might get through.

Walks Far felt both admiration and hatred for the ploy. He

dragged his reins aside to swing his pony clear of the melee, but he smelled it, felt it, knew it for the dangerous battle it was. White men and Indians met in a close, tight knot where arrows and firearms were useless. Weapons could not be aimed where men grappled skin to skin.

Walks Far reached the river side of the battle and began pressing in from there. One blue-coat crawled out of the mud and blood, and he shot him neatly. Another weak-kneed *ve'ho'e* tried to run for the bridge, and he cut him off, rearing his pony high above him to shaft an arrow into the back of his neck. But it was not enough. Their deaths were so clean, so painless.

Frustration seemed to make his vision red as Walks Far considered again their insidious theft of the most precious things in his life. He gathered his reins to charge into the fight again when another roar of cannon fire diverted him. Somehow, impossibly, the supply wagon had managed to get through.

Walks Far stared at it disbelievingly. One wild-eyed driver drove his team of ponies on. As the wagon lurched over the rough terrain, a dead blue-coat dropped from the back onto the loamy, churned-up earth. Others sniped from the bed, hidden by their sacks and crates, and five spider soldiers rode in front, their guns cracking and smoking.

But Walks Far had the bridge.

He threw a glance at it over his shoulder. They would survive only if they got past him, but they were twelve desperate men against his near-empty repeater and his arrows. He shrilled a cry for help to those warriors who were his closest comrades. Once and then again, it rang out over the howls and the screams and the fire.

Most of the Dogs swarmed over the wagon, cutting it and its frantic driver from view. But one warrior reacted, answering his summons, racing toward him over the tortured ground of battle as though the very demons of the *mis'tai* world chased him.

IV

Fire Wolf was one of the first to reach the wagon. His black's eyes were white with terror, and foam flew from his lathered flanks. Still the stallion danced to the pressure of his calves, dodging and plunging to avoid the staccato threat of the *ve'ho'e* bullets that came from the bed.

Fire Wolf leaned into the wagon and found a hank of hair. He whipped his pony about, away from the fight, pulling the spider free of the crates he hid behind. The man thumped, screaming, over the slatted side of the conveyance.

Fire Wolf dragged him along beside his pony, his legs bouncing uselessly over the rough, tangled ground. When they cleared the melee, he heaved the man upward until he laid partially prone across the black. He knocked his gun away angrily and laid his knife to his throat.

"For my mother, for the babe who will not walk, for the woman whose life you have tormented," he snarled. "Know what you die for, white man, and tell me if a land you can never truly possess is worth it."

The blue-coat screamed. The sound gurgled and died as Fire Wolf pulled the blade across his throat.

He pushed the body off in disgust and turned about, looking for another soldier who sought to seize a country the Cheyenne had already claimed. Then he heard the unique, pitched signal of one of his closest brothers. *Come quickly. Help.* He drove his heels hard into his pony, pushing him back through the deadly fracas. The cry had come from the river on the other side.

A soldier lunged to his feet, making a stabbing effort toward the dog rope man's thigh. Fire Wolf lashed out with his foot and kicked him away. He looked up again to find familiar broad shoulders ahead of him. They were bent over a pale-skinned corpse clad in blue.

Fire Wolf began to dodge around Bear as well, then he reined in suddenly, heaving his stallion around to look back at his brother. The same unwelcome impression that had nudged him as he passed hit him again, punching into him with the strength of a *ve'ho'e* bullet this time.

Bear's mind had truly gone.

The big warrior looked up vacantly from his chore of methodically severing the dead spiders' scalp, his fingers, his genitals. The orders had been to strike, to kill, to go on until as many white men as possible were dead. Later there would be time to show the warriors' disdain. But for perhaps the first time in his life, Bear had given in to his hatred now.

Blood clumped on his hands and smeared over his mouth, and his smile was blissful, his eyes mad. Then a second signal came from the river, and he focused again, turning Fire Wolf's blood as cold as the river.

No, friend, no.

The big warrior shot to his feet, his trophies forgotten. He roared for his pony, and the roan lunged from the tangle around the wagon. Bear caught him, heaving clumsily onto his back. He rode toward the call of distress like a maddened throng of *mis'tai* ghosts was behind him.

Fire Wolf knew it intimately, that look in his brother's eyes, a screaming, fleetingly sane need to go in honor. *Let him go. Allow him a warrior's death.* Bear had had his vengeance, killing a man as his wife had been slain. Now he chose to give his life away in battle, rather than go on without the woman who had been his treasure.

Let him go, Fire Wolf thought again, but he could not do it.

Another brother, one sane and strong and able, had given the deadly signal, and he could not allow Bear to recklessly jeopardize his life. He could not allow him to steal more kin from his sister, kin her heart could not bear to lose.

He made his decision as Night Fighter answered the signal as well, breaking from the battle at the wagon with his teeth bared. Together, they flew over the tortured ground and down the last slope, toward the brother who had called them and the one who did not want them.

They found Walks Far's agile little pony dancing in the center of the five mounted blue-coats who had sought to protect the wagon. The warrior grinned calmly at his tormentors, prodding them with his rifle when they got too close, but there was something different in his eyes, something lethal and hot.

He did not acknowledge their approach, nor did Fire Wolf and Night Fighter betray their arrival. But ahead of them, Bear screamed, an eldritch sound of release and fury as he raced for the death he craved.

A *ve'ho'e* veered to shoot. Night Fighter took him out, his bullet smashing through the bone between his eyes.

Walks Far howled and drove his pony free of the circle at the

moment of impact. He clubbed one spider hard with the butt of
his gun as he shot by, then he pushed the emptied, useless
weapon to his back and notched an arrow.

Fire Wolf careened into the melee. Four blue-coats remained, their ponies jostling each other until they ended up
shoulder to shoulder, flank to flank. The spiders began retreating toward the fight at the wagon, peppering the air with their
shots as they went.

Night Fighter dogged them from the right, driving them
back. Bear rode at them from the left. The air fluffed at his
cheek as a bullet grazed him, and he swatted at the spot
impatiently, as though it had been a fly. The blue-coat who had
shot looked baffled at his near miss and paused a lethal
moment before taking aim again. Fire Wolf shot him down.

Three left. And when they were gone, perhaps that would
save this brother who did not want to be saved.

He attacked from behind the three survivors as Night Fighter
closed from the front, killing one, distracting the others. He
notched an arrow, and the shaft thudded into another man's
back with a wet, meaty sound. The spider dropped face-
forward over his pony's neck.

He left his last *ve'ho'e* brother wild-eyed, with spittle
drooling from one corner of his mouth. The blue-coat dragged
a hand there, his gaze darting back and forth with the first true,
sick knowledge of his death. A dark blue stain appeared at the
crotch of his *ve'ho'e* leggings. He cried a thin, senseless sound
and shot off a wild bullet that plucked up the grass in front of
Night Fighter. Then he broke for the safety of the bridge as
Bear roared in fury and went after him.

Fire Wolf spurred his black to cut his brother off. There was
a time when their eyes met, when each understood what the
other would do. The rage and betrayal that came to Bear's face
bored a hole in the dog rope man's gut.

For you, little Eagle, may Ma'heo'o *and this brother forgive
me.*

He found the roan's reins and pulled him around savagely,
making him rear. Understanding hit Night Fighter like a
thunderbolt. He struggled with himself for a moment, then he
rode up behind them to cock his arm around the bigger
warrior's throat, spilling him into the dirt.

The *ve'ho'e* raced toward the bridge, his eyes disbelieving as he looked back over his shoulder to see the Indians skirmishing among themselves.

Only Walks Far noticed him go. *None, not one, could live to spawn more.* He howled a war cry and thumped his legs against his pony. The wiry animal strained and sped until Walks Far could feel his muscles quivering beneath his thighs. They reached the bridge first, angling in front of the *ve'ho'e*, and Walks Far twisted backward to aim his arrow.

The spider dodged at the last moment, plunging into the water.

Walks Far felt a bellow of anger hurt his throat. He yanked hard on his reins, his pony's eyes going white as the animal staggered to his knees and struggled up again. Then they were galloping once more, crashing down the reedy bank into the river.

But the *ve'ho'e* was gone.

The soldier's pony lurched up the far bank, shaking water from his hide. The stirrups of his saddle slapped loosely at his ribs, but there were no boots in them. He was riderless.

Where was the soldier?

Walks Far felt his own pony find his footing even as the current tugged at them. He saw the white man rear up from the reeds ahead of him. From somewhere deep in his head, he heard his name-giver shout. *Go back! Get back out of the river!* He pulled his pony around hard, fighting the river. The animal struggled to obey as the water roared into them.

The *ve'ho'e* shot.

Walks Far took the bullet with his arms raised high, embracing the light that rained suddenly and beatifically down from the sky. He felt the pain distantly, a heavy thump that hit into his chest, stealing his breath.

Then there was warmth, only warmth, and the face of a child, young and strong and proud. He saw her breasts straining against her new dress and the sudden, sweet blush of heat on her neck. *My mother had to make this new for me last season . . .*

I could maybe not take my rope off . . .

I will be here waiting for you when you return . . .

As his pony lunged up the bank, all guidance gone, Walks Far slumped over his neck. It chilled the *ve'ho'e* to his soul to see that the warrior was still smiling.

17

Moon When the Cherries Get Ripe, 1865
Ohmeseheso Country

I

The moon was thin with the beginning of a new season as the *Hotame-taneo'o* rode into the copper-colored dawn.

Behind Fire Wolf, Night Fighter, and Bear, the Dogs were silent and strained. Somewhere to the north of them, the remainder of the raiding party returned home. On this detour across the southern Ridge People flats, the Dog Soldiers would say goodbye alone.

Grief for one of their own was impossible.

Something roared up inside Night Fighter's head, telling him that it could not be. They had ridden together for six circles of seasons, had laughed and killed together. He had carried Walks Far's wife to him on the night he was wed. In sacred and lonely times, they had mourned together.

Goodbye?

Beside him, Fire Wolf stopped, scanning the horizon as the moon left. On the back of his pony was lashed the body of the solid, grinning man who was somehow gone.

Night Fighter stopped as well. Their eyes touched and slid away, protecting the pain there.

"This would be a good place." Fire Wolf's voice was tight and strange. Night Fighter found he could only nod.

The dog rope man dropped to the ground and untied their brother's body. They left their ponies and carried it into the wild plain. Behind them, still astride, Bear followed quietly, a look of childlike curiosity on his big face.

Ma'heo'o, do not give him his sanity now.

But even as the prayer came from Night Fighter's heart, even as Fire Wolf laid his burden down into the grass, Bear's eyes focused and knew. A rasping sound of anguish cut from his throat.

Fire Wolf flinched. Night Fighter groaned, and then silence came again as they stood, awkward and aimless, a broken brotherhood.

The sun that had forsaken them for days finally rose. When the heat blistered them and the sweat began to roll into their eyes, death's scavenger came.

The coyote slunk low, belly to ground, lip curling. His eyes were bloodshot and wary on the silent men as his jaws closed over Walks Far's arm. He snarled and backed off, dragging his prize with the effort of short tugs, defying them to stop him. They did not.

Somewhere distant, in an echo of their own mourning, the dog's brothers howled. This warrior was theirs now, to be scattered over the beloved prairie he had died for.

Night Fighter finally dropped to one knee and bent his head, his eyes wet and hot.

Goodbye.

II

The Crazy Dogs rode into the home camp first, and then there was a gaping hole between them and the throng of other societies, a hole where the *Hotame-taneo'o* should have been.

Eagle did not need to see anything more to know.

She screamed. On either side of her, Wind Woman and Falling Bird grabbed her, shaking her so that her voice wavered and her teeth came hard together. But even as they protested that she could not know it was one of their own men who was gone, she knew.

Grief peaked and shattered within her. She felt someone pull her babe from her back, someone else slap her hard. Her head jerked about with the force of it. There was a shout as she groped for her knife and managed to sever one braid. Then someone wrestled with her wrist, taking her knife away.

They thought her grief premature, her frenzy unfounded. They did not know.

She had been punished for the Dance, and it had killed one of her own.

III

The Dogs appeared as the next sun set.

Bull Bear led them, with Fire Wolf and Tangle Hair flanking his sides. Even as they closed in on the home camp, Fire Wolf heard the wails of the grieving families. The *ve'ho'e* had been routed, but they had taken eight warriors with them. The warriors had lost seven Sioux and a Dog.

A Dog.

He had known as he had wrestled with Bear at the river. The single shot that had taken Walks Far had sounded impossibly loud in his head over all the other fire. He had felt a violent, ripping pain in his own chest, and he had lunged to his feet to see his brother fall.

There had been no single moment when he considered the pact they had made with the Dance. That had been with him always, a certainty deep at the core of his soul, taunting him, warning him, each and every time he touched his bow.

Where was she?

Suddenly he needed Eagle as he never had, because for all the barriers he had learned to build against grief, she alone made him tolerate the pain when it edged through. She prodded him and believed in him. She made him strong.

Now, this time, they would be strong for each other. *But where was she?*

The other Dog wives emerged from the lodges. Behind them, the glows of fires beckoned, offering respite and peace. But the women were grim and stony-eyed, waiting to know who the spiders had stolen from them this time.

They braced themselves, Falling Bird and Wind Woman at the fore of them. Wind Woman seemed to sway with relief as she picked out Night Fighter's pony and its cocky jog-trot. But when they rushed forward, neither woman went for their own man. When they moved, they came for him.

"Where?" he demanded. "Where has she gone?"

Falling Bird began keening, a wild, ragged sound as she saw which wiry little gelding and which rider were missing.

"Who told her?" Fire Wolf shouted.

Wind Woman elbowed her friend hard enough to cut off her

breath and silence her for a moment. In the quell, her own voice sounded unnatural and flat with her grip on grief.

"No one. She knew. I think she has gone to the river."

"How long?"

"Two suns. We could not stop her."

Too long. Too long alone.

He rode out again, scattering the men who had reined in behind him. He galloped for the water, not surprised but only sick, because of course she had known, just as he knew another death would break her. They would always know each other now with the feral certainty of instinct, because they had shared the Dance.

With Walks Far. Walks Far had known, too.

Suddenly he understood the uncharacteristic ferocity that had goaded the warrior into fighting so relentlessly he had died. He had known that the spiders had taken everything from him, had taken his most precious possession. He had understood that having given his wife once, he would never truly possess her again.

Ma'heo'o, I could not save both him and Bear, he thought savagely. He wanted to rage against the injustice of such a hopeless tangle, but then he saw her.

She was a huddled, fetal figure near the bank, curled in upon herself against a loss too great. The water rushed by, chugging and mingling with the sound of her sobs. He dismounted and went to her, dread building in his gut, because again he understood without words, without being told. Now that he finally knew how to love her, he thought he might lose her to demons all her own.

She straightened at the sound of his footfalls, looking back. Something unseen slashed through his gut at the dull look in her eyes. Her long, thick hair was hacked off, its flyaway ends lifting and floating in the breeze. Through the blood and grime on her face ran the tracks of her tears.

"Eagle," he said, and something flared in her eyes.

"So," she said hoarsely. "It was my husband, then."

He only nodded, because his throat felt strangled as he waited for some fresh outpouring of her grief, wondering how he would stand it, what he could do. Instead, she rose unsteadily on legs that did not want to hold her. He grabbed her to steady her, and the shudder she gave penetrated deep into his soul.

What he could not know was that she did not recoil from his touch, but from a memory. Suddenly Walking Spirit was with her again, beautiful and vivid-eyed. *Even Hotame-taneo'o fall in love, more fiercely, I think, than other men*, she had said. Eagle gave a strange, strangled laugh. Too late she knew; now she understood. Walks Far had loved her and their child so deeply it had cost him his life. He had given her the very sun, and then he had died so that she might pay for it.

In the end he had been the strongest, the fiercest, of them all.

"*Eeeeiaaa*." Her knees buckled, and this time she let Fire Wolf hold her. She sank into his arms and clung there for what she knew would be the last time. Her duty to the Dogs was finished. Ultimately she had failed them, taking from them one of their own.

"Oh, friend," she began when she could speak again, "I need you to take me home."

IV

Fire Wolf waited outside the lodge Eagle had once shared with Walks Far. Frustration brought rage, a violent pounding at his temples that made him press his hands to his head. In all the years since his wife's murder, he had controlled his destiny. He had offered his life freely to *Ma'heo'o* rather than allow it, or anything more, to be wrenched from him. Now he would lose the woman who was his soul and his purpose, and he sensed that there was nothing he could do to stop it.

Wind Woman came out of the tepee, cradling a bawling, red-faced Stick. She looked haggard and drawn.

"She will not feed him. I think . . ." She shook her head, struggling with something her heart could not fathom. "It is as though she blames him for his father's death."

And then Fire Wolf knew. He understood the monster he faced, the demon that would steal this woman from him, the friend he had vowed with his blood to protect.

"There is a squaw of the *So'taa'e* who is nursing," Wind Woman went on. "She can feed this one—"

Fire Wolf gave a roar of anger that made her back off, clutching the babe protectively. He snatched back the hide flap at Eagle's door, shoving his way inside.

"You are wrong," he snarled at her.

It was as though she had been waiting for him.

Eagle watched him with a sorrowful expression that sent another bolt of fear through him. He had not seen her in the two suns since he had carried her back here to the camp, thinking this is where she meant him to take her. But home for her now was a distant river where a peace-loving *Vehoo'o* let the world of his people slide through his aging fingers. The strong, bright flame inside her seemed to have sputtered and died.

"We did not profane that Dance," he went on, because he had to, because it was his nature to fight to the end. "We did not make a mockery of it by wanting each other!"

A resignation filled her eyes that was even more horrible than her grief. "It does not matter," she whispered. "It is done."

"No! This is still part of it."

She studied him for a long moment, then she nodded. "We touched the sun and captured all its heat and glory. It was what my husband gave us. He gave me you, the Sun, my child." She got to her feet, hugging herself as though to hold her body together. "It was wrong," she managed. "To have it all was . . . too much sweetness for one woman to possess.

"I . . . made my choice . . . when I touched you. I chose you . . . over my husband. I chose my child."

"You made a vow to come to me if he fell!"

"Because I knew you would not claim me. Because you have your rope, and heartache of your own."

He sucked in breath as though she had struck him, but he knew, *Ma'heo'o*, he knew he had told her time and time again that he would never wed her. She would believe him, had always believed him, because he had never lied to her.

But he had not told her that he had learned to fear death again because it would mean leaving her. He had not told her that he had taken her in the Dance because he could not bear to watch her go again to another. She did not know that he had shared the sun with her because once again he had been given a choice, and he had come to love her too much to let his demons steal her away from him again.

He had not told her, and now it was too late. He saw in her eyes that if he said it now, she would doubt him. Her heart was there, true and unjudging. Her love was there for a torn, rogue warrior she had once befriended, never knowing or expecting that her love would make him whole.

He used a cruel, desperate ploy, but he was not a gentle man. "Your husband meant for you to come to me. If you do not honor his wishes, then his death has been in vain."

She cringed visibly, but then her chin came up. "Not in vain," she murmured. "No, never that."

She turned away from him to begin pushing odds and ends into her parfleches. "I have thought about it," she went on. "He knew you well. He knew your memories and your pain. He gave me a man who would not take me, a man I would not hurt even if you tried to stake your claim to me.

"Another choice between a woman and your people would destroy you!" she burst out with a flash of her old spirit. "Now you hold the rope. You cannot give the *ho tam'tsit* away. It cannot be passed on to another until you die! I know what such an obligation would do to you, the knowledge that in any battle you would have to choose again between returning to me and staying with your brothers, planting your rope into the ground! Oh, no, my friend. I will not ask it of you. I will not destroy you, too."

He felt it burn at his hip, and he cursed her and his god because he knew that he could not sway her. To change her mind would be to change the very nature of her love. No vow or promise would ever force her to make him choose in such a way again.

He laughed bitterly at *Ma'heo'o*'s twisted fate.

Eagle watched him until his voice was spent. "He knew I never chose him as husband, that I was given to him. He lived with that all the suns of our marriage, and with his death, he cut me free again. I cannot marry. I must go back to my kin. I would mourn there. I would honor him that much."

She waited, praying that Stands On Clouds had been right all those moons ago, her heart breaking with the certainty that he was. The dog rope man respected her enough to allow her to choose her own path this time. He would take her back to the land of her people, where she could live alone, away from their village, and pay homage to the man who had loved her so much more than she deserved. She would go back to *Wu'tapiu* country, and she would release this beloved friend from a vow he should never have made.

Fire Wolf finally nodded, a hard, angry gesture, and she breathed again. She did it very carefully so that she would not cry out loud.

18

Cool Moon, 1865
Flint Arrowpoint River

I

It was a changed land.

Eagle noted it dispassionately as they crossed the southern prairie. The rich, green blankets of grass she remembered were brown and tangled. She mentioned it to Fire Wolf, but his cold silence hurt her as much as their awkward attempts at conversation.

"It has been a dry summer here," she murmured.

It had been a hungry summer, the dog rope man thought. He saw it in the shoots of tough, hard greenery that punched up from the game trails. Too few animals had passed by here to nibble them down.

He understood why. He had seen signs of other life, alien life that gnawed Grandmother Earth's choicest parts and spit out as waste her most valuable essentials. Twice on their journey they had passed *ve'ho'e* forts where there had been none before. The white-skin spiders had sneaked in here even as the Dogs had driven their brothers out of the north.

It is a hopeless war.

But he did not believe that, could not believe it, because the ache it brought to his heart was too great. Somehow, he knew, the Dogs would kill them all. But now Black Kettle's people would still be starving. How would this woman beside him survive a mourning exile in a place where even he could not detect any strong signs of game? He wanted to chastise her, but when he turned to her and saw her eyes, he felt her pain like it was his own.

Who knew better than he what a gnarly animal guilt was? Only she could set herself free of its strangling hold, and then only when it was ready to let her go.

"Cross here," he said tightly instead.

Their ponies splashed down into the Flint Arrowpoint, committing to the last part of the journey. They rode along a sweeping bend where the cottonwoods and cedars were bare and crooked. When the trees finally tapered down, a smudge of distant smoke appeared on the horizon. The wind that rushed at them began to carry the smell of humanity.

As the camp became visible, the *Wu'tapiu* noticed them as well. The people stirred among their lodges, and then Eagle was able to pick out her kin. She saw their poverty, and her heart hurt anew.

Little Moon, once so robust, was thin and haggard. Sun Roads looked up from her work disinterestedly, giving a lie to her name. There was her father and her grandfather and Black Kettle, looking on stoically as though to learn what new tale of horror this small party would bring. Then Sun Roads seemed to recognize her, and she shot to her feet. She ran to meet them, horror in her eyes.

"What has happened? Where are the others?"

Little Moon reached them, and though her body was wasted by hunger, her eyes were the same, sharp and intrusive.

"My boy—"

"Blind Fox is alive," Fire Wolf answered. "He has learned to fight well."

Her aunt's breath came out of her more easily, but still her eyes searched until they found Stick's cradleboard. "We had word that there was a Sun Dance."

"The babe is healthy enough. Her husband is gone."

Medicine Woman Later approached and began the keening sound of grief. Sun Roads joined in as they led the ponies back to the camp. Then the others began it, too, a slow dirge of respect and empathy, but it was an empty sound that chilled Eagle to the bone.

To them, it is still part of Sand Creek, she thought, *just another death, another tragedy.*

She slid from her pony, bone-weary. Caught the Enemy made a move to steady her, but she pulled herself up one more time, her hand against Wind Runner's flank.

She looked to Fire Wolf. He had not dismounted, but she understood, as it seemed she had always been able to read his heart. He would leave her now, quickly, because it angered and hurt him to leave her at all.

Oh, friend, this little grief now is so much kinder than the torment I would cause you later.

"It was her husband's wish that I take responsibility for her, and her wish that I return her to you," he told Black Kettle. "Care for her well if you do nothing else wise and strong again."

There were some indrawn breaths at his disrespect as the dog rope man jerked his pony around. He heeled him hard, so that the animal plunged forward, and then he galloped back the way they had come.

"He should stay to eat and rest," Little Moon grumbled. "He will ride that pony into the ground."

But Eagle knew he would not do that. Soon he would be the dog rope man again, cold and sane and strong, as though she had never touched him, had never savaged his life.

He stopped once on a low crest to look back at her. Something cruel caught her about the throat at his beauty, at the way the prairie wind lifted his unfettered hair. His spine was straight and arrogant. She cried out without meaning to as the wind moaned his name.

Her wanting of him had destroyed them all.

II

The sun was low and red before she managed to leave the camp. So many wanted news of those in the northern country, and she told them in meticulous, weary detail, flinching only when they asked of the bridge fight. Then she pulled away, the urge to be free from them nearly a physical pain.

Still, her kin went with her as far as the bend in the river, where the trees began. Sun Roads was quiet and watchful as she marked a return trail for the later visits that would ease Eagle back into society. Little Moon instructed her gruffly on her behavior in her solitary moons.

Eagle barely heard her. She clutched Stick hard against her chest as she walked.

She could not do it.

If once she had turned away from this child in the darkest time of her anguish, now she could not bear to let him go. She

had lost everything, had given everything, in her treacherous
fight to save him! It was not fair that that fight would be for
nothing if she kept him by her side now.

She knew that Fire Wolf feared for her life, camping alone.
A raw, harsh laugh escaped from her. She would not die. She
would survive, as she had always survived. But this little one
needed warmth and food and good shelter. There was a
Wu'tapiu woman who was nursing and who would feed him.
She knew that Sun Roads and Little Moon would cherish him.
With her, in exile, his precious life would snuff out.

A moan of protest came from her, drowned out by a faint
shout from the direction of the camp.

She whipped about, her heart stumbling even as her skin
turned red-hot with shame. She longed for the dog rope man to
return, to ignore her wishes and take her back. But it was
Medicine Wolf who hobbled after them, tugging his robe back
against the wind that would rob it.

She felt her eyes grow hot and painful. Her grandfather's
love and kinship had been the first casualty in her struggle to
save Stick's life. She knew then that she had to let Stick go to
him, had to give her forgiveness and regret to Medicine Wolf
if this nightmare were ever to end.

When he reached them, she let him pry the cradleboard from
her clutching fingers. "He will . . . want to . . . try to walk
soon," she tried.

"Once before I helped a man with a short leg. I think I can
fix this boy." His voice was gruff, matter-of-fact, but she heard
the tremor in it. "I will not fail him this time, Granddaughter."

And she knew he would not, knew that he had never truly
failed him at all. He had only been older, wiser, far more
familiar with the deadly bargains that death made.

She pressed her cheek to her babe's one last time. But she
could not speak, could not say what was in her heart. There
were too many words, and the sun was setting.

She let Stick go, and ran before the last hard, small kernel of
her courage could fail her.

III

She wandered aimlessly for three suns until she found the spot of the old *Wu'tapiu* summer camp. She stumbled in exhaustion and stared at it.

On the close side of the river were hundreds of neat, round circles where the grass was thicker and more verdant. The indentations of old fire trenches were still there when she ran the toe of her moccasin over them.

So many of them, so many lodges.

But once the *Wu'tapiu* had been hundreds of families strong. Once, when she had been young and frightened and bleeding for the first time, they had been healthy. When her grandmother had taught her about marriage, when the Ridges and the Dogs had come for her joining with Walks Far, the *Wu'tapiu* had been able to greet them with feasts and gifts.

"Ah," she breathed. She did not want to do it, could not bear to see, but she knew that *Ma'heo'o* had shown her here for a reason. She turned about slowly, her eyes scanning the lonely, windswept prairie.

The Dogs had camped to the west of the *Wu'tapiu*, she remembered, and the Ridge People had set their lodges across the water that sun. Walks Far had set his marriage lodge among his mother's people.

Suddenly she was running, crashing through the dried underbrush that tangled the banks, sliding down into the water. She waded across and clawed her way up the other side. There were no circles here; the Ridges had not camped long enough to spill their tears and sweat and cooking paunches into the dirt, making it fertile. But she knew where Walks Far's lodge had been. There had been a double-trunked tree, and a swell of protective ground beside it.

There.

She went to the spot, dropped onto her knees, and remembered.

The fire had been shallow and banked, more for light than for warmth, and his lodge had been so manly and stark. *He had wanted her so much.* She trembled, knowing that now, remembering his moan when she had reached out a hand to touch his hardness. She remembered his curse when her rope had tangled at her feet. *This once I will hurt you, and then I promise, my woman, I will never do it again.* And oh, how he had tried not to, how he had cherished her and touched her as though she had been a newborn fawn! And she had hungered greedily, never understanding, wanting so much more.

"Oh, husband, oh, *Ma'heo'o,* I am so sorry."

She put her head to her knees and wept.

IV

Cold Maker came insidiously, creeping up on her. She began waking with his frost riming her nose and her hair, and she knew she needed some sort of shelter, but she clung perversely to the misery of cold until the first drenching rain fell. Then the small, hard kernel of her will rebelled.

She did not want to die.

That sun she fashioned a lean-to beside the low knoll at Walks Far's lodge-spot. She used its bulk for a wall and wove a roof from the trees' water-hungry branches. She dug it into the sod on one side and braced up the other with stronger limbs.

When she was finished, she stood, her back aching. A sudden cramp gripped her belly, and she slid down the bank to relieve herself. Her bowels twisted and burned from a lack of meat. For the first time since the moon had begun to wane, she felt a stab of hunger, thinking of food. She fought it back. She had noticed no game since she had come here.

But she knew how to catch fish.

She straightened abruptly and began moving along the river, peering into it. Then she went still again, her heart spasming again with memory.

Even then, even all those seasons ago, she had put her babe first, before her husband.

Her hunger slid into nausea, and she sat down hard, staring unseeingly across the water. She had turned away from Walks Far so that her child could be born safe. But he had come back for her and had found her with the fish, and their reunion had been feverish. *I did love you, I did.* But she had loved her child and her dog rope man more.

No!

Something reared up in her at that, something angry and strong. She had loved them all, each differently, each with a part of her soul that no other could claim.

Suddenly the memories of Walks Far came faster and fiercer. There was the turnip fight on the Cedar River, when he had bounced over the back of her contrary old mare. And the hunt feast when she had told him that he had put a babe inside her. She remembered him holding her after she had killed the boar, and dancing with him the night Stick had gotten well. The ache to touch him again, to feel his smooth skin beneath her palms, was suffocating.

Oh, *Ma'heo'o*, they had known so few seasons, but through them all, when she saw his face, she saw him smile.

Through those few seasons, he had been happy. She had made him happy with the love she had been able to give.

She cried again, but this time her laughter chugged out too, mingling with her sobs.

V

The fish skittered wildly along the bank, flapping itself about until it was perilously close to sliding into the water again. Eagle gritted her teeth against the cold river and clamored out into air that was even colder. She lunged at the fish with her knife, but a vine caught her up short, tangling painfully in her cropped, matted hair.

She yanked her head back, and a thick hank of strands snarled with the weed and brought tears to her eyes. She pinned her evening meal, then she sat back on her haunches, rubbing her scalp. For the first time since her exile began, she looked down at the water and thought longingly of washing. But that was not the way of a wife's true mourning.

She pushed the oily strands behind her ears instead, then got to her feet to see if her kin had left her any dried barley or turnips. They had begun dropping things off for her as the Cool Moon had waned. At first she had snubbed the gifts because it was too soon, and she needed to hurt. But gradually she had come to know, as her kin seemed to, that this starved land would not treat her mourning kindly. It seemed crazy when she considered all the lean times she had known at the hands of the wretched spiders, but she had begun to fear that this time she was actually starving. She felt her body wasting, noticed its functions shutting down.

She had not bled in so long she could not remember when it had last happened. Her milk, no longer needed, had dried quickly and painlessly. Not even her tears would work anymore.

As she left the fish dying on the bank, she felt a flicker of shameful hope. Perhaps her father had been able to bring down a kill by now. Perhaps there would even be meat waiting for her this time.

In the distance she saw a darkened line of trampled grass that told her a pony had come this way recently. She turned into a copse of trees, then she heard a whinny. Her heart thrummed and she took a quick step back.

She could not see anyone else just yet; that would be blatantly bucking *Ma'heo'o*'s rules of mourning. Her gaze flew about and she sought a place to hide, but before she could move, Sun Roads came out of the copse.

"Oh!" Her sister's eyes widened, as startled as her own. But when she would have turned back, Eagle heard her own voice call out, hoarse and unused.

"No, please. Wait!" Oh, *Ma'heo'o*, maybe it was wrong, but this was not something silly and vain like washing. Besides, how much more worse could her crimes against Walks Far become?

"Tell me," she went on. "Please, tell me how my son is."

Sun Roads hesitated, then her old, familiar grin flashed. "First, there is pemmican," she said. "Fresh. Caught the Enemy got a buck. You should eat."

"Ah." Eagle felt her belly twist hungrily. Together they pushed through the vines to the place they had established, a gutted hole with rocks and branches to protect it from the elements and rodents. Eagle thrust her hand inside and came out with a small, warm bundle.

She pushed the sweet little mounds into her mouth. As she chewed, licking the grease and crumbs from the corners of her lips, Sun Roads talked fast, as though trying to get everything out before the powers could hear and punish them.

"Our grandfather has fixed Stick a little moccasin with many layers of our old hides stuck together. It makes that bad leg almost as long as his good one. It is still weak, but Medicine Wolf rubs balm into it every sun and pushes it this way and that, making it stronger. He thinks that soon Stick will be able to put weight upon it, enough to limp. But for now, he can kneel on it and crawl pretty well.

"Oh, sister, he is like your husband. When it hurts and he has to drop back to his tummy, he gurgles and laughs."

A sharp pain went through Eagle's belly, though she could not be sure if it was because of the food, her longing to see her child again, or the fresh memories of Walks Far's jaunty grin. "Yes," she managed. "My husband would have been like that, had he been lame."

"I care for him well, sister. I never take my eyes from him—"

Eagle shook her head at the bleak shadows that came back to Sun Roads' eyes. She knew she was remembering Pot Belly again, but the look was fleeting. Caring for Stick had given Sun Roads some purpose again, a fresh chance.

It was another small bit of healing that the wretched Dance had wrought. And she realized anew that for all the horrors that had been unleashed, there were indeed far-flung seeds of rebirth as well.

"You are happy again?" she asked cautiously.

"Oh, yes. The *Se'senovetse-taneo'o*, the Comanche, have come to share our camp, and that is good, too."

Eagle's jaw dropped, and for a moment she forgot to swallow. The Comanche? What had happened in the moon she had been sequestered here?

"The *ve'ho'e* are calling this country In-di-en Ter-a-tor-ee now," Sun Roads went on. "It has always belonged to the *Wu'tapiu*, so we do not care what they say. But some other people who do not choose to fight the spiders have come here to share it with us."

Eagle's heart lurched. "There is not even enough food here to feed the *Wu'tapiu*."

Sun Roads scowled at that consideration. "But we do not eat less than before," she mused. "I think there is even a little bit more food. With more men, some can travel farther in search of game while others stay in the camp to defend."

That, too, was a new scheme, Eagle realized, brought about

by the travesty at Sand Creek. Something uneasy squirmed inside her. "Tell me more."

"One of the *Se'senovetse-taneo'o* is a warrior named Snake Under The Rock," Sun Roads went on willingly. "Even though I have a babe to care for now until you come back, he has asked for me anyway."

"You have bled?" Eagle asked absently. Her mind was still whirling with the implications of such a thing as an In-di-en Ter-a-tor-ee.

"Last season," Sun Roads announced proudly. "At the next spring hunt, Snake will talk to Blind Fox, and then I will wed him."

"Did Black Kettle put his mark on anything to agree to this Ter-a-tor-ee?" Eagle interrupted. She knew, suddenly, what her sister's answer would be.

"I do not think so, not yet. The spiders want to make amends for the massacre, to be friends again. They say they are sorry and we can keep this land for our own. Later they will give us papers saying this is so."

Papers, always more papers. They would say that the spiders gave the Flint Arrowpoint, but Eagle knew they would not mention those western hunting grounds, the ones so many of her loved ones had died for. Her head hurt with thoughts suddenly sharp and focused again. Somehow, she knew that when they omitted that land from what they were giving, they would somehow manage to claim it for their own.

Soon the *ve'ho'e* would invite Black Kettle somewhere like that Den-ver place. And once again, her uncle would go. Eagle's skin crawled.

Who would die this time?

"The Kiowa are with us, too . . ." Sun Roads rambled, but Eagle did not hear.

She stood unsteadily. "I . . . this is not good, for me to be talking to you so long."

Sun Roads looked crestfallen and guilty. She stood as well. "I can bring you a little meat with the next sun. And Twin Rivers, a woman in the Comanche camp, has a torn lodge cover I could bring. We could meet maybe at this time, when the sun is at its highest."

"That would be good." But even as she spoke, Eagle was already walking, back the way she had come.

She went to her camp to curl up under her lean-to, images of Sand Creek burning through her mind. The dread that built in her tummy was so thick and roiling it made her scramble out from beneath her robe to rush outside and vomit. She sat, shaken, on her haunches. And suddenly she was furious at *Ma'heo'o* and the powers, at the *ve'ho'e* and the *Vehoo'o* and the Dogs. She was a squaw, only a squaw, resigned to follow their whims while they destroyed her children and her world. She knew, oh, *Ma'heo'o*, she knew that what Black Kettle would do was wrong, but there was nothing she could do to stop him this time. The Dogs would be furious, but the ones who would truly suffer, who always suffered, were the women and the babes. *Her* heart would bleed, and Stick would go hungry and this unborn one would—

Oh, Ma'heo'o, *how long had she known?*

She palmed a sudden sweat from her brow, but she could no longer convince herself that she was starving. She knew why her body functions had changed, and why she had not bled. And she knew the last time she had bled.

She had a babe inside her again.

She wanted desperately to believe that another small part of Walks Far lived on, but something in her heart knew it was not true. Fire Wolf had put this babe inside her. She had been with both him and Walks Far that sun of the Dance, but she knew instinctively that it was him.

Her hands began to shake until she had to clamp them together. Oh, *Ma'heo'o*, that was the truth that she could not face, that Sun would heal the dog rope man, too, would give him a second chance and a rebirth. Walks Far had died for all of them, strong and selfless, as he had lived. To believe that her guilt alone had been the cause of it was arrogant and small.

"Aiy-ee," she whispered. She knew what she had to do now. She could no longer hide from it.

VI

Eagle huddled beneath her lean-to for what she knew would be the last time, watching as Sun sank low in the western sky.

She would leave when it was full dark. She thought she would get away cleanly then . . . if Sun Roads had waited for her.

They had agreed to meet at the height of the day, and she thought her sister would be frightened that she had not turned up as promised. She hoped she would wait to assure herself that she was all right. She needed her cooperation; she needed to get her ponies back and what meager stores she would bring this sun.

When the sky became a deep, murky gray, she pushed to her feet. She adjusted her robe around her shoulders and went to find her.

Sun Roads had waited. She heard her stirring restlessly inside the grove of trees.

"Oh!" she gasped when she saw her. "I thought . . . when you did not come . . ."

Eagle put a hand out to calm her. "Hush. Everything is good." And it *was*. Suddenly she felt calm and strong in a spot deep inside herself. How much better to work for the fight Walks Far had died for than to weep and starve here in this forsaken land! She had once been given to Walks Far so that she could work for the Dogs, and now *Ma'heo'o* would have her serve in that capacity one last, desperate time.

She brought her shoulders back. "I need your help. I am breaking my mourning."

Sun Roads looked aghast, then confused. It would take too long to make her understand all of it, but Eagle tried. "I must return to the Dogs," she went on. "I do not believe that these papers Black Kettle would accept are as simple as he thinks. The *Hotame-taneo'o* need to know of them."

She thought of the new babe within her. She could not tell Sun Roads of Fire Wolf's child; it would only make her more determined to keep her here, safe among her kin. But she had to birth him in the northern country; she had to give Fire Wolf this gift. Then, and only then, would Walks Far not have died in vain.

"So you would go alone? That is crazy!" Sun Roads burst out. "You are just a squaw!"

"I have always been just a squaw, but the spiders have not yet destroyed me," she answered quietly. The flat determination in her tone made Sun Roads fall into a miserable silence.

"It is nearly the time when the streams freeze," she muttered finally. "There might be snows before you get there."

Eagle flinched. There *would* be snows. It had taken her and Fire Wolf nearly a full moon to travel down from the *Ohmeseheso* camp, and she did not know the trails and landmarks as well as he did. But she knew some of them, and she had been cold and wet before.

"I will need my ponies," she explained as though Sun Roads had made no protest. "You must go back and move them outside the herd so that I can slip away with them. And for several suns you must tell no one that I have gone."

"But what of Stick?" Sun Roads wailed, and then, finally, Eagle faltered.

She had not allowed herself to think of him. When her heart had tried to touch upon his image, she had pulled it away viciously. If only she could steal him away with her as well! But the journey would surely kill him.

"I will . . . take him back at the spring hunt, when we all meet again. . . ." There *would* be one, she promised herself, and Fire Wolf would take her to it. He had vowed to care for her; he would help her retrieve her babe.

"Love him for me until then," she whispered wretchedly. "Please. I must do this thing."

She gave her a little push so that the girl stumbled to her pony and mounted. Sun Roads looked back at her one last time and opened her mouth as though to speak, then her shoulders slumped and she trotted off.

VII

The moon was just coming up when Eagle reached the *Wu'tapiu* pony herd. She pulled herself up onto Wind Runner. The mare seemed to feel her tension, and was rigid and quiet.

For a moment she did not think she could stand it. She could bear no more loss; she could not leave him. Then she thought of the new life within her, and her heart seemed to shred in two. Her throat closed over a quiet, keening sound.

Sun Roads moved from the nearest lodge as though she had heard it anyway, cradling Stick in her arms.

Tears gathered thick and choking in Eagle's eyes. She memorized the chubby, round silhouette of him against the fire-glow of the lodge wall. He was not in his cradleboard, and one little leg curled oddly beneath him as Sun Roads glanced about to make sure no one was watching, then held him high.

"I will return," she whispered into the night. "Oh, babe, I will come back for you and take you where you belong."

He belonged with the Dogs; she knew that now. Both Stick and this unborn one were as *Hotame-taneo'o* as their fathers.

19

Moon When the Water Begins To Freeze, 1865
Eastern Hunting Grounds

I

The first snows came when she had ridden fifteen suns. The spare, stinging flakes whipped in at her on the wind, clinging briefly to her blanket and to Wind Runner's mane.

It was too soon for snows.

Had she counted wrong? Eagle reined in to fret with the leather strip that kept her old ponies close to Wind Runner. Each sun, when she woke, she marked it carefully so she would know when she had traveled long enough to be nearing her goal. Had she dragged herself up from her blankets one dawn and merely rode on, forgetting to make a notch? Her thoughts were beginning to feel thick and sluggish, and she could not remember.

But if she was wrong, if the snows came now, she did not think she would make it to *Ohmeseheso* country.

She had run out of the stores that Sun Roads had brought her on that last sun, but she had found some of the season's last, rotting berries on the trail. Still, her belly was so hollow it put up a steady ache.

She dropped her reins and let Wind Runner nose among the tough, dry grasses for something she might find palatable. Groaning, she swung her leg over her withers and dropped to the ground. She held tight to her neck for a moment while a cloud of dizziness pushed in on her, then she trudged to her old roan, slipped the bridle over her head instead, and pulled herself onto her back. Wind Runner needed a respite from carrying her weight.

She nudged her with her heels and set them moving again. When dark came, the snows stopped. The moon rose, big and white and cold. A dull pain spread up Eagle's spine and across her shoulders, and the roan mare began to stumble.

She closed her eyes, trying to think. She should be near the Smoky Hill River by now. If only she could find it, she could stop and sleep for a while. She cocked her head and listened, smelling the air. The wind rushed and the grass whispered. The air was bone dry. She changed ponies again and went on.

Her gelding was a bit younger and moved more gently. His swaying motion lulled her and she dozed upright. Then, abruptly, she was jarred awake again.

She was close to the river now. Dawn threw enough vague light that she could see. Her pulse skittered as she picked out the dark shapes of trees ahead of her. She nudged her pony harder to urge him to follow his nose, knowing he would scent the water.

His gait hitched awkwardly, and she knew then what had awakened her. One of his legs had gone.

"No," she moaned. She dropped to the ground and her own knees buckled. She fell bonelessly to kneel, running her hands over his pasterns and shins. She found the heat in his right front leg, a bulging, swollen knot of it.

He could go no farther. She dropped back onto her bottom and stared up into his sorry old eyes, fighting the urge to cry.

Oh, Ma'heo'o, *what had she done, setting out on such an impossible mission alone?* She could not make it on two ponies, not quickly enough, not before Cold Maker settled fully over the land.

The wind groaned, mocking her. She wanted to lay her cheek against the cold, hard ground and give up. Then she felt the gentle flutter of the life she carried inside her. Staggering, she pulled herself up again.

The plains surrounded her, silent and beautiful and starkly naked except for the trees at her back. Somewhere, there were herds out there, buffalo with thick, shaggy coats and rich, moist meat. *Black Kettle would not give the last of them away before this babe even had a chance to hunt.*

She pressed a hand to her tummy, and then she thought of Stick. If she died out here, he would live forever, hungry and impoverished, in an In-di-en Ter-a-tor-ee.

He is a Dog, and I am a Hotame-taneo'o *wife.* She pulled her knife from her belt and closed her eyes, keening, to drag it hard across the gelding's neck.

She jumped back to let him fall. His eyes rolled, stunned at her betrayal. His blood soaked into the ground.

"So sorry," she gasped, "so sorry."

She mumbled a choked prayer to send him up the death road, then she dropped to her knees again to slice the meat from his flanks. She leaned over once, hard on her palms, to wretch emptily. Then she dragged a hand over her mouth and went back to work.

When she had the meat she needed, she worked on the bone, severing it until she had something with which to dig into the ground. The wind was wild with no lodges to break it. When she had a fire trench deep enough to thwart the gusts, she scavenged through the trees for some dead branches and laid a fire.

She skewered the meat over the flames and sat down to wait. Long before it was truly cooked, she groaned and hacked a piece off, pushing it into her mouth.

The pony's flesh was sweet and stringy, and her belly heaved. She swallowed convulsively, pushing down the meat, chewing desperately. "Thank you, old friend," she whispered. "Thank you."

This new babe would live. *She* would live another few suns, as long as this meat lasted her without going rancid. She could not wait long enough to dry it, and she did not want to weigh down her last two ponies with too much of it. But for now, for this one precious dawn, she was full.

Exhausted, she curled up on the grass, pulled her robe over her head, and slept. The wind dried her tears on her cheeks.

II

The next time she was jolted awake, she immediately knew why.

The tall, tough grama that surrounded her rustled with a treacherous sound, a stealthy *chh-chh-chh* that was different from the steady buffeting of the wind. Eagle sat up quickly, her body cold and stiff and sore.

No more trouble. Please, no more.

She had slept most of the sun away, but wan light remained.

She looked out to the prairie and saw nothing unusual. She knew her ponies' foraging snorts too intimately to be disturbed by that. She twisted around to look over her shoulder, and her heart staggered.

Ve'ho'e.

Here? This was the Smoky Hill! This was Dog Country!

She scrambled to her feet, stumbling over her fallen robe, and whipped her knife free of her belt again. Terror made her feel dizzy as she eyed the white-skin. He was alone, and he moved toward her on foot, limping. She knew somehow that the war had lost him, that he had run from his comrades, or had been banished by them. His clothing was ragged and torn, but beneath the dingy dust of the prairie, it showed blue. Her knife nearly squeezed out from her sweating palm.

Her fire, he had seen her fire. Oh, stupid, stupid of her to leave it burning!

She wondered desperately if perhaps he only wanted to share her meat. *Let that be all it is, please,* Ma'heo'o, *let him only be hungry.* Then she mocked her own prayer. His kind had slaughtered her kin for far less cause.

He began speaking in twangy, pleasant-toned words that she could not understand.

"They ain't gonna know it's a squaw scalp. Ain't nobody gonna tell it ain't warrior's hair. Gonna take me back a trophy, I think, eh, girlie? Something to show I ain't the coward they say. What d'ya think?"

"His meat has not turned rotten yet!" she called out, stabbing in the direction of the pony carcass. "Take it! Take all you want."

But he did not understand her, either, though he looked where she gestured, his eyes red-rimmed and bleary. Then he moved toward her, past the pony. He did not want it.

She screamed, warning him off, and raised her knife arm. *The boar, remember how you hit the boar, and what Fire Wolf taught you!* But she had practiced on bush clumps and trees. She did not know if she could kill a man, even a white man.

He was close enough that she could smell him, and her nostrils flared at the intrusion of sweat and urine and grime. "Stop!" she shrilled. "Turn around! *Go away!*"

He lunged for her instead, his eyes as intent as if he were stalking a mule deer. He caught her sleeve, and she screamed again, twisting away. Her doeskin tore when she wrenched free, a swatch coming free in his hand. She fell hard to her knees, and her knife skittered free of her hand.

"*Noooo!*" she howled and hurled herself belly first after it. He did not possess enough of a god to concern himself with the lives he had taken; she could not worry about *Ma'heo'o*, either.

Her fingers closed around the hilt as she felt his grip at her nape. She rolled away from him, kicking, and came up on her haunches. *Move with him. Face him always.* She heard the dog rope man's voice again, and she inched about, sobbing, until she found the right angle to hurl the weapon.

It arced in a dead aim toward the center of his chest. She groaned a sound of revulsion as he dropped, his face frozen in shock. The pony meat, what was left of it inside her, tried to climb up her throat again.

"*Aiy-ee,*" she whispered, beginning to shudder. Her teeth chattering, she moved crablike toward him.

She needed to get her knife back. Oh, *Ma'heo'o*, she needed that as much as she needed ponies to carry her.

She picked up a rock and hurled it at the white-skin. It thunked solidly against his shoulder, but he did not grunt or move. *Oh, please, please, let him be truly dead.*

She edged up close beside him, gagging again from his smell, worse now as his bowels emptied. She was ready to spring into flight at his slightest movement, but still he remained quiet. She pushed hard on his shoulder until he rolled over. Her knife came free with a tug, and she jerked her hands away from it, keening as she dropped it again.

Then her eyes narrowed on a lump faintly visible further out in the grass. She grabbed the knife up, wiping it clean against the grama, and hurried to the spot.

It was some kind of sack. He had dropped it in his effort to creep up on her. And there was a rifle. *A rifle.*

She tucked that grimly under her arm. Then she dug through his canvas pouch, tossing aside what she could not use. There were some of the dry, hard cakes she had first seen in the Dogs' war camp. She kept them and the ammunition that Fire Wolf would covet, but scorned his ratty blanket.

She did not want to pass him as she returned to her campsite, but something drew her, pulling her there even as her skin

crawled. She looked down at him as tired, hot tears filled her eyes
again.

"I am sorry," she whispered, "but I did not want you to come
here. I never wanted to meet you."

She backed away from him, then she ran to snatch up her
blanket. Before darkness fell, she was mounted again, riding
hard and desperately for the safety of the *Ohmeseheso* lands.

III

She woke on the fortieth sun knowing that she would not
make it after all.

It was something that came to her even in her shallow sleep,
a penetrating cold that settled so deeply into her bones that she
ached with it. She stirred beneath her robe, the ground hard and
pitiless beneath her. She smelled snow again and knew it would
stay this time. The clouds were bulging and heavy with their
burden, as eager to empty themselves as a woman was to push
out a ready babe.

She brushed her hair out of her eyes, studying a landscape
she had seen only in darkness when she had arrived at this spot
last night. She had crossed the Moon Shell with yesterday's
sun. Somewhere in this vast land there was a camp full of life
and meat and warm fires, but she saw no telltale lodge smoke
on any horizon. She could not seem to find the place, and now
Cold Maker would spill his snows.

She staggered to her feet. There was nothing to do but go on.
She could not conceive of simply stopping and letting the
Heaven Road call her. It would be easy, so easy, she thought,
looking longingly at the grass she had crushed in her sleep. She
could curl up there again, and perhaps she would never wake.
But that was wrong. It was too . . . hopeless.

She did not want to die that way.

She went to Wind Runner where the mare stood, her big
head drooping. "You are tired, too," she murmured. "Do you
want to stop now? Do you want to give up?"

At the sound of her gentle voice, Wind Runner's head rocked
up again, her eyes vaguely accusing.

"No. We will go on," Eagle whispered. "Of course we will
go on." Somehow, she was unreasonably sure that as long as

this last pony lived, they would survive to save the babe in her womb and the world Black Kettle would give away. She was her only companion now. The roan mare had given out as well, blessing her with more bitter meat to gag down.

Eagle found the leather thong that had once kept the other horses close. With her knife in her teeth, she counted down the notches she had made each dawn. *So many of them.* As she cut one more, they seemed to blur, then sharpen again, her vision pulsing with her heartbeat. The first big, fat flakes began to fall.

Grunting, she pulled herself up onto Wind's back, and the blood-red pony began trudging onward. Left or right? Eagle wondered. East or west? North was wrong; the war camp had not been that far off the water.

In the end it did not matter. She did not think they would find it anyway. They angled slowly west.

After a time she leaned down to rest her cheek against the pony's mane. The snow came faster and heavier, lying upon her.

It made her warm. She thought it was the warmest she had been since leaving her sorry little lean-to on the Flint Arrowpoint. Wind's body heat rose up from beneath her, and the blessed snow was her blanket. It seemed she could not even feel her belly gnawing emptily anymore.

She sighed and closed her eyes. When Wind stopped suddenly, her neck high, her ears alert, the jolt made Eagle roll off her back into the whiteness of Cold Maker's winter robe.

She landed with a thud that jarred her teeth together and made her bite her tongue. For a brief moment pain shimmied through her head, clearing it. She groaned, and then she sat up to follow the mare's keen gaze.

Fire Wolf.

She saw him perfectly, sitting astride his black, his shoulders straight, his hair free. Then the snows closed in once more, her vision dimmed, and she laid back again.

He was a *mis'tai.* Of course, that was it. She had not made it, had failed in her mission, and she was a ghost-spirit, too. *Heammawihio,* the Heaven Road, led to Cold Maker's home, and her friend, her dog rope man, was here waiting for her.

He had died too, then. He had finally found his demons.

But Walks Far should be here. If they were all dead, then

Walks Far would meet her as well. He had loved her more than any man should.

She wanted to struggle upright again, to look for him, but something inside her ebbed and gave up.

20

Freezing Moon, 1865
Ohmeseheso Country

I

Fire Wolf was distressed by Cold Maker's billowing white arrival as well.

He reined aside as the rest of the *Hotame-taneo'o* rode on toward the home camp. For a moment his eyes followed them, their images stark against the swirling snow. Then the freshening blizzard obscured them again, and he turned away to look pensively at the prairie.

He thought briefly of the last, long robe season in this northern country. There would be no more big raids now until the thaw, and such an impasse was frustrating and irritating to him. There had been no true disposition of the *ve'ho'e* as the demented Bear had been promised in his vision. Instead, they had brought more men from the east to spawn and populate behind the tall walls of their forts.

And those men were not fighting back anymore.

Once, in their Den-ver place, the white-hair-faced chief had boasted that his tricksters battled well in the cold. But lately the Dogs' strikes had been suffered by them without any measurable response.

Why? What were they planning?

He did not know, and then, for the first time in his experience, he did not care.

His eyes narrowed on a distant, dark speck in the blur of white air and gray sky. He knew, against all reason, that it was her; it was Eagle.

Not a sun had passed in the last moon that his heart had not pumped without self-recrimination. She would die in mourning exile; he had known that as surely as he knew that her soul

217

would wither from guilt if he made her stay. Now he knew that it had happened. She was surely a *mis'tai* ghost, come to torture him for being a part of the Dance that had destroyed her.

A horrible grief clamped around his gut, then her pony stopped suddenly, and she rolled off into the blanket of white that Cold Maker had thrown down. *Mis'tais* did not fall from their ponies. They rode as though borne on the wind.

He was stunned.

He drove his heels hard into his black as his reaction turned to fury. *Why?* Why had she risked her life to come back here at a time when not even a stupid beast would risk journeying? He wanted to shake her and rage at her for the terror he knew; he wanted to hurt her as harshly as her death would hurt him. Then he reached her, and he let out a strangled sound of disbelief.

She lay sprawled on her back in the drifts, the snow already beginning to blanket her. But he could see that her cheeks were sunken and her arms skeletal where they were flung free of her worn robe. She looked worse than a *mis'tai*, but her belly bulged with life.

His child, his babe.

He knew it with that same instinct he had learned in the Dance, and his ruddy face blanched. She had come back to gift him with this life, with this second chance to nurture and to protect, to make all the right choices.

For a wild moment the old fear gripped him again. He knew, suddenly, that when he had left her in *Wu'tapiu* country, he had done it as much in deference to his own fears as her wishes. Oh, *Ma'heo'o*, he had never truly prepared to keep her, to hold her. He had smoked the Dance pipe only because he could not bear the thought of losing her again to another.

She had known that. In the end she had known his heart better than he knew it himself, and she had granted him his selfish, cowardly freedom, never judging him for it. But *Ma'heo'o* would not let him go as easily. The Wise One would return his demons to him, again and again, until he slayed them or succumbed to them once and for all.

He closed his eyes against the sight of her. Then, slowly, he dismounted and went to his knees beside her.

He gathered her against his chest, bracing her ice-cold body with his own heat. Then he wept for the first time since he had found his wife's butchered corpse.

He had given a young man's heart to Sweet Grass Woman, but he had only a scarred warrior's pain to give to this woman and his child. His heart recoiled one last time from the possibility of failing them, and the rope thrummed at his hip, alive.

He would not use it this sun, but he knew he would use it again. And when he did, he would once again have something precious and sacred to fight for. Once she had banished his wife's ghost; now, with her heroic devotion, she took the last of his fear and left him whole.

II

The eerie warmth that had first come to Eagle at the end of the trail kept with her until it became a discomfort. She tried to struggle away from it, but she could not move, and that, more than anything, brought her back.

She came awake irritably, pushing at the robes that confined her. She heard a sharp voice, one so familiar and precious it made her remember. She was a *mis'tai* now, with her dog rope man.

But that could not be, because she was in a lodge, and the death road had led to a snow-crusted prairie. What was more, she *felt* the heat from the fire trench as it beat at her. And if she and Fire Wolf had died, then Bear had as well, along with Falling Bird and Wind Woman and Night Fighter, because they all surrounded her.

So many of them? Then she knew she could not have died. Somehow, impossibly, the camp had found her.

She gave a hoarse, glad cry. There was something important she had to tell them, but she could not remember now what it was. She struggled again with the blankets they had put on her and finally sat up. When too many hands began tugging at her to help, she swatted them away.

"I am fine," she rasped and was rewarded by the rich, rare sound of her dog rope man's laughter.

Fire Wolf came beside her, hunkering down to sit on his

haunches. His strong face was close and grinning. She stared at him, shivering, marveling at the transformation.

"You should not be fine. I think any other woman would have died, but you are more stubborn than any spirit-monster who would call you to his road."

"Perhaps she will die yet if we do not feed her and that babe she carries," Wind Woman snapped, ever practical, and then Eagle laughed as well, a hoarse, stitching sound that felt as delicious as it was painful in her throat.

She was home.

Falling Bird scrambled up close to her, fretting with her robes nervously. "Your other babe?"

"Ah." They thought Stick had not survived the journey. For the first time since leaving the Flint Arrowpoint, Eagle was able to think of him with a good, strong feeling. Oh, yes, she had done the right thing.

"He stays with my kin," she explained. "I suspected the troubles I would meet on the trail, and I did not bring him. I will get him back at the thaw."

She looked around at them, as though defying anyone to tell her that there would not be a grand hunt this season. Falling Bird nodded eagerly, and Bear's big, empty face smiled so that she felt a pang go deep into her heart.

Wind Woman pushed close with a bowl. *Food.* There were tangy strips of smoked buffalo and more of the flat, hard cakes from the spiders' wagons. Eagle reached for them hungrily, but Wind Woman pulled back.

"Nibble a little at a time," she warned, "until your belly gets used to being full again."

She ripped off a piece of the meat, chewing until her jaws hurt. She thought despite Wind Woman's warning that she would eat forever, that the hole in her gut would never be filled. But almost as soon as she began, an aching weariness settled over her again. She slid back down into her robes, so blessedly thick and warm. The babe inside her moved, as though snuggling down as well.

"This one will push out this season," she murmured. "That is why I had to return." And then, suddenly, she remembered the other reason, and her eyes flew open again.

"Black Kettle would give away the western hunting grounds!" she blurted.

At once their indulgent faces turned sharp. Fire Wolf made a sudden, triumphant sound of understanding that she could not fathom. But she was too tired to figure anything anymore. She turned her cheek to the fur side of the hide and slept.

III

When she woke the next time, they were all there, even Bull Bear and Tangle Hair and Tall Bull. The smells of the lodge made her moan with gratitude that she was alive and whole. There was a pervading odor of damp doeskin and hides mingling with the more subtle, woodsy smoke.

She did not wake gently this time. As soon as she stirred, Bull Bear's haughty gaze pinned her.

"Did this uncle of yours put his mark on anything yet?"

She realized that they did not even attempt to speak of Black Kettle with respect anymore, and she flinched. "He had not done so at the time I left."

"That was forty-two suns ago," said Fire Wolf. Her eyes flew to him, and she knew he had found her traveling notches.

"I think those *ve'ho'e* will invite him somewhere again, like that Den-ver place," she ventured. She waited for their uncomfortable impatience at a squaw's right to an opinion, but it did not come. To her surprise, Bull Bear nodded slowly.

"It is not likely that Black Kettle will travel anywhere until after the thaw," contributed Tangle Hair.

"So we have time," Bull Bear mused.

"I do not like it," Fire Wolf argued.

She looked at his face, his brown eyes narrowed ominously, and felt a trickle of alarm.

"I understand now," he went on. "The spiders have not been fighting back because they plan to have this treaty soon. They are cowards, and they think that by the thaw, they will have what they want anyway without dying for it."

"Sun Roads did not say they are taking the western lands, only giving this In-di-en Ter-a-tor-ee," Eagle tried, but Fire Wolf continued to glower.

"They would not stop fighting because they are giving an In-di-en Ter-a-tor-ee to people who already claim it."

Tangle Hair grunted. "That is true. I think we should go to this *Vehoo'o* as soon as it is clear enough to travel."

There were murmurs of agreement all around, but Eagle felt a shudder of worry anyway.

The last time they had tried to dissuade Black Kettle, she remembered that they had not succeeded.

21

Big Hoop-And-Stick Game Moon, 1866
Ohmeseheso Country

I

Cold Maker rushed over the plains that season with a wrath
and a fury that surprised even the Cheyenne who claimed them.
Confined to the home camp, unable to journey south, the
Hotame-taneo'o warriors were tense and angry. The women
were irritable with their own tribulations; paths had to be dug
in the drifting banks to allow them to do the simplest chores,
and utensils gave out with no fresh kills with which to fashion
more. Those who had not scorned the raided *ve'ho'e* goods of
the autumn moons became envied.

Wind Woman was one of those squaws; she possessed an
alarming, curious cache of spider plunder because she was far
too practical to waste anything. While the wind howled
outside, she dragged it all out for Falling Bird and Eagle to
inspect.

"There are no more of those metal kettles," Falling Bird
complained.

Wind Woman shrugged. "I can only use one at a time, and I
thought extras would be too cumbersome to carry on my ponies
when we move. Try this." She pushed a chamber pot across the
floor toward her.

Eagle pinged a finger against it critically. "I think it will
crack when the flames touch it."

"I can find some use for it," Falling Bird mused, setting it
atop her head like a hat while she dug farther into her friend's
stores.

Eagle laughed, then sat back wearily against some bedding.
The wind eddied up from beneath the lodge wall, chilling her.
Once the cold touched her bones these suns, it seemed she

could never get rid of it. She knew she had not yet recovered from her journey, and she had been home for more than two moons now.

She remembered the agony of pushing Stick out, and she swallowed a moan of fear when she considered having to do that again. She did not know that she possessed that kind of endurance right now. But this new babe would come soon, whether she was ready for him or not.

She could not fail Fire Wolf now, could not lose this child, his gift from the sun.

Wind Woman looked her way and saw her shudder. She scowled as though reading her thoughts. "Do you have any of those turnips left that we gave you? Bring them here for the evening meal," she suggested. "I will cook. You need more rest and food."

Eagle did not argue. She struggled awkwardly to her feet. "That would be good," she murmured. "I will tell Fire Wolf."

But when she left the lodge, staggering slightly as the gales hit her, she moved toward her own tepee rather than Bull Bear's, where she was sure to find him. She ducked inside, sighing as she dropped her damp robe from her shoulders. She let it lie where it fell and went to her bedding. She was so very tired, and she did not want to meet the dog rope man right now. She did not know what to say in answer to his harsh, probing eyes.

She knew he expected her to wed him now. She sensed deep inside herself that something about him had changed and he would not easily be swayed this time, but she could not go to him yet. She understood Walks Far's death now, but the Dance would not be over until she pushed this child out safely and brought Stick back among the Dogs he belonged to.

She dragged her bedding around herself. She would rest for a while, she thought, then she would go find Fire Wolf and take her stored turnips to Wind Woman.

But as soon as she closed her eyes, she felt a dull, warning pain at the very deepest part of her.

She knew what it was, although this was not anything like how it had started with Stick. She struggled upright again, suddenly very warm and breathing hard. The first weak spasms built quickly. This was happening too fast. She got to her knees and began frantically pushing her scant belongings up against the lodge walls.

She would have to get the others, too, she thought. But as she sat back on her haunches, she realized the pain was gone. She held her breath, waiting, disbelieving. For those brief moments, the babe had indeed felt ready, but now it seemed that he had gone back to sleep.

She stood up carefully, hugging herself. Then new pain came, crashing in on her with such sudden, unexpected force that she screamed and doubled over. The howling wind outside snatched her voice and ran away with it. She knew no one would hear her.

She felt another gripping cramp and dropped clumsily to her knees again. Warm, murky water gushed suddenly down her thighs. She whimpered and groped for the rifle she had taken from the dead spider.

It would do; it would have to do. Wind Woman thought she was with Fire Wolf; Fire Wolf thought she was with Wind Woman. She would have to do this alone.

She dug at the floor as the pain came back again, too relentless, too soon. Somehow she managed to stab the gun down into the earth and tamp the dirt back in around it. She squatted and clutched it just as her body gathered itself again.

She screamed as she pushed, but this time it was a thin, helpless sound barely audible even in the lodge. Her head began to swim as the pain closed in on her, leaving her disoriented. Once she thought she heard Little Moon again, scoffing. She swayed in that direction, needing her aunt's bulk to brace herself as she had once before. But no one was there, and she fell clumsily, curling in on herself as the next pain swept her.

If only she had had help.

Suddenly she was angry again at this cruel game *Ma'heo'o* played with her. Why had He not let them die out on the plains in that first blizzard, painlessly warm and sleepy? If she was not meant to save this babe, why, oh, why, would the Wise One taunt the dog rope man with the sweet knowledge of its existence?

She could not let it happen. She made a growling sound in her throat and labored back to her knees.

She grabbed the gun again. When the pain came back, she gritted her teeth and pushed with it furiously. And this time the child came with an easy gush, sliding from her so quickly that she had no time to catch him. She stared down at him, stunned, before she barked a hoarse sound of triumph.

She gathered him up, gnawing through the cord with her teeth. He mewled once, then let go with a thin, strident cry. She gasped and put her cheek to the top of his damp head.

Emotion shuddered through her, but that was different from the way it had been with Stick, too. She had been stunned and overwhelmed by the reality of her first son, and this greeting was sharp and fierce, a glory.

Oh, *Ma'heo'o,* this child was indeed Fire Wolf's son.

He was red and scrawny, for he had suffered just as terribly on their long trek north as she had. But his eyes were touched with gold-brown light and his tiny features were so strong and dominant he should have been ugly. But he was not. He was so beautiful, as beautiful as the man who had sired him.

As her hot tears splashed down upon him, Sun broke through the woolly, snow-laden clouds at the smoke-hole, slanting in red-orange from the horizon. She looked up and cried out. She knew then that if the Wise One had taken life from them, then Sun had truly given it back twofold.

II

Wind Woman heard a shout from the camp, and her heart jolted. But when she ran outside, wrestling the wind for her robe, she found only a small knot of people staring slack-jawed at the western sky.

Heavy, gray clouds hugged the land there, but just above the horizon they burst open, revealing a slice of indigo sky. Sun streamed through the hole in a glorious flood of rose and orange. For a stunning moment the wind ceased, and the snow floated gently down. Then the hole closed again and the storm resumed in earnest.

Wind Woman felt a shiver of fright and awe, then she ran for Eagle's lodge.

She shouted and slapped at the door flap. Behind her, women gathered curiously.

"Does she push it out?" someone murmured uneasily.

"It is true, I think. This babe's life started in that Dance." There had been much talk and guessing about that.

Wind Woman turned on them angrily. "Hush!" she hissed. She could hear no sound from inside, but perhaps that was because of their voices and the wind. She started to call out again, but then she felt rough movement at her side.

"Go in," Fire Wolf ordered. "Go!"

She ducked inside, then clapped a hand over her mouth. They had come too late.

The lodge was a shambles, parfleches and robes strewn against the hide walls. A rifle stuck up incongruously from the center of the floor, and the dirt there was stained dark with blood.

Mother and babe were curled on her bedding.

Wind Woman eased close to them, whispering a prayer. But when she reached them, she cried aloud in relief. The boy-child fretted, and Eagle slept deeply.

Wind Woman crouched and eased the child from his mother so that he could be wiped clean and powdered and snuggled in doeskin swaddling. Eagle did not stir. Wind Woman tucked the little one inside her own robe and went back outside.

Fire Wolf waited, and none of the others dared to speak or speculate in his presence. But Wind Woman had known this man long and as well as anyone could. She reached out for his arm, touched deep by the fear in his eyes.

No man loves like a *Hotame-taneo'o*, she thought, and there is no Dog quite like this rogue warrior. It was good that he had made this child with the woman inside.

She peeked down again at the eyes of the babe nestled at her breast, just to be sure.

"You have a son, dog rope man," she murmured. "I will take care of him now, but someone should be with Eagle when she wakes."

III

The night yawned on and on, and twice Falling Bird brought wood to build up the fire. Fire Wolf kept his ready vigil at Eagle's robes. She did not even move, but once she gave a little moan, as though remembering the terror of birthing his son alone.

His son.

He could not help wondering if the first had been a boy-child or a girl. Now, finally, he did so without rage and guilt. His Eagle, his friend, had made him so strong.

He reached down and took her hand, turning it and studying the dirt beneath her nails. He looked back at the rifle stabbing up from the floor.

I thought I knew courage, but it was fear that drove me every moment until I met you.

It was a thought that humbled him. And though he had not spoken it aloud, Eagle seemed to hear it inside her own head because finally she stirred.

A ghost of a smile touched her mouth at the sight of him, then, content, she began to roll over again to doze. But panic took her as memory returned, and she fought up suddenly, pushing the bedding away.

"He is fine. Wind Woman has him, to care for him while you get the sleep you need."

Eagle settled back, but eyed him warily. "This is not right. You should not be here." She needed to spend her first suns in seclusion with her child. She did not want to risk *Ma'heo'o*'s wrath again by snubbing His laws now.

But the dog rope man only gave her an odd smile. "I cannot think that the old traditions hold true for a child born of the sun."

She shivered, because she knew this babe was just that. Then she met Fire Wolf's eyes, so brown and unique and steady, and she knew that she could no longer deny the need and determination in his heart.

She remembered the first time she had been captivated by that gaze, seasons ago at the hunt. From that moment on there had been an awareness between them of the kinship of their souls. She thought they had recognized each other then without ever having met before.

"This babe will have a father," he said, catching her hand, hurting it.

"Soon," she whispered.

"Now."

"No."

The blaze of anger in his eyes almost frightened her. "Wait before you growl at me. Try to understand.

"I have learned to see my husband's death for the beauty he has given. If you are strong enough to claim me and this child in spite of your rope, then I will have to fight beside you. You have dwelled in my heart forever, and already, always, I have been yours. But the guilt and the loss of the Sun Dance must truly be over before I can touch you again."

He recognized her reasoning as clearly as he had seen that sudden burst of Sun through the snow-laden clouds. "Stick," he said tautly.

"Until I bring him back here, I have failed his father's effort to provide for him. Do you see? Walks Far did not only give you to me. He gave you to his son as well. With his bad leg, that child's trail will be rocky and crooked, and he will need a father who is stronger and more forbearing than most. Ah, love, I know you are that man, and I will come to you once I reclaim my son. You have my promise, my vow. But when next I love you, I must do it without any guilt or doubts. I would have that for us!"

He hated it, but he knew it was all true, and his jaw set hard. As a brother, Walks Far had given to him this woman. He could not live with himself if he did not honor that brother's son now.

"So be it," he said roughly.

She thought he would push to his feet again, angry and frustrated. But he settled back and brought her robes to her shoulders.

"Close your eyes."

And Eagle found that she could, with a peace that settled as deep as her bones.

IV

"No."

Eagle held her son close and backed up in her lodge. Night Fighter looked appalled and miserable. It was not dignified to argue with a squaw, but he could hardly wrench her sun-child away from this one.

He tried reason. "The dog rope man would have your brother name him now."

Eagle felt a rush of remorse at that. Walks Far had so easily granted kindnesses to others, but she knew that with the dog rope man, kindnesses came pensively, from his very heart. That he had chosen to honor Bear touched her, but in the end her chin came up.

She had her own sort of name for this child, and she would see him called by something of its kind.

"I throw tradition to Cold Maker's wind," she retorted. "I have done it before and still stand here to speak of it."

Night Fighter's sharp features pulled into a scowl. Then there was a sound at the door flap, and they both turned toward it sharply. The dog rope man ducked inside.

"She will not give him to me!" erupted Night Fighter, relieved to have help.

Fire Wolf's eyes narrowed. "You are not pleased with my choice?"

Eagle flinched. "It warms my heart," she admitted, "but I do not trust that Bear will understand this child well enough to call him aptly. I would name him."

"You cannot do it," he replied evenly. "A warrior cannot be named by a woman. Think what you would make him."

Her jaw set angrily because he was right.

There was another sound at the flap, and she snapped an invitation for the person to enter. *Ma'heo'o*, she thought, the whole camp would be here soon to argue with her. But when she saw the frail, old form of Stands On Clouds, her breath faltered in surprise.

How had he known she needed him yet again?

"Will you allow me to settle this for you?" He looked from her to Fire Wolf. "I would very much like to name this babe, if you would honor me so."

"Does Bear know yet that you chose him?" Eagle whispered to Fire Wolf. Sometimes, briefly, he was lucid, but more often he was lost in clouds of the past.

Fire Wolf shook his head, then he nodded slowly at Stands On Clouds. "So be it. You honor us, Grandfather."

The old shaman pinned Eagle with his shrewd eyes. "And you, Granddaughter? What do you think of such a change?"

It was right, she thought. This man had once led them to the sun. "Yes," she whispered. "Yes, name him, please."

She finally let Night Fighter take the babe. They made their way slowly to the camp center, allowing all the people to see, to drop their work and follow. Their gazes were fast upon the cradleboard Night Fighter carried. She knew they had gossiped of this child, sometimes maliciously, sometimes reverently, and her heart went once again to Stands On Clouds with a rush of gratitude. They respected him so; they would never speak ill again of any child he named.

They stopped at the campfire, and the shaman moved around to face the throng. Night Fighter passed the babe to him, and he freed the babe from his cradleboard. He held him high for all to see, his naked little body squirming in the shaman's gnarled old hand. His swatch of doeskin blanket whipped in the cold wind, and the babe gave a howl of discomfort. Voices murmured and chuckled, pleased that such a strong voice came from the distressingly scrawny child.

Stands On Clouds brought him down quickly to sprinkle sage upon him and wrap him in warmth again.

"I will give him this name. I call him for the glory of his conception, for the power that breathed life into him. I call him Sun Stalker."

The voice of the crowd sounded again in a wave. Now it was told; it was true. The child had come into the sacred woman in the Dance, and that had to be good because the shaman had honored him.

Eagle did not hear the people. Her pulse was beating hard in her ears. She caught Stands On Clouds' gaze and nodded. Yes, it was good. It was a name she would have chosen, a name that said everything that was in her heart.

She looked to the dog rope man, and for one brief moment she allowed herself to remember that sun again, touching him and feeling his solid warmth all around and inside her. Hunger and longing made her shiver, but even they were not strong enough to sway her mother's heart.

She closed her eyes against the sight of him, because deep beneath her pleasure at the shaman's gift, she felt an ache for the swarthy babe White Antelope had named, the crippled son she had left behind.

V

The snows remained crusted over, hard and impenetrable, well into the time when thawing should have begun. When Cold Maker did not relent, the *Hotame-taneo'o* did what it was in their natures to do. They went up against him anyway.

The sky was an unbroken bowl of vivid blue on the sun they decided to strike out from the war camp and head south. Their women broke down their lodges with a great clatter that rang out in the clear, frozen air. The clamor of activity left no doubt as to their sentiments. They were tired of the interminable cold of this alien *Ohmeseheso* country. They wanted to go home.

Eagle saw Stands On Clouds in the crowd that gathered to watch them depart. There was a gladness in her heart, and she grinned at him beatifically. His creased face broke into a tired smile for her, then he put his cane to the crunching snow and made his way toward her.

"You will be fine now," he wheezed when he reached her.

She felt something twist at the spot of her heart. "I will miss you."

"You do not need me anymore."

Her heart kicked with premonition. "I will always respect your wisdom and your medicine."

He shrugged one bony shoulder. "In time you, too, will possess true wisdom. Now you are still young."

"I have seen sixteen winters."

"And you grow stronger with each, but you are not strongest yet. Still, I think you will do well now. Sun has smiled on you."

She knew that, and she nodded ingenuously. "The worst is behind us."

"No. The worst is always ahead. That is what you must learn. But life and the *ve'ho'e* will teach you. I have given you all I can, and I come to say goodbye."

"No!" But she knew then that she would not see him again. The pain in her gut was real. He had guided her through a time when her clouds were darker than most women ever had to bear.

She put a hand out to him, and he covered it with his own.

"Take care of that babe," he went on. "I have named many, but none as unique as he."

She shifted Sun Stalker's board up onto her back while he gurgled as though speaking intently to himself. He was as strangely garrulous as his father was laconic. "Yes," she promised. "And soon I will have my other son back as well."

Stands On Clouds smiled. "Soon is relative. Time can seem to fly as though on the wings of a bird, even when it is moving at its own tortoise's pace."

She did not understand what he meant by that, but there was no time to question him. The others were mounted and riding out.

"After we camp at the Smoky Hill, Fire Wolf will go to dissuade Black Kettle from this In-di-en Ter-a-tor-ee paper. He will bring Stick back with him."

But the old man did not answer, and the *Hotame-taneo'o* were shouting for her. She turned away reluctantly. The Dog ponies began their slow progress, lifting each hoof high, then punching it down through the snow that would impede them. But Sun remained true above them, and Eagle knew the farther south they went, the more the thaw would be evident.

She put her face into the frigid wind and breathed in deeply. Stands On Clouds watched her go, feeling a sweet regret in his heart.

22

Spring Moon, 1866
Smoky Hill River

I

Dog Country. Oh, it felt so good to be back in this wild, unpretentious heart of Cheyenne land that the *Hotame-taneo'o* claimed for their own.

Eagle stood on a swell of ground looking out at it, the river moving busily behind her. At her back, Sun Stalker kept up his gurgling while the prairie wind beat at them and rushed over the river valley. A covey of birds rose squawking from a nearby copse of trees.

Eagle grinned, savoring it all, then her heart skipped and her smile faded. Those birds would not erupt like that unless something had startled them.

She began running along the river, and when she came to a higher rise, she scrambled up it. At first she saw nothing unusual as she scanned the prairie, just a wolf loping along, head down and tail low as the birds harassed him. Then, out on the horizon, she saw what he had run from, a hundred black, jogging dots of ponies.

It was the Dogs. *Oh, please, let Fire Wolf have brought Stick back to me.*

Eagle began yipping to alert the other squaws as she ran back for the camp. She went to Falling Bird's lodge, because that was where their men would go to talk of all that had happened on their journey. She helped to skewer antelope ribs over the fire while Wind Woman brought in some berry cakes and pushed them into the ashes.

Falling Bird shook out a small piece of painted elkhide. She placed her husband's horn pipe and smoking weed upon it. As they finished readying the lodge, a shout went up outside, and the first tattoo of hoofbeats could be heard.

Eagle could contain herself no longer. She shoved through the door flap, her eyes searching the riders hungrily.

Fire Wolf rode alone. There was no cradleboard or toddling babe with him. Dear *Ma'heo'o*, what had happened?

The dog rope man's brown eyes touched on her, but she found no answer there before they moved off again. Hurt and anger caught her about the throat. She wanted to grab his bridle, to make him stop and tell her. But the squaws pressed past her to crowd all around the warriors, cutting her off.

Bull Bear led the way to Falling Bird's lodge. Eagle hurried after them until the small throng of their brotherhood dismounted there. The other warriors went after their own women, spreading throughout the camp in the noiseless way of raids gone wrong. *But there had been no raid.* Had there? Eagle looked around wildly. There were no injuries as far as she could see, and no one was missing.

She ducked into the lodge and moved up close next to Fire Wolf. "Tell me," she whispered helplessly. "Why? Where is he?"

His eyes turned to hers, and this time she saw the fury there, smoldering dangerously. It seemed to take him away from her, putting a barrier of heat between them.

"We found your uncle at Fort Dodge," he said shortly.

"Dahj?" She rolled the word off her tongue with cold premonition.

"It is a new soldier place on the Flint Arrowpoint. Your people are not with him. They have gone south of there to a res-er-va-shun. I did not see your son. We did not go that far."

Silence fell as the women all looked at him in disbelief.

"I do not understand what this is," Falling Bird murmured finally. "Res-er-va-shun?"

Bull Bear rubbed the trail dust from his strong, tired face. "We were too late to stop Black Kettle," he answered. "He put his mark on a new treaty before we got there. He gave the hunting grounds to the *ve'ho'e*, so his people had to move to a country the spiders chose for them."

II

In the suns that followed, a strange grief swallowed the camp. No one wept or keened, but the squaws went about their chores with hollow eyes. Eagle knew the warriors had not yet counciled about the treaty. It was a stunning, staggering loss, one they would have to consider long and hard before they spoke of it.

As she squatted down at the river to collect some live water, she looked across to the northern banks. *Gone? A mark on a soldier paper says I can never walk there again?* It was impossible to comprehend, but it must be real, must be true, because somehow with that paper they had also locked her son away from her on a res-er-va-shun.

The pain of him dwelling in such a place was a live, angry thing inside her. She snapped to her feet again and noticed Night Fighter moving purposefully toward Falling Bird's lodge. Fire Wolf walked behind him. They would council now. She dropped her water sac to rush after them. She would hear what they planned; no one would stop her.

She ducked into her friend's lodge and curled her hands into fists, ready to argue for her right to be present. As Fire Wolf watched her, something flared in his eyes, a half-amused respect that she had not seen in too many suns. It made her hurt with missing him.

"Sit, then," he said quietly.

She nodded gratefully, moving around behind him to squat on her haunches. Falling Bird followed and settled down beside her. For a moment their eyes met, dark with worry.

"I have thought long and hard about this," Bull Bear began finally, "and here is what I think.

"Only four chiefs made their marks on that paper. There are forty-four *Vehoo'o*, but only Black Kettle and his *Wu'tapiu* chiefs made any marks. Stone Forehead did not, nor did Dull Knife or Sand Hill, so that is not enough to give away land claimed by all of us with our warriors' blood."

"The spiders think it is so," Night Fighter snapped. "They have chosen Black Kettle as chief over all the People."

"They have no right!" snarled Tangle Hair. "If a Pawnee said that Skinny Toes is to be first war chief of the *Hotame-taneo'o*, would that make it so?"

Tall Bull shook his head sadly. "Only the Council has a right to elect new *Vehoo'o*, although they might bow to the sentiments of their people, as happened after Sand Creek."

"None of them bowed this time!" Tangle Hair erupted. "Do we obey the spider white-skins as if we are mongrel dogs to be kicked out of our own lodges?

"I say let Black Kettle go to this res-er-va-shun if that is what he wishes. He is a traitor to pretend to his spider friends that he has any right to consign the rest of us to that place as well."

Bull Bear nodded. "Yes, that is what I have decided. The Dogs will stay here and live as we always have, on the land our brothers have died for."

Tall Bull made a stark smile. "When do the mighty Cheyenne obey *ve'ho'e*? This is all my country. I will hunt on it wherever the buffalo go across it."

"Why?" Eagle croaked suddenly. "Why would Black Kettle do this thing?"

They all looked at her sharply, as though they had forgotten she was there. She put her chin up because she needed to understand. The betrayal of her kin was still sour in her gut.

"The *ve'ho'e* told him they would give him land and presents to say they are sorry for the murders at Sand Creek," Night Fighter explained. "They think they can allot some country to each survivor, as though they own it to give. But the land is down near where the Flint Arrowpoint meets with the Cimarron, south even of the *Wu'tapiu*'s own. Once the People are upon it, they cannot leave it. That is called a res-er-va-shun. And once they leave their own country to go there, the white-skin spiders think they can move onto the ground our people have vacated."

Eagle's belly twisted. She had been right. What the *ve'ho'e* did not give in their paper talks, they cleverly kept for their own.

Falling Bird was the first to snicker disbelievingly. "The spiders would say they are sorry for killing us by giving us land we do not want, then when we are gone they would steal the fertile land of our home?" she repeated. "To that I say thank you but no."

Night Fighter stared at her and her blunt appraisal, then he barked a sound of laughter as well. The others all began hooting until their eyes streamed.

Only Fire Wolf remained silent, his strange eyes setting

angrily on them all. And Eagle keened softly to herself, rocking gently back and forth. Perhaps the Dogs would not honor the treaty, but the *ve'ho'e* still had her son.

III

Eagle left the lodge when Falling Bird passed around horn bowls of simmered antelope and prairie turnips. Fire Wolf's gaze followed her, but he stayed until the moon showed at the smoke hole, long after the others had gone. When he finally went outside, he gazed across the moonswept darkness to Eagle's lodge.

Go to her now.

But he could not. Already he felt the futility of being needed by her and by his people, when he could not satisfy either of them without hurting the other. She had asked so little of him over the seasons. Now all she wanted was her babe so that she could come to his side.

He closed his eyes and saw the haunting pleas in her own that hurt him in a place he could not tolerate. He knew he had already failed her, and he had not even used the rope yet that was hanging heavily at his hip.

"I hurt for you."

The sound of her voice when he had been thinking about her made him jolt. He snapped about to face her, but the words he had been about to say died in his throat. Her eyes were deep and knowing, as it seemed she had always known his soul. All the loss of the past seasons had aged her, but he realized for the first time that maturity had made her achingly beautiful.

"You have heartache enough of your own, I think," he answered tightly. "You do not need to bleed for me."

She seemed to flinch, but then she drew herself up. "This is not your fault."

She understood that now, had figured the heated distance in him since he had come home from the fort. It was anger that he could not do what he had sworn to his dead brother to do. He was her protector, but he could not protect her from this loss, and to the fierce warrior who carried the *ho tam'tsit*, that made him less of a man.

"Our people cannot leave this country and allow the spiders

to think we are ceding," she went on carefully. His face only grew harder.

"The *Hotame-taneo'o* will go nowhere."

"And so the *ve'ho'e* tricksters will come to us."

His eyes narrowed on her. "They believe they have a treaty," he allowed finally.

"Then you must show them that they do not." She took a deep, shuddering breath. "Your people need you now more than I do. You cannot leave them to take me to Stick. If you did the spiders might come here while you were gone."

Her words began coming faster. She had a feeling that if she did not get them out quickly, she would never be able to say them at all. "Stick can wait for us. My kin will love and care for him, and the *ve'ho'e* will not kill the people on the res-er-va-shun, because they are where they want us to be. Now—this warm season—is a time for fighting."

She turned away quickly so he could not see her eyes. She would not hurt him any more with her regret.

"When the season turns, when it grows cool again, I will take you to him," he called after her. "I vow it."

"No! I do not take that vow. I do not hear it!"

She spun back to him, and he looked at her as though she had gone mad. But suddenly cold premonition rustled inside her again. She was afraid that if they did not go to Stick now, right away, the *ve'ho'e* would somehow steal him from her forever. And if Fire Wolf failed in his vow to claim him in the autumn moons, she thought it would destroy him just as his guilt once had.

"Please," she whispered, moving close to him again, looking up into his beautiful strange eyes. But he did not seem to feel her same panic. Surely if her premonition were true, she thought, then *Ma'heo'o* would tell him, too. Surely he would feel it as well if Stick were to be lost to them.

"We can hope that we might go when the moons cool," she said fervently. "But I will never, ever trust the *ve'ho'e* with a vow like that. It is enough for me that we have a plan now, a time I can look forward to when we can fill this hole in my heart. Before you were my lover, you were my friend. I will not see you destroyed by a vow the spiders can make impossible."

It was more than she had meant to say, and her heart

stuttered at the way his nostrils flared. It was so dangerous to speak of the time they had touched. If she dwelled on it, she knew she would not be able to stand strong against capturing it all for herself again.

And that would be wrong.

"Not yet," she breathed. She made a quick movement backward, but the dog rope man's reflexes were as quick as lightning. His hand flashed out and caught her shoulder. She did not twist away from him, though heat swam in her belly at his touch and she had to close her eyes against the hungry intrusion of his.

Finally he made a growling sound in his throat and released her. But a small piece of her died as he turned back into the night, and she watched him go. Suddenly she wondered if any of them would survive what these white men were doing to them.

23

Cool Moon, 1866
Red Arm Creek

I

Autumn came early to the *Tse-Tsehesestahase* plains, and Eagle greeted it with cautious gladness. But the spider trickster men did not arrive in Dog Country at all. They swarmed into the western hunting grounds from their Den-ver, but the *Hotame-taneo'o* met them there, allowing them to come no farther.

Their camp became rich again with plunder and tall blue-coat ponies. It was a defiant spot for the warriors' home base. The path of Red Arm Creek angled north and west, directly into the territory that Black Kettle had forsaken. It was a wild land, more untamed than even the Smoky Hill, and it touched Eagle's heart restlessly with its beauty.

Its grasses were thick, baked to a rich gold and beaten flat and tangled by the winds. There were jutting crests and promontories, swales and gulches. The cottonwoods at the banks were rich and dense, and game appeared among them to drink with belly-filling regularity. The big herd to the north broke up, and the foraging buffalo began to return, their calves grown strong and meaty. It was a place to sustain a large number of people, and many came to support the arrogant stance of the Dogs as they remained, proud and conspicuous, in a place the white-skin spiders thought they had tricked them out of. Pawnee Killer brought a hundred and forty lodges of his Sioux to camp just north of them.

The Oglala were an auspicious addition to the Dogs' ranks, and Eagle thought Fire Wolf seemed less grim at their arrival. One sun she even heard him bark one of his rare sounds of laughter.

He had brought down a calf and a cow, letting their tough old bull run to freedom so that he might sire some fatter meat come spring. Eagle and Wind Woman and Falling Bird rode out with their knives and fleshers to break down the kills. But the rutting moons were scarcely past, and bulls sometimes remained dangerous and cantankerous well into the early fall. Fire Wolf stayed mounted nearby, his repeater cocked on his hip, his eyes scanning the horizon to make sure that the old one he had spared did not return.

Eagle watched a snake pass by Sun Stalker as it angled its way toward a promising prairie dog hole. She eyed the serpent warily, making sure he kept on his way and did not stop to visit the babe whose cradleboard sat propped against a sturdy tuft of rabbitbrush. When he was gone, her gaze flicked hungrily, unconsciously, to the dog rope man where he sat astride his black. She bent quickly back to the kill again even as a startling impression registered in her mind.

Fire Wolf had been grinning.

She looked back at him just as he laughed. The sound tickled her skin into gooseflesh. In the next moment he stood high on his pony's back, holding his rifle to Sun, whooping out a cry.

Falling Bird gasped. "Has he gone mad?"

Eagle shook her head and scrambled to her feet. "What?" she called to him. "What is it?" It could be anything, she thought, from more buffalo to foolhardy spiders. But it was neither. It was Roman Nose.

Standing up, she could see him coming across the plains, leading a throng of fierce *So'taa'e* warriors to bolster the Dogs' numbers even more. The party stopped long enough for him to don his hat.

Eagle fell hard to her knees again and grabbed up her knife. "Hurry! Finish! We will have a feast tonight. The *So'taa'e* come."

Her heart skipped a beat, then tried to soar. She wrenched it back firmly, but her lips still curved into a smile.

Roman Nose and the So'taa'e *and the Oglalas.* Suddenly, she dared to believe that her dog rope man's promise might come to pass after all. With so much strength in the home camp, it seemed entirely possible that he might slip away briefly when the moon chilled some more, just long enough to

make one fleet journey into In-di-en Ter-a-tor-ee, to a place
called a res-er-va-shun where the spiders held Stick.

II

Many lodges were eager and willing to accommodate
Roman Nose, but Eagle knew the visitors would stay with Fire
Wolf and his brothers. She watched them as they shared a pipe
at the camp center. Then Skinny Toes was sent to tell the
Oglala of the *So'taa'e*'s arrival, and she hurried back to the
jutting knoll by the creek, where she and Falling Bird and Wind
Woman had set their lodges.

She began working out a large fire trench there. The air was
barely lukewarm as nightfall gathered, and she knew it would
get colder, but Night Fighter and Bear would want to council
with the others, and the *Hotame-taneo'o* chiefs would come,
too. A lodge would soon become hot and uncomfortable with
so many men crowded inside it.

She had saved the much-favored hump steaks and several rib
slabs from Fire Wolf's kills. As she skewered the pieces over
the fire, she heard the soft pad of moccasins on the flattened
grass behind her.

She straightened quickly and saw Woman With White Child.

"Ah!" she greeted her.

"Friend."

They grinned at each other for a moment, then Woman With
White Child went on, "I have come to see those boys of
yours."

Eagle felt the familiar stab of loss that never truly left her.
Her smile faltered. "Broken Stick is still at that res-er-va-shun
place," she explained. But then a sibilant voice of promise
whispered in her heart.

Soon. Soon now the dog rope man will take you to him.

"At least he is safe from the fighting there."

"Yes," Eagle mused. "That is what I think, too, when my
heart grows lonely for him. But come, I will show you how
bright and lively Sun Stalker has become."

She took up his cradleboard from where it rested against her
lodge wall. He began cooing and gurgling. Eagle bent her head
close to her friend's, and they untied the lacings so that Woman

With White Child could approve his healthy growth. They were still talking quietly when the men began arriving, even more of them than Eagle had anticipated.

They settled around the roasting hump steaks, and Eagle left her friend to hand out the livers and galls she had left on stones near the fire to keep warm. As the men licked the last of the delicate green ooze off their fingers, she hung back, waiting to know when they were ready to eat again.

That was when she noticed that something was wrong.

There were no shouts of bravado and good-natured ribbing as there always seemed to be when warriors of different bands gathered to feast. She looked from face to face in the orange light of the fire. The tense mood seemed to be coming from Roman Nose, and the others felt it and were subdued.

"I fear that being so well known as I am is not always a good thing," that warrior mused finally.

"It lures spiders to their deaths!" said Bear loudly and happily, for he was oblivious to the tension growing at the fire. "They all wish to be the one who kills you, and when their guns are empty, they die instead."

"That is true," Roman Nose allowed. "But because my name is one of the few they know, they send messages to me. They would make me *Vehoo'o* when I am not."

Fire Wolf stiffened. "What have these messages said?"

"Your Dog and Sioux comrades have been fighting well. You have the *ve'ho'e* as riled as hornets when the bear disturbs their hives. They have brought a new chief to replace Shiving-ton, the Sand Creek madman. He is called Han-cock."

Pawnee Killer rubbed his jaw, grinning. "And is he no longer so sure about this treaty his spiders got?"

"He says we have broken it. Still we hunt here and molest their people when they try to cross our country. He says we should vacate this land and go to the res-er-va-shun at once."

Suddenly Eagle realized that Roman Nose was no longer morose. The undeserved honor of *Vehoo'o* had disturbed him, not the blue-coats' messages themselves. Those he would greet avidly and hungrily.

"And if we do not?" Bull Bear asked too mildly.

Roman Nose grinned outright. "Then they say they will send their pony soldiers here to kill us."

A roar of voices rose from the warriors. Let the *ve'ho'e* come.

Eagle looked for Fire Wolf's eyes, for something there that would tell her that what she heard beneath their words was not true. They were saying that the fighting would not taper off with this new season. It would begin in earnest.

The dog rope man would not look at her. Finally she understood.

It was not simply a matter of reaching that dangerous place called a res-er-va-shun. Nor was the problem one of leaving a brotherhood alone at a time of war. He could not go to the Indian Territory and take her son away because those who went would appear to obey the white-skins' edicts.

Sudden anger made her temples hurt. Fire Wolf should have known that all along.

Suddenly she got to her feet and left the council. It was breaking up anyway, but she did not want to hear any more. She got as far as her lodge before the dog rope man reached her, catching her as silently and surely as the first time she had seen him.

She turned on him, her heart thumping, her hands clenched to fists. "I have suffered too much, survived too much, to be coddled now!"

His eyes flared briefly in response, but in the end he only appeared tired. "This war will never truly end until the *ve'ho'e* are gone."

"You knew that when you said we would go in the fall!" Oh, *Ma'heo'o*, she hated the way she sounded, petulant, like a child. And she loathed herself for the flash of pained frustration she brought to his eyes, because it was true she had never let him make that promise. But her premonition of the spring moon was alive inside her again, and fear made her wild.

His fingers bit into her arm, and he dragged her close. "Would you send me in there now, knowing they would think to put tethers upon my feet and lock me away there?"

"No, oh, *Ma'heo'o*, no!" But the hope she had clung to for so long would not gently die.

Each time she dared to reach for happiness, the spiders smacked her hand away as though they were gods, not men, mere men. They invaded and terrorized, and they had taken from her nearly everything she had ever loved. But she would not give them this man and her son as well. Somehow, she would wrench something back, show them they could not have it all.

She was already so close to him she could feel his hot breath on her face, could see the torment in his own eyes. She moved closer in a rush, her eyes wide. She pressed her mouth greedily to his in the way Walks Far had first taught her. But only this dog rope man had ever made her burn.

She felt him stiffen, then he made a deep sound in his throat like a growl. His hand curled into her hair, and he pulled her head back until his eyes found hers. His grip was hard, almost painful, but his voice was tauntingly soft.

"Have you changed your mind, little Eagle?"

She opened her mouth to tell him so, but in the end nothing came out.

"I did not think so. You will not betray his memory now any more than you would betray his heart when he was alive. So take this back with you to your cold sleeping robes. Ache with it and remember it, so that when you finally come to me, you are as trembling and damp as I have been hard and hurting all these moons."

He crushed his mouth down on hers again.

Her eyes widened. "You hate me," she gasped. Had she driven him to that? Then her heart stopped at his rumble of laughter.

"No, vixen fox, I love you, but when you tease me you must expect to be tormented in return."

Her heart staggered until she thought it would stop. He had never said that; she had not thought they were words he could speak. She had seen fever in his eyes and had felt hunger in his touch, but his heart was too scarred; she had never dared to believe there was more.

I love you.

She leaned into him, hungry to tremble, to feel coiled and damp, to take all that sweet agony with her into the nights she would wait for him alone. "I have loved you since before I was born, and I will love you until Sun burns clear of the sky," she breathed. Then she covered his mouth with her own again until he groaned and opened to her.

Mine, she thought, mine, and no one would take him from her. Her hands were on his forearms, but she slid her palms up over his smooth skin, over muscles clenched against a desire that could both soothe and destroy them. It had been so long, so very long, but still she remembered. She found his shoulders again, so broad and uncompromising, and drove her fingers into his hair.

He was her dog rope man, one unlike any other. He found her tongue with his own, and she bit his lip, tasting his blood and his breath as they mingled.

His arms tightened once, hard around her, before he let her go. She stumbled backward, breathing hard.

"Go back to your robes before I am unable to let you go at all," he said tightly. "We will speak more of Stick with the new sun."

But she knew they would not; there was nothing more to be said until the *ve'ho'e* came and were defeated, until this land was recognized as theirs once more. And that would take so many moons, so many seasons.

She turned away and ran back to her lodge. But she did not do it for Walks Far this time. If she gave in, if she loved the dog rope man now, it would be like conceding that Stick would never come home.

24

Spring Moon, 1867
Red Arm Creek

I

Eagle grunted softly as she hefted her lodge cover up to pack it over Wind Runner's rump. She looked out one last time at the cottonwoods, their naked branches rattling in the wind. The Dogs and all their allies had worn out this wild land that had so captivated her back in those moons when her heart had been hopeful. Now it was time to move on, to let it grow lush once again.

The Dogs had decided not to leave the creek itself. They would only travel upstream until they found another place where there was good breath of wind and rich swales to lure the game when the thaw arrived. They would stay at the core of this disputed land until the *ve'ho'e* came to try to drive them out.

She shivered at that as she reached down for Sun Stalker where his board rested against her calf. "What do you talk of, little one?" she murmured as he gurgled. "Do you speak of the sun power who watches over you? Tell him to hurry, please, with his warmth."

As she pulled herself up onto her mare, she gazed out at the prairie, still patched with white. She yearned perversely for the weather to thaw so that the blue-coats might appear. If such an attack came, it would end things and she and her dog rope man could finally travel. This had been Stick's third winter. The *ve'ho'e* had robbed so much of his young life from her, first the moons that he had lain near death and now these seasons spent so far from her side. Did he stumble now when he should walk?

Did he remember her face at all?

She bit down hard on her lip so she would not cry out, then ducked her head in confusion and shame. She did not really want the soldiers to come here as they had once descended upon Sand Creek. She could not wish that upon her people, not even if it meant reclaiming her son.

Could she?

Fire Wolf rode up beside her, reading her eyes. "Soon," he said quietly. "I do not think it will be much longer now. White men do not truly know how to wait."

She believed him because she had to.

I love you.

She said it again with her eyes, and read it in his. Then her mouth twisted into a bittersweet smile as she put her heels to Wind Runner and they rode out.

II

Thirty-five miles to the east a spring storm gathered, testing its strength upon Fort Larned. By nightfall gale winds had blown the snow into great drifts. It did not deter Major General Winfield Hancock, however. His expedition had traveled all the way from Fort Riley to begin this campaign, and begin it he would.

He sent his bugler ahead to the gates to signal their arrival, but the soldier's breath froze in his horn. In the end the column was forced to march in without ceremony. Hancock halloed loudly into the storm and tried to stomp the snow from his boots as he waited for someone to greet him.

Finally a private rushed out from the barracks to take his mount. When no one else appeared, Hancock approached the neat, brick edifice of the commanding officer's quarters and pounded his fist hard upon the whitewashed door.

Major Wynkoop responded almost immediately and stood staring at him, slack-jawed. Hancock pushed past him into the hall, throwing off his overcoat.

Beneath it, he wore his finest dress uniform, its epaulets glittering with gold. "Don't tell me you weren't expecting me," he muttered. "I sent word weeks ago."

Wynkoop shook off his confusion and ushered him into the parlor. As he watched him silently, a dull ache of foreboding grew behind his eyes. There was an impatience and pomposity about this new commander that told him any dealings he had with the Indians would likely be as disastrous as the Sand Creek debacle.

"I received your message, General," he replied evenly. "But I assumed you would hold up a few days, given the weather."

Hancock accepted a snifter of warming brandy as he surveyed the neat room. "Chivington's political demise went well enough by you, sir," he observed.

For the first time Wynkoop gave a genuine smile. He had been removed to this post as punishment, but he had kept his commandant's position when Chivington had lost favor in the East, and Fort Larned had thrived.

"Chivington failed to use his keen wit to its full advantage," Hancock mused, "and he has suffered for it. I have never known a career to survive a court martial. Were the East not full of bleeding-heart liberals, he might have gone on to great heights of glory."

"It was my impression that you're fresh from that coast yourself, General."

"Indeed. I was quite active in some of the more decisive Civil War battles."

"And your experience with our tribes and their customs?"

For the first time Hancock looked confused, but he recovered quickly. "I have never met one of the rascals, but it is my understanding that they are little more than uneducated savages. As Lieutenant General Sherman says, they must be exterminated, for they cannot and will not settle down. The Cheyenne were offered fine land in that treaty, but they did not respond properly. Therefore, I intend to launch this campaign against them. I shall target these Dog Soldiers I hear so much about. They appear to be as deserving of chastisement as any other." He paused a moment. "They are Cheyenne, are they not?"

Wynkoop nodded wearily.

"Of course, if they will agree to abandon their habit of infesting this country, we will spare them," Hancock went on.

"I sincerely doubt that the Dog Soldiers will do that, but I informed all bands that it was in their best interest to report to the reservation immediately."

"Have they quieted down any?"

Wynkoop shrugged. "It's winter."

"Ah, an Indian with a fat pony is quite different from one with a starved mount, you mean. Well, then, this is indeed the time to strike, before the spring grasses can strengthen their herds for battle."

"You might wish to address this storm first."

"We will depart as soon as it clears sufficiently, Major. Have your men prepared to march at a moment's notice." Before he finished, Hancock was up and pacing. "My word," he muttered, "I do hate delays."

III

The late blizzard swept west to Red Arm Creek. Where the snows had once thinned enough to reveal patches of barren earth, now fresh banks had the ponies in the new *Hotame-taneo'o* camp gnawing on the trees for sustenance.

Eagle's heart went out to Wind Runner, her neck craned to reach high on a trunk where the bark had not already been stripped bare by the warrior ponies. She pushed her way up a slope toward her, thinking to shovel her way through the drifts to clear some frozen grass for the mare. But when she reached the top, she found herself looking south again, toward that distant place where Stick remained trapped.

The day was old, and the light was murky. Still, with so much white, it was impossible not to notice the many dots of black that were moving in the distance.

A trailing herd? She squinted, frowning, then a knife blade of terror drove into her chest. Riders. Soldiers.

It was finally happening.

She had waited so long for this. Now all the remembered carnage and anguish of Sand Creek returned to her, rushing in on her until she could smell the blood congealing in the cold wind again. She tried to scream a warning to those down in the camp, but her throat was frozen, and she could only gasp.

Finally sound ripped from her, shattering the quiet.

The *Hotame-taneo'o* spilled from their lodges. She heard their shouts as though from far away, her eyes fast upon the soldiers. And then she was running, not for safety, but toward them, all the hatred of seasons filling her.

She would kill them. She would kill them herself for all they had taken from her.

Hands caught her roughly from behind, spinning her around.

"Do not do it!" Wind Woman shouted. "Do not give them another life. Think of your children."

"They have my child!"

"Then live to bring him back!"

Wind Woman began dragging her toward the hill again. In the camp below them, the Dogs painted themselves and got ready for battle. But the squaws were not willing to wait and witness another *ve'ho'e* invasion of their village. They remembered Sand Creek, too. Even the ones who had not been there knew terror. Some lodge poles clattered down, but more tepees were abandoned amid the whinnying ponies that the apprentice boys drove into camp.

When Eagle and Wind Woman regained the hill, Fire Wolf was there, looking out to the south, studying what she had seen first.

Eagle felt her heart move hard. There was a sweet, fierce exhilaration about him, in the way his eyes shined and his nostrils flared. Finally the *ve'ho'e* had come.

He tried to tell her, but it was not something he could find words for. There was something hot and fast moving in his blood, something he had forgotten and had no longer ever expected to feel again. Finally he had something to fight for. He would meet the blue-coats and he would destroy them, then he would claim this woman and take her to find her son. He would be a man again, only a man, and he would know a man's sweet, simple joys.

He could not tell her, but she felt it. She wrenched away from Wind Woman. "It is all right," she muttered to her. "I am fine now."

And she was. Her dog rope man was whole again.

She felt a shiver trace down her spine, and she whispered to him fiercely. "Kill them. Oh, love, kill them all for me."

"Go to the Sioux camp to alert Pawnee Killer," he told her quietly. "Tell him we will try to delay this skirmish long enough for his men to join us."

"Yes."

She began running again. Wind Woman followed her, and they left their lodges to plow through the snow toward the neighboring Sioux village.

Sun Stalker murmured complacently at her back. She stopped only once to wrench him around to her breasts, then she rode on, holding him protectively and close.

It was the blue-coats' turn to pay.

IV

The warriors drew up hard at the tree line, just before their ponies plunged through onto the open expanse of prairie. Bull Bear put his hand up to signal to the others to hold back.

"What is it?" Fire Wolf hissed.

He did not wait for an answer but dropped to the ground to creep close to the edge of the copse. *Sweet* Ma'heo'o, *there were so many of them.* There were easily fifty hands of spiders out there, probably well more than a thousand.

He knew then that they had targeted this camp, had come intentionally for Dog scalps. This was no random, arrogant sweep of the prairie they thought they had claimed.

Night Fighter slid up beside him, belly down in the cold. That warrior noticed something new, and nearly choked on his astonishment.

"They are laying down their guns!"

"They would pretend to make camp. I do not trust them."

"Darkness comes," mused Night Fighter. "Perhaps they do not know our camp is near and would merely settle for the night."

"They know," bit out Fire Wolf.

One particular blue-coat was striding back and forth in front of the others, alternately throwing orders back to the ones behind him, then scanning the plains up ahead. The soldier chief's eyes paused more than once on the copse where the warriors waited.

"Ride out," snapped Fire Wolf.

After a moment's hesitation Bull Bear nodded his agreement. The warriors pushed out into the snow.

Hancock shouted a wordless sound of triumph that had them

stiffening, but they did not stop again. They drew their weapons up and ready as they saw two familiar figures approaching behind the stranger soldier chief. The dog rope man's eyes narrowed. The first man was the disheveled, dirty trader who spoke two tongues. The other was Win-coop, a man who had betrayed them before.

"Ain't many of them, Gen'ral," John Smith observed. "Reckon you can wipe them out here if you've a mind to."

"There are more," Wynkoop warned tightly. "They've not all gathered yet."

Hancock pushed out his chest. "Regardless of their number, I do not intend to make the mistakes of my predecessor, gentlemen. I intend to give these heathens every chance to surrender before we open fire. Soldiers!" He turned to his troops. "You may stop preparing camp for the time being. Let's display our weapons, shall we? We will show them the might of this United States Army."

He strode to a fire that was beginning to leap in the gathering twilight. "This will do excellently for a backdrop," he went on. "Now then, we will have these Dogs gather there" — he pointed to a spot between himself and the approaching warriors— "and behind me, you men will show the many medals of courage that decorate your uniforms."

There was a bemused murmur of agreement.

Hancock turned back to Wynkoop. "I do believe they are coming to surrender peacefully, Major," he decided. "There are so few of them. They cannot possibly mean to attack us."

"No more than a wolf intends to bring down a buffalo by hamstringing it," Wynkoop muttered.

Fire Wolf, too, thought of his namesake.

He considered taking some warriors around to the back of this beast of swarming, busy white men, just as a wolf would creep up on a bull. They could tunnel in close to the spiders, on their bellies through the snow. But they would be able to snipe down only a few before the battle broke out.

He had only two hundred *Hotame-taneo'o* and *So'taa'e* warriors, and another eighty or so Oglala men on their way. The spiders outnumbered them nearly four to one. The dog rope man did not mind fighting against odds. Spiders especially took their superior numbers to mean superior strength, and it made them cocky and arrogant and careless. But this was different. He smelled a certain doubt among these men, as though the white-skins did not entirely trust their leader.

Disorganized enemies made for the most dangerous fighting; it could not be predicted what they might do next.

No, Fire Wolf thought, it was best to wait. He leaned close to Bull Bear to explain his thoughts in an undertone.

Almost immediately the two warriors leapt apart again, their mounts spinning nervously. From among the spiders one man bleated heartily on his horn. Night Fighter raised his repeater as though to blow the offensive instrument from the bugler's hands.

"Welcome, welcome," Hancock called out. "Make yourself comfortable, sirs, right over there, if you would." He pointed to the place where he envisioned the Indians would sit and listen to him.

"Reckon I'd put that bugle away first," Smith grunted, "'afore Tenely there gets his hands blown off."

"They certainly have no appreciation of ceremony, do they?" he murmured, eyeing the Cheyenne again.

Smith shrugged. "Nope."

"Well then, let's get on with this." He moved back in front of the fire, pleased with the way its light played on his uniform and its ornaments. "Sit, gentlemen, sit," he tried again.

Smith translated his intentions, and the tall, arrogant warrior in the lead grunted something in response. For a moment their conversation barked back and forth.

"Well?" Hancock asked. "Why won't they move?"

"They don't want to get off their ponies. Anyways, I found out that you want to talk to that one in front. What you got yourself here, Gen'ral, is the Dog Soldiers, and that 'skin there is their chief."

"His name?" demanded Hancock.

"Bull Bear."

Hancock's face began to mottle red. "They are playing with us, sir. I am not familiar with that name."

Beside him, Wynkoop groaned. "They appear to be listening, General. I would talk to them now while I had the chance, regardless of your acquaintance."

The general looked back to the Indians, scowling, then motioned to Smith to translate. "Very well.

"As you can see, gentlemen, I am not here to fight with you. I am prepared to hold a council and offer you an opportunity to surrender now without having your camp devastated by the strength of my men."

Smith choked, but repeated. A wave of furious disbelief rose from the *Hotame-taneo'o*, a drone of voices that made the hair rise at Wynkoop's nape. Fire Wolf felt a tightening of his chest at the impossible irrationality of these men he was sworn to fight.

"I told Major Wynkoop some time ago that I was coming to see you," Hancock went on. "But I don't find any of your important chiefs waiting for me. What is the reason? I have a great deal to say to the Indians, but I want to talk with you all together. I will take your surrender when all of your chiefs are present. That so many are missing indicates to me that you're not honorable in your intentions."

"My intentions are honorable, *ve'ho'e*," Bull Bear spat suddenly. "I come here to kill you."

Hancock sputtered at the translation and turned back to his troops. "These scoundrels are clearly not amenable to discussion. Pack up! We shall go to their camp ourselves to find Chief Roman Nose, and perhaps then we will get some satisfaction."

Immediately the *ve'ho'e* fell back to their half-erected tents. A howl came from the warriors that made Wynkoop's blood curdle and his bowels feel weak.

He spun about to find a monster of a warrior coming off the line. Livid rage showed in Bear's face as sanity touched him fleetingly with the horrible memory of his disemboweled wife. Once before *ve'ho'e* had entered his village while women trusted their *Vehoo'o* and their men to protect them. He would not see it happen again.

"Arm yourselves!" Wynkoop shouted and dropped to the snow-packed ground. Then his jaw fell open. Rather than joining the forward surge as Wynkoop expected, two warriors moved to cut off the renegade.

Why? Why are they restraining themselves from a fight?

Almost immediately Wynkoop answered himself. There had to be more of them coming.

Cautiously he moved to his knees again, and then he saw them coming through the copse of trees in the distance, easily eighty to a hundred more warriors. His belly crawled down into his groin.

"Ah, here we go," Hancock murmured as he, too, spotted them.

Roman Nose galloped up with his closest *So'taa'ee*. His medicine seemed to flow into him from the hat he wore, making him look bigger, his eyes deeper and darker.

"No more parley," he snapped. "I say kill him now."

He spurred his pony and drove into the throng of white-skins. No Indian batted an eye, but a frightened blue-coat shot wildly. The bullet seemed to ricochet off the air above Roman Nose's head. Roman Nose reached Hancock unharmed and slapped his quirt against the soldier chief's cheek.

"*Ah haih'*," he said into the quiet, counting coup on him. "I am the first."

Behind him, the Cheyenne roared in mighty approval. Hancock's skin split and seeped red. His troops were too stunned by the missed shot and the inactivity of the other warriors to react immediately.

"I am Roman Nose!" he went on. "If you would speak to me, then speak! But know that I am not *Vehoo'o*, only a man whom your bullets cannot kill!"

Hancock took out his handkerchief and dabbed at the welt on his cheek, looking stunned. "I would speak to all of you together," he decided after a moment, struggling to make his voice strong. "Let there be no woman, child, or brave who misunderstands my words. Soldiers, I believe you have your orders. Let us make for their camp."

"You will find no one there," challenged Roman Nose. "We have not been able to hold back our women and children. They are frightened and have run away, and they will not come back. They fear your soldiers."

"Then, sir, you must get them back. It is treachery on your part that they have fled like this." Then caution shook some of his forced bravado. "It is dark now. You may have until dawn to regroup your people. But I fully intend to move into your village at that time, and I expect to find all of your number there to greet me appropriately."

"So now we're stayin', Gen'ral?" a soldier called out.

"We are staying," he answered.

Fire Wolf backed his pony carefully into the throng behind him as more fires began to spring up from the area of the white-skin's encampment.

"That is it, then?" Night Fighter wondered. "They think to stay here until dawn? Should we move in on them when they sleep?"

"I would rather not fight them in the darkness," Bull Bear mused. "Too many of our men would fear for their souls, that they might not find the death road if they went down."

The others nodded. No one fought at his best when that eventuality lurked sinister at the back of his mind.

"There is something else," Fire Wolf said tightly. "We might delay another invasion of the camp, but some spiders are likely to get through our ranks. Where have our women gone? When those blue-coats find our camp empty, they will push on until they reach some fleeing squaws to kill."

"This is not a fight we can win," Bull Bear said woodenly. "We can spill blood easily, and perhaps die ourselves. That does not bother me. But our women run on weak, winter-hungry ponies. If these blue-coats follow them with their seed-fed mounts, they will catch them easily." He paused, his heart torn. But in the end he was a *Hotame-taneo'o* chief, hot-blooded but wise. "Our mission is to protect," he finished. "Our time for glory is not now."

Fire Wolf's hands tightened on his black's reins. But finally, his jaw hard, his heart hurting with a new kind of frustration, he dropped to the ground.

"Find the women," he agreed tersely.

As the night grew deeper and darker, the warriors slipped away in pairs and in threes. They slashed grimly at their breechclouts and bundled their ponies' hooves in swatches of the buckskin. As they backed their mounts away, what softened, obscure tracks there were appeared to be leading into the parley rather than into the night.

By the time Hancock thought to send a sentinel over to check on them, his Indians were gone.

V

Eagle was not that far ahead of the retreating warriors.

She had returned after summoning Pawnee Killer and his Sioux, riding back up to the herd hill to watch. As the sky fell into night, first one blazing fire, then a handful of smaller ones appeared at the place were the spiders stopped.

Fires?

She did not understand, did not know why the warriors did not just kill those men. But soon it became too dark to see anything, and she pulled her pony around pensively to go after the squaws.

North again.

Anguish built in her. Oh, *Ma'heo'o*, none of this was right. She knew, instinctively, that they would leave this camp for good now, putting even more uncrossable distance between her and Stick.

Suddenly her heart began beating hard. She could not go with them! In a moment, any moment now, she knew it was going to be too late. Her premonition of the Spring Moon bloomed in her again, stark and horrible, and she knew somehow that if she did not go to her son now, she truly would lose him forever.

The first warriors began passing her, returning from the parley, making her even more sure that something had gone dreadfully amiss. She had heard no gunshots, no war cries or sounds of battle.

She groped down along her saddle, her hand slick and trembling as it fell on the rifle she had taken from the dead soldier so many seasons ago. She pulled Wind Runner around again, put her moccasins to her, and began trotting.

Suddenly, another pony jostled hers and a hand came out of the night, snicking down hard over her mouth to stop the scream that built in her throat. Fire Wolf. She could not truly see him in the blackness, but she felt him, knew it was him. She fought him until he made a guttural half-sound of anger and shook her hard.

"It is too late," he hissed, knowing her heart. "It is already too late. Look."

Her eyes went to the camp they had deserted, her eyes wild above his hand. It bloomed suddenly with the horrible, orange glow of fire. Even as she stared, there were flares and eruptions as the enraged spiders burned the lodges and the depleted winter stores the squaws had left behind.

There were sporadic gunshots sounding here and there across the prairie. Even she knew them for what they were, signals from one blue-coat to another as they fanned out, searching for the warriors who had eluded them.

The white-skins were all over now, effectively blocking them from the southern lands and the place where the *Wu'tapiu* had taken her son.

25

Moon When The Horses Get Fat, 1867
Red Shield River

I

The air was warm with springtime, as it had been four circles of seasons ago when all the People had gathered at this place for the grand hunt. Eagle shivered as she had done then, hugging herself as she stood outside her lodge. But it was not pleasure and anticipation that touched her. Her heart was like a stone, heavy in her chest.

The *Hotame-taneo'o* had been on the Red Shield since the Red Arm Creek camp had fallen to the spiders' wrath. Some *Ohmeseheso* and *So'taa'e* and Brule Sioux had already been here, but no one was gathered to hunt this time. It was a war camp.

Eagle sighed and made a move to turn back into her lodge. Abruptly she stopped to stare at it and giggle a little hysterically. How many new covers had she made in the last circle of seasons? She looked down at her hands, still red and sore from the laborious chore of stitching the last hides together, the ones the man Han-cock had burned.

She finally ducked inside to gather up Sun Stalker. Fire Wolf and his brothers were gone, out on the warpath. She had some fat and marrow left over from the dog rope man's last kill, and she thought she would take it to Wind Woman's lodge; they could eat together to stave off some of the loneliness.

It was, she thought helplessly, just another way of waiting.

She pushed what she needed into a parfleche and pulled Stalker up onto her hip. He had seen six seasons now, and he was agile and energetic. He wriggled in her arms as she moved across the little clearing that separated her lodge from her friend's, then she paused, cocking her head. Someone at the camp center was hooting a greeting.

She changed direction, moving that way. More and more warriors from other bands had been coming to join in the fighting. She knew from the news they brought with them that the *ve'ho'e* were not honoring Black Kettle's treacherous treaty. The tricksters thought to keep the land, but they would not give the *Vehoo'o* any of the strange money or food or presents he had been promised.

A dangerous feeling of hope had begun squirming in Eagle's heart again. Perhaps some *Wu'tapiu* would get angry enough to join the Dogs, too. Perhaps one of them would think to bring her son.

She reached the camp center and searched the new faces. Then, suddenly, her heart kicked so hard it made her feel faint. She took an unbidden step closer to the warriors who had just arrived.

It was true; sweet *Ma'heo'o*, this time they really were *Wu'tapiu* warriors.

One man stood at the head of the little group, being greeted by Black Shin, the *So'taa'e* chief. He was Far Away Fox, distant kin of her mother's.

II

"I do not understand your impatience," complained Wind Woman. "You said this warrior did not bring your babe."

Eagle stopped her quick pacing to scowl at her. "But he can tell me of him, how he fares."

"Warriors do not notice such things." She pushed some pemmican in her direction. "You should eat something while you wait. That man could council with Black Shin until the moon leaves."

Eagle bit her lip. She knew what Wind Woman was thinking. There was an unspoken warning in her tone that if Far Away Fox had known he was coming here, why had the warrior not brought Stick if her babe was alive?

"I am going to wait at the camp center," she muttered.

She left Stalker with her friend. The moon was high and full, and as she looked up at it, she took a deep, steadying breath. Then she marched her way toward the water again where the chiefs of all the bands had put their lodges.

There was no communal fire this night; the air was too sultry and still. Crickets screeched in the silence, and Black Shin's lodge walls were rolled up high. She was not *So'taa'e* and had no particular right to eavesdrop here, but after a moment she tossed her braids back and went just close enough to be able to hear.

She hunkered down in the grass, chiding herself. *Stupid, stupid.* Far Away Fox would not say anything to this chief of her boy. But hope was wild and clawing and alive in her now; she felt almost sick with her fear of it.

"I can no longer sit idle in that peace camp," she heard Far Away Fox say angrily. "I will not shrug like an old squaw while the *ve'ho'e* rob us."

"They are not having much success with their war," Black Shin answered, and another warrior grunted in a sound of pride. "Their only serious coup was our village on the Red Arm. Any white men who dare to settle on these grounds soon find their stock gone and their women scalped."

"You have many allies, and I think there will be more. Many men of my band will join this fight as their bellies grow emptier and emptier without the food the spiders promised."

Eagle's pulse thumped hard at that. Then, suddenly, Black Shin got to his feet. She scrambled up as well.

"We are glad to have you with us," Black Shin said. "Put your lodges among us, and together we will show the *ve'ho'e* they do not possess this country. We will talk more of those plans with the next sun."

A dark figure filled the door opening. Far Away Fox moved outside.

At first his glance only skimmed over her curiously. Then he turned away, and Eagle cried out to him.

The warrior looked back at her. He began to close the distance between them, then he stopped, stunned.

"I am Eagle Voice, born to your people, to Caught The Enemy and his wife, who has died. I must speak with you."

He backed up and began a medicine song that chilled her to her bones. He was a warrior, but even warriors knew a healthy fear of ghosts. His song was one against *mis'tais. A song against her son?* But no, that was crazy. She thought on it a moment, then a gasp of relief burst from her.

He thought *she* was a *mis'tai*!

"Oh! No! I live! Did someone tell you I went up the death road?" Who would think such a thing?

Fox paused in his retreat, eyeing her warily. "When you did not return two spring moons ago for your son, your kin thought you did not survive your journey."

Her son. "Tell me, please, tell me of him."

Fox shrugged. "The old medicine man talks of that boy often. He is proud of him. He is big and strong, even with that lame leg. But he gets around well enough by dragging it. Medicine Wolf made him a special moccasin."

Stick lived. A spot deep within her trembled with joy, but she wanted more. "Is that all you know?" she persisted.

Fox scowled and shrugged.

Her eyes felt hot and wet. "I . . . thank you. *Ha ho'.*"

It was so little, and she seemed so grateful. Fox searched his brain for something else he could tell her. "All our kin are well enough," he said. "The girl who cares for him . . ."

"Sun Roads," Eagle breathed. "Yes?"

"She was wed a short time ago to one of the *Se'senovetse-taneo'o*, those Comanche. Your boy is provided for, at least as much as the game in that Ter-a-tor-ee allows."

"Good, that is good."

Eagle turned away dazedly. Ah, *Ma'heo'o*, her heart felt so full and warm.

Stick was well. It was enough; it would have to be enough, because she was no closer to reclaiming him than before.

III

Her hope died painfully this time, over several suns, like a vicious little animal that would not stop clawing and snapping as it went. Fire Wolf returned to camp to find her looking haunted, and Wind Woman told him why. Her *Wu'tapiu* kin thought her dead, failed in her winter effort to reach him. No one would send Stick to her with the warriors joining the fight.

Fire Wolf had not even known she was harboring that thin, desperate wish.

As he watched her across the fire of Falling Bird's lodge, something in his belly crawled. *She was so unhappy.* The truth of that dragged at his mind at dangerous moments, creeping up on him as he rode after a *ve'ho'e* wagon, or deflecting his thoughts in council. When he was with her, he often caught her eyeing him from beneath lowered lashes, when she thought he could not see. The aching uncertainty he felt in her tore at him.

There was nothing he could do about it.

If it were a live thing, this war, he could kill it, but he possessed no weapon against the will of men. He knew she was ready to come to him now, without waiting any longer, but he knew, too, that she could only do it when she thought all hope of reclaiming Stick was gone.

And that would destroy her.

Frustrated, he drove the knife he had been toying with deep into the dirt of Falling Bird's floor. Bull Bear paused in midsentence and raised a curious brow at him. He was saved from explaining by the sound of someone's arrival at the door flap.

Young Blind Fox came in. He had become a strong and accurate warrior over the seasons, but he was still awkward in the presence of so many elite and honored fighters. Bull Bear had to prompt him to speak.

"There is a runner here from the Flexed Legs People," he said. "I think it is important."

The men surged to their feet. Eagle watched as they went out, then she met Falling Bird's eyes. The same weary, fearful question was in both of them.

What now?

IV

Eagle was curled on her bedding when Fire Wolf returned to their part of the camp. She laid looking out beneath the rolled side of her tepee at the moonswept grass. When she saw moccasins approach, she knew him by the hard purpose in his stride, and she had to close her eyes against the sight.

Oh, how she wanted him.

It was time; she knew in her soul that it was time to give up. She could not make things right for Walks Far. It was not within her power. She bit down on her lip to keep from keening her sorrow aloud, and when she opened her eyes again, she saw the dog rope man's feet falter.

Her heart stopped a moment, and she pushed up on her elbow. He was coming for her lodge, but why had he hesitated? Did he have something horrid to tell her, something he knew would break her heart again after so many seasons of shredding and healing?

His voice came to her, unnaturally hushed, from just outside. "Do you sleep?"

She scrambled to her knees. "No, no. What is it?"

He ducked in and stood rigidly for a moment. He was only a dark silhouette in the moonlight that crept inside, but how well she had come to know this man, this friend, through all the seasons. She sensed that his belly was not churning with anger or sadness, and her breath came a little easier.

He squatted down to rest on his haunches, watching her, wondering how to tell her what he had learned. His throat tightened. He did not know how to be kind.

"That runner brought a proclamation from Stone Forehead," he explained finally.

Eagle crawled closer to see his eyes in the darkness. "Tell me everything," she whispered. "From the beginning. It is good."

"And bad."

She flinched but did not back off.

"Stone Forehead has had a dream," the dog rope man went on. "He has sent runners all over the plains to spread word to all the People. *Ma'heo'o* spoke to him and told him that we are in far worse danger from these *ve'ho'e* than we know.

"He says that while our warriors have managed to kill many of them, more will keep coming in ever larger numbers. He says we see only the ones crossing the plains, and in places like their Den-ver. But if we count the ones in their eastern lands, they outnumber us many thousands to one. For every white man we dispose of, that many will come someday to take his place."

She felt an ache in her head. "There cannot be that many of anyone," she breathed.

"They will come here," he insisted grimly. "They will try to kill the buffalo for their hides and let their meat rot, as I saw in that Den-ver place. They will attempt to lay claim to Grandmother Earth herself as though she could be owned. They will defile her with their stinking, permanent villages. That is what Stone Forehead says, and he thinks there is only one way to save the *Tse-Tsehesestahase* from destruction at their hands."

Now she reared back, a fighting horror in her eyes. Fire Wolf caught her arms as he saw that she feared the worst.

"No. Stone Forehead does not want to go to In-di-en Ter-a-tor-ee. Not that. He says the time has come once again to pay homage to the *Maaho'tse*, the Sacred Arrows."

At first she stared at him as though not understanding. It was not what she had expected to hear, and her heart was slow to accept. Then, like a gentle, drizzling rain, the truth came in on her.

The Sacred Arrow Renewal was an even more hallowed event than the Sun Dance. It was done in times of desperate trouble for the People. The *Maaho'tse* were displayed for one of the rare times in the history of the Cheyenne, ceremonially revealed from their protective wrapping to bask in the life-giving rays of Sun.

They were the very strength and soul of the *Tse-Tsehesestahase*. When the arrows were strong and happy, the People were strong.

Dread for the Shaman's prophecy was still sour in her mouth, but her heart began to pound with wild joy. *Ma'heo'o* said it was mandatory for every man, woman, and child of Cheyenne blood to attend this rite. If anyone stayed away, disease and misfortune would strike all the People and those who abstained would die a wretched, painful death.

Black Kettle would go. He had to go, and the *Hotame-taneo'o* would be there, also. She would see Stick again. She would be able to touch him, hold him, bring him home.

"It is over?" She mouthed the words, terrified to say them aloud lest she dreamed and her voice would shatter it.

It was over.

She put her forehead to Fire Wolf's chest and wept. For a long moment his hand hovered awkwardly over her hair, then he made a strange sound in his throat and stroked her.

She had taught him to love again, and now he found he could be kind and gentle after all.

26

Moon When The Cherries Are Ripe, 1867
Chikaskia Creek

I

Stone Forehead chose a place for the Sacred Arrow Renewal that was not more than half a sun's ride from his own claimed Medicine Lodge Creek. When the old shaman rode into the camp, it seemed to Fire Wolf that he was in some trance. His eyes, one sharp and black, one milky with a cataract, surveyed the bands already gathered. But he seemed to look into the People rather than at them, seeing a spiritual place that grew in their souls and bonded them all together as the *Tse-Tsehesestahase*.

Not all the bands had arrived yet. Some of the *Hotame-taneo'o* were fighting until the last moment, as well as their *So'taa'e* and *Ohmeseheso* comrades. But their own early arrival was one small gift Fire Wolf could give to Eagle.

He watched her now as she scanned the plains, feeling his heart swell strongly. Suddenly he barked a sound of laugher, and Eagle looked up at him.

"You search the land as though you can see into the next sun," he told her. "Looking to the horizon like that will not make your *Wu'tapiu* come any sooner."

Her lips curled, too. "Someone comes," she answered complacently, "and I can see them."

He frowned and shot a hard look back to the horizon. There was a place on the flat, southern prairie that was pitched in shadow. But there were no clouds in the sweeping blue sky, and when he stared at the place long enough, Fire Wolf could tell the spot was moving. It was a band coming toward them. Judging by its shape and direction, he thought it was probably the Hair Ropes. They drove a large pony herd ahead of them, and the Hair Ropes were judged to be the greatest horse thieves of all the People.

Fire Wolf's glance came back to the Renewal camp. There would be smokes to be shared now, and his place was with the Dogs.

"I must go, little Eagle. Enjoy watching their arrival."

She nodded without taking her eyes off the Hair Ropes. This was, she thought, a very good way to wait.

It seemed incomprehensible to her that this effort of Stone Forehead's could fail. Peace and bountiful hunting would soon be restored to the People. Stick would be a warm, soft, energetic boy in her arms, among the people his father had pledged to. Only once, on their journey south, had she thought to question it, and sudden panic had made cold sweat stand out on her brow.

"What if the *ve'ho'e* attack us in the middle of the rite?" she asked Fire Wolf. "What if the *Wu'tapiu* are so frightened of that they do not come?"

"Every warrior of the People will be there. What cowardly white-skin would risk such odds?"

She had relaxed, knowing it was true, needing only to hear him say it.

As the Hair Ropes began arriving in the camp, she saw the same certainty in their faces. The most ancient grandparents came in on travois, their tired old eyes crinkling above wide, toothless grins. Babes dangled in cradleboards slung from saddles and over squaws' backs. The women gossiped and laughed as their men trotted behind them. The village soon spread out in every direction. Boys yelled at the ponies, whistling and hooting as they drove them away to graze. Eagle was forced to leave the spot where she stood because she could no longer see around the People to the horizon.

She moved to the new edge of the camp and turned herself to face somewhat southward.

Soon now, she thought. Soon.

II

They came before the sun passed. When Eagle first saw their impoverished, ever-dwindling numbers, her heart bled for them. Black Kettle came ahead of the others, riding with a torn, ragged imitation of his old pride.

Her gaze flew over him only in an effort to get to the others. A terrible tension built in her as she searched behind him. *Not again, please no more disappointment.* And then she found him. She shrieked her joy so that a nearby squaw dropped her cooking paunch in surprise, then she began running, her vision blurred with tears.

She blinked furiously. She would see this moment so that she could hold it in her heart's memory forever.

Stick was perched precariously atop his own diminutive mount. His eyes moved over her without recognition, but she could not care. It was enough that he kept up with the other boys now that his pony walked for him.

"Ah." Her breath blew hard out of her, and then she was beside him. For a long moment she only looked at him greedily, filling her eyes with him, then she pulled him from his pony to clutch and kiss him.

A horrible, anguished, keening sound came suddenly from behind her. She whirled, her nape prickling, letting Stick slide down her side so that she could grab her knife. But it was only Little Moon, wailing in terror and shock.

This time Eagle understood immediately. "No! Oh, Aunt, I am not a *mis'tai*! I am here, I am alive."

Fire Wolf approached in that strong, arrogant way he had, his loose hair lifting in the wind. "They are here!" she blurted unnecessarily, reaching for Stick's arm again, hauling him close, unwilling to stop touching him.

Fire Wolf half turned about again, and then she saw Bear behind him. He waved her brother on, coaxing him with the tense, deliberate kindness that came so deep from within him. Somehow, with all else this moment meant to him, he had paused to remember and collect her brother.

Her knees finally wobbled until she dropped to sit and pull Stick into her lap.

He squirmed, embarrassed and uncertain. "Ah," she whispered again, touching his cheek, his hair. His round face had become even more the image of Bear's as he had grown, but his crooked grin was like Walks Far's.

She felt a hand on her head and looked up at Sun Roads. The girl's round face was wet and streaked.

"Mama?" Stick asked of Sun Roads.

Eagle gasped, the pain deep but bearable compared to all the others she had borne. "No . . . yes . . . your other mother," she answered him. "I am your true mama."

Sun Roads knelt beside her, moving awkwardly around the swell of a new life in her own belly. Then their other kin began dismounting and pressing close.

A fierce-looking warrior, dressed in the odd way of the Comanche, hung back. Sun Roads motioned the man over, but he took only a few steps in their direction and nodded. Still, Eagle thought she could see a good love in his eyes.

"This is Snake Under The Rock, my husband." Sun Roads sighed, then her chin came up. "Blind Fox will be disgruntled, but I did not wish to wait for his approval, and Caught The Enemy agreed to give it."

"Blind Fox has had his mind on the trouble," Eagle murmured.

"Bah!" a familiar voice snapped from behind her. "That was a crazy, foolish thing to do, running off from your mourning! Do you know the grief you put us through?"

Eagle stood unsteadily to face Little Moon. "It had to be done," she said. "I had this one to think of, too."

She pulled Stalker from her back, where he was angrily muttering to himself over the cradleboard she had forced him into while she kept her vigils for her kin. Little Moon's jaw fell, then hardened again, then she looked to the others.

"I told you. Did I not tell you, again and again, that this girl was too determined to die before reaching her goal?" Then she thumped away, but not before Eagle saw that tears pooled in her aunt's eyes as well.

Her throat closed as Sun Stalker began a more determined protest. Eagle untied his lacings quickly.

"Yes, little one, yes. You can come out now. There is someone here you must meet."

She gathered her boys up, one on each hip. Laughing, she touched her brow to Stick's. Stalker tangled his little fist around her braid and was silent long enough to look across her chest at his brother.

She went to Medicine Wolf. "Thank you," she whispered. "Thank you for caring for him so well."

She turned to Medicine Woman Later, pressing her cheek to her fat, furrowed one. "I am sorry if I frightened you, if I let you grieve before it was time."

Her old aunt patted her shoulder and peered at Stalker. "He is a fine boy, but small," she said, and Eagle laughed like the sound of a hawk bell jingling.

"Only in stature. He has the heart of Grandfather Bear when he does not get his way. . . ." Then her voice trailed off as she stepped sideways to greet her father.

But Caught The Enemy's eyes were on his son, the proud, robust man who had been the first of their kin to earn a place among the Dogs. Bear looked back at him with an unfocused, childish grin.

Eagle felt her father's pain. "Please," she said softly, "try to see that he is happiest this way. When his mind comes back to us, it brings a soul that is tortured."

Caught The Enemy glanced sharply toward the girl-child who had twice now spoken to him like no daughter should. Once she had chastised him for staying with her uncle, and now her eyes were sharp and knowing, too wise for her seventeen winters.

"They say he still fights well, only dangerously when his full mind is upon him," Eagle went on.

Caught The Enemy nodded. "Thank you," he said hoarsely. "Thank you for telling me."

She smiled for him and began to go back to the others. Then her eyes snagged Black Kettle's gaze as he stood nearby, his arms crossed over his chest beneath his favorite robe.

A deep-rooted anger stirred inside her. This was the man who had taken Stick from her side, the hand that made an X on the treaty paper, the *Vehoo'o* who had run from the strife. Suddenly she wanted to hurt him for all she had suffered herself at his hands. She could no longer feel any kinship for him. But he was still *Vehoo'o,* and she was still a squaw.

She held her tongue and turned away silently, unwilling to let him spoil these precious moments of reunion.

Even Stick's easy nature had its limits, she discovered, her grin spreading again. He squirmed in her arms, too well taught to complain, but obviously unhappy. She set both him and Stalker on the ground again, her heart spasming as she watched Stick lurch away from her.

But he walked, oh, sweet *Ma'heo'o*, he walked!

"They are both fine boys," Fire Wolf said from behind her.

"Yes," she whispered, turning back to him.

Now, now he could be hers.

Her heart had been empty and waiting for so long, this wealth of happiness felt almost painful. Suddenly she knew that she could not wait until after the Renewal to claim him. It would be proper, but she did not dare it. The *ve'ho'e* had taught her well. She had to grab quickly every precious thing that was rightfully hers.

"This night," she decided. "We should be wed this night."

A rare smile touched his mouth. "Brazen squaw. I am the dog rope man. I should say."

"Not this time." She lifted her brow in imitation of his own haughty look, then she turned slowly to face the others.

"We will wed," she announced, "this night."

Her black eyes flashed out at her kin, challenging any of them to defy her. And behind her she heard a sound she thought she loved above all others.

It was a slow, rough rumble of Fire Wolf's laughter.

III

Their joining shared none of the lavish appointments of her wedding to Walks Far, but Eagle thought it would be even sweeter for its simplicity. They had waited so long; it seemed right that they should finally come together with little more than a sigh. But her kin did not feel the same.

"There are no presents," Little Moon grumbled as they stood outside her lodge. "There should be presents."

Eagle watched Stick thump happily after some older boys. She shrugged peacefully. "I have everything I need.'"

But the *Wu'tapiu* did not. They were far too impoverished to part with any of their meager possessions this sun, and Fire Wolf had no true kin anyway with whom they could exchange things. Because of Black Kettle, her people could not truly celebrate.

"It will be better for you soon," she promised. "You are my kin. Fire Wolf will not allow you to suffer any more than you choose to."

"Sometimes it is not choice," Little Moon responded flatly. "A woman can become too old and too beaten to change."

Could she? Eagle thought helplessly. Change was the *Wu'tapiu*'s only salvation. She wanted to tell her that, but then she saw Falling Bird and Wind Woman coming toward them.

She grinned at her friends as they unloaded dried meat and fresh pemmican. "It is not much," Falling Bird lamented even as Little Moon greedily snatched up a strip of the buffalo.

"There will be more. Tall Bull has gone out," Wind Woman told them. "In all my seasons with the Dogs, I have never known that man to return from a hunt empty-handed."

Eagle nodded, but she could not help thinking that this was the southern country, and she had gone hungry here many times before.

Squaws were beginning to come back into the big camp, leading ponies laden with baskets and parfleches. At least the land was alive with fresh roots and wild onions and cherries. Sun Roads finally returned when the sun was orange and swollen against the horizon. She looked aghast to find Eagle on her knees, mashing berries for more marrow-cakes.

"It is nearly time for your dog rope man to come, and you are not ready!"

Eagle laughed aloud at her chagrin. "I have been burned out and chased from my lodge so many times I have little of beauty left," she explained. "It really does not matter now."

"But it can be fixed," Falling Bird decided. "Go bathe. Come with me," she ordered Little Moon.

Eagle went to a far bend of the creek with Sun Roads and Wind Woman. They washed her hair until it streamed past her shoulders, jet black and shining with glints of gold and red from the sunset. Then she redressed in her old doeskin.

"It will do, truly," she protested as they dragged her back to Little Moon's lodge.

"I do not think it will have to," Wind Woman answered.

Falling Bird and Little Moon were inside waiting for them. When Eagle saw the array of borrowed finery they had collected, her throat tightened and her eyes burned all over again. Falling Bird gave her the doeskin she herself had been wed in when she had joined with her *Hotame-taneo'o* chief.

"I knew there was a reason I kept grabbing this parfleche every time those white-skins flushed us from a camp," she muttered.

The dress was soft as dew, fringed along the hem and down both sleeves. A shiny row of deer hoof beads marched across her breasts. It was too warm for leggings, but they had found some yellow-painted moccasins that fit just right. Someone had contributed some brass wire bracelets, twisted out of a warrior's plunder, and there were wrappings of cat fur for her braids.

She closed her eyes, hugging her happiness to her heart.

Falling Bird stuck her head out past the door flap and mischievously gave the hoot-whistle a squaw usually reserved for her husband. "You look fine, dog rope man," she teased. "You will leave broken-hearted squaws all over the camp when this is over."

Eagle felt her heart jump and settle again. "He is here? He is ready?"

Wind Woman and Sun Roads inspected her slowly and critically, one tugging on her sleeve, the other pushing up a bracelet. "Please," Eagle protested. "We must go out now."

"No, I think—" Wind Woman began.

"Now!" she interrupted, and her friend's face cracked into the smile she had been trying to hold back.

They ducked out, Eagle leading the way. Fire Wolf did indeed look magnificent in his untamed, uncompromising way. His clothing had not been borrowed but earned, time and again over the seasons; he wore his war dress, even the scalp-trimmed leggings she had first seen him in so very many seasons ago.

She looked him over hungrily, then stopped, shivering, when she met his eyes.

There were no demons there anymore.

Night Fighter broke the moment when he came up jauntily beside them. He pushed a handful of lead-leathers at Fire Wolf; seven ponies nickered and snorted and crowded each other at the opposite ends of the lines.

Fire Wolf had brought presents for her people after all. Eagle's heart rolled over.

He handed the stallions to Caught The Enemy and Medicine Wolf, and even gave one to Black Kettle. Four ponies remained, three of them mares carrying assorted trinkets of plunder. Little Moon tried to look stern as she inspected the gifts, but even her haggard face broke into a grin as she and Sun Roads and Medicine Woman Later thanked him.

One lanky, black colt remained, obviously the get of his stallion. Her dog rope man held that lead-leather out to her, and Eagle felt confusion swim in on her.

She gave a little shake of her head. "No. It is too much. He will be a fine war pony," she protested.

"He is the future," Fire Wolf answered.

And then she understood what he was giving her, and she closed her eyes weakly. It was the promise of a distant sun when he had been beside her through everything, when she had patched his wounds and bled for him, and the birds were only silent in awe of it. He gave her a weanling that would grow to sire foals that their sons would someday ride after the buffalo when the *Hotame-taneo'o* had reclaimed the prairie.

"Yes," she breathed, "I see." She took the lead from him, trembling.

"I will wait for you," he told her, his voice low and aware.

Her heart kicked and she looked up at him again quickly. Night was only just gathering, but he was telling her he would not be feasting; already he would be in his lodge. The suns ahead would be replete with camaraderie, but this time when they could finally touch again was priceless.

With shouts and laughter the other Dogs and the *Wu'tapiu* moved off to feast on what the squaws and Tall Bull had been able to gather. Eagle looked after them bemusedly, then to Little Moon, who remained beside her.

She thought of Small Blanket, who had been here with her the first time. Her heart constricted with a pain it never seemed to lose. *So many missing.*

"It is different this time," she whispered. "I would go to him now, Aunt. Please do not argue with me."

Little Moon opened her mouth as though to do just that, but

in the end she only muttered, "The others expect you to eat with them."

"And I will. Later." When her soul was full, then she would fill her belly, but oh, her heart had been empty for so, so long.

She began hurrying toward the *Hotame-taneo'o* part of the camp. After a long moment she heard Little Moon trudging up behind her, leading the colt. They stopped in front of Fire Wolf's lodge door. Around them the Dog people muttered and shrugged, then went back to their eating. Tradition did not entirely hold in this joining; the woman had already been given to the dog rope man in the Sun Dance long ago.

Eagle murmured a fervent prayer to Walks Far's *mis'tai* that he could know her soul-deep gratitude for this gift she had finally accepted. Then she caught her breath and ducked past the door flap.

Fire Wolf stood just inside, tense and ready.

Suddenly it was all there in the air between them, all the memories of all the seasons. He remembered the way she had healed and haunted him with the covert, innocent awareness in her eyes. She remembered him arriving in the Dog camp after her first wedding, a near-naked renegade with a distant pain in his own.

Threaded through it all, she realized, was the inevitability, dark and destined, that everything would come down to this moment when she would be his without doubt or guilt or reservations. She shivered and her hands moved down her thighs to the hem of Falling Bird's doeskin. She brought it up and stepped out of it carefully, but before she could reach for her rope, his hand was there.

There were no gentle kindnesses or tender ploys in the gesture. Naked, hungry need filled both of them, two people who had suffered and fought back and lived to wrench this moment from the *ve'ho'e*. His hand tightened over hers and he tugged sharply at the knot so that her rope unraveled to the floor.

"I have waited all I care to," he said quietly. "I want you fast and hard, right now, but know that that does not mean I love you less than a man who would dwell over you. I want you more."

She smiled, slowly and catlike. "I know, my friend. That is how I have wanted it from the first time I saw you."

His breath snagged, and he pulled her suddenly to her knees so that they knelt together. Then their hands were searching and groping, their bodies pressed tight and close. His mouth was bruising against hers as he claimed her, finally making her his.

Eagle gave a fierce growl of satisfaction. She tasted him, truly tasted the musky, masculine flavor of him this time. He was like the fire, she thought, warm and smoky, then his hands caught her about the waist, bringing her beneath him.

She cried out as she drove her fingers into his hair, dragging his mouth back to hers. She wanted more; she wanted the danger and the raw, wild tumult that was Fire Wolf alone. She arched into him, pulling at his breechclout, freeing the waiststring there until it fell aside. His *ho tam'tsit* uncoiled, forgotten, dropping to the lodge floor.

He drove into her as he had promised, fast and hard. She had shared his pain and he had lived hers, and in the end, it made them one.

27

Cool Moon, 1867
Chikaskia Creek

I

The last of the bands arrived before the Cherries Moon shrank from the sky. As the People waited for Stone Forehead to begin his sacred rites, they visited and smoked and began healing in subtle, small ways. Eagle gifted her last lodge cover, almost new, to Sun Roads, and moved her salvaged possessions into Fire Wolf's tepee. They camped with the Dogs; there was never any question that the dog rope man would dwell among the *Wu'tapiu*.

She could not truly bring herself to care. She enjoyed her visits with Sun Roads and Little Moon, but her true heart hungered for the nights when she could be with her babes and her husband. When the boys slept peacefully, they touched again, and nothing, nothing could stop them now. Her nights were covetous; only her suns were easy.

The hunting was spare, but the Dogs and Sun Roads' Comanche warrior made it adequate. There was always a doeskin to be chewed down, or sinew to be stretched and twisted into thread. On the sun before the Renewal was finally to begin, Eagle worked with her kin over some moccasin pieces. She had thought to get Medicine Wolf to show her how he had layered the soles together for Stick's shorter leg, but neither her grandfather nor her father was about.

Her eyes went curiously to the *Vehoo'o* lodges near the creek. More and more men were beginning to congregate there.

Sun Roads came outside and followed her eyes. "The four principal *Vehoo'o* are all together for the first time since the new ones were chosen. Many of the men will want to hear the talk."

Eagle nodded. Her eyes left that gathering and moved greedily to Fire Wolf. She could just make out his strong, dark shoulders as he bent over something in the clearing between the *Vehoo'o* camp and the *Hotame-taneo'o* lodges. Night Fighter and Bear leaned over him. She squinted, and when she realized what they were doing, her jaw dropped.

Gambling? The dog rope man was gambling?

She laughed aloud as she watched. Night Fighter protested a roll of the buffalo-bone dice, and Fire Wolf came to his feet so that they went chest to chest, shoving each other. Their hooting derision collapsed into laughter, and Eagle bit her lip, loving him so deeply it almost hurt.

It took several long moments before she realized that heated shouts were coming from the water. She looked sharply toward the nest of four painted *Vehoo'o* lodges again.

"What?" Sun Roads muttered as something in Eagle's gut twisted.

Three of the principals were clearly furious. Dull Knife's strong face was florid and contorted. Stone Forehead looked aghast, and Sand Hill pounded one gnarly fist into the grass as he shouted.

Oh, Uncle, what have you done now?

She knew it was Black Kettle; it was always Black Kettle. She scrambled to her feet, her heart moving sickly.

In the clearing near the Dog camp, Fire Wolf kicked the game away. Night Fighter broke into a jog in the direction of the chief's council. All over the big camp warrior chiefs from other societies began moving hurriedly toward the *Vehoo'o* as well.

Eagle grabbed Stick. "Please!" she cried to Sun Roads over her shoulder. "Bring Stalker. Come with me, hurry!"

She was already running before she finished, other women falling into place behind her. When she reached the *Vehoo'o* lodges, her blood turned to ice. Dull Knife had stomped off to his lodge and had returned with his lance.

Bull Bear arrived, shoving his way angrily among the chiefs. "Would you kill him?" he demanded of Dull Knife. "Do it, and these people, your people, are lost beyond saving!"

Someone in the growing crowd keened softly. Stone Forehead pushed between the war chief and the still-livid Dull Knife.

"He is right," he cautioned. "To kill one of our own demands exile from the tribe. I cannot consider what the punishment should be for the murder of a principal *Vehoo'o*."

Eagle watched narrowly as Fire Wolf stepped into the council, his hand strong and restraining on Dull Knife's shoulder. She saw him speak to that chief.

"I will not kill him now," Dull Knife spat finally. "But I challenge you to tell the People. Tell all those who are hungry and grieving what this traitorous mongrel has done now!"

A sibilant hiss of horror went through the crowd. "What?" a woman cried. "We would know!" And then others took up a chorus of demand.

"Our *Wu'tapiu Vehoo'o* brings word to the Arrow Renewal that the white men are gathering a short ride away in my country," Stone Forehead told them gruffly.

Someone screamed, and the crowd surged crazily. Squaws tried to flee while others blocked their way, crowding in to hear more.

"I do not sanction this!" Stone Forehead hollered over the noise. "They are on Medicine Lodge Creek, but I do not welcome them!"

Black Kettle labored to his feet. *Oh, Uncle, do not say it!* But he would; Eagle knew he would, because in his old, misguided heart he truly believed in what he was doing.

"Hear me!" he called out. "This is not a cause for alarm. These blue-coats will not harm us. They wish only to make another treaty. Our shaman *Vehoo'o* has said they are too innumerable to fight. This Arrow Renewal will save us only if we learn to live beside these white brothers! We must talk to the *ve'ho'e* as well as honor the Arrows, so that our People can remain strong!"

"Live beside them to die!" someone challenged.

A roar came up from the crowd, seeming to fill the very earth. Eagle clutched Stick closer and screamed reflexively. *Her people, these were her people.* But they were as wild now as any enemy, shoving against each other, waving fists and dibbles. Something cracked down solidly on her crown, sending pain shimmering into her neck. She pushed her shoulder desperately between the two bodies in front of her to thrust free of the horde.

Fire Wolf swung toward her as she stumbled into the clearing. "Make them stop!" she shrieked to him. Then she spun around to face the crowd again. *"Stop this!"*

A grandparent seemed to heed her. "Let the shaman lead this talk!"

A tense, short quiet fell. The *Hotame-taneo'o* moved their bodies to form a protective ring around the chiefs, guarding a man they would prefer to kill themselves.

Stone Forehead nodded. "I will tell it to you. The *ve'ho'e* wish to meet while all our important men are gathered together this way. They tell our *Vehoo'o* Black Kettle that they think perhaps the reason we still raid is because only he signed their last arrangement for peace. This time they want the marks of all the *Vehoo'o* and the society chiefs, for they think this will bring about a lasting truce.

"I say this. There can be no murder at this Renewal. I will use all my power to put a curse upon any man who tries to kill this *Vehoo'o* for what he has done. It is unforgivable that he told his spider friends that we would be gathered for this sacred ceremony. It is unconscionable of him to disrupt it with treaty talk. But spilling our own blood into this soil will only destroy every man, woman, and child who ever treads upon it.

"You heard me first. I have spoken."

He moved angrily into his lodge again. Eagle looked sickly after him, then at all the faces around her. Fear, stark and vivid, glittered in their eyes.

They knew, Eagle thought. No blood need be spilled. It was too late. One of their own *Vehoo'o* had betrayed the ceremony, had brought the white men nearly to it.

The sanctity of the Renewal had already been shattered. Hope was lost.

II

The rite did not begin the following sun. The *Vehoo'o* camp fell silent, and Black Kettle did not come out of his lodge again.

"That shaman is wrong," Fire Wolf growled suddenly one night over their evening meal.

Eagle watched him pensively as she bent over her cookfire where she tended strips of antelope. The man who had laughed and gamed with his brothers on that one precious sun was gone. She had lost her strong, healthy-hearted husband before she had even had time to appreciate the glorious change in him.

She, herself, could easily have spilled blood in her rage at that.

She pulled the meat off the fire and crawled close to him. "How?" she pushed quietly. "What do you think?"

His eyes flashed up to her and narrowed as though wary of the chance to mull his thoughts aloud in the privacy of his lodge. But in a strange way he could not have anticipated, it made his heart feel strong.

"Stone Forehead postpones the Renewal, as though waiting for the white-skins to go away," he answered. "But they will not, and to keep silent about what has happened will make it like a wound that festers from within. There must be a council."

"Should I get Bull Bear?"

He pushed to his feet, rubbing his face tensely. "No. I will go to him. You should find Blind Fox. Have him run to all the bands to say that the *Hotame-taneo'o* call a council at the place by the creek."

He went out, and she woke her boys gently where they were curled together on a pile of bedding like puppies in a litter. She worked a groggy Stalker into his board and slung him over her back so that she could cradle the heavier Stick in her arms.

She went to her cousin's lodge and passed on Fire Wolf's message, then she hesitated. She knew she could no longer wait obediently in her lodge for her husband to return and tell her what had transpired. Those days had died with Walks Far. Grimly she turned in the direction of the council place.

She settled herself and her babes in the shadows nearby, close enough that she could hear. The *Vehoo'o* and the warrior chiefs who gathered were stern-faced and stubborn-jawed. After a smoke was offered to *Ma'heo'o* and his powers, Bull Bear began the talk.

"First I would address this treaty. The spiders wait nearby and they expect it. It cannot be ignored. If we do not respond in some manner, I think they will come here to fight. That, above all else, cannot be allowed."

His voice was flat and calm. Many of the men nodded.

"If this *Vehoo'o* signed away the western hunting grounds with that first mark he made, then the marks of all our council and societies would result in giving away even more. Who among you, even the most peacefully inclined, would condone such a thing? Speak now, for if we are truly divided, this is the time when we must know."

Black Kettle hitched his weight beneath his tattered blanket, but he made no sound.

"Look at this *Vehoo'o*'s men and ponies!" Bull Bear charged, gathering the arrogant force he was renowned for. "The *Wu'tapiu* mounts are ribby and thin even in this season of long grass. His warriors are hungry and lazy. That is what comes from consorting with white spider tricksters!

"I say we must never touch the hand of a white-skin again unless it is to kill him! We should save ourselves as we have always done, with this sacred Renewal, not with paper treaty words."

The men began talking, some shouting opinions across the fire, some standing to speak their views with dignity. After a while Eagle got to her feet to carry her babes back to her lodge. Such a council could well last until dawn.

But the talk escalated much more quickly than she could have imagined. She took only a few steps before a shout erupted, and she looked back sharply.

Dull Knife was on his feet, still spittingly angry. "If you will not let me kill him, then I say this man should leave us!" he charged, pointing to Black Kettle.

Eagle's heart staggered.

"Let him go to that camp on Medicine Lodge Creek with his spider trickster friends," Dull Knife went on. "To keep him here now, among us, is to defy *Ma'heo'o*. If we are to salvage the terrible damage he has done to the *Maaho'tse*, then he must be cast from us. We must show the Wise One we do not condone his actions!"

Voices rose strong in the night. Had he forgotten that all the

People had to be together for the Arrow Renewal? Eagle clutched Stick tight, but she knew in some small, terrible part of her heart that there was some truth to Dull Knife's point. It was a desperate measure, but in this terrible time of disruption, little else could be done to salvage the rites.

She watched Fire Wolf move close to her uncle, and felt a shiver of pride and alarm as he dared to turn his back on the others. Tempers were vicious now and untrustworthy, and many had already talked of murder.

"It is best, Uncle," he said with strained, cold respect. "And I would ask you to take your family with you."

All her kin? No! Eagle blanched.

"This is a dangerous place for them now," he went on. "I do not think they can go about without fear for their lives if they stay among so many people who think you have destroyed them. Take them, Uncle, where they are safe, if only until we can put thoughts to this dilemma and the wind can blow away some of this bad feeling."

"And what of your wife?" Dull Knife snarled from behind him. "She is kin to this traitorous fool!"

Fire Wolf turned on the *Vehoo'o* with deadly quickness. "My wife is *Hotame-taneo'o.*"

A tense murmur rose and fell among the crowd. Bull Bear moved quick as a cat between them.

"I have respected you long and well," he said to Dull Knife. "Once, after the bloody suns at Sand Creek, I put you up for this council. Hear me now. There are three of *Wu'tapiu* birth dwelling in lodges near to my own hearth. The man who strikes against them strikes against me."

Dull Knife grunted, but he sat again. Eagle bit down hard on her lip to keep from crying out as her uncle rose.

It happened in swift, silent despair. Blind Fox trotted for his mother's lodge, his face stony with a pain he could not reveal. Black Kettle rearranged his robe about his shoulders and ducked into his own lodge to summon Medicine Woman Later.

The *Wu'tapiu* rode out as the moon began to rise, a cool, white slice that offered no comfort. Eagle stared up at it as she tried to pull her strength into her heart so that she could stand this. Then she felt a body, warm and solid, come beside her.

Eagle knew then that somehow, she would survive this, too.

She had the man who was her wisdom and her strength. She was no longer alone.

III

"The Arrows can be denied no longer," Night Fighter said several suns later. The Dogs as well as several chiefs were all gathered around Eagle's fire trench. Fire Wolf sat at the head of the hearth, looking stiff and nonplussed. He wore authority well in battle, but he found it awkward to have so many men crowded into his own lodge, a place that had been solitary and private for a very long time.

Eagle almost smiled at his chagrin as she passed around horn bowls of water. Then Dull Knife interjected, and her heart squeezed with fear.

"Black Kettle and his kin must either be killed or accommodated so that he agrees to return and we can get on with this rite."

The *Ohmeseheso Vehoo'o* still sanctioned death in an effort to put an end to the turmoil. Her hands fumbled and the water spilled.

"Before anything is decided, someone should go talk to Black Kettle," Bull Bear advised.

"He has already sent all our runners back with the message that he will not return unless we do this treaty!"

"He thinks to bend us to his will with our need to see quickly to the *Maaho'tse*, the Arrows."

"If the water begins to freeze, it will be too late in the season to renew them," Dull Knife declared. "Then we will be doomed. I think *Ma'heo'o* would be angrier if we disperse without honoring them than He would be if we take drastic measures to see that they are worshipped as intended."

Too many men nodded, but then Fire Wolf spoke for the first time.

"I will go to him," he said shortly. "If I fail to make him see reason, I will not interfere in whatever the council chooses to do after that."

He stood abruptly, and Eagle felt her heart tear, part going to her kin in some distant, unseen enemy camp, but more of it stuttering in fear for her dog rope man. This was a responsibility she would not see him risk. If he failed in this, he would never enjoy quite the same respect again.

But she believed in him. She trusted in his intuition and his will. If anyone could fix this sanely, he could. She closed her eyes helplessly, letting him go.

IV

Fire Wolf's delegation came back with the last sun of the day. While they were gone, word of their mission made its way stealthily through every camp. Eagle watched women and warriors begin to gather silently at the creek, awaiting their return. Finally she gathered up Stick and Stalker again and followed.

When Fire Wolf rode in, she searched his face desperately. He did not look at her, but neither did he appear defeated. His jaw was hard, his eyes unreadable as everyone waited to hear what had happened.

"Black Kettle refuses to relent," he said finally.

"*Aiy-ee*," Eagle whispered. Her heart seemed to slide down inside her, deeper and deeper into a part of her where it could not be touched by this new grief.

"He will not return unless we compromise," Fire Wolf went on. "But he does say he is willing to do that much."

"Anything!" a squaw wailed.

"What compromise?" demanded a warrior.

"He asks that our *Vehoo'o* and warrior chiefs travel to that camp to hear what the spiders would say. He will tell the white-skins that he cannot achieve more than that. He will not hold out any hope for them that we will comply with another treaty. He says that if we only come and talk to the *ve'ho'e*, then he will return for the Arrow Renewal."

Stone Forehead's eyes narrowed thoughtfully. "*Ma'heo'o*'s taboo against murder is so harsh, and in this case complicated, that I do not know how we would deal with it," he reiterated. "I think we should go."

"We can placate these spiders," Sand Hill said suddenly. "They are stupid."

All eyes turned to him, and Eagle scarcely allowed herself to breathe.

"We would have to be very, very sure that no treaty is agreed to," Bull Bear warned. "To even allow those white-skins to think they have acquired something is almost as bad as giving it to them. Look how many of our men have died in these last seasons, trying to reclaim what Black Kettle professed to give."

Sand Hill nodded. "One *Vehoo'o* could remain away, and we will tell those spiders it is so. Then they will know that no two-tongued, convincing lies will bind us."

Stone Forehead cleared his throat. "I will stay and keep the Arrows here with me. They have graced every true peace we have ever entered into. Nothing is binding without them."

Even Dull Knife was forced to nod at that.

"Please," a squaw moaned. "We cannot deny the *Maaho'tse.*"

The council looked to Dull Knife. His jaw hardened, but he saw that the eyes of his people were pleading and desperate. After a moment, he grunted.

"So be it."

Eagle's legs buckled. She dropped to her haunches, wrapped her arms around her knees, and gave her heart into a silent prayer.

V

Black Kettle returned the following sun, his followers looking gaunt and hollow-eyed. They kept their gazes down, but they were back, they were safe, and Eagle did not think she dared to ask more of *Ma'heo'o* than that. She went to them briefly, but then she made herself move away before any desperate watcher could question her loyalties.

Reverently, carefully, Stone Forehead laid out the sacred *Maaho'tse*. Their fur was unwrapped, and all the men of every band passed by them to pay their respects. Fresh, clean feathers were affixed to them, and for four days there was singing and dancing and feasting in praise of them. They basked in the sun, absorbing its strength.

Eagle watched the Arrows critically. Sun glinted off them in a way that made her shiver, but she could not tell if they were truly happy now or not. They had been so nearly defiled. A worm of doubt remained blasphemously inside her.

On the fifth sun the Dog wives began breaking down their lodges to move to Medicine Lodge Creek. Eagle worked grimly among them, her fingers clawlike with her apprehension.

Oh, *Ma'heo'o*, she did not want to visit the blue-coat place, did not want to take her boys there. But this gathering was finished now. It was time to go home, back to Dog country. The *Hotame-taneo'o* would only stop at the soldier place on the way.

Her dog rope man would go, and she belonged beside him.

28

Cool Moon, 1867
Medicine Lodge Creek

I

She would keep Stick and Stalker close, Eagle vowed. Nothing could ever be permitted to happen to her family again.

The move to the *ve'ho'e* camp was short because the warriors rode hard; she realized that the men were wary of this trip as well. They sent wolves out to scout the trail ahead and behind, as though they expected soldiers to ambush them as soon as they drew close. If they did, they would die trying; the *Hotame-taneo'o* were ready for them.

When they drew near enough to see the place, the warriors went wild. At first Eagle did not understand what they were doing. Her heart pounded and she sawed on Wind Runner's reins, ready to whip her about and gallop the other way. A hue and cry went up from the blue-coat camp.

"Cheyennes! Cheyennes!"

"You would think we are spirit-monsters, the way those spiders act," Falling Bird muttered.

"That is what our warriors would like them to think," Wind Woman pointed out.

The *Hotame-taneo'o* charged into Medicine Lodge Creek in a glorious display of horsemanship, waving their scalp-trimmed lances as they surged across into the camp. They rode four abreast, the chiefs and their dog rope man at the head of each column. Several shot their rifles off, the cracking echoes splitting the air. Others screamed the ululating cry of the warpath that many of the blue-coats remembered from skirmishes they had barely survived.

The soldiers scattered in alarm, then, abashed and blustering, they began to regroup when the *Hotame-taneo'o* quieted.

Eagle looked about at the place, her skin crawling.

So many people. The Arapaho were present; she recognized Little Raven's lodge. There were men in the dress she now knew as Comanche, and scores of other lodges sat beside theirs. She thought they were probably their allies, the Kiowa. The white-skins were threaded all through the commotion, popping up here and there in the sea of red faces. Never before had she been so close to so many of them, and her breath started falling too short. Wind Woman reached over and slapped her pony's rump hard so that the mare bucked forward, carrying her into the camp.

"The longer we sit here fearing it, the worse it will look," Falling Bird agreed, then she nudged her pony as well.

As they trotted past the lodges and *ve'ho'e* tents, one of the spiders cat-called his appreciation of them. Eagle shrank back, dragging Stick's pony close to hers. But then, somehow, she found Fire Wolf.

He was still trotting around the white-skins' tents, antagonizing them, but his eyes searched for her as he went. Suddenly her fear felt foolish. He was here, and nothing could happen to her or her babes. She owed him her courage and pride.

She squared her shoulders and went on, and Stick took her lead and followed. Her heart squeezed as she kept one eye on him. He rode so much like Walks Far, jauntily, a crooked, curious grin on his small face.

Oh, little one, you do not know all they have done to you.

Someday, soon enough, he would learn, but for now Eagle took her eyes from him long enough to consult with Falling Bird and Wind Woman.

"We should find a good, safe place to put our lodges."

II

As the suns went on, the *ve'ho'e* talked endlessly. With every dawn several *Hotame-taneo'o* warriors and the principal *Vehoo'o* went to the place that had been set aside for the council. But Eagle kept close to the Dog lodges.

The smell of the place bothered her more than anything. It reminded her of the blue-coat she had once killed, a lingering hint of sweat and urine as though these men never bathed. It was most pervasive near their tents, but it hung faintly everywhere, and she wondered if it could get into her food, tainting it.

Fire Wolf came back from the talking and hunkered down by the communal fire trench that she and Wind Woman and Falling Bird had dug outside. He rested on his haunches and ripped off a piece of meat with his teeth. His gaze moved warily over the *ve'ho'e* part of the camp, then, suddenly, he choked, spitting the food out into the dirt.

"What?" Eagle asked suspiciously. "Does it taste like the air smells?"

"Worse," he muttered.

She moved up close to him, and Bull Bear and Night Fighter returned to stare down at the food as well.

"Cat-tul meat," Night Fighter offered. He looked to the women. "Did the blue-coats give you this?"

"Sand Hill's woman did, but I think she got it from those wagons," said Falling Bird. She pointed toward the *ve'ho'e* vehicles, more than fifteen hands of them, lined up at the perimeter of the camp. They were laden with presents and food, and Eagle would not go near them, either.

"I thought it would do . . . it was fresh . . ." Falling Bird trailed off and shrugged.

"Problem with the provisions, folks?"

Eagle wheeled around to find that a blue-coat and a shabby white-skin translator had approached them. She stepped back warily as the warriors met them.

"Provisions?" Night Fighter snorted.

The blue-coat nodded. "We're here to take you by the hand and make a good road for peace and happiness. We give the meat freely. There will be more to come when we all finish counciling."

Suddenly Fire Wolf stepped forward angrily. "A mongrel will eat provisions," he snapped. "The food you give us makes us sick. We can live on buffalo. What we truly need from you are items that we do not see. We need powder and lead for our guns so that we can protect the country you would try to steal. When you show these to me, I will believe in your talk."

He turned his back on them in contempt and strode away. Finally Eagle saw what she had been too preoccupied to notice earlier. She had been so absorbed in keeping her boys out of harm's way that she had not seen the tight-lipped restraint in her dog rope man. There was something dangerous and simmering about him that told her the talking was not going well at all.

Fear began coiling in her again.

III

"No more counciling after this sun," Tall Bull decided as the Dogs moved back toward the *ve'ho'e* tents. "We have done what we promised Black Kettle we would do. There is only one moon left for hunting. We need to settle in somewhere before the snows come."

Fire Wolf made a rough sound in his throat. "It is senseless anyway. This talking is like it was in Den-ver. It is what the spiders do not say that alarms me the most."

Night Fighter snorted. "If they give many more presents, they will begin to sway the Council. Those *Vehoo'o* will not hear their sweet lies for what they are."

Bull Bear ducked under the treaty tent. "The *Maaho'tse* are not here," he reminded them. "Stone Forehead has gone south. Our *Vehoo'o* know nothing can come of this but a short hunting moon."

Fire Wolf barely nodded. His gut tightened as soon as he stepped beneath the blue-coat half-tent.

They had put it on the north bank of Medicine Lodge Creek, in the midst of some cottonwoods and elms. As was their way, they had chopped down trees to clear a space for it, rather than move a short distance away where the land was free. Far in the distance a long, flat-topped hill crested the horizon, and lower ones swelled before it. His skin itched with a feeling of confinement, with a longing to be out there, riding away. But these white men would try to take that land from him, and so he paid attention, turning back to the meeting.

There were seven *ve'ho'e*, some dressed in the kind of finery he remembered the man Han-cock wearing. They had put panels of wood on cross-beams, raising them up from the ground, and they sat behind these tables. Fire Wolf went to rest lightly and tensely on one of the logs strewn about to seat the Indians.

There were men here from every tribe, and that bothered him, too. The *Tse-Tsehesestahase* had their own land to protect. He did not care about the Comanche's Tex-us.

A white-skin who called himself Hen-der-son began the talking, as he had every sun.

"Two years ago we entered into a treaty with your chief Black Kettle at the mouth of the Little Arkansas, and we hoped then that there would be no more war between the tribes and the government," he said. "We are sorry to be disappointed. Peaceable white persons, engaged in building our railroads, have been attacked, with women and children scalped as well. These reports have made our hearts very sad. The Great Father has sent us here to hear from your own lips what were these wrongs that prompted you to commit these deeds. We now ask you to state to us if you have at any time since the treaty committed violence."

Bull Bear stood, erect and arrogant. "There was no treaty. We disappoint no one."

Henderson's tone became conciliatory. "We have come to hear all your complaints and to correct all your wrongs. We have full power to do these things, and we pledge to you our sacred honor to do so.

"We wish to feed you, to house you, to educate you, if you will only lay down your weapons. The Great Father has authorized us to provide you with comfortable homes upon our richest agricultural lands. We can build you schoolhouses and churches, and provide teachers for your children. We'll give you implements with which to work the soil, as well as cattle, sheep, and hogs. Now, then. I shall cease and wait to hear what you have to say."

A Kiowa chief rose first, a slain general's coat draped over his shoulders. "The Cheyennes are those who have been fighting with you. We have not fought you and we want nothing from you. I do not want any of those medicine houses built in my country to put things in my babes' heads. I want my babes brought up just exactly as I am.

"I have told you the truth, but I do not know how it is with you co-mish-un-ers. Are you as clear as I am? A long time ago

I had my own land. It belonged to my fathers. Now you have taken that and given me some elsewhere. I do not want it. When I go up my old rivers, I see a camp of soldiers, and they are cutting my wood down or killing my buffalo. I do not like that, and when I see it my heart feels like bursting with sorrow.

"I have spoken."

The commissioners exchanged blank looks. Henderson coughed. "Well, then. Would anyone else like to speak?"

A Comanche stood, his red-shot eyes narrow and accusing. "I, too, do not want your medicine houses."

"Schools, damn it!" a blue-coat interrupted. "They're *schools*."

Ten Bears shrugged eloquently. "I want to live and die as I was born. I love the open prairie, and I wish you would not insist upon putting my people on a res-er-va-shun. The best of my lands the Tex-ans have taken, and I am left to shift as best as I can do. That is done. But now I do have a problem you could help me with. I love to get presents, for it reminds me that the Great Father has not forgotten his friends the Comanche." He sat, then scowled and stood again. "Also, I want my country to be pure and clean."

Henderson cleared his throat. "You say you do not like our schools, but you like the buffalo and the chase, and that you wish to do as your fathers did. We say to you that the buffalo will not last forever. They are now becoming few, and you must know it. When that day comes, the Indian must change the road his father traveled, or he will probably die. We want you to live, and we now offer you the way."

Dull Knife shot to his feet. "There were buffalo before you came here. They will stay when you are gone."

"The whites are settling up all the good lands!" Henderson protested. "They have come along the Arkansas River. When they come, they drive out the buffalo. If you oppose them, war must come."

"Then I say let there be war." Dull Knife moved to the edge of the tent. "I did not wish to come here. We told you first there can be no treaty because my people are not all present. But these words of mine will hold: Before I give you this prairie, I would rather let you steal my breath and turn my soul into the ground eternally."

Henderson took a deep breath and looked back at those who remained. "We are many, and you are few," he continued to try. "You must see that. You may kill some of us, but others will come to take our places. And finally many of the red men will have been killed and the rest will have no homes. We are your best friends, and now, before all the good lands are taken by the whites, we wish to set aside a part of them for your exclusive home."

"We have our home now," said Sand Hill, rising. "We have no problem with it. We sprung from the prairie, we live by it. As yet we have no need of your medicine houses and tee-chers. When we desire to live as you do, we will take your advice, but until then we will take our chances. You think you are doing a great deal for us by giving us these presents, but we prefer to live as we do now. If you gave us all the goods you could give, my women and my warriors would still prefer our own life. You give us presents, and then you take our lands. That produces war.

"I have spoken."

He, too, strode out of the tent, and the *Hotame-taneo'o* rose as one. There was a stirring along the *ve'ho'e* ranks.

A man of the press leaned close to a soldier. "My word, I look forward to writing this, sir. These Cheyenne are as proud and haughty and defiant as men who are to grant favors, not beg them. They truly are masters of the plains."

The soldier waved him irritably into silence and leaned closer to Henderson. "You're not getting through to them."

Yet another commissioner spoke into the hushed, private conference. "Perhaps if you rephrase things a bit, they'll think they're getting what they want. If you tell them they can continue to travel their hunting grounds until the game runs out, they'll think we're granting it to them for all time. Indeed, let them hunt there for the time being. They think their damned buffalo are as numerous as the stars in the sky, but we know they're running out. As long as they dwell on their reservation and take passes from their agent when they wish to go out hunting, we should be able to keep track of them efficiently enough. It will be years before Colorado and Kansas are truly settled anyway. Until then we can accommodate them."

Henderson scowled. "How exactly does the treaty read now for this faction . . . the, er, Cheyenne?"

"We retain all the land between the Arkansas and the Platt rivers, essentially Colorado and Kansas."

"Sir?" A young corporal, standing behind the table, cleared his throat. "I believe that country includes the Smoky Hill River, and that, I believe, is to be considered the Dog Soldiers' hunting grounds."

"Well, they'll have other hunting grounds," Henderson muttered, studying the treaty map. "I believe you're right. I believe it's all in the way we've phrased this." He rose again. "Well, gentlemen, we can understand your problems with all this," he said to the Cheyenne.

"We're willing to compromise. We will not ask you to cease hunting the buffalo. You may roam over the broad plains as you have done in years past, but we still feel that you must have a place you can call your own. We propose to make that home on the Red River around the Wichita mountains, and we have prepared papers for that purpose. In the meantime, you can continue to hunt as long as the buffalo remain. However, in doing so, your hunters must stay ten miles clear of any white roads or settlements. Now, will you make your marks?"

There was deep silence before Bull Bear drew himself up to his full height. "When the buffalo leave our country, we will let you know. By that time maybe we will be ready to live in your houses."

"Good, good," Henderson responded absently.

Fire Wolf felt his belly tighten again. He elbowed his way close to Bull Bear. "We will hold all that country between the Flint Arrowpoint and the Moon Shell. We will not give up as long as the buffalo and elk are roaming through the country. Is that what we say?"

Henderson nodded quickly. "So, can we have your marks?"

"There are no need for marks," sneered Bull Bear. "We do not trust your papers."

He moved out of the half-lodge, his warriors following him. In the end only Black Kettle moved up to the table.

"I will put my *X*. My people will live as they have been. We would like to take your presents so that you do not kill us."

The blue-coat holding the treaty looked awkwardly at Henderson. The senator shrugged.

"Yes, well, we spoke to all of them. I suppose one should be enough to sign for each nation. Someone get that Comanche chief back here, and the Kiowa."

IV

The *Hotame-taneo'o* wives began packing up as soon as the warriors returned and gave them the word. The *Vehoo'o* families were inclined to linger and travel with the new dawn, but Eagle did not want to spend a moment longer at this place than she had to. None of her friends disagreed with her.

She mounted and rode restlessly in little circles, waiting for Wind Woman and Falling Bird to finish. Each time a voice rose in the white man's talk, her head snapped in that direction and her heart bucked. But no *ve'ho'e* made a move to stop their departure. They seemed inexplicably pleased with the inconclusive council.

As Sun began falling in the western sky, the last of the *Hotame-taneo'o* loped out of the camp. They traveled hard and steadily to the north, their ranks stretching magnificently across the prairie, the black feathers on their lances snapping in the wind. When they reached the first hill, Eagle finally dared to twist around and look back at the place they had left behind.

No white-skins followed them. After two summers of battling over it, the *ve'ho'e* had finally given their land back to the *Tse-Tsehesestahase*. The Arrows were happy, and all her loves, her family, were together and whole.

She had not known peace in so long, she could scarcely believe it was hers.

29

Spring Moon, 1868
Arikaree Creek

I

"Cannot!" Stick cried mutinously.

"You can. There is strength in your thigh. Use that," Fire Wolf answered him, his eyes critical on the boy as he bounced on the back of a new colt. "This pony is yours," he told him. "He will grow with you and learn to respond to whatever signals you decide to teach him. He does not have to learn the same cues as every other mount. A man's war pony should be unique, an extension of himself."

Stick's lower lip still protruded, but he tried again to make his bad leg work for him. Eagle had to bite down on her own lip to keep from protesting aloud as she watched.

It is the only way he will survive.

She hugged herself in the freshening spring breeze. Oh, yes, she knew it was true. In his hard-kind way, Fire Wolf pushed Stick on to feats just slightly beyond him because he knew that come any sun, he might have to keep up with the others or perish. Life was good now, but Eagle could not quite lose that lingering fear that at any moment she could blink her eyes and everything would change.

"Good, that is enough," she heard Fire Wolf say, and she glanced up again to see Stick reining in. He looked as if he would protest the end of his lesson now that he had finally achieved whatever it was the dog rope man had been trying to teach him. But Fire Wolf swung him down from the pony's back.

"It is far better to stop while the lesson is going well," he explained. "That way both you and your mount will look forward to learning more next time. Those things a man does for pleasure are often his best feats."

His eyes moved to hers in a gaze that was both brief and telling. Then he bent to lift Stalker up from where he toddled in the grass at her feet. He tossed him high into the air so that the babe squealed. Eagle shivered a bit. She saw it more and more as the suns unraveled, how truly needful of this kind of peace her dog rope man had been.

He cocked a brow at her. "I noticed some sign out there while I worked with Stick's pony." Eagle felt her mouth go dry.

"What kind?"

"Buffalo. Just buffalo. It is a very small trailing herd, a bull and five cows. I would like to see where they are heading this season, perhaps even catch up with them and bring some down."

"Tall Bull has probably already thought of that—" she began.

"Come with me," he interrupted.

He turned away, back toward the herd. Her heart jumped. She looked to the camp and saw Woman With White Child working outside her lodge. She hooted to her and motioned to Stick and Stalker, knowing the squaw would be more than willing to keep watch over them for a while.

She ran back toward the herd where Fire Wolf had already flushed out Wind Runner and his black. He was astride, waiting for her, and she grabbed a hank of Wind's shaggy mane and swung up. Grinning, her heart giving another little thump of goodness, she drove her heels against the mare so that Wind leapt off into a sudden gallop.

She heard the dog rope man behind her, gaining on her, the rumble of his hoofbeats growing steady and fast. She laughed aloud, guiding Wind with her legs as she pulled the rawhide thongs from her braids. It was a delicious, wild feeling as her hair whipped in the wind, and Walking Spirit's voice was suddenly close again.

Think of the freedom! Think of it! There is only you, and your man, following the wind.

In that moment Eagle finally knew that for all the heartache and strife, once tasted the *Hotame-taneo'o* life was the most glorious one of all.

Beside her, Fire Wolf's muscled body moved as though he

were part of his black. She laughed again. He was not looking down at any tracks at all. His gaze swept the land.

It was magnificent country, craggy and rough with ravines etched into the hills. They were on the southern brink of Sioux country; the Dogs had joined those allies and the *So'taa'e* once again, this time to pass the winter.

They raced along one of the high slopes, but when she thought Fire Wolf's rangy animal would pull ahead of her, he crowded close beside her instead. She gasped as he caught her around the waist, pulling her from her pony, then she scissored her leg over the black's head to settle in front of him. Wind Runner kept apace with them; she belonged to the black stallion now as irrevocably as her mistress belonged to the dog rope man.

Fire Wolf pulled her hair aside where it lashed his face. They thundered down the hill into a valley, the incline forcing him closer into her. She felt him hard and ready behind her, and another sweet shudder went through her. *Oh, to be his woman.* It was every wild, dangerous thing she had ever known that it would be.

He felt the change in her body, felt the excitement dance through her. *How well he knew her.* She had grown through the seasons, tempering and bending to the harshest winds, but still she responded to him the same.

He pulled hard on the reins, bringing the black around in a skidding circle, driving him into one of the deep, hidden gulches that flanked the hill. Before the stallion plunged to a stop, Fire Wolf pushed off behind him, coming around to pull her down as well.

Her hands went into his hair, the untamed cascade of it that was one of the first things she had ever noticed about him. But he caught her wrists and stepped back to snag the waist string of his breechclout with his thumb and break it free. Then he waited for her, naked, his eyes hot and searching, hungry for every flare of her nostrils, every skip of her breath.

She gave it to him, a yearning moan as she went to her knees, sliding her hands covetously down his hard belly, his strong thighs. He had shown her this, another *ve'ho'e* way of loving that delighted her with its shattering effect on him. She wrapped her hands around him and moved her tongue over his hardness, teasing until his hands curled into fists in her hair. Then she took him into her mouth.

A sound ragged and rough came from his throat before he finally dropped to kneel in front of her, wrenching her doeskin up over her head. Then his mouth was on hers again, hungry and hard. His weight leaned into her until she fell back into the scrubby grass.

And once again the sun baked down on them with its elusive springtime heat. The breeze tickled their skin so that she gurgled a half-laugh, half-gasp as she brought her legs hard around him, pulling him into her. He buried his face at her neck and plunged deep, almost hurting her, but not quite, leaving her on the edge of rapture.

He rolled away, pulling her with him until she sat astride him. And then, as her nails dug into his shoulders, he gave her what few warriors of his stature could sacrifice. He gave his will over into her keeping, letting her use him fully and well until his eyes closed with the torture of restraint.

When she had spent herself, he struck out like a snake, suddenly and fast. He moved her beneath him again, staying with her, and rode her with exquisite urgency until he took his own release. Groaning, his skin slick and smooth with the warmth of the sun, he dropped on top of her again, his breath damp and hot at her neck.

"How did we do it?" she murmured. "How ever did we survive so long without feasting on each other?"

He did not tell her that the worst part was after he knew what it was to love her. He did not have to; he felt the memory of it in the way her breath changed.

He stirred first, sliding off her with quick irritated tension. She thought he would swat at a gnat or pull a burr from his skin, but he sat up instead, cocking his head.

"Riders," he said. And then she felt it as well, a faint shifting of the breath of the earth beneath them.

He was not alarmed, and she sat up languorously, reaching for her doeskin to pull it back over her head. "Tall Bull got the trailing herd while you played," she teased. His brown eyes came back to hers, simmering a moment before a corner of his mouth lifted.

"No hump steak could have been sweeter," he murmured,

but already he was a warrior again, his eyes moving up the gulch. "Wait here."

She knew then that there were too many riders for it to be Tall Bull's party returning. She watched her dog rope man move up the gulch, and some unbidden voice whispered a prayer in her heart.

Not yet, it is too soon yet for trouble. She was only just learning what it was to have her heart full and sated.

Fire Wolf only glanced over the rim of the hill for a moment, then he turned back to her and slid down. *"Wu'tapiu,"* he explained laconically as he bent for his breechclout and dog rope again, tying them back on.

Then he was up and mounted again. Eagle scrambled onto her mare as well, but even as they broke into a gallop, something tense and uneasy curled around her belly.

.There was no good reason why the *Wu'tapiu* should be visiting them now.

II

The newcomers went to Black Shin's lodge, and Eagle glared at the closed flap in helpless frustration. Fire Wolf had gone in there as well as Bull Bear, but Night Fighter stayed in camp, greasing the scalps on his lance. He had decided not to interrupt the chore for what would surely amount to a quick smoke.

"When there is nothing to worry over, you look for something," Wind Woman chided. "Those *Wu'tapiu* are only hungry. They said as much when we greeted them, and they told you your kin are well, too."

Eagle sighed and nodded. It had been gratifying to learn that Sun Roads had pushed out a healthy girl-child, but she knew the warriors had not come to tell the Dogs that.

"If their bellies growled, then why didn't they just go to Stone Forehead or the Hair Ropes or the Ridge People, some band who dwells closer to them?" she persisted.

"Those people probably had a hard winter, too," Night Fighter answered. "None of those southern lands are fertile anymore—"

He broke off suddenly, and Eagle twisted around to follow

his gaze. The flap had finally snapped back at Black Shin's lodge, and Fire Wolf and Bull Bear came out.

Eagle saw it, too. She had lived with the *Hotame-taneo'o* for six circles of seasons now, and even if she had not been able to feel the anger coming off her dog rope man as he strode toward them, she would have recognized the way Bull Bear's arrogant jaw jutted forward.

"What is it?" Night Fighter demanded, thrusting to his feet.

"We ride out," the dog rope man answered tightly. "Now. Someone must keep Bear behind."

"Why?" Eagle asked. *Oh,* Ma'heo'o, *what now?*

"I do not want him to see this. We are only going to sneak in and witness this thing for ourselves. I do not want to be spotted, and sometimes memory makes him unruly."

"See what?" she wailed, then she bit down on her lip in an effort for control.

Finally, distractedly, her dog rope man looked at her. "None of the things promised to your people in that Medicine Lodge council have come to pass," he said tightly. "Neither the *Wu'tapiu* nor the Kiowa or Comanche staying in In-di-en Terr-a-tor-ee have received any food since Cold Maker's Freezing Moon. Instead, they have been driven even farther south, to a new res-er-va-shun, and told to hunt where the old one was, a place already stripped bare of game."

He paused. Eagle waited. There was more. She knew it, because nothing he had said so far was much different from what any of them had expected.

"The *Wu'tapiu* came north to hunt with us and take some meat home to their kin," he went on. "On their way they came upon a new fort at the headwaters of the river, not very distant from here."

"A fort?" Wind Woman scowled. She looked quickly to her husband. "You said at those stupid talks that the *ve'ho'e* finally agreed this land was ours."

"They did," Night Fighter answered tightly.

"And now they settle upon it?" Eagle sputtered, anger and despair building in her. But somehow she had known it would happen. Sooner or later the treacherous white-skins would be back.

Fire Wolf ducked into their lodge and came out with his

repeater, burnished and gleaming from much idle winter cleaning. "There has not been a promise yet that their forked tongues have honored," he muttered, then he moved off toward the herd. Only Eagle seemed to hear his last words, and they were like a death song for the sweet, lazy robe season behind them.

III

Fort Townley was where the *Wu'tapiu* said it was, but the Dog Soldiers decided to wait to retaliate until the Spring Moon had urged lush grasses from Grandmother Earth. It would be a long campaign, wearing on the ponies, and they wanted them to be strong.

It was a strange time for Eagle, a time of war cloaked deceptively in robes of peace. All through the moon, the *Hotame-taneo'o* kept wolves on the fort, watching it to learn the number of blue-coats there and their routine. But the place was only half a sun's ride away, so the warriors were rarely out of camp when the moon rose. It was a cruel, taunting time, because when she was naked beneath their bedding robes with her dog rope man, she could almost believe that nothing had changed. But then Sun would come, and he would leave her to stalk the blue-coats.

By the time the moon waned, the ponies were as fat as they could be in early spring, and the Dogs began their siege of the compound. They had avid allies this time; the place was alarmingly close to the Sioux's country, and it was in the very heart of the *So'taa'e* grounds.

It crouched toadlike within strong wooden walls, reminding everyone of the Platte Bridge fort. This time the Dogs would not try to lure the blue-coats out of that smugly safe place. Instead, they harassed them persistently, goading them into leaving the country entirely.

Whenever the blue-coats crept out from behind their walls, they found themselves engaged in a skirmish. When sprouts of tenacious buffalo grass pushed up around the compound, the *Hotame-taneo'o* and their comrades burned it back again, effectively killing the soldier ponies' hay supply. With the coming of every sun, they infiltrated the hills banking the fort, one band of warriors relieving another so that their eyes were always keen, their senses sharp. They posted men at every strategic path, and when the white-skins tried to get in with mail or supplies, they died for the effort.

It was a smooth, powerful campaign that pleased Fire Wolf in that spot of his heart that was hard and cunning. As he rested lightly on his haunches in a waist-deep culvert above the fort, he gave a flat, flashing grin. He looked up at Sun, squinting against its glare, gauging that Roman Nose should relieve him with a party of *So'taa'e* warriors at any time now. Then he went still at the sharp howl of a wolf, a signal that had been echoing through the hills and prickling the hair at the blue-coats' napes since this assault began.

Fire Wolf howled back, giving his location. A moment later, Blind Fox crawled into the culvert behind him.

"Another wagon approaches on the supply road," he reported.

"How many spiders?"

"Fifteen blue-coats and nine of other white-skins."

They were getting desperate for food, the dog rope man thought. It was a larger party than any that had attempted the run yet.

"Where is Night Fighter?" he asked.

"Leading twelve warriors in to cut them off."

"That may not be enough. Where are the others?"

Blind Fox nodded toward the southern hills and gulches where the other parties hid.

"They are posted all over that road those soldiers ride in on when they come up from the other fort to try to rescue these men," he answered.

Fire Wolf scowled. Reinforcement soldiers had not tried to approach for several suns now, and he was sure another attempt would be made shortly. He did not want to pull his men off that place, but this supply wagon was so strongly manned, he had little choice.

"Get them," he snarled, angry that the perfection of their surveillance would have to be altered temporarily. "Send them to the fight, and watch for Roman Nose. If he comes before these blue-coats are disposed of, tell him I need his men to watch the soldier road."

Blind Fox moved off through the grass on his belly. The dog rope man risked a crouched run, his repeater low at his side.

Before he reached the supply road he heard the first war cries shriek through the air and the sporadic sound of rifle fire. When he came upon the trail, the fighting was already in earnest. He dropped down into a swale to collect his stallion from the concealed herd.

He charged up out of the copse again, screaming, and came immediately upon one of the blue-coats trying to flee on foot. His horse was down nearby, twitching and spasming in its last moments of life. Fire Wolf heard another young wolf coming in behind him, and he decided to give the soldier to the boy. The white-skin was already winded, and he would be a sure coup for the apprentice warrior.

"Take him," he spat to the boy behind him and drove his black into the melee.

He chased down a quartermaster pony galloping for the safety of the hills, but he knew his stallion did not possess the endurance yet to hang in there with the seed-fed mount. The ponies struggled up the slope side by side, and as soon as the dog rope man came abreast of the spider civilian, he gave another curdling scream and came up in his saddle.

The white-eyes turned on him viciously. Fire Wolf lunged at him as the *ve'ho'e* brought his rifle around, and the weapon caught the dog rope man against his ribs. His in-drawn breath made pain bloom there. Snarling, he snagged a handful of the spider's long, greasy hair and clamped his arm down, trapping the spider's rifle against his side.

He dragged the white man's head back. The pain in his chest peaked with the effort, but the white-skin somehow, impossibly kept his seat. He held his stallion close to the *ve'ho'e* mount with the pressure of his right calf and let go of his hair so suddenly the man had to grapple for balance.

Both guns exploded at the same time. Fire Wolf felt the searing heat of the white-eye's weapon burn against his bare skin as that rifle percussed. But the bullet went past him, thudding into the tangled brush of the gully wall. Fire Wolf's shot smashed through the white-eyes' chest, killing him instantly.

The body dropped backward into the grass, and the dog rope

man grabbed for the reins of the *ve'ho'e* pony. A seed-fed mount would be of good use in the coming suns. The white-skin's scalp was less valuable; he would come back for that if he had time. Stick might enjoy waving it around the camp, although Stalker was too young yet to appreciate it.

He rode hard for the copse where the warrior ponies waited, delivering the wild-eyed pony there. Then he spun his black around and headed toward the skirmish again. The dust of the fight was still lifting and swirling in the wind, but the blue-coats and civilians were dead. Night Fighter was helping to strip the wagon of its supplies and load what was usable onto the ponies. A small herd of cat-tul bawled behind the conveyance.

"I caught sight of Roman Nose back there. I will take our men back now," Fire Wolf said stiffly, trotting up beside him.

Night Fighter looked up, startled. The dog rope man was always the last to have a skirmish. Then he saw the glistening red blisters along his ribs, the rifle burn from the spider's gun. Night Fighter nodded.

Fire Wolf reined away, howling out to the others to follow him. A *Wu'tapiu* man galloped abreast of him, eager to return to his woman with something to feed her. His pony was laden with the fatty salt-meat Black Kettle had been promised in his latest treaty talks. It had not been given freely, as Hen-der-son had promised, so the warrior had wrestled it away.

Another warrior passed him, then another, but still there was too much commotion behind him for the clever retreat that was the Dogs' tactic. Scowling at the poor time they were making, Fire Wolf looked back. More *Wu'tapiu* were trying determinedly to herd along the recalcitrant cat-tul.

"Leave them!" he snapped. "They are stupid and slow, and no one cares for their taste anyway."

A man grumbled, but he gave in to the sense of the dog rope man's objection. As the *Wu'tapiu* drove their ponies through the herd, the cat-tul scattered and lowed.

IV

Within moments after the last Indian departed, the wind whipped the dust clear of the supply road. A turkey vulture hung in the air against the cobalt sky, then made a flapping, awkward landing on the shoulder of one of the slain blue-coats.

But this man wasn't dead.

Blood seeped into his eyes from his stripped, livid scalp. A raven-tipped arrow shot up from the back of his thigh. Captain Nathanial Carver gave a dazed grunt of agony and managed to roll half over, dislodging the talons of the bird so that it lurched up again angrily and settled nearby.

Grimly he hung on to consciousness and began to crawl up the road toward the fort.

His disjointed thoughts slid to his horse, that loyal beast that had gone down in the first volley of fire when the savages had swept, howling, from the hills. For one indescribable moment, as Carver had leapt free of the staggering animal, he had truly believed that he would escape the carnage. The Indians had been intent upon the wagon, and he had been thrown far from it. But then another grease-slick warrior had burst from a copse ahead of him.

Incredibly that brave had passed him, but another young buck had come on to chase him down. He had been preoccupied with screaming his coup cry and taking his scalp. He had done both so frenziedly he had not realized the blows he struck were not fatal.

Carver suspected he was going to die anyway. The path behind him was smeared with his blood, congealing puddles of it baking in the sun at the spots where he had rested. But he would survive long enough to get to the fort; he would make sure of it. If it was the last thing he did with his life, he would let those red-skinned heathens know that their savagery would not be tolerated by his countrymen.

It was nightfall when he reached the compound, collapsing just outside the gates. By the will of some white-skinned God, a picket chose that moment to stick his nose out beyond the planked walls. Carver managed a groan that brought the soldier's attention.

He turned back into the fort, bellowing. In a moment someone lifted Carver beneath the armpits and dragged him inside. He screamed at the pain of it, and they settled him on the ground again as the commanding officer leaned close over his face.

"Let's get him to the infirmary," he ordered.

"Wait," Carver grunted. "Major Forsythe . . . at Wallace . . . I heard he was coming this way."

"Won't get through," someone muttered.

"Already has!" came a jubilant shout, and there was a grinding, creaking noise as the big gates swung open again.

Major George Forsythe trotted in, his fifty Solomon Avengers on his horse's heels. They were a body of scouts enlisted from among the frontiersmen living in Colorado Territory, men he had begged the Department to allow him to organize. They were scarcely more than another batch of irregulars, and his superiors had been skittish enough about using such men again, but, by God, they had managed to get through to Townley.

Forsythe waved a hand to halt their progress and dismounted near the crumbled form of Carver. The commanding officer pushed to his feet again.

"Another quartermaster wagon was intercepted, Major," he reported tiredly. "By the looks of things, this young man managed to squeak through."

"Cheyenne?" Forsythe demanded of Carver, ignorant of his injuries.

"Two . . . tribes, I think. Dressed . . . different."

"Cheyenne and Sioux, no doubt," said Lieutenant Fred Beecher, second in command to Forsythe. "It would help us immeasurably, Captain, if you could remember which way they went."

"West . . . and north," Carver supplied.

"That explains how we managed to get so far up that south road," Beecher observed. "The Indians were busy over here on the other side."

Forsythe nodded, though he preferred to think it was the stealth and cunning of his men. But in truth, the road had been open only as long as the howls and gunfire had sounded from the opposite hills. It had been barely enough for him to bring his men in close and conceal them until sundown.

"Well," he decided, turning back to his Avengers. "I do believe this is the opportunity we've been waiting for. We'll follow them at first light."

Beecher was excited. "They won't be expecting our pursuit a day later. They'll lead us straight back to their home village."

A trapper who went by the name of Lucky Tom shook his head. "Don't count on it none." But despite an ear missing from an aborted scaling attempt at the hands of the Crow, his superiors were too zealous to listen to his experience.

Forsythe and Beecher led their men out just before dawn. Their enthusiasm peaked into righteous anger as they left several soldiers to collect the scalped corpses of the quartermaster party. With full light they fell upon the warriors' tracks with full steam of indignation. Then Lucky Tom made a sound of disgust and dismounted. Forsythe rode up beside him and scowled.

"What's the problem?"

"They're Cheyenne all right, Major." He had often thought that if he had fought with them instead of the Crows, he'd be missing his whole head. "They don't never get lazy. Lookee there.

"The bucks separated bit by bit, one or two taking off faster 'n the others. Reckon they'll all come together again in some prearranged spot we ain't never gonna see. This pony here, staying slow"—Lucky Tom pointed to the hoofmarks of a strong pony, probably a stallion—"he's their leader. After a while he'll be the only one left. Then he'll take off for some hard ground that don't track easy, and his trail'll be lost, too."

"So what do we do?" complained Forsythe.

"Keep going, I reckon, just to make sure. Maybe he made a mistake."

When even the stallion's tracks disappeared, Forsythe cursed mightily. The trapper silenced him with a sharp gesture.

"What?" Beecher asked, then he heard it, too, a distant lowing. "By God, it's the cattle they took! We've found them!"

"Don't reckon they kept those steers with 'em," Lucky Tom cautioned. But he led the way in that direction, the remainder of Forsythe's Avengers following him.

The beeves were in a low, grassy culvert, milling aimlessly, but the fresh trail of some bone-thin, winter-ravaged ponies was visible here. The scouts followed it avidly until it moved out onto the springy, young green of the season's first prairie grass. That growth was too new to hold prints for long, and soon it sprang back healthily, revealing nothing to the beleaguered scouts.

Forsythe reined in, his jaw set.

"Whatcha wanna do now, Major?" Lucky Tom asked.

The officer was sure only that he did not want to give up. "They were heading west. We'll circle back to the fort that way," he decided. "Maybe we'll get lucky and stumble across them."

Tom grunted. He didn't think stumbling upon any Indians was a good idea, least of all these Cheyenne.

30

Moon When The Horses Get Fat, 1868
Beecher's Island, Colorado Territory

I

Eagle winced as she touched the *o nuhk'is ee yo* medicine to the raw skin at Fire Wolf's ribs, then he sat up so that she could wrap his broken ribs above and below the blistered flesh.

"You need to eat," she decided when she had finished. There was little fresh meat to be had these suns; the men had been so devoted to their assault on the fort they had not hunted much. But she had made a sweet porridge from some lily bulbs, and she squeezed some out of her paunch into a bowl for him.

A shout went up outside as she handed it to him. She guessed from the pitched excitement in the voice that it was one of the younger warriors, probably coming back from his stint at the *ve'ho'e* fort with another scalp.

She fixed Fire Wolf with a hard glare. "They will still be dancing out there after you put that in your belly."

He cocked a brow at her bossiness.

"It is the first time you have come back to me hurt," she explained. "I do not like it."

"I will try to remember that next time." He twisted away when Stalker would have toddled into him, lifting him painfully to settle him between his thighs. "When a white-skin comes after me, I will tell him to stay back because my wife will get upset."

Eagle gave a choked little laugh. She could not ever remember him teasing before. Her heart filled with a fierce swell of love and possessiveness. He was the dog rope man, his heart was strong again, and he was hers.

Then another hooting cry went up outside, and this time Skinny Toes appeared to hunker down in front of their door.

"Some hunters have returned," he said. "They bring word of soldiers approaching. The spiders have finally left their protective fort, and they have come right to us."

Fire Wolf sprang to his feet, his pain forgotten as he ducked outside. Eagle's heart bucked as she dragged Stalker onto her hip and ran after him. Stick limped behind.

In a moment the camp turned chaotic as the word was spread. Apprentice warriors raced about, driving the ponies in from the herds to keep them safe from capture. She saw Night Fighter yelling for his war mount, and Blind Fox ran up with Fire Wolf's black. There was not anger in the air, but an edge of elation, a sense of victory almost grasped.

Something cold and unsettled began to fill her belly all the same. Bull Bear strode up to them, and she whipped about to face him.

"I have told Two Feathers to cry out that no small parties will be allowed to leave camp," he announced. "I do not want anyone to attack these blue-coats too soon. No one can be permitted to alert them. We will wait and ride out in one body, Lakota and Cheyenne together."

Fire Wolf was already working on his stallion. "What of the *ve'ho'e* numbers?"

"The hunters say there are maybe five hands of them, and they are fumbling around in the darkness. They do not seem to know they are so close to our camp."

The chief looked to Skinny Toes. "Go out to the Sioux camp and alert them," he ordered. "Roman Nose is there, having his evening meal. Bring him back."

The orphan rushed off, and Bull Bear went away to tend his own mount. Medicine symbols were painted on the ponies' hides, and feathers were fixed to their bridles. Fire Wolf was finished before anyone. He began to duck inside to paint his own face and put on his war clothing, but when Eagle remained still, he glanced back at her curiously.

"What is it?"

She did not know.

Suddenly she realized that the fear was not just blooming in her now. It had begun haunting her as long ago as the Medicine Lodge *ve'ho'e* place, a feeling that all this goodness and victory was too easy, too sweet. Somehow she knew it was about to shatter and destroy her.

The dog rope man grew impatient; the fight called to him now, and his blood was rising hot. "It will be all right," he muttered, moving inside, leaving her alone in the night.

Two Feathers trotted by her, his strong voice calling out the orders of the battle. As she listened, her blood began to chill even more.

"Roman Nose says to go on to the fight and do not wait for him! When he is ready he will come! Meet at the five trees at the creek when you are ready to ride!"

Night Fighter was still outside, binding up his pony's tail. "Why?" she demanded. "Why would Roman Nose wait?"

The warrior answered absently as he worked. "It always takes him a long time to complete the ceremonies of preparing his hat for battle."

She squinted toward his lodge. Silhouettes moved there in the flickering light at the open flap. It was a sight of peace and warmth, but her heart had started to pound hard.

The warriors began riding out for the five trees. Her dog rope man was among them, magnificent in his scalp leggings, his bronze skin shining in the moonlight with paint and grease. She hugged his son tight as he looked back at her, then he was gone into the darkness.

Once, many seasons ago, she had known in her soul that the Dance was not finished, that the Platte Bridge raid was another insidious part of it. The Dogs had come back then without her husband. Now, again, *Ma'heo'o* was telling her that something was wrong, terribly wrong, with this fight.

Her palms went slick-hot, and she began to shake. She could not, would not lose her dog rope man, too. The spiders would take no more from her.

She looked around in the darkness for Stick and found him beside the lodge. She grabbed him up and took him to Wind Woman's lodge, Stalker wriggling on her other hip. The expression on her face froze her friend.

"Please, run with them if the fighting sounds close."

"Where do you go?" Wind Woman gasped, but Eagle only spun back toward the water, running now.

Woman With White Child let her inside her lodge, and Eagle

stood for a moment, staring at them. Roman Nose was seated at the head of his fire trench, the items of his war bag strewn about him. His war bonnet was on his lap, and he smoothed its feathers gently before offering it to *Ma'heo'o* and all the four directions. They were the actions of any man going to battle, but his eyes were without fire.

"What is it?" she whispered. "What has your medicine told you?"

She knew he would not answer her. He was the strongest man of all their people, and she was only a woman. His eyes did not even move up to acknowledge her, so she turned on Woman With White Child instead.

"Do you know? Has it something to do with my man? *Tell me that much.*"

The squaw began a low, keening death song in her throat. Eagle felt herself sway.

"Something was done at the Lakota camp that I was told must not be done," Roman Nose acquiesced finally. "I ate food touched with the white man's metal. A squaw gave it to me without knowing. This breaks my medicine."

"Fix it," she begged. "Surely there are ceremonies . . ."

"They are long and elaborate. The battle begins now. I have no time." He stood, and Woman With White Child screamed.

"Do not go! They can fight this one without you!"

He looked at her as though she had lost her head. "My warriors do not know my power is broken. They fight best just knowing I am there."

He put the bonnet atop his head.

"Now," he said, "I am ready to die."

II

Eagle waited in the shadows behind his lodge until she saw the great warrior ride out. Woman With White Child howled inconsolably within.

She did not know what she could do by going after the warriors, but the sick urgency in her gut was growing stronger, filling her. She dragged a palm across her sweating brow and sprinted to her lodge. She dug past her parfleches until she found the rifle she had taken from the dead *ve'ho'e,* then she moved outside again, hooting for Wind.

The mare was close and her head came up, her ears flicking. Eagle hurled herself up onto her back. The earth was pummeled with the warriors' tracks. She thumped her heels hard into her pony and flew along them.

She came upon the warriors almost too quickly, nearly thundering into the midst of them. She reined back savagely and slid down into the tall grass to crouch and wait.

Where were the white men?

The moon was thin, but it gave enough light that she could see the Dogs and the Sioux and *So'taa'e.* They were settled into a cold camp. But they knew the enemy was near, and Bull Bear had said that the white-skins did not. There should have been fires from that *ve'ho'e* camp.

She put her weapon down to rub her hands on her thighs, then her eyes narrowed. Eight shadows moved away from the warrior camp, creeping stealthily away into the blackness.

Lakota. No apprentice Dog, no Cheyenne warrior under their lead, would dare defy Bull Bear's edict about not attacking without the main party.

"No!" She started to hiss the word aloud, then choked it back. None of the warriors turned in her direction. Some of their comrades were still creeping in; her noise had been taken for one of them.

She grabbed up her white-skin rifle again, and keeping low, scuttled after the defectors, skirting the warriors. They went up on their ponies when they were a safe distance away. Eagle groaned; she could not hoot for Wind without being heard. Finally she sprinted after the Sioux on foot.

She followed them up a rise, and then she saw the *ve'ho'e* fires below, easily two hands of them flickering off in the distance beneath this hill that protected the warriors from their sight. The Sioux boys approached the camp quietly enough, but then they charged for the blue-coats' herd, howling and waving their robes and blankets.

The night exploded.

Eagle screamed reflexively and flattened herself in the grass. Behind her, she heard a single shout of confusion from the warrior camp, then Bull Bear's voice roared out instructions.

The spider ponies heaved and screamed at their pickets, and some broke loose. The Sioux drove them away, and the *ve'ho'e* scrambled from their bedding, opening fire.

Grandmother Earth began to tremble beneath her, tortured by hundreds of galloping hooves. The *Hotame-taneo'o* and their allies thundered past her, the feathers on their equipment sending up a strange *burring* sound in the wind. But the *ve'ho'e* had been warned. Shooting wildly back toward the hill, they leapt upon their ponies that remained.

Eagle pushed up on her arms. The white-skins gained the creekbed of the Arikaree, splashing across the low, pooled water. An island rose in the middle of the shallow channel, and as dawn began to spread across the sky, she saw that it was thick with willows and alders and tall grass. The spiders reached it and dived in, falling from their ponies into the concealment of the brush.

As the warriors reached the creek, they split their numbers to circle the island. The air cracked and whined with their bullets and arrows, and the spiders' screams of agony rose as they died.

Their ponies dropped as well, and the spider survivors hunkered down behind them, using them for breastworks. Screaming in triumph, the warriors began to retreat for another charge.

NO!

Suddenly, Eagle knew why she had been meant to come here. Understanding brought her to her knees again, scrambling and screaming. She spotted Roman Nose, his pony's ears flat as he broke into a dead run toward the island. *Ve'ho'e* bullets spit at him, but his men followed him fearlessly up the first grass of the island. Some white-skins were hidden there, and one of them reared up, shooting. Red burst at Roman Nose's back.

"*Aiy-ee*," Eagle breathed, but the fearless warrior kept his seat, turning his pony about to ride back across the bed. Unobtrusively, without a death song, he dropped down to lay himself out on the prairie.

Without their most fearsome warrior, the men would be aimless. They would come back here to the high ground swelling up from the water, and she could see that they would be easy targets.

Oh, sweet Ma'heo'o, *they would come back unless the dog rope called them to return.*

III

Fire Wolf felt the loss of Roman Nose like a breath of cold air at the nape of his neck, as though his friend's *mis'tai* had slipped by to alert him on its way to its death road.

He left his black in the bed and crawled up the island on his belly. He thought the *ve'ho'e* there would have to stand if they wanted to shoot down into the creek at the warriors, and he knew their impatience would urge them to do it soon enough. Any men here at the grass level would see them first, killing them as soon as they rose.

He bellowed for other warriors to join him. When he got no response, he looked behind him.

He could not spot Roman Nose, but it did not matter. He knew he was gone, and now the others knew as well. Someone had found the prone form of the fabled warrior, and reaction raced through their numbers, breaking them, scattering them.

"Come back!" he shouted. The warriors either did not hear him or chose not to heed him. They went for the high land on the far side of the creek.

Viciously, with all the venom of a lifetime of loss and choices, Fire Wolf cursed whatever powers gave him the insight to see the trap. Only those who were in the bed, beneath the white-skins, were safe and could effectively take the offensive.

He gripped the rope at his hip, and it was hot and alive under his touch.

He wanted to live.

Too late, it finally came to him, a passion for each breath *Ma'heo'o* granted him, for the woman and boys who had given him life again. He could not let his men die, but if he planted the rope, he would sing his death song with the action.

With an anguished roar, he pulled it free of his breechclout, and then he saw her.

She was far back on the prairie, standing straight and hauntingly beautiful. For a lethal moment, he considered that she was a vision from *Ma'heo'o*, some cruel, taunting joke in this final moment. Then her words came back to him from a sun long ago, on the day his son had been born. They were words he had not truly heeded then, but he knew they would destroy him now.

"If you are strong enough to claim me in spite of your rope, then I will have to fight beside you."

He remembered, and memory sealed his choice. If the *ve'ho'e* shot across to the high prairie, she would die with the other warriors. He could leave nothing over there for them to shoot at. He had to bring the Dogs back to his side.

With a tortured cry of rage, he stabbed the picket pin into the earth.

IV

Ma'heo'o gave Eagle the chance to spare herself. Darkness swam over her vision so that she would not have to witness it, would not have to watch Fire Wolf go down. She fought back against the blackness with every bit of strength in her soul.

She swayed, putting her gun against the earth to brace herself. She blinked, and saw that he still stood with the rope in his hand. Then she howled a bloodcurdling scream and ran for him.

A bullet ripped up the grass near her feet, and she leapt, sobbing. When she looked up again, he had put the pin in the ground.

"Nooooo!"

But it was too late, it was planted, and he was bellowing to his warriors.

"See me! See what I have done! Come back, not to save me, but yourselves!"

Behind and above him, she saw a spider rise. He leaned down across his breastworks, taking aim at the dog rope man.

Suddenly her heart felt cold, her breath slow. She brought her rifle up and pulled at the trigger until the gun went off.

The percussion was stunning and painful. It slammed her off her feet, but she crawled to her knees again, weeping. The white-skin slumped over his breastwork, dropping over into the sand at Fire Wolf's feet.

She gave a thin sound of exhilaration and relief as the last of the warriors rode back to Fire Wolf's bank. He did not need her any longer. She had done what *Ma'heo'o* had sent her to do. The rifle dropped from her nerveless hand, and she pitched into blackness.

31

Moon When The Cherries Are Ripe, 1868
Arikaree Creek

I

Summer fell sweetly across the land that season, but it could not seem to warm Fire Wolf's heart.

Eagle watched him as he moved around outside their lodge, adjusting and cleaning his weapons. Her heart squeezed with something like fear. More than once his attention wandered, and then he would gaze stonily out at the prairie. She was beginning to give up hope that he was only angry with her.

Something had changed inside him since the dog rope fight. It was nothing so simple as the return of his demons. It was both deeper than that and new; there was a brooding distance to him that was different from anything she had ever seen in him before.

She could not explain it, but she knew that she could not stand it anymore. To go on like this, without his nearness, would break her soul as surely as if he had died that sun.

She moved toward him, her chin rising determinedly with each step she took. He turned sharply at the sound of her approach.

"I am not a *ve'ho'e* enemy," she teased, "only the woman you claimed as wife." But he did not smile or soften.

Was that it? she wondered. Was it this endless war with the white-skin spiders that preoccupied him? It had reexploded after the island fight. Soldiers seemed to fill the country, crawling into its every nook and cranny as they never had before. The People moved tensely after the buffalo this season, always looking back over their shoulders.

A great deal of their fear and hatred was for the new chief called Cus-ter. He had had an alarming number of coups against the warriors and had flushed out far too many camps.

"Is it that new one?" she asked. "The new white-skin who stalks us?"

Fire Wolf focused on her, then shrugged. "He is troublesome. He concerns everyone."

"But is it he who darkens your mind?" she persisted.

A deep pain touched his eyes. It scared her. "Tell me," she begged suddenly. "Your heart goes away from me. Why now, when we have been through so much?"

He did not answer; still, somehow, Eagle knew she had reached him. His eyes closed as though shutting out the sight of something he could not bear.

When he dragged her close, she gasped in surprise. His mouth crushed down on hers. She was not ready for him, and they were out in the plain view of the people, but her heart began skittering crazily. This edge to his love was different, too, but she could not turn away from him. Hunger flared in her as it always did, and they pulled each other into the lodge.

There was a frightening urgency to his touch, as though he was trying to memorize her. He pulled her doeskin over her head roughly, and his hands moved over her skin as though he would imprint the feel of it on his fingers. When his mouth came back to hers, it was like he would capture the taste of her forever on his tongue. She moaned and writhed up into him. If this was what he needed, if it would make him strong again, then she would give it.

They came together feverishly, but when he finished it was with a groan that tore at her heart. He rolled off her, and she looked over at him, her breath still coming hard.

"I do not chastise you for what you did," he said finally. "You cannot believe that."

"No." She didn't, not with her instincts. She sat up to hug herself.

"I cannot begrudge the fact that you were real in that fight, and not a vision. Your presence saved my life."

Did that unman him somehow? She wanted to ask, but a hot, angry look came suddenly to his eyes. He rose to push his breechclout back down and pace.

"How can I berate that very fire in your nature that drew me, body and soul, in the first place?" he went on. "I cannot, but neither can I live with it, not yet, not now."

She didn't know what she expected him to say, but it wasn't that. Her breath seemed to freeze somewhere low inside her. "What do you say?" she managed. What did he want from her?

"After you shot that white-skin, when you fell back into the grass, I thought I had lost you. I fought crazily because there was nothing left."

Eagle nodded carefully. She knew he had killed seven white men, more than any other warrior, while some of the Dogs had crawled to her and dragged her back to safety.

"I cannot fight like that again, or I will die next time," he said flatly. "You must leave me until this last rash of fighting is over. I want you to go back to In-di-en Ter-a-tor-ee, where they will not kill you. Then I can fight this war to the end, knowing you are safe."

She had thought she could bear any problem that haunted him. She was strong; he had given her that, and it had made her survive everything the *ve'ho'e* had thrown at her. But his last words struck something inside her like nothing else through all the seasons.

"Leave . . . you?"

Rage gripped her. She lunged to her feet. "Until this last fighting is over?" she repeated incredulously. "Do you not see it yet? Have you not figured it out? *It will never be over!* No victory over these white-skins will drive them out, and no paper talks will stem the greed in their hearts! Our blood will seep into Grandmother Earth, and our women and babes will scream at the scepter of their own slaughter, *but it will never, ever be over!* In the face of that, we are all we have. If you choose to live without me until the victory comes, then you will live without me all your suns!"

She thought she saw him flinch, but in the end his jaw only hardened. "I will take you as soon as the next moon fattens. It is a dangerous time now. We will have to travel by night."

"Noooo!"

He had started to duck out of the lodge, but now he turned back, his expression every bit as fierce as her own. "I learned much at that battle on the island. I know I was right in doing what I did when I lost Sweet Grass Woman. I am strong enough now to face doing the same thing again. I am a warrior, and I can fight anything, but having you wrenched from my world would destroy me as nothing else before. I would hide you where there is no chance of losing you. Understand me. Roman Nose is gone. My people need me. They need me to fight sanely and well, because if I do not, all is lost.

"Perhaps you are right. Perhaps this war will never end, but I think you are wrong. This time the white-skins will try to take everything from us, and either they, or we, will have to die first."

He left with a hard slap at the door hide, and Eagle felt her heart shatter.

"Understand me as well!" she screamed after him. "I belong here with you while you kill them!"

He did not come back.

"I am Hotame-taneo'o!"

II

Every step Wind Runner took was one in which Eagle's heart threatened to rise up in violent protest.

She rode behind Skinny Toes across the low, flat southern lands she had once loved so deeply, her heart aching for the high country she had left behind. Her mind wandered back to it again and again.

Did he mourn her yet? What was he doing, now, in this moment?

She slumped on her pony, then dragged herself upright again to stare at the orphan's back. All his seasons of subservience to the Dogs had not prepared him for this bizarre request. She had asked him to travel with her because she knew that saying goodbye to her dog rope man was the one thing in *Ma'heo'o*'s world she could not do. Skinny Toes had pleaded with her, and in the end Night Fighter had had to intercede on her behalf. He had instructed the orphan to take her south, and Skinny Toes had led her away one high noon while the warriors had been away, spilling *ve'ho'e* blood as though that could possibly change anything.

Eagle knew, somehow, that her dog rope man needed this from her more than anything she had ever given him. If she had not gone to that fight, he would be dead, but in the saving, she had lost him.

32

Big Freezing Moon, 1868
Washita River, Indian Territory

I

Eagle arrived in Indian Territory to find that her kin had not changed.

Little Moon was still angular and sharp-tongued. Caught The Enemy was distant and remote, harboring an impotent anger at Black Kettle that she knew went deeper than his heart. Only Sun Roads seemed happy enough, content with her girl-child and her Comanche husband. Eagle thought bitterly that her smiling, placid sister had never asked much from *Ma'heo'o*, so there was little the *ve'ho'e* could take from her.

Of them all, only Medicine Wolf seemed different. He had aged terribly.

He walked slowly, as though each step pained him horribly. Eagle took it upon herself to see that he moved no more than he had to. When there was food enough to fill her paunch, she took it to him to share it. She was shocked one sun when she carried a thin gruel of cherrywood bark to his lodge, only to find him laboriously mounting his pony.

"Grandfather!" She nearly dropped her paunch, and skewered the carrying stick through the top quickly to keep it from spilling its precious contents. She set it beside his lodge and ran to him, not knowing whether to push on his rump until he was astride, or drag him down again.

"Ride! Ride!" Stalker cried, running toward the pony, his arms outstretched so that some adult might lift him upon the mount. Medicine Wolf finally settled himself without Eagle's help and looked down at the boy.

"Yes, Grandson," he wheezed. "That is exactly what I would do this sun."

"Why?" Eagle demanded. "Where in *Ma'heo'o*'s name would you go?"

He slumped in the saddle as though already weary. "Your uncle would go to Fort Cobb, and I should be with him. Sometimes he listens to the advice of men older than he."

"Would he try to beg food?" Cobb was the res-er-va-shun fort, the place where supplies were to have been issued had any been forthcoming. The *ve'ho'e* said there was none because the Cheyenne were warring again, but they had given nothing even during the last peaceful robe season, just after Black Kettle had marked his treaty.

Medicine Wolf shrugged. "We will ask for some as long as we are there, but I do not think it will do any good."

"Why then? Why go?"

"Black Kettle is concerned that so many of our young men are slipping off the res-er-va-shun to fight."

Eagle sighed. The warriors told the a-jent at Cobb that they were going hunting, but more often than not they returned with plunder, and sometimes they did not even bother to get passes for their trips at all. In the end, even *ve'ho'e* food was digestable, and starvation had pushed them beyond caring if it went against the terms of a treaty that did not seem to exist.

"Your uncle would ask the spiders not to be angry with him because he cannot control his warriors any longer."

"He grovels," she spat.

"It has been nearly six circles of seasons since the last great hunt. He is a beaten man."

Medicine Wolf turned his pony toward the *Vehoo'o*'s lodge. Eagle chewed on her lip for a long time, staring after him.

II

Black Kettle and Medicine Wolf, along with a handful of lesser *Vehoo'o*, stood solemnly outside the planked porch of Fort Cobb's commanding officer's quarters. Once again, Black Kettle would dearly have liked a smoke, but there was little pipe weed in this country, either, except for that possessed by the *ve'ho'e*. General William Hazen did not offer him any.

The spider soldier stood on his porch, his arms crossed against the north wind that howled at him across the parade ground. He was impatient and it showed in the way his eyes moved. Indians from all the reservation tribes came to him daily to beg for rations he could not give them. There had been too many red-tape glitches in the Medicine Lodge treaty for the pact to be ratified, and too many altercations since for it to be feasible.

All Hazen could do was stall. He had confidence in the new man the Department had spearheaded to mop up these bloody Indian wars. George Custer would put an end to the skirmishes soon enough.

Now, however, Hazen still had six sorry-looking chiefs eyeing him hopefully. "So what is it you're trying to tell me?" he prodded them, wanting very much to go back inside where it was warm.

"We would like peace," Black Kettle reiterated. A young half-breed leaning against the porch rail translated and yawned. "I come to remind you that my *Wu'tapiu* are complying with your treaty."

Hazen scowled. He knew for a fact that the old chief was lying. Custer had pursued too many plundering warriors heading south into the southern hills of Indian Territory.

"Men have left your camp to raid," he snapped.

Black Kettle shrugged eloquently. "They are young, renegade warriors who are determined to get food for their families. I cannot control them when their babes wail with hunger and their bellies twist emptily. You should give us provisions. Then they would not want to go out."

"Don't have any to give you. I told you that last time."

"Still none?" Medicine Wolf asked.

"No, sir. Sorry."

Black Kettle sighed. "Most of my people do not ever leave this place. There should be no blood spilled."

Hazen shifted his weight uncomfortably. He did not dare risk his reputation by offering these characters sanctuary near his fort. Their leader had as much as admitted that some of his bucks were raiding, and sooner or later Custer would nail them. Hazen didn't want it happening in his backyard, as had happened to Anthony at Sand Creek.

"I think the best way to prevent bloodshed is to take your people farther away from this compound," he decided. "Try to keep them as quiet and peaceful as possible. Looks like snow," he finished, looking up at the sky as he turned back into his quarters. "Maybe you'd better be heading back now."

III

Medicine Wolf hurt badly as they rode back to their camp on the Washita, but he suspected that his bones were not aching from the cold. They hurt with foreboding.

He had outlived much of his usefulness, he mused, and his woman was gone. If Hazen's soldiers came to them, he would not mind dying. But now there was his granddaughter. There were her boys, one he had struggled badly to heal and who had stolen his old heart. Thinking of them, Medicine Wolf could not stop considering how Ha-zen's eyes had not met his, not even when he had tried very hard to catch them.

"What do you plan?" he asked Black Kettle.

The *Vehoo'o*'s face creased deeper. "We will take our people farther west with the next sun."

"I would urge you to move on this night."

Black Kettle thought about it. "I do not think any soldiers will hurt us," he answered at length. "I told them we are not guilty of much."

Medicine Wolf stiffened. At Sand Creek his wife had not been guilty of anything at all.

But too many other men nodded. The first snowflakes were beginning to sting their faces, and a cutting cold was blowing up in the wind. "It is not a good night for any man to be moving about," Caught The Enemy agreed, "whether he is red or white. No one will come this night."

"Then why did that soldier warn us away?" Medicine Wolf demanded.

"I am not sure he did," replied Black Kettle.

They dispersed to their lodges, and the pain in Medicine Wolf's bones settled deeper.

Inside his tepee he crouched close to his fire. His body put up an ache of protest as he dragged some bedding atop his travel robe. Then his gaze fell on Eagle's cooking paunch.

She had left it for him, sliding it just inside his door flap so that he might fill his belly when he returned. The sight of it sent another pang into him. Grunting, suddenly decisive, he labored to his feet again.

He dug into one of his parfleches, then carried a small, rawhide bundle back outside into the night. It was late and the snow was blinding. He put his meager weight into the gale and trudged to his granddaughter's lodge.

Eagle started at the sound of his voice outside. The wind seemed to snatch it from his lungs and hurl it into the night. She gasped, urging him inside.

"What is it?"

She knew something had happened at the fort. His arrival in this cold could mean nothing else. But she had known too much fear to cringe, too much loss to fear. She cared more for the man in front of her than for any *ve'ho'e* trouble that would come whether she fought it or not.

"Here, sit." She began to pull him closer to the fire trench, but he shook her off with surprising strength.

"I am not sure there is time." He pushed a small parfleche at her. "Once I turned my back on you, on your son. I vowed never to do that again."

Eagle shook her head. "You did not—"

"Hush," he interrupted. "I think *Ma'heo'o* will call me up *Heammawihio* soon to his Place of the Dead. I think that is what my bones are trying to tell me. The *ve'ho'e* will come here and kill me this time, but you must live."

She had thought she could not feel anymore, but still she shuddered. She did not doubt him.

"I have been saving this for many seasons. You should have it now. I no longer wish to fight for my life."

She opened the bundle. Inside was a small cache of powder and lead.

"Get that gun you brought here with you," Medicine Wolf said.

Eagle flinched. She had scarcely touched the weapon since the deadly, pivotal sun of the island fight. But she found it and handed it to him. He squatted down with it on his lap.

"Now I will show you how to put those bullets in here. You tell me you already know how to shoot it."

He demonstrated, loading the rifle. Then he stood slowly and started for the door flap.

"Why do you think the spiders will come here?" she demanded.

"Because once again they spoke many words without saying anything at all."

IV

She was so very tired.

Eagle pushed her bedding robes aside to crawl back to the fire trench and feed it again. But she knew that the cold she felt came from inside her. It came from the place where Fire Wolf had once dwelled, the place of the strength that she had called on so very many times.

Now that place was empty. This fight was endless anyway, and her dog rope man was gone. Still, she waited, awake, to see if her grandfather was right. She settled back against her bedding again and laid her gun across her lap.

The snow eased at her smoke hole, then the white, unforgiving orb of the moon passed by. When the sky began to pale, she heard the first aborted scream come from the direction of the valley where the ponies were grazing. She winced, then pushed to her haunches, shivering once. But suddenly she was not cold anymore.

She had been wrong. She could still feel. Hatred settled in her, strong and bracing.

The white mongrels had taken everything and left her nothing, and now they would strike their cruelest blow to the warrior who was her heart. It had taken all of Fire Wolf's courage to send her here. Killing her would be the coup that shattered him once and for all.

She would not allow it.

She crept to the door flap, then, impossibly, she heard some sort of music. Had she slept without knowing it? Did she dream? There was no thunder of soldier ponies this time, but the bleating strains of a horn scraped over her skin.

She pushed at the flap. The snow was deep and banking outside. She shoved her full weight into it, spilling out into the cold when it gave.

She sat up dazedly, brushing the white off her. But now she knew why she had not heard any blue-coats approaching. The storm had been a strong one. The snow was thick enough to muffle their hooves.

There were other sounds, though, now that she was outside. *Ve'ho'e* harness metal jingled, and there was the sickening, distant crack of bullets. *No more. Not again.* Her hands began to shake with her deadly rage.

She scrambled back inside to her boys, shaking them awake. They focused on her with startled cries, and she gathered them close one last precious time.

"This is very important," she managed. "You must listen to me well.

"Stay close to me, very close. You must do whatever I tell you to, and do not pay too much attention to anything you see or hear. Can you do that?"

Stalker felt her emotion, and he began chugging as though to cry. Stick took his brother's arm.

"I have him, Mama. I will pull him along."

He had only one good leg. But she could not carry them. They were both too heavy for her now.

She pushed Medicine Wolf's powder sack down into her belt, then she led them outside. The familiar trickster shouts were beginning to fill the air as some white-skins came on from a dip between the distant hills to her right.

There was more commotion behind her, and she veered to find it. More blue-coats poured out from behind the hills behind her lodge. She yelped and pulled back, dragging Stick and Stalker with her, and then she saw still more soldiers spew out from the trees on the other side.

So many of them. Dragging her boys, she began running for the creek at the far side of camp. There was dangerous, open prairie beyond it, but there was nowhere else to go.

Custer's military band exploded into sound again, and Eagle screamed this time, whipping about to look in disbelief. But she could see little because all around her, her kin were staring, too.

Then the blue-coats stopped their merry music and charged.

She lifted her rifle and took aim at the first loathed *ve'ho'e* who galloped past her. She was ready for the percussion this time, and she only staggered back a few more steps while the blue-coat rolled off his pony. She took a precious second to reload.

"Good, Mama!" Stick howled.

"Yes, my babe, it is very, very good." She grabbed them again and turned and fled.

The *Wu'tapiu* screamed and swarmed. Not even Black Kettle could tell his people that this carnage was yet another mistake. She saw him ahead, running along the river, crashing through the brush that pushed up from the snow. Medicine Woman Later lumbered after him, and then some of the pony herd trotted by as well. Her old *Vehoo'o* uncle snagged a mount and clambered up on it, pulling her aunt behind him.

Medicine Woman Later took the first bullet. She was driven sideways by the blast, tumbling down into the ice that crusted the water. Then a hail of fresh fire drove into Black Kettle.

Her voice ripped from her, screeching and crazed, then it broke into sobs. "Oh, Uncle, they are . . . your friends!"

She pushed her babes to make them run, and followed them before she could see him fall. She came upon Medicine Wolf next, but that old man did not flee. He remained in front of his lodge, bravely and uselessly shooting his arrows into the soldier ranks until the white-skins shot him down.

"*Aiy-ee!*" She was deep in the knot of her own kin's lodges now. They began moving toward the water again, then she stumbled over a body.

It was one of her own. She knew it without looking, willed herself not to look. But her eyes were dragged down as she hefted the lame Stick across the corpse, pulling Stalker after him.

Caught The Enemy.

She could not stop to mourn him, either. She prayed to his *mis'tai* to understand. *Please, my father, think of my boys. They still live, and live they will until they are old enough to fight themselves against these men who would destroy them.*

She did not lose control until she met Sun Roads. She burst free of the last lodges and saw her sister ahead, fleeing to the creek with her babe. Her Comanche husband held off the soldiers, but then the warrior fell, and Eagle screamed as Sun Roads turned back to the blue-coat who had killed him.

Eagle saw it in her face, the end of all hope and forbearance, and finally she wept, thick, hot tears.

"What is it, Mama?" Stalker cried.

But she could not tell him, could not explain. Sun Roads could no longer struggle against these men who had taken her simple life from her, but neither would she surrender anymore.

Eagle screamed at her to be heard over the fire. But it was too late. The blue-coat's face whitened to the color of ashes as Sun Roads fell upon his pony, wresting his gun from his hand. She did not kill him. She shot her child, then she pressed the weapon to her own belly.

Eagle spun away, howling, as the rifle exploded. But a hysterical edge of triumph began to fill her. *You see, white mongrels, you cannot have everything. There are still some things we can take from you. She would not let you have her own death or her world.*

She reached the creek and shoved her boys down into it, then she turned back again to the edge of the bank. She could still avenge Sun Roads. There was that much she could do for her.

She gripped her rifle and ran back to the soldier. He still gaped, stunned, at Sun Roads and her babe. She knew he did not know her tongue, but it did not matter. Somehow, in his heart before he died, he would know her message.

"You think you can wrench this land for yourself by any means you choose!" she hissed. "You think you have the right to take lives as the People know only *Ma'heo'o* can do. But you are not a god, *and you have tormented me enough!"*

She lifted her cumbersome weapon again before he could react, and then she shot him.

Keening, she raced back for the creek, grabbing up Stalker and Stick as she crashed down into the ice. She hauled them up the other side, and then, cresting the hills in front of her, she saw salvation.

Comanche and Kiowa warriors, alerted by the distant sounds of carnage, swept down toward the camp to help. But it was an incomprehensible fight that had already been lost.

Ponies crashed through the river behind her, fleeing, and one of them was a lost *ve'ho'e* mount. She lunged for his reins as he passed and caught them. He dragged her a little way, then quieted.

"Stick!"

The boy came limping, hitching up to her as quickly as he could. She dropped him hard on the pony's back.

"Remember what Fire Wolf taught you. Now gallop, gallop hard. Over there toward those men!"

She slapped the pony's rump, and Stick raced off proudly. She said a prayer to the man she fought for. *Thank you, love, thank you for teaching him hard and well.*

She looked back to the camp. Squaws fought there, heaving kettles and hurling knives. Too many warriors were down, but in the face of yet another undeserved massacre, the women held on, viciously defending their own.

Stalker pressed close to her as she searched wildly for another pony. Then she felt a rough warrior's grip snatch her up by her belt. She screamed for her babe, and another strong, red hand came down to snag him. She watched her son settle in front of the man on the pony, then she pulled herself up to ride behind the warrior who had saved her.

Finally a wail of mourning ripped from her throat. All her kin were gone. Fire Wolf had been right.

The war had ended for the *Wu'tapiu*. They had been exterminated.

33

Hoop-And-Stick Game Moon, 1869
Comanche Reservation, Indian Territory

I

The snows kept coming that winter, and the cold ached as though in sympathy for her. The Comanche band who had rescued her watched her with their own pity, but Eagle was not concerned. She was waiting, and she had waited before.

What unnerved Ten Bears' people the most was the way she watched the sun.

She did it sometimes at the height of the day, staring up at it until her eyes teared, but eventually she always turned away to work for one of the squaws who helped to shelter her. Of them all, Eagle preferred Last Bead's company the most, and she stayed at her lodge as often as she could without snubbing the others. She was a guest among these people, living off their charity when they were as hungry as any southern tribe. They all shared stoically with her, never questioning, but Last Bead was blunt and inquisitive.

"If you would stay with us, then you should let one of our young men take you into his lodge," the woman said once as they worked at boiling dye.

Last Bead communicated well enough with an odd mixture of Comanche and Cheyenne learned from her neighbors. Eagle knew she had not misunderstood her, but she forced her features into blinking confusion.

"I am wed." *And my dog rope man will come for me. He will find me.*

Last Bead made a sharp sound against her teeth. "I did not take you for a fool."

Eagle shrugged. She knew they all considered Fire Wolf to be dead. Even if he hadn't fallen yet, surely he would before he could find her. Cus-ter and his men were savagely crisscrossing the prairie. But Eagle knew that Fire Wolf would get through. He was *Hotame-taneo'o*, and the country that the white-skins sought to shoot him from was his own.

"Fights Blind would like to take you," Last Bead persisted. "He is kin of mine and a good hunter, and he admires you. You have two fine sons, one so strong of heart he defies his lameness to do everything our boys do."

Eagle nodded. "My husband taught him to be that way."

Last Bead puffed out her breath. She had heard that these Cheyenne squaws were loyal to a fault. It would take some work to lure this one from her husband's ghost.

"You are young yet. You have a lot to offer a man."

Eagle gave a little laugh. She felt as old as the moon.

"I have seen nineteen winters."

"Well, we are all hungry," Last Bead said, trying another tack.

"I will be gone by the Spring Moon, and I will not forget you. My husband will give you food."

"How can you be so sure he will come?" Last Bead grew exasperated. She was beginning to fear that when this girl learned her faith was unfounded, it would bend her mind into craziness.

Eagle only gave her another ageless, unbreachable smile. "He will come. The sun still rises."

II

When word reached him of the massacre, Stone Forehead sent grim word to the *Hotame-taneo'o*. Then he called in his warriors and moved his people south from their Medicine Lodge homelands. He took them to a place on the northern rim of In-di-en Ter-a-tor-ee, but they did not give Cus-ter their weapons and they did not intend to stay. They established a winter camp on the Wolf River to collect those survivors who had escaped Cus-ter's Washita slaughter.

The *Wu'tapiu* who lived limped in to his place over the course of Cold Maker's moons. Most had been surviving in little bands of four and five, stealthily and carefully making their way north by night. Stone Forehead's runners haunted the

People's trails to find them and brought them in wounded, their spirits torn.

Little Moon was among those they found. The Flexed Legs men brought her back on the same sun that the *Hotame-taneo'o* stormed in. Blind Fox fell upon his mother with unmanly grief, but she held him as though not knowing he was her kin.

Fire Wolf's face never changed when his eyes fell upon Eagle's aunt.

To consider Eagle's fate now, knowing that he had sent her to it, would destroy him. The truth of that was like flames licking at the edges of his soul. He could not let them consume him, not yet. He would wait until he found her bones.

Then he would die arrogantly, gloriously, in a coup that would remind the white men of his hatred and rage until the sun burned clear of the sky.

Now he looked narrowly at Blind Fox as the young warrior crouched down beside him near the big *Hotame-taneo'o* fire. "What does your mother tell you?" he demanded.

Blind Fox could not meet his eyes. "She does not remember anything of the fight at all."

"She should remember her kin," the dog rope man snapped.

"No. I think her mind stopped when she lost another husband, and when the *Vehoo'o* she followed went down."

There was no room in Fire Wolf's heart for pity. He hurled his meat into the fire angrily and stalked off into the night.

Wind Woman hesitated, then pushed to her feet after him. She had forced her way on this trip knowing there would be bloodied, bereft survivors who needed her. Now she realized that her own men might need her most.

"What can you do?" Night Fighter asked, watching her.

"I will tell him she lives."

Night Fighter scowled. "You cannot know that. They say it happened at dawn again, with no warning." *And she was only a squaw.* But he did not speak the thought aloud.

Still, Wind Woman understood his expression. "She is *Hotame-taneo'o*," she said fiercely. "We all are."

She trudged off the way Fire Wolf had gone. She followed his tracks through the snow into one of the many copses of trees in this disorientingly wooded country, but then they vanished. She planted herself, scowling, turning about in small circles to look into the brush.

The chuckling sound of a stream was distant, and she went that way, thinking it would be a good place for a man to soothe his mind. But when she reached the brook, splashing coldly over some stones, she found herself still alone.

A sound farther upstream had her narrowing her eyes. She moved along the path of the water, then froze in midstride, her heart slamming.

Blue-coats.

She took a single step back, moving silently without turning about and taking her eyes off them. There was enough snow on the ground to muffle her sounds. She did not run until she was back at the place where she had started, where Fire Wolf's tracks had disappeared. Then she raced back into the camp, her robe flapping.

"White-skins," she hissed, running up to the *Hotame-taneo'o* fire.

The warriors surged to their feet in the way of men who never truly rested. They shot questions at her in quiet urgency while the Flexed Legs men and the few remaining *Wu'tapiu* warriors gathered around them.

"There is a stream to the west of here," Wind Woman gasped. "Follow it north and you will find them."

"Are they camping?"

"They were watering their mounts."

"Where is the dog rope man?"

To that, she could only shrug miserably. "I could not find him."

But the dog rope man was already aware of the intruders.

He crouched low in the brush near the place where they rested, coldly weighing his options. There were three hands of them, and he could not take them all down by himself. When they showed an inclination to move, he thought he would return for his brothers, then track them.

He melted back into the woods, then a hand reached up against his back to stop him. He whipped around to find Night Fighter.

The other Dogs moved up silently into the wooded growth,

encircling the *ve'ho'e*. Then the night was shattered by a howl of blood-hungry rage.

All stealth was lost. Fire Wolf felt his heart come up hard as all around him the Dogs rose to their feet. They swarmed into the knot of startled white-skins, and the *ve'ho'e* reacted in fumbling terror, going for their arms.

Fire Wolf leapt down from the knoll he crouched on, kicking one rifle away as a white hand reached for it. He came up behind a spider and brought his rifle hard across his throat. He pushed the tip of his knife into the soft skin below his ear, trapping him against him.

He would not kill him. Not yet.

The warrior who had screamed first was *Wu'tapiu*. He ran to them, snarling as though to kill the man himself.

"That is him," the warrior spat. "He is the one. *Cus-ter.*"

Fire Wolf's grip tightened, and his own blood began to pump with a hatred that could easily craze him. The officer stood haughtily and lazily in his grasp. There was no tension coming off him. He was either crazy or full of himself beyond sanity.

Fire Wolf closed his eyes briefly for control. *If he has killed her, I will cut his belly open and let him watch his own guts spill out before he dies.* Yes, this was a coup he could die with. He looked to the *Wu'tapiu* warrior again.

"Find out if anyone here speaks two tongues."

A new voice came quietly to caution him. "Above all else, remember you are the dog rope man. Be wise."

Fire Wolf's eyes flashed to Stone Forehead as he stepped into the clearing. Old man, you do not know, he thought. Above all else, I was her protector. I promised the sun.

The *Wu'tapiu* warrior dragged forward a scrappy trader. Fire Wolf pushed the knife almost gently into Cus-ter's neck until a thin trickle of blood seeped out.

"Talk, white man. Talk."

Because he owed it to himself, to his woman, to his people, Fire Wolf let the white mongrel turn around. He met the soldier chief eye to eye.

The *Wu'tapiu* survivors had told of an unprecedented stealing of their squaws this time. It was not a *ve'ho'e* custom, but clearly a new twist of this devil soldier.

"You took some of our women," he challenged.

Cus-ter nodded calmly when his words were translated.
"They're at our forts, waiting for you to come in."

Again, Fire Wolf choked back his rage. There would be time
later to tell him that such a thing would never happen. "What
fort?"

"What women?"

He pushed his rifle into his belly so that Custer gave a little
grunt. "The ones you took when you massacred the people in
your protection."

Custer lifted a brow. "You speak of the Cheyenne in the
Territory? They were protected only as long as they desisted in
their depredations."

"You had a paper talk with them."

Custer's eyes narrowed. "I have done nothing I will not
cheerfully confess to my God."

An ungodly howl came from a *Wu'tapiu* man. A Dog held
him back from a suicide rush.

"Where are the squaws you took from that fight?" Fire Wolf
snarled.

"I believe those were taken to Fort Cobb's camp supply."

"Did you take all who survived?"

"Every one," Custer sneered. He saw no need to admit to the
heathen that too many squaws had escaped for his liking.

Night Fighter stepped forward, reading the death intent in
his brother's eyes. "Was there a woman with two young boys,
one limping on a bad leg?" he demanded. "Did you take her to
your camp?"

Custer's chin came up a notch, and he eyed the first warrior.
He waited a heartbeat before he lied.

"I remember seeing no such woman, no boys alive."

Fire Wolf screamed an unearthly sound of loss and rage. He
brought his knife arm back, but Stone Forehead came close so
that the man could not sweep the weapon down without
stabbing the shaman. Not even to grasp his own death could he
assault the revered medicine man. He would die honorably,
above all else.

"Move, Grandfather." His voice was like the snow, still and
cold. *"Move."*

Stone Forehead remained planted. "You think with the heat
of your heart, not your head. We know these *ve'ho'e*. They lie.

"I see the pain of your loss in your eyes, and my heart tells me it is bad. I do not ask you to live. I ask you to wait for another time to die."

Fire Wolf's eyes went thin and suspicious. Stone Forehead sighed.

"*Ma'heo'o* has told me there will be another battle when your life is needed more."

He turned to the soldier chief, and his voice took up an eerie tone of conviction. "Hear me now, white chief. If you are lying to us, a sun will come soon when you and all your soldiers will perish by red hands. This war is not over. We will meet again. Until then, I curse you."

He pulled some ashes from his medicine pouch and sprinkled them on Custer's boot before the soldier could react. But several other *ve'ho'e* jumped back.

"What the holy hell?" someone muttered.

Custer stomped his heel, curling his lip in disgust. Stone Forehead smiled at him, then he looked to Bull Bear.

"Let them go."

The war chief's face twisted in disbelief. "He is ours, *Vehoo'o*. Do not speak to me of peace when this man still has Cheyenne blood on his hands!"

"I am not Black Kettle. Hear me. I have good cause for what I ask.

"My camp is full of the wounded and the dying, and I am sworn to the *Maaho'tse* and to the People's salvation. Your *Hotame-taneo'o* will kill here and move on, but my people must remain until they are strong enough to move. Even if you destroy every man here, other *ve'ho'e* will come back to us and retaliate. If you trust my medicine, you will wait and give my people a chance to get away. This one will die eventually anyway."

Bull Bear turned away, his lips white. He looked to Custer. "Take your life and go. But know that if you try to pursue us, your scalps will hang from my lance."

Warriors growled and howled, and Bull Bear walked away.

The Dogs slipped after him. Fire Wolf went after the others, leaving the blue-coats to mill about, disorganized, many gripping their weapons in tense, stiff hands.

"Guess I'd get that stuff off my foot if I was him," someone muttered, his eyes drawn again and again to Custer's boot.

"You think they really have powers?" someone asked.

"Oh, Jesus," moaned another soldier. He looked the way the last warrior had gone, a chill in his blood.

He had been close enough to see that old medicine man's eyes when he spoke of his prophecy. There had been something there, something bright and not quite of this world. Worse yet, the soldier knew for a fact that Custer had been lying.

"Oh, hell, it's just a 'skin looking for his squaw," he snapped to the others. "What's the harm in telling him?"

"You spooked?" his friend demanded.

The soldier hesitated a moment. "That squaw ain't worth my life, whoever she is."

He trotted after the Indians, shaking off his comrades. He paused only long enough to grab the translator by the arm and drag him with him.

"Wait!" he called out to Fire Wolf.

The dog rope man stiffened, looking back coldly, but something kicked in the area of his heart.

"I saw her. That squaw you talked about, I saw her. She put some kids in the water, then she killed one of ours. One of those boys didn't walk too good."

In the silence Fire Wolf let his words sink in.

"There were some Comanche and Kiowa bucks on the other side of the river," the blue-coat rushed on. "Your women went that way. Maybe they took her. Maybe one of those other tribes is holding her."

He backed off wearily, having appeased his conscience. Fire Wolf turned slowly and thoughtfully to find Night Fighter beside him. There was no doubt in his heart that the blue-coat spoke of his Eagle.

She pushed her kids into the water and killed one of ours.

He saw her again as he had first known her, spitting threats at him if he would harm her mother's lodge. She will do that sort of thing, he thought, when you threaten those in her heart.

"Come along, friend. We ride this night. If she is alive, I do not think we have much time before she takes it into her mind to come and find me."

III

Eagle woke as she had every dawn since she had come to the Comanches, slowly, her head filled with tangled dreams. She shook them off as Sun touched the smoke hole of the lodge she shared with Last Bead and her husband.

This time it speared brightly into her eyes, sharp and strong, without clouds. Perhaps that is a good sign, she thought.

She pushed her bedding back, taking a gourd from Last Bead's pile of parfleches, and went to the water. As she hunkered down, she gazed over at Sun where it peaked above the eastern horizon. She breathed in its sacred strength, then she tilted her head back to savor its weak winter rays. Finally she sighed and filled the gourd, pushing up again.

This time she saw them.

She could not scream out her joy or run for him. There had been too many deaths, too much elation and despair in her world for her heart to explode over something she had always known. Once, long ago, she had loved this man on the prairie. They had touched the sun for one glorious moment, capturing its strength, taking its life-forces into their souls. They had honored it with their passion, and if Sun would take this warrior, it would take her, too, by his side.

She had waited for him too long, and there was still a desperate fight to be fought.

She dropped the gourd, letting it slide slowly from her fingers. Then she gasped, a sweet, whispering sound, and went to meet him.

As she drew closer, she saw that they were all here, all the Dogs. Even Wind Woman rode among them. Eagle laughed aloud and finally she began running, faster and faster until her breath burned.

Their line moved out across the land as they approached, straight-backed and haughty and strong. Their raven-feathers snapped in the wind, and their lances stood high. Then she was upon them, and her dog rope man's hand came down for hers. She grasped it, strong and sure, and he heaved her up behind him on his pony.

She rested her cheek against the warm skin of his back and held on to him.

For a long time they watched the sun come up, feeling quiet and whole again. Then she straightened and put her face into the wind.

"What do we do now? Where do we go now that everything is gone?"

"We go home, back to the north country, and we fight on."

She nodded, knowing they would do it together this time. They would fight until the last blade of grass was trampled by white feet and the last buffalo was gone. It was in their blood, in the wind that carried them.

They were the Dogs.

"All we ask is to be allowed to live, and live in peace. We bowed to the will of the Great Father and went south. There we found a Cheyenne cannot live. So we came home. Better it was, we thought, to die fighting than to perish of sickness and hunger. You may kill me here, but you cannot make me go back. We will not go. The only way to get us there is to come in here with clubs and knock us on the head, and drag us out and take us down there dead."

Tahmelapashme, Dull Knife
Northern Cheyenne
Fort Robinson, 1877

If you enjoyed this book, take advantage of this special offer. Subscribe now and get a

FREE
Historical Romance

No Obligation (a $4.50 value)

Each month the editors of True Value select the four *very best* novels from America's leading publishers of romantic fiction. Preview them in your home *Free* for 10 days. With the first four books you receive, we'll send you a FREE book as our introductory gift. No Obligation!

If for any reason you decide not to keep them, just return them and owe nothing. If you like them as much as we think you will, you'll pay just $4.00 each and save at *least* $.50 each off the cover price. (Your savings are *guaranteed* to be at least $2.00 each month.) There is NO postage and handling – or other hidden charges. There are no minimum number of books to buy and you may cancel at any time.

Send in the Coupon Below — To get your FREE historical romance fill out the coupon below and mail it today. As soon as we receive it we'll send you your FREE Book along with your first month's selections.